IF YOU KNEW HER

IF YOU KNEW HER

a novel

EMILY ELGAR

HARPER

NEW YORK • LONDON • TORONTO • SYDNEY

HARPER

P.S.™ is a trademark of HarperCollins Publishers.

HarperCollins books may be purchased for educational, business, or sales promotional use. For information, please email the Special Markets Department at SPsales@harpercollins.com.

Originally published in 2017 in the United Kingdom by Little, Brown Book Group.

Epigraph p. vii © Paulo Coelho 2003

FIRST EDITION

Library of Congress Cataloging-in-Publication Data has been applied for.

ISBN 978-0-06-283404-1 (library edition)
ISBN 978-0-06-269460-7 (pbk.)

18 19 20 21 22 LSC 10 9 8 7 6 5 4 3 2 1

For my sister Amy

At every moment of our lives, we all have one foot in a fairy tale and the other in the abyss

PAULO COELHO, *Eleven Minutes*

IF
YOU
KNEW
HER

Prologue

The darkness seems to pull her towards it, holding her in a freezing embrace as she moves down the lane and deeper into the treacle-thick night. The air electrocutes her lungs with each icy inhale, and her legs feel slick, sure of their new direction. She hears the stream bubbling by her side and the branches from the silver birch trees creak over her head like arthritic fingers knitting together.

The moon shines its mottled, kindly face, silvering her path like a fairy godmother; she smiles up at it before it vanishes again behind a fast-moving cloud. She feels entirely of the world; it moves easily along with her, as though some invisible force has, with a small sigh, been released within her, and she's in step with life. She starts to hum, surprising herself, something made-up, childlike; it's nonsense but she doesn't care and she doesn't feel ashamed.

Why didn't she notice before how smooth the world can be?

Her hum turns into a name. She calls out long and light, "Maisie!" She stops and calls louder this time, "Maisie!" She listens. The silence of the night is like a presence itself, taut and endless. Any moment now, there'll be a scampering in the hedgerow, a sweet snap as Maisie's nimble paws break delicate twigs. But for now there's just a thick silence. She chooses not to worry; Maisie will be running in some nearby field, her body tight with adrenaline, nose to the ground, tail wagging, deaf to everything except the cacophony of smells around her. She adjusts her bag on her shoulder, calls again and keeps walking along the familiar pockmarked lane.

The flash of the car lights from behind startles her, like they're intruding on her private moment and have caught her doing something no one else should see. The car is familiar. She waves, casting shadows on the lane, her arms preposterously long.

She breaks into a little run; the lane widens ahead, they can stop and talk there. But it's as though running has caught the car's attention—exposed some weakness in her—and she feels as if the car lights have locked onto her back with an animalistic ferocity, like the glazed eyes of a wild animal in a trance of instinct, nostrils full of prey. She feels the lights coming faster and faster, galloping towards her. A scream rips from her throat, but the wind whips her voice away, as if it's needed elsewhere, at another drama. The car growls, so close behind her now.

Her bag falls from her shoulder and her neck whips round as the car bites into her hip. She feels her bones crack as easily as porcelain; the impact makes her spin, an insane pirouette to the edge of the stream. Her feet can't keep up and she falls back. Thorns shred her useless hands as she clutches the hedgerows for support, but it's just brambles and loose branches; it doesn't even slow her down. She hears herself scream, distant, as if it's coming from someone else far away. Her head sounds like a piece of meat slammed down on a butcher's table as it hits something hard.

The stream is quite narrow; it fits her well, snug as a coffin. Her heart beats energy around her body with such force she can't feel anything else. Even the ice water that busily trickles around her, trying to find its new flow with her in the way, doesn't sting anymore. The freezing air smells of wet, rotting things and her breath leaves her in blowsy clouds like small spirits, as if part of her was escaping, dissolving into the night.

She opens her eyes; the sky is still inky with night-time, and raindrops sting her face like tiny wet kisses. The car has finally come to a mechanical panting halt above her.

She places her hand between her thighs and raises it to her eyes. There's no blood. Thank God, there's no blood. Maisie, naughty Maisie, barks. She hears footsteps against the lane. They pause above her. She wishes they wouldn't. It's a relief when they walk away again. Predawn silence seems to cover her, tucking her into her new bed. She feels held by the stream, calm in the silence, and she decides to drift off, just for a while, and when she wakes up, everything will be clear and she'll feel free again.

1

Alice

I sit down in my usual chair, facing him. His head is turned towards me, patient, waiting for me to begin. I don't expect a welcome, which is good because he never offers one. He just waits, professional, for me to start talking, which eventually I always do.

"Hi, Frank—Happy New Year. Hope your Christmas was all right. It's good to see you." I smile at him.

He doesn't move; his expression doesn't even flicker.

"It feels like I've been away for ages." I look around; his sparse little area is just the same. After all the rain, the bright January light from the window is a relief; it catches dust motes floating in the air.

"Our Christmas was quite fun. Remember I told you David and I went to the New Forest to see my folks? Claire's moved my mum and dad into the barn they converted, so now her, Martin, and the kids have the old house. I thought I wouldn't mind but it was pretty weird. The house we grew up in but with someone else's stuff. Anyway, David thought my folks seemed pleased with the setup and that's the most important thing, of course."

The plan had been hatched and carefully executed by my sister, Claire. Younger than me by just eighteen months, Claire decreed it was ridiculous our parents were rattling around in the four-bedroom Georgian house we grew up in when she and her family were squeezed into a three-bedroom rental. An annex conversion was designed by my architect husband David and hastily constructed in just six months from the old black-stained barn. My parents gathered up their bird books, their mugs and the old oak table that still has "Alice Taylor" engraved with a protractor on the long edge and, in their usual quiet way, shuffled across the driveway to their new home. Claire rented a dumpster for everything else.

Frank waits for me to start talking to him again.

I shift in my seat.

"The kids were sweet. Harry, Claire's five-year-old, had head lice recently and realized my name spells 'A-Lice' so he called me 'Auntie Lice' or 'A-Lice' all Christmas. David thought it was hilarious. I sort of hinted that Martin might want to tell him to stop, but either he didn't get the hint or he couldn't be bothered to do anything. I never can tell with Martin."

The jury was still out on my languid, shoulder-shrugging brother-in-law. I thought he was either a quiet genius or not at all bright. David just thinks he's figured out how to have an easy life, which, if true, makes him a genius in my book, considering he's married to my sister.

"Claire and I didn't piss each other off too much, thankfully, but, oh god, there was one thing on Christmas Day." I lean in towards Frank. I can't tell stories about the kids to most people, so I'm going to enjoy this. "I'd just given Harry a bath and went down to the kitchen and caught Claire peeling grapes for Elsa . . . peeling grapes, for God's sake! I mean I get it for a baby but a three-year-old? I think Claire knew what I was thinking, and immediately said Elsa wouldn't eat them with the skin on. David came in though, thank God, and stopped me from having a go at her."

This last bit wasn't strictly true; David's presence stopped a full-blown argument erupting but I hadn't been able to stop myself from muttering, "You are wrapped around her finger," at the sight of Claire bowed over their new kitchen table, chipping away at the grape skin with her nail while Elsa had sat in her booster seat, kicking the side of the table like a tiny dictator.

Claire had snapped up from her work. "What did you say, Ali?"

Elsa had stopped kicking the table to look at me, her cheeks flushed red, rashy, glistening with grape juice. She'd looked affronted by my interruption when she'd had things working so nicely.

"Oh, come on, Claire. You're seriously still peeling grapes for her?"

Claire had finished the grape she'd been working on and handed it to Elsa who, without shifting her gaze from me, had snatched it from her mum and steered it greedily into her mouth with her chubby fist.

"I just want her to have more fruit and this is the only

way," Claire had said with forced restraint. Elsa had started sucking the grape, trying to get her teeth to grips with its slippery, skinless surface. Claire had taken a swig of wine before saying, "Just leave me to it, OK, Alice?"; the subtext being, "You don't have kids, so how could you possibly understand?" That's when David had come in, perfectly timed as always, his paper hat torn at the seams, his prematurely gray hair poking out at strange angles. He'd known I had been drunk and tired enough to pursue a petty row.

"Come on, Alice; come and help your dad and me beat Martin and your mum." They'd been playing board games in the sitting room while I'd helped Claire with the kids. David can't bear rows so I'd sidestepped around Elsa's seat and had gone to play Trivial Pursuit. As I'd walked away, I'd seen something like a light green eyeball pop out of Elsa's little mouth. Later, David had stepped on the peeled grape and I'd apologized to Claire and the two of us had laughed at the grape trail David had smeared all over the slate tiles.

It would be at this point in my story that a therapist might ask, "And how did your sister's comment make you feel?" But not Frank, it's not his style.

I pressed on. "Everything else was fine really. Mum and Dad were sweet and quiet as normal. Still completely obsessed with Harry and Elsa; they love having them so close. I guess it's like how families used to be: grandparents mucking in, teaching their grandkids things, telling them what it was like when they were children, all that stuff." I pause, swallow, unsure how I fit into this wholesome family picture. I wonder if Frank notices how quickly I change the subject.

"We had Simon, David's dad, to stay for a few days and then we went to our friends Jess and Tim's for New Year's—they're the local friends I told you about—so it was pretty low-key, more board games and wine." I shrug, "It was nice." A widower for five years, since David's mum, Marjorie, died from breast cancer, Simon has found love again with golf. He seems content enough. I can't think of anything else to say. I sense Frank knows there's something I'm not telling him, a promise I've made that I keep trying to bat away like a persistent fly.

I sit back in the visitor's chair. Frank hasn't changed during the break. His cadaverous head rests heavy on the pillow. He is partly obscured by breathing apparatus; his tracheotomy is attached to a great blue plastic tube like an octopus tentacle, which runs cruelly from the middle of his throat. His body is shrivelled, like a line drawing, but his head is as hard and heavy as a marble carving. The respirator and monitor screens behind him click and beep away endless seconds. They seem louder, more intrusive than I remember.

Lucy, Frank's daughter, once told me he has a broad West Country accent. I love accents. It's a pity I may never hear him talk. I look down at his face; it's a tired suggestion of the Frank I've seen in photos. Like some over-loved old teddy bear, his skin is sallow from hospital air and his hair is white and spidery like frayed cotton.

When he was first admitted, two months ago, it was mahogany, like my hair; I remember one of the nurses—Carol maybe—saying we could be brother and sister. Perhaps it was that comment that made me start talking to him like this. Or maybe it was because he's been here so long and weeks go by without anyone coming to visit, or maybe it's just because Frank's such a good listener.

My instinct is that Frank's more conscious than his brain scans and test results show, but instinct doesn't count for anything on 9B; everything must be proven by a machine or a graph before anything changes. When Frank was first admitted, talking to him was like talking to an empty box—he was off somewhere; I don't know where—but now when I sit with him, I can feel his presence. I know he's listening. Without moving a muscle or saying a word, he comforted me just before Christmas on the anniversary of my first miscarriage. I told him about the first as I cleaned his tracheotomy; I think it surprised us both. Then I told him about the seven that followed. I even told him about the ones David doesn't know about, my body snuffing out tiny life as efficient and silent as a candle in a jar. I felt better after talking to Frank. I suppose it helps that he can't move, that I don't have to watch the familiar struggle to hide the pity I see on most peoples' faces. I stroke Frank's downy hair, soft as breath on the back of my hand. This New Year marks the end of trying and the beginning of trying to accept we won't have our own family. I promised David; I agreed eight years of trying is all we can take. It's over.

I bite my bottom lip. I mustn't get into a habit of talking to Frank about myself too much—it's not fair to him—so I pull my hand back and look away from Frank. The nurses working over Christmas have wound some purple tinsel around the frame of Frank's bed, by his feet. I know their intention was good but now it looks a bit silly.

I get up from the chair, grateful for something to do. I

pick the sticky tape off the bed frame and unwind the tinsel. I imagine Frank thinking, *Thank God for that*, and I smile and say, "You're welcome, Frank," as I drop it in his bin.

Apart from the purple tinsel and a plastic Santa and sleigh with reindeer that look like they're hiding forked tongues, 9B has got off quite lightly this year. The only other decorations around Frank are a couple of Christmas cards stuck to the side of his bedside table. I leave them for now.

I hear voices at the end of the ward: the other day-shift nurses arriving. I've got rounds in five minutes so I say goodbye to Frank and walk down the wide corridor that makes up Ward 9B at St. Catherine's Hospital, or "Kate's" as everyone calls it. We're part of the "Nines": the three critical-care units at Kate's. 9B is a small High Dependency Unit with four operational bed spaces. All our patients here teeter on their own personal tightrope between life and death. Us nurses share patient care but since he was admitted in November, I always put myself forward to nurse Frank.

My white running shoes squeak against the tacky dark green plastic floor as I walk back towards the entrance of the ward, the sound as familiar to me as a kettle boiling. Today, everything seems the same but Christmas has subtly altered the ward somehow; there's a sense of possibility this morning. There are some new members of staff, fresh calendars and the carpet in the nurses break room has been cleaned. The smell's the same though, the air like another presence in the hospital, a humid puff of overly boiled potatoes and hand sanitizer. Visitors find it stifling, but when you work here you get used to it.

I'm on my way to join in the post-holiday chatter that bubbles out of the nurses break room like foam when Sharma, one of the attending physicians, walks stiffly out of his office, ready for rounds. He looks much older than his forty-seven years, as if Christmas has aged him. He's even more precise and starched than normal, as though Santa Claus brought him a steamer, a ruler, and fixing spray. His small moustache, like his hair, is jet black, shiny and symmetrical. His shoulders are right angles and the three pens in his breast pocket—black, blue, and red—rest ready for action. It's unsettling. How can anyone like him work in a world of piss and vomit? I always feel a little anxious doing rounds with him, as though I'm dirtying him by proxy, talking about bedsores and bowel movements.

In the break room, I hear Mary chatting to the new junior nurse, Lizzie. Lizzie starts laughing at something Mary's said. Both of them were working over Christmas. Mary can be an acquired taste, so I'm pleased it sounds like they got on.

I pick up the ward-notes folder from the reception table. Sharma likes to do rounds with the most senior nurse on duty instead of with each patient's nurse; I suspect it's to avoid talking to too many of us. As ward manager, I've been called up today. I turn towards Sharma.

"Hello, Mr. Sharma. How was your holiday?"

"*Bonum.* Thank you. Shall we proceed?" Sharma sprinkles his speech with Latin, which incenses Mary—"The pompous arse. Who does he think he is? Julius Caesar?"—but it just makes me laugh.

There are only three patients on 9B at present. Just after

Christmas, Caleb in bed two caught a nasty infection after his cancer-ridden spleen was cut away. He was ready to go, as they say; even though he was as weak as a lamb, he still found the strength to try and pull out the IV that pumped the antibiotics into his arm. His wife, Hope, wrote us a thank-you card after he died; it's still pinned up behind reception. Winter is usually a busy time here, with pneumonia for the old and more accidents from slippery roads and revelry for the young; odds are Caleb's bed will be filled by the end of the day.

Rounds start with bed one: a cardio patient called George Peters, recovering from a recent bout of pneumonia. Sharma moves on to Ellen Hargreaves in bed four, an eighty-nine-year-old with multiple organ failure, dementia, and cancer, before lastly coming to Frank Ashcroft. Sharma finds Frank the most vexing patient on the ward. Not because of his symptoms but because of his prolonged presence. Frank has been on 9B for too long in Sharma's opinion; most other patients stay for a few weeks, maximum. Frank's been here two months already. On our way to Frank's bed, we pass Lizzie who waves, grins, and blushes at me. She's already making up Caleb's old bed, bed two opposite Frank, sticking "I'm sterilized" stickers onto everything that has been made ready by the healthcare assistant.

"No tinsel for Mr. Ashcroft, I see," Sharma says as we stand at the foot of Frank's bed. His voice still contains some notes from Hyderabad. Accents can't be bleached.

"Oh, no, I already took it down actually."

"Can you see to it that all the other stuff is removed as well?" he asks as he looks down at Frank's notes.

I bite my bottom lip as he talks.

"Righto, Frank Ashcroft, fifty, our brain stem stroke. Coma for a month and now probably PVS since some involuntary eye movement was observed. EEG showed extensive damage with some upper and lower PON activity. He's been on a ventilator since he arrived, is that correct?"

Sharma knows about Frank's medical care, of course, but he still likes to go through the motions. I nod.

"It was thought we'd try and encourage him to breathe independently, check his diaphragm function, so we tried a reduction but he suffered another minor stroke."

"Yes, that's right."

Sharma likes pliant nurses. He decided Frank was in a Permanent Vegetative State after a few minutes of looking at his scan results and less than two minutes of being with Frank. The protocol for diagnosed PVS requires approval from two other attending physicians. Sharma only has approval from one. If Sharma gets his diagnosis, that would be the end for Frank; he'd be moved to a facility, a morgue waiting room, kept alive until he got an infection and the antibiotics stopped working. I have to hope for something better for him; otherwise, what's the point?

"I recall he doesn't have any family to speak of. None that are involved in his care anyway?"

I wish I could shush him up; Frank is just a couple of feet away.

"He has a daughter." I speak quietly. "Her visits are infrequent. He's estranged from his wife; a couple of his friends and his mum visited once or twice but she's now moved abroad. She wanted to come over for Christmas, but I think it was too expensive. But, no, apart from them, I don't know about anyone else."

Sharma looks down at Frank and then back at his notes, his forehead creasing. "Well, as you know, he's been here a long time. It's a huge drain on resources. I'm afraid it's the times we live in; we have to find somewhere for him to move on to. I heard a care home in Reading is looking to invest in new equipment. I'll make some enquiries." Out comes the blue pen and, with that, rounds are over until this afternoon. I imagine Sharma, retreating to his office, doing sums with his red pen, working out how much money Frank's life is costing.

I peer through the square window leading to the little break room at the end of the ward. Carol—a middle-aged matron with short, permed hair, a quick laugh and big boobs that make her back ache—is sitting behind her desk, which overflows with policy and procedure manuals, lists and memos. On the far wall of the small, windowless room Carol has framed a photo of all the permanent ward staff on the "Nines." Everyone on the ward hates the photo, our tired faces ghoulish and aged by the fluorescent lighting, but we all like Carol too much to take it down.

With five years under my belt, I'm the second-longest-serving nurse on 9B. My friend Mary—who is, this morning, sitting opposite Carol, eating a half-priced mince pie and drinking a cup of tea—brings home the medal with twenty years' service on 9B.

Nearing retirement, Mary is small and, in her words, "shrinking fast"; she's thin but always eating. She has short, gray, cropped hair and huge, goggly eyes, which she says grow the more she sees. Even the attending physicians revere Mary, who's been known to diagnose patients faster and more accurately than the most senior practitioners. In the safety of the break room, Mary treats them with a mixture of pity and disdain, calling them the "Ists," her catchment term for the Intensivists, Neurologists, Chemists, Oncologists, Cardiologists, and so on who visit the ward daily, most of them like nervous insects, hovering by a patient's bed before scurrying back to the safety of their desk and their books.

Carol and Mary both give me a hug. We ask about each other's Christmases, and then Mary gets back to the rant I interrupted.

"The Ists don't get it. They don't get it at all."

She's angry; she'd been nursing Caleb with her usual painstaking care and attention when he died over Christmas. Caleb's wealthy family sent the physicians tickets to an England rugby game as a thank you for looking after Caleb. The nurses got a dozen donuts.

Mary, as usual, keeps talking. "They think everything they could possibly need to know must be in a book. Most of them don't even bother looking properly at the patient, let alone speaking to them. But here we are, day in, day out with our patients, their families; we see it all. Nurses are like hospital furniture. Everyone else constantly moves, the Ists get promoted, patients go home or die but we stay, steadfast, waiting to be sat on, leant on, perhaps kicked about a bit."

Carol chuckles at Mary and Mary rolls her round eyes at me. I turn to the rota board so neither of them see me smiling; I know how irritated Mary gets with Carol's perpetual jolliness. She comes round to stand next to me and squeezes my shoulder with her thin, strong hand that has lifted, wiped, squeezed, and caressed so many sick and dying over the last two decades.

"Here we go again, eh? Happy New Year." With that Mary walks back out on the ward and starts calling to the ward technician, "Sue, hey, Sue!" before the door shuts behind her.

I take the seat opposite Carol, where Mary had been. Carol's shaking her head at the door and beams at me as she says, "Something about old dogs and new tricks, huh?"

Carol, who is already wearing one pair of glasses, starts fishing in her permed hair for her reading glasses, which are, as usual, roosting somewhere in her thick hair.

"I know," I say. "She keeps talking about retiring, you know. I can't tell if she's doing it for attention or if she's serious. Either way, I can't imagine this place without her."

Carol nods at me as she swaps her glasses and, opening a file, she says, "So, what's happening today?"

As ward manager I'm part matron, part nurse. At Kate's the matrons are managers who perform hundreds of administrative duties on the three critical care units of the hospital. 9B has a core nursing staff supplemented by roaming "bank" nurses. It is a reflection of the strange hospital hierarchy that the amount of patient contact within a role dictates that role's position in the hospital food chain. Many hours of patient contact—healthcare assistants, porters, cleaners and nurses—are the plankton and krill, yet positions with very few or no direct hours with patients—most of the "Ists"—are the sharks and whales of this peculiar ocean. Despite my increased administrative duties, I'd never give up the patient contact. I studied medicine at the University College London but failed the first round of doctors' exams. I was devastated at the time, of course, hated the way my parents quietly hinted I was more suited to nursing. As it turns out, they were right; I am more suited to the human part of medicine. I administer drugs, change sheets, comfort families, and hold the hands of dying patients until their last breath. I'm with them. I'm happy to be plankton.

"OK, let's see here," Carol says, reading from the schedule. "Well, you'll continue with Frank, Brighton has requested bed two for a thirty-year-old head trauma, GCS 4 coma patient, but she won't be arriving until this evening or maybe even tomorrow. Lizzie is getting the bed ready now. If you could take on Ellen Hargreaves, she's got all sorts of appointments today; Paula said she's been bad, especially at night, getting very agitated. She keeps calling out like she's back in the Blitz, poor love. Oh, and the notes mention something about mouth ulcers and her G-tube needing to be checked. We have a meeting with her children at two o'clock. Then if you could do afternoon rounds, check in with George Peters's family—he was with a bank nurse over Christmas so I think they need some attention—and then get going with the nursing schedule that would be great. I was also wondering, Ali . . . you wouldn't mind keeping an eye on Lizzie for the next few weeks as well, would you? Just make sure she's finding her feet, that sort of thing." She lobs a grin at me again and I smile back, before walking onto the bustling ward to meet the long day ahead.

I pull in to our drive at 22 Blackcombe Avenue just before 7:30 p.m. David and I have lived here since we got married, seven years ago. It's one of those houses that's shrouded in evergreen bushes, giving the impression that it's much smaller than it is. Like something from a children's book, the dark front door seems to peep out of the shrubbery like a kindly eye. Built in the fifties, the house was considered indescribably ugly when we first bought the redbrick two-story house—perhaps that's why the previous owners planted the shrubs—but now it's called "retro." David tells me that—as he knew it would—mid-century's become cool again, so we're right on trend apparently. David describes the house as "Old Hollywood," a phrase I'm sure he picked up in one of his architecture magazines, which he now uses to make me laugh and give me an excuse to call him an "Archi-wanker." I have to admit, though, it's a fairly good description. The house has a balcony around the back, with glass sliding doors that overlook the sloping garden. David loved the generous proportions and the opportunity for building an extension; I loved the three bedrooms and the opportunity for building a family. Of course, now we just have two spare rooms.

It's dark in the house so David must be out. David works for the Planning Permission Trust, and for the last six months he's been working from home, which suits his budget-minded boss and also suits David who I know carves out extra hours to work on his private architecture projects. David said this year will be the year he reduces his hours at the Trust to finally practice full-time as an architect. His job at the Trust, where he pursues and debates controversial planning applications for local government, was always supposed to be just a stop-gap, a year tops, while we settled into our new semi-rural Sussex life. But as the financial crisis hit, people stopped planning expensive home conversions while Tesco's still needed their parking lots, so David dug his heels in and clung onto his desk and we talked at night about how it'd just be for another year or so, until the economy improved.

David's out now though; he's taken Bob, our black Labrador, with him. I fondle the wall for the light switch and shrug my coat off, dropping my bag with a thud on the stone floor in the hallway. Claire once described our house as "adult tidy." No muddy shoes or wooden toys dot the floor. There are no safety locks on the cupboards or potties behind the toilet.

Our kitchen is a miniature farmhouse kitchen with a little pantry and big windows out to the garden. David, I know, would prefer something modern but I've always been a sucker for anything rustic. I step over Bob's chewed sleeping rug and stare into the fridge. I quite fancy a glass of wine but we always try and do a month off booze for "Dry January," so I pour myself a large glass of fizzy water instead and lean against the trough-style sink to text Jess.

Can you guys come for dinner next Thursday? David wants to catch up about the extension. I'll get him to cook and we could make a night of it? x

As I press "send" the outside light flashes on and through the kitchen window, I see David. He looks like he's recently been on fire; white clouds of sweaty heat billow around him like smoke, puffing up from his Lycra running top. He's breathing hard and puts one hand flat against the driveway wall as he uses the other to grab his ankle and stretch out his long thigh, the muscles in his standing calf tense with his weight. He only holds the pose for a couple of seconds, before he does the other side. Stretching's never been his thing; he'll be sore tomorrow.

There's a light scratch at the front door. I open it and Bob's slick black head pushes forward, pink tongue lolling out, urgent for affection. I give him a pat on his cold, muscular shoulder. He's breathing hard but still manages to raise his eyebrows in pleasure as I look in his loving eyes and reassure him he's a good boy.

David walks through the door, kicking off his ancient running shoes. His graying hair clings to his forehead in sweaty curls as he leans towards me for a salty kiss. His eyes rest on mine, taut just for a second, scanning to check I'm OK.

To reassure him that I am, I look down at his sweaty running outfit and say, "I'm impressed. New Year's resolution number one."

He laughs. "I know, big bloody thumbs up for Bob and me. I have to say though, Bob didn't do much for morale, did you, Bobby?" Bob, at the sound of his name, only has the energy now to thump his tail a couple of slow, heavy times against the floor where he's already collapsed in his basket on his side of the kitchen, his black flank moving wearily up and down.

David refills Bob's water bowl before pouring himself a glass from the tap. He drinks it in three gulps and says, "He was doing that stopping thing he does, you know, where he just sits down, refuses to budge and then starts trotting home. I had to drag him along."

I laugh. Bob can be as stubborn—and heavy—as a mule.

David strokes my bottom as he passes me to get to the tap for a refill. "How was your day?" he asks.

I drop the mail I was flicking through onto the counter and bend down to take my running shoes off. After the break my feet hurt more than usual.

"Busy," I say, "but fine. You know, Mary's been at Kate's for twenty years now? Seriously, that woman's got stamina. I don't know how she's done it. That's another resolution actually: I need to make a plan, think about what I'm going to do next." I'm pleased I keep my voice breezy. Our first few years together in our tiny Hackney basement flat—me as a newly qualified, overwhelmed nurse, David finishing his architecture training—we'd talk over pints in our local pub about the future; Hackney at that time was more associated with "Murder Mile" than flat whites and pop-up restaurants. In my plan, we'd have kids in our late twenties and early thirties, I'd stop nursing while they were tiny and maybe do something completely different when they went to school, like working in an art gallery or designing jewelry, something creative that would allow me to always be there for any sick days and holidays, by which point, David would have his own flourishing practice. We'd live in a rambling farmhouse near the sea and our kids would grow up with dogs, chickens and goats and they'd be the boisterous, ruddy-cheeked type, unafraid of adults and the future. I had it all figured out.

David turns to hug me; he probably knows what I'm thinking. I fit perfectly under his shoulders and instinctually he bends to kiss me somewhere on my face. His lips land near my eyebrow.

"How was your day?" I ask, my voice muffled against his chest. He kisses me briefly on the lips this time before we let each other go.

"Oh, fine, you know. I did some more drawings for Jess and Tim's extension; it's starting to come together pretty nicely." David's charging our friends a mates' rate but it's worth it to get his name more visible locally.

"That's exciting!" I say, opening a mobile phone bill and immediately putting it back on the counter top without looking at it. "I just texted Jess actually. I invited them over on Thursday next week. I thought you and Tim can geek out on the drawings and Jess and I can have a proper catch-up."

David rinses out his glass. "Sounds good, I'll make one of my famous lasagna." He winces at what's in the fridge. "What shall we have for dinner? God, it's a jungle in here." He's talking about the bushels of spinach and kale I bought. Resolution number five: actually use the juicer I bought David for Christmas. David pulls all the green stuff out of the fridge until he finds an old block of cheddar, which he starts slicing directly on the counter top and eating in chunky pieces. Through a mouthful of cheese he puffs his cheeks out and nods. "Looks like it's going to be good old kale with lettuce on the side and spinach for pudding tonight. God, I miss Christmas."

I laugh as he drops his head dramatically down onto the wooden counter and I pinch the last bit of cheese as he murmurs in an injured voice, "Promise me the year is going to get better than this."

I grin at him, but I don't reply. I start walking upstairs towards our bedroom instead, because I don't want to make David anymore promises I can't keep.

2

Frank

When I was a kid, around six or seven maybe, my mum got ill. Nothing too serious it turns out but she had to go away for a couple of weeks, and me and my brother went to stay with our grandparents. They were nice enough to us, but the point is, it's the first time I can recall missing someone. Not a vague everyday kind of missing, but a sort of reverse umbilical wrench. Without my mum I felt embryonic, incapable on my own; every instinct wanted to be back inside her, where it was safe, where I couldn't be alone. Then we went home and everything was normal again and in the way of kids, all the crying and calling out for her, well, it was as if it never happened.

Without Alice, I remembered that time, how I felt when my mum was ill. I've been panicky these last few days, scaring myself imagining her never coming back. She told me she wouldn't be around for Christmas but I thought it'd just be a day or two. There were a couple of bank nurses over the holiday who didn't even bother to learn my name. To them, I was just "the patient."

That new one, Lizzie, tries the odd joke with me.

"It's turkey flavor today, Mr. Ashcroft," she said from under her Santa hat on Christmas Day as she emptied a syringe into one of the tubes that spools out of me, pumping brown ICU mush directly into my stomach. Nice of her to try, but she should know I couldn't tell the difference between turkey and turpentine. Lizzie's new to us veggies as well; it's obvious. She moves my head in hesitant, cautious jerks. It's quite sweet really. She doesn't want to hurt me, but she could take a cheese grater to my chest and a lighter to my balls and I'd feel it, every grate and burn, just like anyone else, but I wouldn't be able to scream. I wouldn't even be able to bat an eyelid.

I often wonder if Sharma had believed Alice and her diagnosis of "Locked In" rather than "Persistent Vegetative State" how different things would be for me here. PVS, as far as I can gather, is a pretty way of saying dead in all ways that count for the living. The PVS patient is balancing between life and death, their brain empty as a cloud but their lungs pumped with oxygen. The docs keep the patient going, like kids with a butterfly on a piece of string, they will not let go, but stick grimly to their game, because to turn off the machines, to let go of that string, would be to lose the game, to let the butterfly float away, and that can't happen. It can't be helped though, I suppose. The living are usually obsessive about life.

So that's PVS, lights on but no one home. My situation is a little different, I'm home but my fuse has blown to the "off" setting, Alice calls it "Locked In Syndrome." An itchy nose, a sense of humor, sex drive, a voice in my head, needing to shit, regret, I've got it all, all those urges, needs and desires, as clear, prickly and torturous as ever. But I'm stuck, I can't "do" any of them. There's no scratching, laughing, shagging, chatting, crapping or crying. It's all done for me or over me, apart from the shagging.

Alice is still the only one who can sense me in here, trapped in my body, like a straitjacket.

This morning, I hear her before I see her; I know her step anywhere now. Her walk sounds like a pianist's fingers across the keyboard. She lifts and lilts, the heel notes low and the toes higher. Relief pulses through me and crests as she comes into my line of vision.

Alice is back. She's here.

A few strands of her wavy brown hair have escaped from her bun and bounce down towards me just inches from my face. Her blue eyes crease a little as she smiles, a dimple on her left cheek, and, yes, there it is . . . there's the gap between her teeth; like a tiny secret cave, it only shows when she smiles. She told me once that when she was a student she tried to save enough money to have the gap closed up, but she went on holiday instead.

"Hi, Frank, Happy New Year. Hope your Christmas was all right. It's good to see you." I want her to touch me, to put her hand against my cheek, to tell me like my mum told me that she's back and she'll stay with me now. I don't think even Alice knows how long ten days can be trapped in here. She chatters away about her Christmas, her niece and nephew, but I know what she's thinking about as she bites her bottom lip. If I could, I'd tell her I know how loneliness gnaws, how rage blisters, I'd tell her we may be different, but she's not alone.

She picks the tinsel off the end of my bed and I think, *Cheers, Alice, not my sort of thing, to be honest.* She hesitates for a moment by my Christmas cards, but she doesn't take them down, and then she's gone, off for rounds. I'm grateful she leaves the cards; I've only seen them once, when Lizzie opened them just before Christmas. The rest of the time they've been stuck onto the side panel of my bedside unit and it's rare they move my neck far enough to the right for me to see them. I only got three this year, which is fair enough, I suppose, considering I didn't send any. I can remember them fairly well; my brain's good at taking photos now. Small mercies. There's one from my little brother Dex who about a year ago moved to Costa del somewhere with his new wife. My mum moved out of the house in Swindon we grew up in, where she lived on her own since Dad died, twenty-nine years ago, to live with Dex and his new wife, Bridget, in Spain six months ago. I was amazed Dex had done something for Mum, for the family, but then I found out the minicab company he's set up is in her name for tax breaks, and she has to be registered as living in the Costa del somewhere. Their card is of a cartoon Santa in his sleigh landing on a roof. My mum would've chosen it; when Lizzie hovered the card in front of my face, I saw the writing is in her spidery hand.

All OK here. Dex's business is going well and most shops sell English food so I can get my Branston and cheddar so I'm happy! No one told me it gets so cold down here over winter but it should pick up again soon. We'll come and see you next time we're over. Sorry we couldn't come for Christmas, love, but things have been tight since the move. Hope you're keeping your chin up! Love Mum, Dex and Bridget.

Dex and Mum visited me before they left for Spain. I didn't see Mum properly; she didn't like looking at me. I don't blame her. Instead she sat in my chair and cried softly while Dex paced around me, wincing at the tubes that plunge into me, and said something about how we're kinder to animals. He's never been the tactful type.

My other card is of a wintery scene with a hare running across the snow. It was from my old mate John, another site manager I worked with for years, before we all lost our jobs. He didn't say much, as I recall. No one ever does when they think you're as good as dead.

The last one—an ice-skating polar bear—was from my Luce. She knows, of course, that someone will read out my cards so she doesn't say much either but she included a photo: me dressed as Santa Claus and a five-year-old Luce sitting on my knee with dark pigtails and a red tartan dress, in our newly built house on Summerhill Close just outside Brighton. Moments before the photo, she'd pulled down my beard, and seeing me underneath, stammered, her eyes wide with the magical truth, "Daddy! *You're* Santa Claus!" It became a Christmas tradition for me to tell that story every year. Imagine if she could pull away my breathing tube, look beyond my putrefying body and see, really see, me here, now—"Daddy! *You're* here!"—but I shoo the thought away. It'll mess with my head.

Celia, George's wife, visited for most of Christmas Day.

She'd been to church and brought along some of her church friends after the service for a visit. I get the impression church is Celia's interest and George's triple bypass and the pneumonia that has led to his incarceration here on 9B have provided Celia the perfect platform to really try and hammer Jesus into George's re-upholstered heart. On Christmas Day, the prayers muttered around George were longer and said with even more gusto than usual, Celia's soft West Indian accent floating above all the other voices for the "Amen!" One of the members of the congregation started humming "Hark the Herald Angels Sing" and by the time they'd got to "Glory to the newborn king!" everyone else had joined in, and before I knew it there was an impromptu carol concert here on 9B and for a moment the ward felt as much like home as any house I've lived in.

At the end of the carol, I heard the curtain between George and me slide back, exposing me. Someone sucked their teeth. Celia stepped towards me and peered into my face. I'd only seen her properly once before, although I hear her weeping over George most days. I've only had a glimpse of George; he's so covered in tubes he looks like a drawing a child tried to scribble out. I suppose he might think the same of me. I saw just a puff of white hair and his lower arm and hand, his skin must have been dark once, but now it's almost chalky; so different to Celia's which is the color and silky texture of milky coffee. On Christmas Day, her eyes were alight either with the Holy Spirit or with the sweet sherry I smelled on her breath.

In a voice that seems to freshen the air, she said, "Merry Christmas, Mr. Ashcroft, here's a little something from us all at the Risen Lord Church." She leant forward and whispered, "It's a Bible," into my ear as if she'd just given me the elixir of life and everyone else on the ward would try and steal it if they knew. Still, it's a happy surprise when someone thinks it's worth whispering to me at all. She left the Bible on my bedside unit. It must still be there now.

Lizzie opened my other present for me, which was a scarf from Luce. It prickled and scratched my skin like sackcloth all day. Although I'm sure the nurses felt sorry no one visited, I'm pleased Lucy didn't come. I'd only make her feel low.

Ellen, an elderly patient, had her quiet, doughy-faced grandchildren with her for a few minutes on Christmas Day. She must have been unconscious. She started her bloody wailing while they were with her. "No! No!" she called. "The siren!" They left a few minutes after she started, their faces singed a sunset pink, probably worried the nurses would think they were doing something to upset her. They shouldn't; she calls out like that all the time.

Today, I watch Lizzie across the ward tuck in the sheets in the bed opposite with aggressive movements. She's not tall; she has to stand on her tiptoes and lean over the bed to pull the sheets taut. She reminds me of one of Luce's friends from school. Her cheeks are freckled and pillow-like, and she has round hazel eyes that look like they've cared for people for many years already. There's a well of feeling in those eyes. She still jumps every time one of our alarms goes off. She'll get used to all the noise soon enough. It won't take long for her to know which alarms are normal and which alarms mean someone is trying to escape. When she's finished, the bed looks like it could be in a barracks not a ward. She sees my eyes are open and she smiles.

She comes over to me and says, "Morning, Mr. Ashcroft," before she moistens my eyes with a cotton bud soaked in saline solution. My eyes burn with relief. Because I don't blink, my eyes have to be moistened when they're open, at least every hour or so, otherwise they'll dry up like raisins. Alice asks all the nurses to moisten my eyes whenever they see them open. I'm troublesome like that; it's why some of the nurses will stroke my eyes shut when no one's looking, as if I'm dead already. I've heard Sharma call my eye opening an "involuntary spasm" and I'll give him the involuntary—my eyelids do seem to follow their own laws—but Alice said it can be a sign of getting better too and although I don't often let myself linger on the thought, this morning, as a treat, I rest there for a while, letting myself believe that it might be true.

Lizzie comes over to me some time during mid-morning, when the sunlight has settled into its space on the ward. She piles towels, waterproof blankets, soap and extra blankets in front of me.

"Alice is busy, Mr. Ashcroft," she says. "She asked me to give you your sponge bath. I hope that's OK."

To be honest, I'm a little disappointed it's not Alice, but I'm in no position to make demands. Lizzie has forgotten to draw the curtains and I'm just bracing myself for a new humiliation, imagining Ellen's kids and grandkids arriving and seeing Lizzie cleaning my arse like a toddler when, with a titter at herself, Lizzie remembers, and draws the curtain around us, saying, "Better to have some privacy, eh, Mr. Ashcroft?"

Lizzie moves a soapy cloth methodically over my skin, over every inch of me. She talks about the weather. The water is warm. I feel each individual skin cell react to her massage, each pore opening like a starved mouth to the cloth. She moves me onto my side to wash my back. Every bed bath feels like the first time I've ever been touched, like an entirely new sensation.

"So my dad reckons this cold snap is going to last for a few more weeks, like last year, remember?" The water runs over me, sheds my old skin, makes me new. Lizzie glances over an area on my back with her sponge. It doesn't have as much feeling as the rest of me. "Oh, you've got a sore here, Mr. Ashcroft. I'll pop a dressing on that later." But now that she's touched it, even so lightly, I can feel the skin around it start to pucker and burn, and I know what's coming and I'm swearing and fucking livid that this moment is going to be ruined and here it comes, the lightest tingle at first, increasing in waves before the whole area explodes in a tsunami of itchiness.

"Of course all my mum can think about is her bulbs; too much cold can kill them off apparently . . ."

The itch burrows itself into my back like a maggot in an apple, the flesh around it rotting with longing, longing to be scratched.

Dear God.

". . . and all my brother can talk about is getting a day off school if it snows."

Please, Lizzie, please.

The itch spreads; like an army of ants marching, it branches from the base of my spine up towards my shoulders.

Scratch it!

I can't enjoy her washing the backs of my legs or my feet; I can't even think about it. I start counting with my breathing machine. It's all I can do to distance myself from the million tiny feet drilling the itch deeper into my back.

SCRATCH IT!

"I don't really care either way, I like snow but I can't stand slush!"

Finally, at count fifty-six she rolls me from my side onto my back and the relief is like a blanket on a fire. I can still feel the itch, licking up the base of my spine, but the worst of it has been snuffed out for now.

The last thing she does is move my head, rub the cloth behind my ears and gently dab my neck, avoiding the hole where my tracheotomy disappears into my throat. She rests my head back on the pillow, at the usual thirty-five-degree incline, and then she says, "That's better isn't it, Mr. Ashcroft. Nice and clean."

I hear a crinkle as she drops the sponge, soap packet, plastic apron and gloves she just used into the waste bin.

Lizzie leaves me and I silently thank her. She's like Alice, with her well-tuned heart. I know my dignity is more important to her than her own. I'm facing forward, staring at the empty bed opposite, the heart monitor, IV and other machines, ready and waiting to slide into the new patient's veins. Caleb went off to a whole orchestra of outraged wails and beeps from his machines, Mary barking at everyone on the ward, following the family orders to "do anything" to keep poor old Caleb ticking. I hear everything that happens on the ward. A side effect, it seems, of being suspended in life is my new supersonic hearing. Like when someone loses a sense, another one becomes more acute, I can hear people talk quietly about ten meters away, at the end of the ward. None of the docs have picked up on it. I'm glad of that; I don't want any tubes in my ears and worse, I don't want people getting nervous, self-conscious when they talk. It's my only entertainment. I never realized quite how much people moan before, about the weather, the neighbors, their children. It's so petty, so mundane, so exquisite. I love hearing Carol cursing her bunions, or Mary bitching on the phone to some poor soul in India about how she still can't access online videos. Small mercies.

By afternoon, my eyes have closed. In, out, in, out. I count along with my breathing machine as I listen to the nurses making the final preparations for the new patient, neat little footsteps checking machines, plastic being torn away from sterilized apparatus. In, out, in, out. I never know whether the next breath will come, whether I'll die here today or whether I'll be cocooned within myself as months turns to years, each day decomposing a little more, as life clatters on around me. People will fall in love, they'll go on adventures, they'll cry and shout, there'll be wars and long, lazy summer days but I'll still be here, staring at the gray ceiling, a statue, longing for some wonderful day when my feeling exhausts itself, and I'll be left with a numbness so complete it'll sweetly smother any memory of who I once was, who I once thought I could be. If I don't die soon, my hope is to be relieved of hope, and even though my body may still be pumped, prodded and wiped, my mind will be frozen and Frank will be gone.

3

Cassie

In a way it was a surprise that Jack and Cassie had guests at their wedding at all. Even before they were engaged, they talked late at night, naked and curled around each other like vines, about getting married in Scotland, somewhere wild and new to them both, just the two of them with a couple of strangers as witnesses. But they'd only been together a few weeks then, and when, eight months later, they were on their way back from Paris flushed and newly engaged, they both knew it wouldn't happen like that.

They both knew it would break Charlotte's heart if she wasn't there to see Jack, her only child, marry. So they agreed to a small ceremony and a drinks-only reception in the beautiful old converted barn behind The Hare, Buscombe village's best—and only—pub. Which was why Cassie was now being passed from guest to guest like a fragile present, for careful cheek kisses, powdery as moth's wings. All their guests tell her she looks beautiful, even the ones she's never met before.

"You look absolutely radiant," they say. "Jack's a lucky man."

Cassie smooths the tight, ivory, lace dress—which Charlotte insisted she try on—over her hips and feels an increasingly familiar bubble swell inside her as she replies, "Not as lucky as me!" And she means it; she is lucky. Bloody lucky.

Her eyes dart around the black-beamed barn, decorated by Charlotte with cheery red-berried holly wreaths, two Christmas trees and hundreds of candles, before they lock on, magnetized to the back of Jack's dark head. He's always the tallest person in a room, floating above the canopy of heads as though he's got more life in him than everyone else. The sight of him—his sure, solid features, his easy smile, the dimple on his left cheek—calms and excites Cassie simultaneously. He bends down to kiss an elderly woman Cassie thinks is his Aunt Torie. She's clutching on to his hand like a child with a balloon she can't believe she's won; she's left a haze of pink lipstick on his cheek. Aunt Torie looks up at Jack, smiling and coquettish as if she's back in her own romance from decades ago, but Jack's not looking at Aunt Torie anymore; he's looking at her, his new wife. She starts moving towards him, and they open their arms to each other, as natural as breath, and Jack kisses her full on the mouth. A camera snaps.

"Wifey," he whispers in a jokey Scottish accent, and she smiles up at him, in rapture that this is who she is now.

"Husband," she says back to him with a little bow of her head.

At home in the Brixton flat where Cassie grew up and where Jack and Cassie have lived together for the last six months, they've been calling each other husband and wife for weeks already, trying their new titles on for size. They fit perfectly. He kisses her again before someone ting-tings a spoon against a champagne glass and a hush like a wave washes over the wedding guests as they form a neat semi-circle around Charlotte. Jack and Cassie, holding hands, are gently nudged forward to the front.

Charlotte strokes the side of her blonde bob with her left hand, and her own wedding ring glows like an ember. Cassie has never seen her take it off, even though Mike died over twenty years ago. Theirs was the kind of relationship Cassie's mum, April, gently told Cassie was make-believe, improbable, a sugary fairy tale for people with sweet heads and hearts. But Charlotte's ring—its position on her left hand—is proof. April hadn't been right about everything.

Some guests are still quietly chatting so Charlotte clears her throat to quiet them. Gentle crow's feet, like quotation marks, punctuate her blue eyes as she smiles at the wedding guests who stand before her, like exotic birds in their best outfits. Jack puts his arm around Cassie. She feels his muscles tense, nervous for his mum. Cassie strokes the back of his hand to calm him.

Charlotte thanks everyone who helped with the wedding, the cousins for the Christmas tree, the local family friends for the wedding cake. The guests keep their eyes fixed on Charlotte, moving only to take blind, occasional sips of champagne. Charlotte pauses for a breath. Cassie stops stroking Jack, her hand clammy suddenly, as Charlotte starts talking again:

"Finally, I just want to say what a rare union we have witnessed today. The coming together of two exceptional individuals who share an exceptional love. The first time I met my wonderful daughter-in-law"—a couple of "whoops" from the younger guests—"I knew she was special. With the beautiful Cassie by his side, Jack is the happiest he's ever been. He came to me just a few weeks into their relationship and said, 'Things make sense now, Mum. Everything just makes sense,' and I knew my boy had found the love of his life."

Jack squeezes Cassie's waist before releasing her so he can clap. Cassie's holding a champagne glass. It's in the way and she tries to clap but her hands are clumsy around the glass.

"Of course," Charlotte says, "we all know there are two very special people who can't be with us today."

The air in the room becomes dense. Cassie feels a familiar lump harden in her throat, too large to swallow. Charlotte looks directly at Cassie, her eyes kind as always, and the lump softens.

"I know I speak for us all when I say how dearly we would have loved April, Cassie's remarkable mum, to be here with us. I'm saddened Jack and I never met April. I've heard stories of a woman who loved color, late-night dancing, a woman who laughed easily and loved heartily. Although we can never fill the void in Cassie's life, I'm certain April would have been pleased that Cassie will forever be part of a family who will love and cherish her.

After all, what more could a parent ask than for the happiness of their child?" Charlotte's voice wavers a little. "Welcome to our family, Cassie. We love you dearly."

Jack's arm snakes around Cassie's waist again.

"We're also missing Mike," Charlotte continues, "Jack's dad, today more than ever. Many of you knew Mike, so you'll know how strongly he believed in marriage, and I know he would hope, as I do, that you are as happy as we were." Charlotte's eyes fill as she looks at her son for a moment before she clears her throat and says, "Now, all that remains is for me to ask you all to raise your glasses to the bride and groom! To Cassie and Jack."

All eyes in the room spin towards them, and, like a shoal of colorful fish, moved by some unknowable, compelling force, their guests form a circle around them and their voices echo Charlotte. "Cassie and Jack."

Jack bends Cassie over his arm as he kisses her to more whoops and clapping, before they both turn to Charlotte who, speech over, is wiping her eyes.

"Thank God for waterproof mascara," she says, and Cassie holds onto Jack's hand as she hugs Charlotte.

"I meant it, Cas," Charlotte whispers in Cassie's ear, "every word."

Cassie wants to tell her again how grateful she is but she can't because Charlotte's turning towards Jack for a hug and there's a hand on Cassie's forearm gently begging attention, so Cassie turns away from Charlotte, letting go of Jack, expecting one of Jack's friends or his uncle perhaps, but the hand on her arm, Cassie realizes with a sudden drop in her stomach, belongs to Marcus.

His smile stops at his mouth. Cassie can't see any real

joy in his face even today, his dark eyes a vacuum. As far as Cassie knows they've been empty ever since April died.

"Got a hug for your old man?" His attempt at an old joke rests like stale air between them. After April and Marcus married, just six months before April died, Cassie used to tease Marcus, calling him "Daddy" in public to embarrass him and to make April laugh.

Cassie's arms feel weary as she obligingly hugs her stepdad. He's smaller than she remembers, and his body feels weak and skittish beneath the fibers of his dusty suit. She keeps herself tense, as though if she were to relax, some of his grief might seep into her. Like rich chocolate cake, Cassie finds she can only manage a little bit of Marcus at a time. Cassie gently pulls away from him, and he keeps hold of her arm with one hand; he knows she wants to float away.

"That was a lovely speech, wasn't it?" His eyebrows bounce as he talks.

"Marcus, you know, we decided not to have too many speeches, it was our . . ."

A small sac of skin pendulum swings beneath Marcus's chin as he shakes his head, trying not to care that Cassie walked herself down the aisle, that he doesn't have a spray of flowers in his jacket pocket, that there was no stepfather-of-the-bride speech.

"No, no, Cas, I wasn't implying that. I thought—what's her name . . . Charlotte?—did a good job. Your mum would've loved it."

Even a year and a half on, there still seems to be no Marcus without April. Cassie feels her dress tighten around her lungs; they feel leaden. Marcus's hand on her arm starts to burn and she feels like she's back in the hospice room, staring down at her mum's empty body, Marcus opposite. Marcus makes her feel stuck, as though she should never step away from April's deathbed.

"I haven't said hello yet, Marcus!"

Cassie turns with gratitude towards the familiar voice, and her lungs instantly loosen. Nicky, her oldest friend, must have seen her with Marcus and known she needs rescuing.

Nicky's long, red hair is braided and coiled like a rope over her shoulder; little wisps hover round her head like gas. Nicky has never liked dressing up. Her older sister told her when she was a teenager that she was too big for pretty things and the comment stuck to her like a burr. Today she's wearing a dark green silk dress to her knee; it flatters her lightly freckled skin.

"How are you, Marcus?" Nicky asks, giving him one of her firm kisses on the cheek.

Cassie keeps her eyes fixed on Nicky, but she feels Marcus's eyes flicker to her face before going back to Nicky, as though he needs reminding who Nicky is, even though he's met her many times.

It was Nicky who used to listen to Cassie moan about how weird Marcus was, how it was even weirder that he was her mum's boyfriend. They got together five years before April died. Cassie could never say it to anyone, not even Jack or Nicky, but she used to think April only married Marcus because she was dying; she knew it would make him happy.

He was a retired civil servant from the Isle of Wight who never married before April, and never had kids of his own. He was not the bon vivant she imagined for her mum; he was too beige to ever be a hero, but he made her mum happy and that made Cassie happy. So she'd decided Marcus was a good man.

There's a pause. Marcus looks stricken for a moment before he says to Nicky, "Long time no see." He squeezes Cassie's arm before he lets go. "How've you been?"

"Oh, I'm good, good, thanks. Just getting over another knee operation, but apart from that I'm fine. Wasn't it a lovely ceremony?"

Marcus ignores her question and instead asks, "Did I hear you got a new job?"

Cassie looks away, over her friend's shoulder.

"Oh, no, that wasn't me, Marcus. I'm still temping." Nicky tilts her champagne flute as an adolescent waiter, face swarming with pimples, refills it for her. "Which is, you know, fine . . . fine, for now."

"Nicky works at the same place I used to work, remember, Marcus?" Cassie says, still not looking at her stepdad.

"I'm afraid so," says Nicky, nodding at Marcus. "I'm still on the waiting list for my Jack-in-shining-armor to appear, unchain me from my desk, and whisk me off to the countryside."

Marcus laughs at Nicky; like he doesn't know what else to do. He shifts his weight from one foot to the other. Cassie wonders if she can just walk away, or if that would be unfair to Nicky.

Nicky perseveres with Marcus. "How's life on the Isle of Wight?" she asks.

"Oh, just the same; quiet, especially at this time of year."

The conversation limps on. Cassie's grateful when Charlotte catches her eye and waves Cassie over to meet an old family friend, a round jolly man whose lips feel like squashed berries as he presses them to Cassie's cheek.

She watches over his shoulder as an old school friend, Beth, interrupts Nicky and Marcus. Beth and Nicky hug, and Marcus, as though suddenly tossed overboard, steps away from them, hobbling slightly; his hip gets worse in the winter. He moves like a lost tourist through the party, vulnerable and hesitant in this new land that is populated by much happier people than he's used to. He pretends to admire the Christmas tree, then finds a waiter to top up his smeary glass. An old twist of guilt ripples through Cassie: Marcus getting old on his own. She thinks about going to say goodbye properly, promising him she'll visit soon, suggesting that maybe they could go for a sea walk along the cliffs and have a pub lunch like they used to when April was alive? But suddenly Jack takes her hand.

"Ready, wife?"

Charlotte takes her other arm, and it's all over so quickly, and, before she knows it, they're outside with the few remaining guests, and Marcus has disappeared into the night already. Probably for the best.

Nicky raises her hand, palm up to the sky and says, "It's raining."

Charlotte opens an umbrella, holds it over Cassie. "It rained cats and dogs on mine and Mike's wedding day, it's good luck."

As Cassie kisses Nicky and Charlotte goodbye before getting in the car to the airport hotel with Jack by her side, she feels the hair on her bare arms rise and she doesn't know if it's the rain or something else that's making her feel so cold.

4

Alice

I don't have long with her. Cassie Jensen still smells fresh, like an aura of the outside surrounds her. The hypothermia has turned her lips and eyelids an unnatural ice blue, like bad makeup, but her cheeks still have the slight plumpness of recent health, helping her look more alive than dead, but only just. They'll lose their bounce in a few days. The surgery team has removed any jewelry she was wearing.

I stroke her left arm, the one that's not pinned by the surgeon like a voodoo doll; it's ribboned with thin red lines, lacerations from the accident. I hold her right hand for a moment; it's warm but there's no ripple of response beneath Cassie's eyelids. A tube runs from the back of her blond head where the neurosurgeon drilled into her skull to insert a temporary probe in the cavity to monitor the inter-cranial pressure and swelling around her brain. It looks like they've done a good job; the horror of the tube as it plunges into Cassie's head is discreetly covered with a small bandage and they've only shaved a small bit of her hair. She's patched with a couple of deep bruises on her neck and chest and there's a nasty cut on her lip. Like tiny, blazing galaxies, the bruises color her otherwise fair skin. I wonder as I always do with new patients who she is, what her laugh sounds like, what she had planned to do today. Maybe she should have been meeting a friend for coffee right now. Even with the bruises, the cuts and her broken fingers, she doesn't look like she belongs here. She looks like she's pretending.

I pick up her folder from the little table by her bed. It says her dog was spooked by New Year's fireworks and disappeared in the early hours of New Year's morning. Cassie went out in the dark to look for her. It was noted there was a puddle close to where she would have fallen, which could have caused her to trip. The form is marked that it was either an accident or a hit and run, so the police will be calling.

"Nurse Marlowe?" It's Lizzie, speaking from behind the curtain, probably unsure whether she's allowed in or not.

"You can come in, Lizzie."

She pulls back the curtain just enough to move her head around. She looks quickly at Cassie before turning to me. "The family are here."

"Her husband?" I ask.

"Yes, and I think maybe her mum?"

"OK, so there's only two relatives?"

"Yup. Yes, I mean."

"OK, show them in, please. Oh, and Lizzie." Her face

reappears from behind the curtain. "Call me Alice." She nods and we smile at each other before she leaves.

I stroke Cassie's shoulder-length blond hair back to try and conceal the bandage on her head as much as possible, a feeble attempt to minimize the shock for her family. Other senior nurses delegate the family liaison duties as much as they can, but I like to do the initial meeting if I'm on duty. What a patient's family is like has a huge impact on the ward. It's often a fine-balancing act: empathy tempered with realism.

I hear footsteps coming towards us and Lizzie says in an appropriately subdued voice, "Here she is," before drawing the curtain back. Lizzie closes the curtain again behind a woman, who's probably in her sixties, and an athletic-looking man with dark hair—Cassie's husband—who looks just a few years younger than me, in his mid-thirties. I stand back. They don't notice me. It's as if they're magnetized towards Cassie.

"Cas, oh Cassie," says the husband, clasping and kissing the hand I just held. The woman stands just behind him; she places one tidy hand on his lower back. "Oh god," exclaims the husband, and starts sobbing. The woman makes small circles with her hand on his lower back and makes "shhh"-ing noises. The woman is wearing jeans and an old, lumpy cricket sweater—the sort of clothes thrown on in an emergency. The husband is in jeans and a crumpled blue T-shirt.

The woman raises her silvery head, as if suddenly aware of where she is. She looks around the curtained area and sees me for the first time. She looks as if she's searching for something but I raise a hand and say as gently as I can, "Please, take your time." I don't think the husband heard me. I don't want them to feel glared at, so I step to the other side of the curtain. The husband is still sobbing.

"Jack, remember," the woman says, "the surgeon said this would be a shock . . . that this is the worst we're going to see her." Her voice starts out clear but crackles at the end of the sentence.

I wait a few minutes while she mumbles some more soft words, and then I step forward, the rattle of the curtain makes them raise their heads. The woman has her arms around him in a small two-person huddle over Cassie. They look at me, surprised, as if they forgot they were on a hospital ward. The woman breaks away from Jack and comes towards me, her palm outstretched.

I take her hand. "I'm Alice Marlowe, the ward nurse. My team and I will be looking after Cassie while she is with us."

"Hello, Nurse. I'm Charlotte, Charlotte Jensen, Cassie's mother-in-law." She smiles, a quick reflexive flicker. She smells subtly of perfume, warm, as if she's been wearing the same scent for so many years, it's become part of her. I'll bet all her clothes carry the same smell.

Unlike his mum's, Jack's hand is clammy, almost lifeless. He's grown a sprinkle of reddish-brown stubble while they've been waiting overnight on plastic chairs.

"I'm so sorry. This must be the most terrible shock for you."

Jack meets my eyes briefly and nods his head.

"Let's go through to the family room," I say gently, "so I can give you an update and then you can come back and spend more time with Cassie, if you like."

They follow me like zombies to the end of the ward. As soon as we walk into the family room I wish I'd removed the decorations in here as well. The Jensens don't seem like plastic reindeer people.

They both shake their heads at my offer of tea or coffee. Someone's thoughtfully arranged three chairs in a semi-circle; I think it must have been Lizzie. Jack pulls his trousers up an inch at the thigh as they sit down; a sweetly old-fashioned habit, I wonder briefly who he learnt it from.

Charlotte takes a tissue out of the little packet in her lap, hands one to Jack, who holds it carefully in his hand, as if it's too precious to be used for wiping and blowing.

Jack is fiddling with something small and delicate in his hands. There's a flash as it catches the light and I know what he's holding: Cassie's engagement and wedding rings. One of the trauma nurses would have given them to him for safekeeping. He wipes his eyes, then puts the rings in the breast pocket of his shirt. A second later, he pats the outside of his shirt, either to reassure himself the rings are still there or to check that his heart is still beating.

He breathes out. "Sorry, Nurse, that was the first time we've seen her since yesterday. It was harder than I imagined." His mum puts her hand on his knee and he stares, unseeing, at the floor.

"Please don't apologize. It's a huge shock to see someone you care about after an accident like this."

A phone buzzes. It's on silent but Jack still apologizes as he lifts it out of his pocket, declining the call without looking at the screen. It gives me a second to look at them properly. The Jensens are an attractive duo. Jack is tall and broad without being gangly or boxy. I noticed earlier that his eyes are amber, like his mum's, the whites laced red with worry. Charlotte's face is a little puffy, from crying or lack of sleep or both; there are traces of old mascara and eyeliner around her eyes.

"Can you give us an update on how she's doing?" Charlotte asks. "It's been over twenty-four hours now and the surgeon didn't say much."

I sit forward in the chair. The same chair I sat in when I told Ellen's blank children that their mother would never leave a care facility, and the same chair I cried in when I couldn't find anyone else to cry for Frank.

"Cassie is obviously in serious condition. She's in a coma but that is the body's natural response to an extreme shock." I talk slowly; shock can mess with people and this is my chance to reassure them that Cassie's in the best place for her.

"Think of it like a building going into emergency-shut-down mode to protect itself. Cassie's body has hopefully only temporarily shut down to assess and eventually fix any damage caused by the accident. The good news is that she is healthy, young, and, most importantly, breathing on her own. The ventilator is just to protect her airways. Her MRI scan showed a lot of swelling around her brain from the skull fracture, which is why she has a tube in her head, measuring the pressure caused by the swelling. We are hoping the swelling is a short-term response from the accident and will decrease over the next few days, so we need to wait to see if it does go down. Before then, anymore scans we do may give us inaccurate results."

Charlotte nods gently; I think through her exhaustion,

she's trying to remember what I'm saying so she can reassure Jack in case he can't remember later.

Jack twists the wedding band on his finger and stares at his feet. Charlotte pats his knee as I talk.

"Hopefully, Cassie won't be here for long before she's moved to a rehabilitation ward but, for now, she'll be receiving the best care possible for patients in her condition. I'll make sure she stays comfortable and that all her needs are met until we know more about what's going on. Until then, I'm afraid it's a waiting game. Her body needs to rest and that's exactly what it's doing."

Charlotte nods, unblinking, before she asks, "Is there anything we can do for her?"

"It's good to come and just sit with her. Talk to her if you can. It's best to visit when you're feeling strong and rested though. I've worked with coma patients for a few years and I'm quite certain they pick up on our mood and how we're feeling." I don't want to overdo it; Jack seems vacant with shock. I smile gently as I hand Charlotte the ward information leaflets and my contact details.

"Mr. Sharma, the attending physician, and I were hoping to meet with you tomorrow morning at ten o'clock?"

They both nod. "Ten o'clock, yes," Charlotte says.

"Good. Well, if you have anymore questions you'll see me around the ward."

Jack and Charlotte are too tired to realize the conversation has come to a close so I stand up. "Try and get some rest," I tell them, before they shuffle to their feet.

They thank me and Charlotte holds my hand briefly in both her own; they feel soft from rich hand cream. Even with gray shadows underneath her eyes, and in a lumpy sweater, she is striking. Her blond hair is sleek, streaked with lightening white and gray. Her wrinkles seem to compliment her round face, like the fine lines in soft, expensive leather. She looks like the sort of woman who at any other time would be well groomed.

"Maisie, the dog . . . she's run off before," she says, releasing my hand. "I can't believe this is happening."

I try to smile reassuringly. "You must try and rest." As they turn to leave I add, "Oh, sorry, I forgot to ask, does Cassie have any other family members you want me to contact? Parents, brothers or sisters?"

Charlotte talks softly, as if she's worried Cassie will overhear even from the other end of the ward. "No, no, her mum died from cancer two and a half years ago and she never knew her dad. So I'm afraid it's just us. We've been a close little family though, haven't we, Jack?" She raises a hand to her mouth.

Jack pulls her towards him, tucks her under his arm and says, "Come on, Mum, you're exhausted. We need to get home." He guides her gently away.

Carol, Mary and I eat our homemade sandwiches together in the nurses break room. We're an unlikely trio in some ways, but we've grown close and keep an eye on each other when a patient dies or the job is getting to us. As Mary says, in reference to the first time we clicked, "Nothing brings people together quite like clearing up a pool of puke at four in the morning."

Today, like most days, Mary is holding court, telling Carol and me about the living will she's drawing up with her husband Pat. Turning sixty has made Mary more aware of her mortality. In November, soon after Frank arrived, we resuscitated a woman the same age as Mary, pumping her with chemicals. None of us wanted to, but the family was desperate. We squeezed three more days of bed-ridden unconscious life out of that poor woman. Afterwards, Mary was maudlin; she told us she'd haunt us for the rest of our lives if we ever put her through something like that.

"I asked for a tattoo for Christmas," she says, running a finger between her eyebrows. "Yeah, I want 'Do Not Resuscitate' tattooed on my forehead."

Carol and I laugh.

"You should get 'Do Not Intubate' on your upper lip while you're at it," Carol says.

Mary opens a packet of crisps. "Not a bad idea, Caz, not a bad idea."

Carol turns towards me. "You haven't told us about your Christmas yet, Ali?"

"Oh, you know, the usual: eating and drinking too much, presents I don't really need, afternoon naps, arguing over Trivial Pursuit . . . all of that traditional stuff."

They both nod, their mouths full. I don't tell them about how, for the whole week with my family home, I felt like I was leading my childlessness behind me, a great elephant crashing into every room. My mum desperately searching for something to say that wasn't related to Harry and Elsa, my dad's silence from behind his newspaper becoming another presence in the room, and my sister's careful, apologetic smiles. Drunk, she told me once she feels guilty that she produced two perfect, healthy, pink babies, and started talking about "other options," which was when I had to walk away. I'm not sure I'll ever be ready to talk about other options. I feel for them, I really do, I don't know what to say either. Sometimes I wish we were the sort of family to scream and shout, that we could exorcise our grief together, mourn our lost grandchildren, nieces, nephews, cousins and children. Perhaps that would make the elephant turn tail and leave us all alone, for a while at least.

There's a pause for chewing and swallowing, before Carol says, "Pretty, isn't she? This new Cassie."

"Yes, yes, she really is," I agree before Carol carries on.

"I know it shouldn't, but it breaks my heart even more that she's young and pretty." Half of the biscuit she'd been dunking falls into her tea. "Shit," she says under her breath and she starts trawling her cup with a teaspoon.

"So what happened exactly?" Mary asks, before putting a handful of crisps in her mouth.

I tell them what I know of Cassie's story. "She came back from a local party earlier than her husband to check on her dog. The dog spooked, ran off, and Cassie went out to look for her. It's happened before, apparently. Her husband walked home a couple of hours after her, heard the sirens just as he got home. They live about ten miles away, near Buscombe, so it was one of those little windy country lanes they've got out there, no lights, raining. You know how icy it's been recently. Well, it must have been worse in the countryside. The police reckon she either slipped or it was a hit and run." Both Mary and Jen tut and shake their heads as I carry on. "She fell into a stream by the side of the lane, badly, hence the bruising. She was in the stream for about forty-five minutes; the water was just above freezing. She was found just in time. Sharma reckons she'll most likely have some permanent damage."

"Of course he does," says Mary. "Old Dr. Doom. So what is the family like then? Weepers and wailers or stiff upper lippers?"

"Bit of both really. Poor things. Obviously, still in shock."

"The husband was pretty easy on the eye."

Carol's like a sniffer dog when it comes to men. Neither Mary or I say anything.

Carol defends herself anyway. "Don't tell me you weren't thinking the same thing."

I stand and put my Tupperware in the sink and wonder whether it's a sign of age or contentment that I hadn't been thinking about Jack, I'd been thinking about how close Jack and his mum seemed, their love for each other active and unashamed. But then, that's what tends to happen, loved ones rally for the initial drama, attracted to the shock, and then slowly people wander away, disinterested in the long grind towards rehabilitation.

"Jack's mum waited with him all day yesterday while Cassie was in surgery. Jack didn't want to leave Cassie and his mum wouldn't leave him alone, so both of them waited all night as well," I say, just as there's a knock at the door and Lizzie appears.

"Hi, Liz," says Mary, "Carol was just telling us she fancies Jack Jensen. Did you see him?"

Lizzie smiles at Mary, blushes, and says to me, "There are two police officers here to see you, I think it's about Cassie Jensen."

I leave immediately. There's one male and one female officer waiting for me. Lizzie showed them to the family room, so I meet with them there. The chairs are still arranged from my meeting with the Jensens. I sit in the chair Charlotte sat in. DI Anderson is prematurely bald and overweight, his head like a sweaty egg glistening above his too-tight collar. He makes a wheezy show of getting out of his chair as I come into the little room. He's twitchy and uncomfortable.

"Sorry, I hate hospitals," he says.

"Most people do," I reply as I shake his pillowy hand.

He introduces his colleague, Constable Jane Brooks, a young woman with short, spiky hair, and ears dotted with old piercing scars, relics from another life. Anderson tells me they've reviewed the case at the station and because Cassie has significant bruising on her right side, concurrent with being hit, and because they found tire marks at the scene, possibly from an old SUV or similar, they currently think it was a hit and run.

"People get so carried away this time of year. There was one guy a couple of years back, killed someone just outside Brighton and swore blind he'd only hit a badger." Anderson is, I suspect, the sort of man who has a story for every occasion.

"What can we do?" Anderson asks no one in particular. "She was walking on a dark lane early in the morning, no witnesses, no nothing. We're talking to the neighbor who found her now, a Jonathan Parker. He called the ambulance when his dogs led him to her. But the nearest cameras are over a mile away on the Brighton Road, so I wouldn't hold your breath that we'll catch the bugger." He shakes his head. "Anyway, we've put signs up around the area and have the incident on our website, but, as I said, I wouldn't hold your breath."

Brooks keeps her head cocked to one side as Anderson

talks. She squeezes the fingers of one hand with the other in her lap, like she's trying to stop herself from saying something. She smiles at me quickly as we shake hands before they leave. It feels like an apology. She hands me her card before she dutifully follows Anderson, who's already left the room.

I knock on Sharma's office door exactly at 7:15 p.m. as he requested. I had been getting ready to go home but he said it was urgent and I've learnt not to ignore him. He calls out, "*Intrare.*" I don't know what it means, so I just open the door.

He sits behind his desk. It's a boxy, bland office and Sharma has made no attempt to personalize it. There are no photos of his family, no homemade cards from his kids. There is no intimacy here. He seems slightly ruffled, less composed than normal. I have the sense that if I had entered two minutes earlier I might have caught him with his shiny head in his hands. It must be about one of the patients. I hope it's not Frank. He asks me to sit and starts talking without preamble.

"Nurse, Mrs. Jensen had a full-body MRI downstairs in trauma before she was brought up to us."

"Yes, I thought she would."

"Well, the radiologist, a—" Sharma pauses to look at the notes before him "—Henry Chadwick, ever heard of him?" He glances at me but I shake my head. He keeps talking. "Well, Henry Chadwick saw something quite unexpected. He saw a fetus. It seems, against all the odds, Mrs. Jensen is pregnant."

"What?" It sounds like a joke; pregnancy, that word

and all its meaning, belongs to a different ward, a different world from the one on 9B. Aneurysm, hemorrhage, tumor; they're our kind of words . . . but pregnant?

"She's pregnant, *praegnas*, pregnant."

"But that's, that's . . ." I want to say "impossible" but at the same moment I realize that's wrong; it's entirely possible. It's highly unlikely, of course—absurd almost that a fetus would survive the trauma of the accident and then almost an hour in a freezing stream—but it's still possible. I feel light with the realization. Sharma and I stare at each other. I'm pretty sure my expression matches his: eyes wide, faces made youthful, lit up by something so improbable, so fantastic, a laugh bubbles up inside me.

Sharma blinks, clears his throat and looks at his notes again. "She's approximately twelve weeks."

I want to tell Sharma to slow down. "Twelve?" I ask, holding onto the back of the chair, but Sharma ignores me, relying on his notes to sober him.

"An obstetrics consultant, a—" Sharma looks at his notes again "—Elizabeth Longe, will be performing more tests on Mrs. Jensen first thing tomorrow morning, to establish the health of the fetus and so on. I know you've been caring for her since she arrived, so I thought it best to let you know, but we are keeping this confidential for now. Did the family mention anything?"

I think of the puffy-eyed Jensens . . . the shadows under Jack's eyes. Although in shock, they would have said something if they'd known, surely?

"No, no they didn't say anything."

Sharma frowns briefly, as if he's smelled something unpleasant.

"OK. I think in that case it's vital we keep this between ourselves until we know more and we've had a chance to talk to the husband. It's curious her GP, Dr. Hillard, didn't mention it either. Anyway, Ms. Longe is going to perform the tests here tomorrow so we don't have to move her. Who's with her tonight?"

I think of the thick-set, vacant-eyed Paula.

"Paula Simms."

Sharma's lip curls slightly; he thinks Paula is sloppy.

"As I said, let's keep this between us for now. I've gone over Mrs. Jensen's medications and checked nothing will impact negatively upon the fetus, so all should be well on that front. We're seeing the family tomorrow?"

I nod, tell him we're meeting them at 10 a.m.

He smiles at me briefly before dismissing me, a fleeting acknowledgement of the miraculous survival of this new, tiny life.

I feel a little high as I walk out of Sharma's office. Did Sharma really say twelve? Or did I not hear him properly? I want to go to the toilet, splash my face with water before taking some deep breaths and passing my day, my patient, this miracle over to Paula's care, but before I make it to the toilet, Carol, who already has her black coat on over her dark blue matron's uniform, calls out to me.

"Alice, love, glad I caught you. Paula just called. She's running late again, something about one of her kids being unwell. She won't be in for about another half an hour. You couldn't hang around, could you?"

I'm often asked to cover into the evening for other nurses; they know I don't have any bedtime stories to read. David thinks I shouldn't, but I find it hard to say no. Tonight, though, this extra half an hour feels like a gift: some time with Cassie on my own.

"OK, no problem," I answer Carol, who doesn't notice the unusual enthusiasm to stay in my voice, and tell her to have a good evening.

With all the curtains drawn around the beds, the ward looks ready for a secret. The portable ultrasound scanner is in its usual place, tucked in a corner. I pointed it out to Lizzie today, as I reminded her where everything is. I wouldn't have believed I'd be using it like this just a few hours later. I roll the little machine down the corridor, the wheels squeak. It's already nighttime-dark outside, the fluorescent lights on the ward ceiling highlight an anemic path before me. Carol said Paula would be half an hour, which means she'll be forty-five minutes. The other nurses won't look in on Cassie; they'll be busy with their own patients and we discourage visitors so late. It's risky, but I can't resist having a quick look . . . a few seconds just to see for myself.

I enter the room and Cassie lies just as before, the light from the bedside lamp covers her in egg-yolk yellow, her hair arranged as I left it a couple of hours earlier, stroked back over the bandage on her head. She looks like she's drowning in her own sleep. Her eyes are open just enough to see a sliver of iris. She looks like she's looking down at her belly, as though she was giving us a clue all along: "Follow my eyes! The secret is down there!"

Leaving the scanner just inside Cassie's curtain, I stand by her head and bend down towards her.

"Cassie," I say, "I just spoke to Sharma." I pause, wondering how best to phrase what I need to say; if the

Jensens didn't know, then is it possible Cassie didn't even know she was pregnant? I'm fairly sure Sharma did say twelve weeks but I've only heard of naive teenagers claiming they didn't know so far into a pregnancy. I decide to risk it and say softly, "You're pregnant, Cassie. You're still pregnant. I hope you don't mind, but I'm just going to take a quick look."

I open her hospital gown. As I apply the gel onto her abdomen, I notice it is a little swollen. I'd thought it was just water retention, normal after a trauma. I don't need to apologize for the gel being cold, but I still look up to see if she reacts. She doesn't even flicker.

The strange film appears in grainy detail; the fallopian tubes, the uterus all measured by a heartbeat, like a little jumping rabbit, the fetus is curved like a strange shell: the brave, tiny proof. Life in this hidden halfway world!

I stare at the image. I'm relieved I was right; Sharma must have said twelve weeks. The baby feels a little safer. The older it is, the greater the chance it'll survive. I stroke Cassie's arm and smile at her briefly a couple of times before voices on the ward spook me and I turn the machine off, wipe the gel off her stomach and, before anyone can see, wheel the scanner back to its place in the supply cabinet before going back to Cassie.

I'd seen a baby. Through it all, Cassie had managed to protect her child, and I want to kiss her cheek, but instead I hold her hand again.

"The baby looks fine, Cassie," I tell her. "We'll know more tomorrow, but you should know, your baby looks fine." I place my right hand over her abdomen and feel the gentle curve, the hill of her belly that now seems obvious.

I promise her silently that I'll look after her, her and her baby. I stroke her dark blond hair, pushing strands behind her ears.

"I'll wash it for you soon, Cassie. I always feel better with clean hair. Maybe you will, too."

I try not to be selfish, and try not to think that if Cassie's baby survived then maybe . . . maybe one could survive in me? I feel my lower stomach, and feel for any change there, some hope, but it's frozen to me, and I make myself remember my promise to David. So, as I wait for Paula to arrive, I just hold Cassie's hand and hope she knows she's not alone.

5

Frank

Cassie's bloke and his mum were all degrees of gutted to see their girl black and blue, pierced by tubes and surrounded by screens, only just on the right side of life's line. They kept on hugging and whispering soft words to each other. There's nothing performative—nothing awkward—in their intimacy. I like to think we were like that, Ange and I, as a couple, even if only for a short while.

We met at her sister Abi's wedding. At twenty-seven I was seven years older than Ange. Abi was marrying an old mate of mine, Phil. Me and my mates couldn't believe Phil with his trophy ears and hook nose had bagged petite, blonde Abi. I didn't even know she had a younger sister until an even better-looking version of Abi was in the queue next to me at the buffet table.

"What's that?" she said pointing to a jelly dessert, wobbling with the movement of the trestle table.

I had no idea, but didn't want to seem thick, so I just blurted out, "Tiramisu."

She made a face. "Bless you!"

I'm not sure it was even a joke, but I laughed like it was the funniest thing I'd ever heard, and she started laughing too and licked a puff of cream off her finger, which I took to be a good sign.

"You're funny!" I said and tried to avoid looking at her breasts as I asked her to dance. Two hours later I was in the pub parking lot with Ange's tongue in my mouth and her hands at my fly. Six months later, and Ange and I had a smaller reception in the same pub, the life growing in Ange's tummy, and my thinly disguised terror now undeniable. She seemed happy enough then, as if a half hour chat outside a pub with me spilling my soda over our shared chips when she said, "I'm pregnant, Frank," was the way she always dreamed she'd start a family. I told her I'd support her through an abortion, and she'd snarled like a dog snapping at a fly and told me never to say that word again. She looked frightened, unmasked for the first time, and I thought in that moment that I loved her, but I didn't tell her. We were always like that, Ange and I, keeping our words sealed and packaged up within our own heads, worried that if we ripped ourselves open the truth would spill out between us, make a mess that neither of us knew how to clean up.

Without telling Ange, I gave up my shot at a managerial placement with an American-based construction company. A few years later, Ange called my giving up the placement her "first disappointment"—she'd always wanted to move to America, apparently—but there was a baby on the way. I thought I was doing the right thing.

That was the first time I felt it: something dark and predatory in my shadow, waiting for me to stumble so it could pounce, and when it did, I didn't come home for three days. I ended up in Reading, miles away from home, by the bins at the back of a pub I didn't recognize, my mouth just an inch away from a thick, acidy pool of my own vomit. Once I compressed my shame, like a wrecked car at a scrap heap, and squeezed it small enough to swallow—a painful, metallic-tasting pill down a dry throat—I thought about how close I'd come to death, how easily Lucy could have lost her dad. Anything could have happened: I could have fallen onto a train track; had I been an inch or two closer to my puke my lungs would have filled and that would have been that. I promised Ange it wouldn't happen again and for a while I think we both tried to believe it. But being addicted to something is like being constantly stalked. It's always there, sniffing out weakness, licking its lips, braced and ready to spring from the shadows.

Eventually the creature would always find me. It pounced when I lost my job. It pounced when I heard Ange telling the other hairdressers at the salon where she worked that she should never have married me. And it pounced when Ange finally chucked me out.

After that, it seemed to take up residence within me, switching places with the man I tried to be, consigning Frank to the shadows, meek and withered as the beast gnawed my bones, sucking out the marrow of my life with every bottle of whiskey. I managed to keep myself away from Luce when the beast was in control; I wouldn't let her see me rabid with booze . . . couldn't do that to her.

I'd watch her sometimes; I got myself on a bus to the airport when she came back from a holiday in Spain once, and a couple of times I followed her home to make sure she was safe after a night out. I think she sensed me keeping an eye on her; I watched her stop and listen, but she never saw me, thank God, grizzled and stinking. I wrote to her instead, told her how proud I was of her, how I was going to get better, make it up to her and her mum. I told her I was going to get myself on a detox program as I swigged straight from the bottle.

When my eyes first slid open after the coma, and my brain finally clicked into place with my body, it was as if the world had been submerged in water. What I soon discovered were ward lights spun a kaleidoscope of color, until my eyes settled enough for shapes to form. Ghostly figures darted around, fast as silverfish. My body lay before me, where it should be, but it was covered in white, contours soft as snow. The air pressed down on me, so heavy I thought it would surely crush me.

Not dead then, but not exactly alive either.

My mind reeled, trying to find the thread of my last conscious thought, but it was like trying to figure out where I was before I was born.

With effort, I focused my gaze higher and I saw a bed opposite, just a few feet away. The bed had high, plastic sides and propped up in it was something that looked like it had fallen out of a formaldehyde jar. Tubes and cables cascaded out of the specimen like slides at a water park.

Poor bugger.

I tried to call out to the person in the bed, but it was like trying to make someone else speak. I was fairly sure

I wasn't dead because my internal voice was still clear as a bell, and my mind felt sharp, nimble with fear and confusion but my body was swollen and familiar with shame. It must have been quite a bender.

It's OK, I told myself, trying to abate the avalanche of panic. You're just a bit rusty.

I tried to talk again but I couldn't fill my lungs enough. I couldn't fill them at all; someone or something was pumping my lungs with air. A blue tube fell off into the abyss from the lower reaches of my line of sight, the angle of the blue thing curled directly towards my lower throat. I tried to feel my throat. It felt blocked, by something hard and cold, as if I'd swallowed a cannonball and then I heard my breathing machine, like bellows pumping at a fire, punctuated by a rude rhythmic beep. On impulse, I raised my arm to pull the cruel thing out of my throat—it felt like it was feeding on me—but I didn't feel my arm muscles flex or my fingers wrap and tug the tube out of my throat. My arm didn't move; it didn't even twitch. Panic coursed through me like lava. If I could, I would have screamed, thrashed around with terror, but I didn't even twitch a toe.

I don't know how long I was like that, until one of the fish, a woman in a dark blue uniform swimming busily between me and the poor bugger opposite, noticed me. I don't know what made her stop and look. She was holding some old sheets all bundled up in her arms. She looked busy, but something, perhaps a glint from my eye, made her look directly at me and I told her with all my being *I'm here* and in that moment I think Alice saw this last little grain of life behind my eyes. She dropped the sheets to the floor and came close enough for me to smell her; like apples and antibacterial alcohol gel. Her eyes were full moons; they crested as she smiled, and, for the first time, I saw that sweet little gap in her teeth.

"Frank, I'm a nurse. My name is Alice. You're in hospital. Can you hear me, Frank?"

I tried to talk but some bastard had poured cement down my throat.

"Just try and blink for me, Frank."

I tried to blink but it was as if my eyelid wasn't designed to lubricate my eyeball.

What is happening? What the fuck is happening?

She stared into my eyes so intently that it looked as if she was planning on crawling in here with me.

Is this some form of extreme rehab?

"Frank, you're safe. You're in hospital. You had a stroke."

A stroke?

"You've been in a coma, Frank. A coma for two months."

Jesus, two months?

My mind wheeled, trying to find a recent memory to prove she was wrong as Alice called over her shoulder to someone I couldn't see.

I need to piss.

"Carol, do you mind getting Sharma?" Alice asked the woman.

"He's on his rounds on 9C."

"Well, can you page him? He needs to know Frank Ashcroft has opened his eyes, and if he looks blank, say Bed three, 9B."

I needed to piss urgently. I didn't know how to tell her, but then the pressure just dissolved and I panicked, waited for a wet patch to appear, to creep across my crotch. Nothing. It was as if my piss just evaporated, disappeared. *This is fucking weird.*

Alice didn't seem to notice or care so I thought I'd got away with it; I didn't know I was catheterized. She kept talking to me.

"You've been doing well, Frank, although it's a huge relief to see your eyes open."

She sounded excited. It was a promising start. I tried to smile at her, but it felt like some sadist had sewn my lips together. She came closer, close enough for me to feel the warm puff of her words on my cheek.

"Can you blink for me, Frank?" she asked gently.

I'll blink.

I tried, but my eyeballs were stone. I saw a pulse of disappointment in Alice's eyes. I tried again and again but I was still as a statue.

"Never mind, Frank, all in good time. All in good time." She stroked my arm, the one without a tube running into it, and I felt a silky, tingly sensation as our skin touched.

There! I thought, *At least I felt that! At least I can feel.*

Alice turned and stood up, out of my view, my lower arm suddenly cold without her touch. She was replaced by a man's crotch at the end of the bed. He had pristinely pressed khaki-colored trousers.

He peered into my face. He was Indian. I read somewhere the best doctors are Indians these days. He squinted into my eyes, puckering his face, and all of a sudden I was blinded again by a light so bright I thought I must have suddenly died after all. But then it was over and my sight returned blotchy, like a watercolor and then I heard it for the first time, that phrase, that godawful phrase that I would love to pulverize like a cigarette butt under my foot.

"Involuntary spasms," he said. "Involuntary spasms."

"Really, Doctor? I'm sure there was something else there." *That's right, Alice.*

"I'm afraid you're mistaken. It's easy to see what we want when looking too closely for improvement, you know that."

No, no, that's bullshit. Ignore him, Alice!

"He is still in a persistent coma," the doc continued. "We should probably anticipate more involuntary spasms, and look out for them around other areas of the body. It's muscle reflex, nothing more, typical in Apallic Syndrome. His eyes may open but he won't regain consciousness is my bet. When his eyes are open, moisten them frequently to prevent infection and let me know if he blinks on demand; then we can think about doing a PET scan."

Alice argued with him for a bit, but he said a scan was too expensive, so that was that. It was a relief when he left me alone with Alice again.

She leant towards me and whispered, "I know this must be terrifying, Frank, but remember you're safe and I think you're getting better. Save your energy and when you can, try and blink, Frank, try and blink as hard as you can."

I saw the gap for the second time when she smiled and I thought, *Of course she's right. Of course I can't just get up, recover straight away. This is going to take time. This is going to take effort.*

She darted around me a bit then, checking God knows what. Occasionally I heard her mumbling numbers, jotting things down in a folder, which she slotted into the frame at the end of my bed. Then she said goodbye, told me she'd be back later and she left.

I heard her shoes squeak for the first time; they reminded me of the guinea pig Lucy had when she was little. I was left on my own again, staring at the poor bloke opposite. I listened to the old clock by his bedside tick, tick, tick, every second identical to the one before. My breathing machine beat slower but just as metronomic, and any calm I felt when Alice was with me was immediately smothered by a panic so visceral, so charged, that I was sure it must make me twitch. But it didn't.

My fear woke up in me then. It crawled from the pit of my stomach, and uncurled itself. With cold tentacles it crept into the rest of my body. My mind crashed around my skull as though it was trapped in someone else. I'm stuck in a prison the exact size and shape of my body.

What the fuck is going on? I silently screamed. *Why the fuck can't I move?*

One month on and I still haven't blinked. I still try; my mind bleeds with frustration. I watch Alice blink, the most basic reflex, and I imagine that brief split second of black, the relief, perhaps unnoticed by Alice, as lid lubricates eyeball, something she does thousands of times a day and I'd give both testicles to do once. Sometimes even I think the doctor might be right. Perhaps I am just a husk; perhaps I am suspended between life and death. Thinking like that is dangerous though. Fear burrows into my bones and I crave relief. I long to slip permanently away, but, of course, I can't even do that. I spent days trying to crash my mind like a computer, find some button that will release me, but my body will be pumped with nutrients and drugs, and air will be blown in and out, in, out, in, out of my lungs, Alice will carry on talking about getting better and I just lie here, inert in this body, locked in life.

Lizzie, bless her heart, didn't close my curtains properly this evening, and as she left me facing forward I get my first good look at Cassie. There's one soft light on her, the darkness looks like it's trying to swallow her up. Only two days since the accident, her first night on 9B, and she's already starting to look rigid, brittle, like she's holding herself up in bed. It must be her muscles tightening. I hope for her sake she's deep wherever she is; otherwise those muscles will soon be agony, like lumps of skewered kebab meat turning over burning coals. Only her face looks serene.

Paula must be late again. Alice should be on her way home by now, but instead I watch as she wheels a little machine down the ward in front of her. I only see it briefly but I'm sure it's the ultrasound. It takes me awhile to believe what I see in glimpses. It's only when I hear Alice crying gently and I hear the word "pregnant" that I know it's true. Cassie's pregnant. Pregnant?

It takes me a moment to wrap my head around that one. How can she be pregnant, here on 9B? And more to the point, she looks like a half-crushed beetle on her back; she barely survived, how could a tiny baby? Besides, medically speaking, I reckon she's even worse off than me. Even coma patients are in a hierarchy. She's GCS 4 so her consciousness is off on a jaunt, God knows where, but her body is here, and unless my ears are going the way of the rest of me, or unless I misheard Alice, she is pregnant. I will her to be brave, wherever she is down her rabbit hole.

Alice leaves Cassie after a few minutes, pushing the ultrasound back to its place, before going straight back to Cassie. I think I can hear Alice's excitement ringing through her footsteps, the movement of her stride.

Be careful, Alice, look after yourself, please look after yourself.

I focus on my breathing machine, and count along with the breaths, like the sound of the sea on the shore, it calms me and I remember, all those years ago, how it was when Ange was pregnant. I was even clumsier than normal around her. Sometimes, usually if someone else was around, she'd grab my hand and I'd feel the baby kick. It made me queasy and panic would rise up like bile as I looked up at Ange's smiling face and the creature in my shadow would start licking its paws. Then Lucy was born, pink and squirming, and one of the nurses said, "She looks like you, Mr. Ashcroft. She looks like her daddy." At that moment I felt the world slide into exquisite focus, like slotting the final color into place on a Rubik's Cube. The creature slept and I felt clear, organized.

"I am your daddy," I said to her red, puffy little face and then she did her first pee on me, which, in years to come, would make Lucy laugh and laugh every time I told the story of her birth. I've been hooked ever since.

Alice told me Lucy came everyday for the first few weeks, when I was like Cassie, deep somewhere I can't explain, but Lucy can't visit so much now. The University College London were good to her and gave her some time off during the first couple of weeks I was in here. I miss her, of course, but I'm pleased she's back in London, focusing on her degree. She's the first from either family to go to university. She's studying English literature. I want to get better to tell her I'm proud of her, of course I do, but when blinking an eyelid seems like a fantasy, the thought of saying words feels delusional.

Still, Alice always seems to think there's hope. "It takes time, Frank," she always reminds me. "It takes time."

Alice stays with Cassie, even after Paula has arrived. She massages her hand, trying to tease blood into her muscles so they don't petrify too quickly.

I watch them, still trying to wrap my head around the news, silent as the moon, when the ward doors sigh open and I hear voices at reception, a low, urgent man's voice first and Paula's laconic response, lazy as chewing gum. I watch as Alice places Cassie's hand carefully back onto her bed, alert suddenly. I haven't heard the man's voice before and I don't think Alice recognizes it either.

Suddenly, the floor squeals like it's alive as a tall, fair-haired man runs down the ward and into my view. He skips to a stop outside our curtains, ignoring Paula's shouts behind him. His hair is wild, and even from here I can see that his breathing is fast and his heart is beating, like something winged and panicked. His eyes meet mine for just a second; they're electric. He has the blanched, unpredictable look of someone who has no idea what they're doing, like a new swimmer who's just let go of the edge. Then he turns towards Cassie's curtain, so I can only see the back of his head. Alice is too quick, her instinct to protect far stronger than his wired energy. She closes the curtain behind her and puts herself between the curtain and the man. Paula shouts that she's calling security, but neither Alice or the man look at her; they're staring at each other. Alice's face is rigid, sharp and uncompromising as a knife. His breath is long and labored now, like something slowly dying.

"We need someone on 9B immediately, there's an intruder here," Paula says into the receiver.

"Let me see her," he says, like he's commanding Alice, but Alice stands firm. She won't let him any closer.

"Security will be here any second," Paula shouts down the ward towards Alice.

"Please, let me see her?" he asks again, but this time, there's begging in his voice.

Alice shakes her head slowly at him.

Careful, Alice.

"My colleague told you; it's past visiting hours. We don't let people run onto our ward, demanding to see patients in our care. Who are you?" Her voice is like a hand on his chest, pushing him away from getting any closer to Cassie.

The man rakes a hand through his hair, shakes his head, as though it hadn't crossed his mind he'd meet with any resistance.

"I'm a friend of Cassie's, her neighbor. I found her, I found her in the stream. I've been at the police station all day, so I couldn't come any earlier so I just thought . . . I just thought I'd try and see her now. I haven't slept for thirty-six hours. I just need to see her."

They both turn towards the tap, tap of hard shoes running down the ward. He turns back to Alice and I don't hear what the man says above the crackle of radios and Paula shouting, "There, he's over there!"

Alice faces the man again and I watch as her face folds

into a frown, and I know that whatever he's just said doesn't make sense to Alice.

"What are you talking about?" she asks, but it's too late. A security man in a black uniform is upon him, and it's clear he's all out of fight as he holds his hands up in submission.

6

Cassie

Underneath the hopeful smell of new wood, and the chemical funk of whatever Jack used to stop it rotting, the shed still smells musty to Cassie, of rust, lawnmowers and long-forgotten garden tools. Jack started calling it her "studio" but she teased him for being pretentious; it is still, after all, just a shed, with its hollow floor and the whorls in the wood that pop like psychedelic eyes. Cassie thinks April would have approved.

Nicky's the first person to see the shed since they finished doing it up a couple of days ago. The door creaks on its hinges as Cassie and Nicky step from the sunny March day into the dark folds of Cassie's current favorite room in the whole of Steeple Cottage.

"It's still a work in progress," Cassie says, a little shy suddenly, as though she needs her old school friend to know it's going to get even better. "There's more I want to do."

"Oh, Cas!" Nicky sighs her name, long and airy as she looks around the small rectangular space. Cassie and Jack spent a few days clearing out the shed, stripping back the old wood, patching up areas that had started to rot. Jack said he could only take one day off from work to help, so Cassie did the decorating on her own. She'd laid one of April's thin Moroccan rugs on the floor, hammered in nails for her painting utensils and carefully unpacked her mum's and her own painting boxes and canvases. Eventually the sharp smell of oil paints would mask the grimy whiff of engine oil, and the shed would—to Cassie at least—maybe even smell like home.

"The view's the best bit," Cassie says, a high-pitched excitement back in her voice as she takes Nicky's hand and leads her to the little window on the far side of the shed. They have to step around April's old easel that stands proud on its spindly legs in the middle of the shed misshapen by dried globs of paint, the once-bright layers now the color of mulch.

Nicky drops her long white arm over Cassie's shoulders and Cassie snakes an arm loosely around her friend's waist as the two women stand to face the window that frames a view of the Sussex Downs, the curvature of the hills gentle as sleeping giants.

"It's amazing, Cas."

"I know . . . I can't believe I get to paint here everyday if I want."

"Not just this, but the whole thing, meeting Jack, moving here. All of it." Nicky lifts her arm off Cassie's shoulders and as she turns to face her friend, Cassie notices Nicky's blue eyes are glossed with emotion, but her thin, lightly freckled lips smile. They've talked about it many times before, of course, how meeting Jack eighteen months ago has led to Cassie slowly gluing her broken life back together like fragments of a dropped vase, patched up to create an unexpected but more beautiful design.

"It's really cool, Cas."

Cassie smiles gratefully; Nicky never gives compliments half-heartedly. She wants to find a way to tell her friend the same thing could happen to her without sounding patronizing, but before she finds the words, Nicky starts talking again, the sparkle back in her voice.

"I mean, imagine how different everything would have been if you'd stayed with Robbie, or worse, that weird hip-hop DJ . . . what was his name again?"

"Daz."

"Yeah, that was it. Daz. God, he was weird." Nicky scoffs and, turning back to the view, says, "By the way, Beth said it's true Robbie got some poor teenager pregnant and has left her to raise the kid on her own."

Cassie thinks—as she always does whenever someone mentions a young, single parent—of her mum, and she feels her joy dampen. She doesn't want to think about her mum now; she wants Nicky to keep sharing in the delight of "Mrs. Cassie Jensen's" new life. It's unsettling talking about her old life here, like remembering a long-forgotten unfriendly acquaintance, someone buried in the past.

Cassie finds she can't stay still, so she turns away as Nicky slouches against the window and starts telling Cassie about Beth's new boyfriend. Cassie busies herself, picks up her newly washed painting apron—one of Jack's old shirts—from the floor, and hangs it back on the nail she hammered in yesterday. She flicks some invisible dirt from the white, silky heads of her new paintbrushes. She waits for a pause in Nicky's story then pulls Nicky's arm and, pointing at a wooden box on the old table, says, "Check these oils out, Charlotte gave them to me. They're amazing. Look." But as Cassie goes to open the box, she can feel Nicky's attention is pulled elsewhere.

She's looking at the two canvases Cassie propped up on the ridge that runs along the inside of the shed. The canvases are small, just a foot square; Cassie painted them in a late-night frenzy in Marcus's cottage on the Isle of Wight, just days after April told her she had stage IV breast cancer.

Nicky pauses in front of them, but doesn't say anything. Both canvases are covered in violent reds in various shades that rip and swirl across the surface. In the far-right corner there's an outline of a small figure. She's facing away from the viewer, her frame just a thin layer of indigo in all the red. In the second canvas, the figure is sitting down. Her hands cradle her chin; her gaze is fixed somewhere outside the canvas, staring at something unknowable to anyone but her. The canvases seem naive, childish to Cassie now, as though her grief was a bit tasteless. She should have put something more cheery, something springlike, up in here.

She wishes Nicky would stop staring. She can see a flicker—something not far off amusement—in her friends' face. The indigo figure is so clearly Cassie: an old, sadder version of Cassie.

Cassie wrinkles her nose at the canvases. "I'm going to

replace those." In fact, she wishes she could start pulling the canvases down right now, but grief always adds a somber significance to even the simplest thing. If she took them down now, Nicky would worry that Cassie was hiding from the past, not grieving "well" enough.

Honestly, managing others was far more exhausting than the thudding loss itself.

At last, Nicky turns towards Cassie. "Has Jack seen them?"

Cassie can't remember showing them to Jack, these souvenirs from her old life, but she says, "Yeah, I think so. Why?"

"Oh, no reason really." Nicky turns back to the canvases. "I just remember when you first met, you found it hard to talk about April with him."

"No, I didn't, Nick. I told him about Mum on our first date, you know that." Cassie feels a queasy twinge of irritation; sometimes it feels like Nicky's searching for drama.

Jack and Cassie met at a friend's party, just a couple of months before April died. Cassie, made wild by her mum's illness, had drunk so much she was sick, but Jack had still asked for her number and kept sending her the odd text until three months after April died. It was Nicky who had persuaded Cassie to put on some mascara and go for a drink with Jack. He'd been living in Islington but came down to meet her in a Brixton pub on a rainy Tuesday evening.

Cassie had wanted to leave as soon as they arrived. She'd been feeling fractious; pissed off with Nicky for making her agree to a date, and pissed off with herself for not definitively refusing his offer.

"So how's the painting going?" Jack had asked.

There was a big group of blokes in the pub, rugby types, slamming their fists on their table, laughing as though they were in competition with each other to have the best time. Jack had ignored them, and kept his eyes fixed on Cassie, as though he could wait forever for her answer. He'd wait for a long time; Cassie wasn't prepared to tell a stranger how she cried every time she tried to paint, how she'd resigned herself to a mind-numbing future in soul-sucking admin jobs.

She'd taken a couple of big gulps of red wine and once the other table had quietened down she'd said, "Look, Jack, I'm really sorry. I probably should have canceled tonight. The thing is that I've had a shitty few months—well, a shitty couple of years actually—and I thought I was ready to go for a drink, but, really, I'm not, so maybe we could do this another time?"

He'd nodded slowly again, and had looked down at his pint briefly as if deciding what to say before he'd asked, "Is your mum still ill?"

The pub had seemed to swell around Cassie before it shrunk to normal again; she must have told him April had cancer when she was drunk. Her jaw had felt rusty as she'd tried to answer; she'd felt it move like a ventriloquist's dummy as she'd fired two words at him like arrows.

"She's dead."

But Jack hadn't looked away, or shifted in his seat. He'd just kept calmly looking at Cassie, as if her two hard monosyllables hadn't hit him, as if they hadn't even grazed his skin. Her tragedy hadn't made him uncomfortable, not like everyone else.

Instead, he'd kept his eyes on Cassie. He'd cleared his throat gently. "I'm sorry to hear that, Cas. My dad died when I was fourteen. It's still, twenty years on, the hardest thing that's ever happened to me."

"Your dad died?" She'd almost heard the hinge of her jaw creak around the words.

"Heart attack," Jack had said simply. "He was the hero of my life, really. I idolized him. When did your mum die?"

Fat tears rolled in waves down Cassie's cheeks; she hadn't bothered wiping them away, and they'd disappeared under her T-shirt. Jack had handed her a napkin from the dispenser on their table.

"July twelfth, eleven weeks and three days ago."

"So you've had, what, twenty-seven years believing she was always going to be in your life and less than three months trying to get your head around the fact she's not alive anymore. I'm not surprised you're not ready to sit in a noisy pub with someone you don't know that well."

Cassie had blinked at him across the table. Suddenly, she'd felt like giving him a chance.

"Most people don't get it at all. They think they can fix things with tea and sympathy and it's like they're pissed off with me that they can't; they think it's my fault somehow that they don't make me feel better."

"I remember that. I got so fucked off with people avoiding the fact that what felt like the worst thing in the world had happened. I was a right little shit for a while. The thing is, I think grief makes people uncomfortable. It's so final, so unfixable. That's why it scares people shitless; they're just trying to make it better for themselves and for you."

"I know, but they're not."

"Of course they're not, they can't. Often, through no fault of their own, they make it worse. It's belittling; they think grief can be cured with a biscuit. Most people don't understand. Grieving is a kind of art. You have to let yourself be creative with it, own it. You can't let other people tell you how to do it, otherwise it won't be done right and you might end up in a pickle." Jack had paused before he'd asked, "Why are you laughing?"

"I'm laughing because what you just said is the best thing I've heard in weeks and you ended it with the phrase 'in a pickle.'"

Jack had looked at Cassie and blinked. "Shit. That's exactly the sort of thing my mum would say."

Cassie had wiped her damp cheeks and neck with the napkin. She'd liked the way Jack had interlaced his fingers around his pint glass, and she'd liked his hands, big, firm hands, the sort of hands she could imagine holding her. She'd wanted to carry on looking at those beautiful, safe hands, and she'd wanted to carry on talking to Jack.

"There's a pizza place around the corner. They give you a fiver off if you can finish their calzone. We could give it a shot if you're hungry?" Cassie had asked.

Jack had drained the last of his pint in one go and stood up from the table. "Starving."

Three months later, Jack had moved into Cassie's Brixton flat, three months after that they were engaged and now eighteen months from that rainy evening in the pub, Jack is making lunch in their beautiful, newly converted three-bedroom cottage.

Cassie, nervous at dwelling on her good fortune too

much, in case it tempts fate, still can't deny that the world has at last been good to her. Really bloody good to her.

Nicky is looking at Cassie, eyebrows raised, like she expects Cassie to cry any moment. She wraps her slim arms over Cassie's shoulders and pulls her friend towards her.

"Sorry, I shouldn't have brought it up," she whispers in Cassie's ear. "I am happy for you, Pudge. You know that, don't you?"

Cassie smiles at her old nickname, and nods her head against Nicky's shoulder. April called her Pudge since Cassie was a baby and Nicky was the only other person allowed to use it.

Cassie thinks about reminding Nicky that it was the sale of the Brixton flat—worth over eight times what April originally paid for it in the late eighties—that paid for everything, but she doesn't have the energy.

April used to say that Cassie and Nicky, friends since they met at preschool, were more like sisters, which is why they could be so close but be mean to each other as well, because they knew, like sisters know, that they share an unshakeable bond. Cassie loved that idea, of having a sister, someone who she would always love, no matter how annoying they were. The sister relationship always seemed to Cassie to be one of the greatest of them all.

"Oh, I just remembered." Nicky pulls away from Cassie. "I got an email from Marcus, about April's anniversary weekend on the Isle of Wight."

Cassie groans inwardly, and Nicky spots it immediately.

"What, Cas? You don't like the idea?"

"No, it's not that exactly. It's just . . . I . . . I just want to spend time here, you know, with Jack."

"Well, Jack's invited too, isn't he?"

"Of course, but . . . we just can't commit right now, you know. We were thinking about going away maybe this year in July, just the two of us."

"Uh huh." Nicky nods, her eyes creasing in recognition of Cassie's bullshit. "What's this really about? The drama last year?"

Marcus had hosted the first-year anniversary of April's death last July as well. It was the first time Jack and Marcus had met. Marcus had become uncharacteristically antagonistic with alcohol and grief and, somehow, Marcus and Jack had started arguing about an article they'd both read about how property developers contribute more to climate change than any other industry, which had led to Jack storming off in a rage and Cassie and Jack leaving earlier than planned. Marcus couldn't remember any of it the next morning, but he'd sent an apologetic text a couple of days later.

"Well, let me know, will you?" Nicky asks. "I won't go unless you do."

The old, dependent mantra of their youth sounds ridiculous now. Cassie wishes Nicky wouldn't use it anymore—she should understand things have changed, that the rules are different—but Cassie nods anyway. She looks around the shed, slightly shy, and, changing the subject, says, "You do like it?"

Before Nicky can reply, from across the garden there's a clatter of stainless steel as something heavy-sounding drops from the oven onto the kitchen tiles.

"Bollocks!" Jack shouts, and Cassie laughs quickly, grateful for the distraction.

She grabs Nicky's arm, and steers them out of the shed. "I love him, but he's absolutely shit in the kitchen."

They decide that, with sweaters on, it's warm enough in the spring sun to have lunch outside. Jack and Nicky set the outside table while Cassie tries to rescue the salmon fillets Jack dropped and makes a dressing for the salad.

She turns down the radio so she can hear Jack and Nicky talk as they lay silver cutlery and fill water glasses. They're still learning how to relax with each other, trying to figure out the subtle alchemy in the relationship between old best friend and new husband. Nicky tells Jack about a recent date she went on, an attractive biology teacher she met online whose tongue seemed too big for his mouth. He kept spraying Nicky in fine fountains of spit when he spoke. Jack laughs, careful to strike the right balance between amusement and horror. Cassie's heard the story before, of course, but she still laughs along from inside the kitchen.

Jonny, Jack and Cassie's neighbor, is preceded by his half-blind Alsatian, Dennis, who trots around the corner of the redbrick cottage from the drive.

His tail wags as Cassie strokes his shaggy head; she'd love to get a dog, but Jack, being slightly allergic, isn't at all keen.

Dennis turns away from Cassie at Jonny's whistle, his eyes cloudy with cataracts, as Jonny follows Dennis around the corner of the cottage. Although they've only met twice before, both times in The Hare, Cassie's never seen Jonny in anything other than shorts and a T-shirt. Today he's in denim cutoffs.

Jack texted Jonny yesterday, inviting him to join them

for lunch. He'd said Jonny must get lonely, on his own in the farm cottage; typical, thoughtful Jack.

Initially, Cassie was mildly irritated that Jack had extended Jonny an invite; she'd wanted the weekend to be about her best friend and husband getting to know each other a bit better. But she was pleased she'd managed to swallow her irritation. She wanted to try to be more empathetic like Jack, and, besides, she told herself, it'd be good for Jack to have a local friend, someone other than her to have a pint with after a stressful day at work.

Jonny hands Cassie a bottle of prosecco as he kisses her cheeks, lifting his sunglasses off his face, using them to pin his sandy-colored hair back from his forehead. It's grown curlier since she last saw him a couple of weeks ago. He's been growing it since he moved to Buscombe from Hackney four months ago, just a month after Cassie sold the Brixton flat and she and Jack moved down. Jonny jokingly said in the pub that he's growing his hair as a symbol of freedom since quitting his job as a graphic designer and going freelance. Cassie wondered if it was also a sign of freedom from his wife, Lorna, but she doesn't know him well enough to ask about her, not yet.

Cassie introduces Jonny and Nicky. They almost clash noses as he tries to kiss both her cheeks, while Nicky only offered one. Nicky laughs in girlish delight, and Cassie immediately recognizes the way Nicky's light blue eyes slide over Jonny, and how Nicky starts fondling the ends of her long red hair between her slim fingers as he talks.

Jack slaps Jonny on the back as they shake hands and Nicky follows Cassie inside to help bring out glasses for the prosecco. Cassie pretends not to notice as Nicky's eyes slide over her reflection, checking her slim silhouette in the mirror as Cassie rifles through drawers trying to find the bottle opener.

"I know I saw it earlier . . ." she mutters, opening another drawer as Nicky picks up a photo of April in a silver frame from the sideboard. It's Cassie's favorite, the one where April's wearing the peacock-blue headscarf Cassie bought her for her last birthday; it's tied at the top of her head, like she's a present to the world. April's smiling hard at the camera, her eyes half moons, the sea a boiling mess of white foam fifty feet below. Just five months after the photo was taken Cassie and Marcus scattered April's ashes into the sea from those same white cliffs. Cassie opens the same wrong cupboard twice before she finds the wine glasses. Nicky isn't looking at the photo though, she's looking at the frame.

"Didn't this photo used to be in that frame we decorated with shells April found at the beach?"

Sometimes, it would be nice if Nicky didn't question everything. Cassie doesn't respond, but she knows Nicky wants an answer.

"Cas?"

"Oh, yeah, it was, but we were given those ones as a wedding present." Cassie glances over at Nicky and shrugs. "It looks so much better in a proper frame, and besides the shells had started to fall off the other one." That was a lie; they hadn't started to fall off. Jack threw away the old frame, assuming Cassie had bought it at a charity shop or something. When Cassie told him her mum found the shells, he tried to go to the dump to look for the old frame but Cassie told him not to bother; she'd never liked it that much anyway and, besides, the shell frame had looked ridiculous in their sleek white kitchen.

Nicky picks up a photo of another lost parent, in an identical silver frame. Cassie knows which one it is without looking at it. It's Jack about eight years old, on his dad's shoulders, in his football gear, Jack's muddy knees hovering by his dad's ears. Mike's holding onto his son's ankles. They're both grinning at the camera, dimples on their left cheeks, dark hair combed away from their faces, like nothing bad could ever happen in their world.

"They look exactly the same," Nicky says, peering into the faded photograph. "You said he died from a heart attack?"

Cassie nods slowly, putting the glasses on the oak kitchen island. She finds it hard to talk about Mike with someone other than Jack or Charlotte. Even though she's family now, it's still not her story; she feels she can't tell it the way it should be told. She starts filling an ice bucket to keep the bottle cool as Nicky puts the photo carefully back in its place on the shelf.

"I loved meeting Charlotte at the wedding. She's amazing," Nicky says, taking the ice and bottle opener off Cassie.

The wine glasses clash against each other as Cassie picks them up by their stems.

"She is," Cassie answers. "Honestly, I don't know how she did it, after losing Mike—coping with her own grief and still raising Jack."

"I guess that's what your mum did as well," Nicky says gently.

Cassie looks at her friend. She doesn't know her face like

she used to, as if her freckles and the familiar notes of her face have subtly moved like stars in a night sky. Nicky always seems to find a way to remind Cassie about the exotic way she grew up, never knowing her dad, the fact that she is basically an orphan now. Nicky always resented her suburban, secure childhood. She'd moan on and on about her two younger brothers, and their family holidays to Greece, while Cassie shared a bed with her mum until she was twelve and stayed in South London all summer.

Nicky, oblivious to Cassie, is still staring at the photo of Jack and Mike.

"I think we've got everything. Come on," Cassie says, turning away from Nicky and walking towards the safety of Jack's low, gentle voice outside before Nicky can say anything else.

They eat salmon fillets, salad and new potatoes, as if it's summer already. After a few glasses of wine, Cassie feels herself soften as Jonny tells her about the dog rescue where he adopted Dennis.

She's pleased she didn't snap at Nicky before. That's Jack's influence, she thinks; he soothes her . . . calms her fire.

As she talks to Jonny, she keeps half an ear on Nicky and Jack's conversation. Jack's telling Nicky how busy he's been at Jensen and Son, the family property company founded by his grandfather and run by Mike until his death. For the last twenty years, the company had been grinding along, managed by an able but uninspiring ex-lawyer hired by the board. Jack was advised to gain experience in another company before taking a position at Jensen and Son, so he worked for the last ten years for huge developers in London. Soon after he met Cassie the board agreed he was ready to join the small, rural company—an opportunity that had been the deciding factor for their move from London to Buscombe.

Now he is asking Nicky's advice on recruiting a new project manager. She won't have a clue, but Cassie knows she'll pretend to be expert, and she'll feel good that Jack asked her opinion. Cassie feels herself relax knowing the two of them are getting on; it seems silly now that she ever thought they might not.

Jonny opens another bottle of red wine. "So, Jack was saying that in your spare time between getting married, doing up a house and moving to the country you've set up a business?"

"Painting?" Cassie frowns. She's too much in Jack and Nicky's conversation to know what Jonny's talking about.

"Oh, that must be another one then. No, he was saying something about jam?"

"Ah, jam." Cassie laughs. In the autumn months after April died, Cassie found unexpected solace in making jam after Jack bought her a box of plums from his mum's garden. She had no idea what to do with the plums, but found a recipe in between the sticky pages of one of April's old cookery books and found the steady preparation of the fruit, the careful weighing of the sugar and the bubbling of the pans to be a sweet meditation, a break from the monotony of the uncertainty, the strangeness of her new life. She gave Jack a jar of jam to give to Charlotte before she'd met her future mother-in-law, and Charlotte and Jack told her it was so good she should sell some locally. She resisted at first, but then worried it might look like she wasn't making an effort to fit in—that she wasn't fully embracing the new, rural Cassie.

Jonny raises the bottle to Cassie's glass. He doesn't pour wine like Jack: a precise, rich tap of wine. No, Jonny tips the bottle so it slops in a wave, creating a tiny tsunami inside her glass.

Cassie raises her hand to get him to stop.

"That's like, half a pint!" she says, looking at the glass. Jonny sloshes the same amount into his own glass and keeps talking.

"So, Jack said you're selling jam next weekend at a local festival?"

"Oh no, I'm not doing that anymore."

Jonny takes a long gulp from his glass, like he's drinking water not wine.

"How come?"

"Oh, it's just I've got a lot on and Jack has to work. I can't drive so it's just too much hassle to sort out really."

Jonny holds the plump bottom of his wine glass between his middle fingers as if he's worried someone might steal it if he left it on the table.

"That's a shame." He pauses for a moment, before continuing, "I've got a van and am around this weekend if that's helpful?"

Cassie looks up at Jonny. It's one of Charlotte's friends organizing the small fete and she'd been putting off making the difficult phone call, telling her she was going to cancel and letting her down.

"Really? You don't have weekend plans?" she asks.

"I was going to be in London but not anymore, so I'm

around. It'd be good to do something wholesome for a change." Dennis stirs underneath Jonny's chair as Jonny keeps talking. "I warn you though, I'm only good for donkey work—moving boxes, driving, that sort of thing. I can't do any sales chat at all and I'll only accept payment as long as it's fruit- and sugar-based, sealed in a jar."

Dennis pulls himself out from under Jonny's chair and rests his big bear head on his master's lap.

Cassie glances over at her husband; he's telling Nicky about Jamie, a monosyllabic solicitor friend of his who's single. She hears Jack suggesting an afterwork drink in London when he's next up, so he can introduce Nicky to Jamie. He's always trying to fix things, find solutions for people. Jack feels Cassie looking at him, and turns away from Nicky to smile, his lopsided, adorable smile at his wife. Cassie feels her insides warm.

She turns back to Jonny, and watches his Adam's apple bob as his throat swallows more wine. Jonny's help would be a neat solution to her little problem.

"You're sure you don't mind?"

"No, like I said, it'll be good to be helpful. So it's a fete, right?"

Cassie nods. "Brace yourself, it'll be all purple rinses and tea cosies." She picks up her wine. "The café in the park is doing cream teas and using my jam so they said I could have a stall, sell a few jars at the spring fete, just to see how it goes. I thought I may as well. You know, get involved in the village and all that." Maybe, she hopes quietly, in a few months she'll be selling paintings as well as jams.

Jack and Nicky's conversation has lulled, and Jack leans

forward across the table and says, "Did I just hear you getting an offer for help with the fete, Cas?"

Cassie nods and smiles at her husband as he keeps talking.

"Funny, I'd had the same thought." To Jonny, Jack says, "Thanks, mate, that's good of you."

"Don't mention it," Jonny says, shrugging and scratching Dennis behind his ear.

Cassie had been prepared for making friends to take awhile. In fact, after London it was a relief to have the peace and time to paint, to enjoy being a newlywed, but she feels it's now probably time to make some sort of an effort. She doesn't want to piss anyone off, so it's good she doesn't have to cancel.

Jack has stood up from the table and come to stand behind Cassie.

She didn't notice, so she flinches as she feels his hands rest on her shoulders.

"Cas, it's too sweet!" Nicky says, smiling across the table at her friend. "Honestly, less than two years ago you were partying in Brixton, and now you're selling your jams at the village fete!"

"I know, who would've thought it?" Cassie says, smiling back at her friend. Above her, Jack kisses the top of her head.

"I'm sure Cas is secretly writing a book: *From Brixton to Buscombe: An Odyssey*," Jack jokes.

Jonny laughs and Cassie slaps Jack's hand.

"It's my gypsy blood," she says with pomp in her voice. "I'm very versatile. I can make a home wherever I go."

Jack kisses her on the head again. "I know you can, my lovely gypsy."

Cassie, emboldened by wine, bends her head back to kiss Jack full on the lips. In her peripheral vision sees Nicky's smile fade and the same flicker in her expression Cassie saw earlier in the shed, and she pulls away from Jack, because something feels wrong. She shouldn't kiss Jack in front of Nicky like that; it feels too much like showing off, especially as Nicky so wants to meet someone.

Dennis starts wagging his tail, noticing the shift in the atmosphere. He barks and Jonny stands up from the table, his wine glass almost empty.

"Right, I think Dennis is telling me it's time to go home for a walk." He looks at Cassie. "Give me a call in the week and let me know what time you need me on Saturday, I'm free all day." Jonny gives Cassie and Nicky a kiss goodbye on their cheeks, thanking them for lunch, and he hugs Jack in the brief, slapping way men do.

Cassie watches Jonny walk away across the lawn, Dennis jogging by his feet. He takes his car keys out of his pocket just before he turns around the front of the cottage. He shouldn't be driving after all that wine, but no one else seems to notice and Cassie reminds herself that the rules are different in the country. Jack carries some dirty glasses into the kitchen, asking who wants coffee and Nicky starts stacking the plates on top of each other. Cassie takes another sip of wine, feeling it slide, silky around her mouth and she's not sure why but as she listens to the sound of Jonny driving away she shudders, cold suddenly.

"Oh, someone must have walked over your grave," Nicky says, turning away from Cassie towards the kitchen, a pile of plates in her hands.

Cassie smiles at the old schoolground superstition. She hasn't heard it in years. Typical Nicky to remember these things.

Cassie shakes again, harder this time, the spring chill spreading into her bones, and she thinks that Nicky's wrong. It doesn't feel as though whoever it is strolling around in the future is walking over her grave; it feels like they've stopped and they're standing on it.

7

Alice

By 4:38 a.m. resisting the urge to get up is more exhausting than still being awake. I gently move David's arm from around my waist and pad to the little alcove desk he grandly calls "The Office."

I love the bottomless peace of early morning; it reminds me of sitting with Frank. The chime of the computer as I turn it on is a shock in the silence, and my fingers freeze over the keyboard. What should I search for? I type "Woman, coma, pregnant" into the search bar. The words look crazy together, but I think of the scan image, remember what I saw, and bite my lip and smile as I press search.

There are two reported cases, both in America. One of the women—Tiffany Prescot in Phoenix, Arizona—had been in a head-on collision. She was sixteen weeks at the time. The baby, a little boy called Noah, was delivered naturally for fear the drugs used for a caesarean at that time would harm Tiffany. A comatose mother giving birth naturally doesn't sound possible, but Noah is the proof. He's now four years old and living with his older sister and father. Tiffany died last year. Her heart, already weak before the accident, withered and fragile, finally disintegrated after his birth.

There's less information on the other woman, only a brief article in *Nebraska News*. The baby, a little girl this time, stopped growing and was delivered by C-section prematurely. She was too small and her lungs were undeveloped. She died a week after delivery. Her mother, at the time of writing, seemed to be recovering. I imagine what it must be like, to discover your body had nurtured and given birth to a little girl, that she died without ever leaving the blankness of the hospital rooms, and all the while you were fast asleep, a red scar grinning up at you, the only proof of her existence.

Sharma thinks Cassie is about twelve weeks. We'll know for sure in a few hours. I've never got that far so I don't know how it feels, but I've imagined it. The swelling, sore breasts, the hormone surges, jeans feeling tighter. I can't imagine not knowing at twelve weeks. But then, if she did know, why didn't she visit her GP? Tell her husband?

"Every woman is different," I parrot to myself, thinking of the countless gynecologists and fertility experts who have said those same words to me. I think of the fair man, who I know now is Jonny Parker, Cassie's neighbor who ran onto the ward last night. I see distressed, emotional friends and family everyday; people are always trying to visit out of hours. But Jonny was different; he said he had to tell Cassie something, and when I wouldn't let him get close enough to her, he told me at least a part of what he wanted Cassie to know. Just before the security guys took him away, he said, "She was scared."

And I saw in that moment in his eyes that Cassie feeling scared was worse than any other punishment he could suffer.

I'll have to write about Jonny's visit in Cassie's notes later today. I'll tell Paula to play it down to Jack and Charlotte. The last thing we want is for them to worry he'll come back. I shut the computer down and decide not to share my internet research findings with Sharma; he wouldn't like the odds.

I get back into bed—my side is still warm—and I listen to David gently snoring and stare at the ceiling for a few minutes, like a patient, before curling myself around his sleeping back.

I pull into the hospital parking lot an hour before my shift starts. The sun rises lazily this morning. Kate's sits on the horizon like a gray arachnid, absorbing any color from the surrounding fields, smudging the dull January surroundings. I always think she'd fit in nicely in Soviet Russia. Kate's was once featured in an "Ugly Buildings of Britain" book—one of those books full of pictures people like to keep in the toilet. We have one in ours, with the top corner turned down on Kate's page. Even if she's a bit rough round the edges, for me, the hospital is like the ultimate mother, beckoning most of us into the world, patching us up when we're scuffed and bruised, and when the outside has tripped us up too many times, she'll see us on our way for the last time. The big, real-life stuff happens inside her sterile walls.

I feel buoyant, too buoyant, as I get out of my car, so I give myself a talking to, as if I were a relative. I cross the parking lot, reminding myself of the hundreds of possible complications, of the delicacy of Cassie's pregnancy. The automatic hospital doors open with a sound like the breaking of a seal on a vacuum.

The receptionist looks up briefly from his newspaper as I call, "Good morning," but he just turns back to his paper as I start walking down the long corridor, where the walls are decorated with watercolors of wheat fields, towards 9B.

Cassie lies just as before, impassive to night or day. Unlike the peacefully sleeping coma patients in films, her face is twisted, as if she's absorbed by a difficult problem, and she thinks no one can see her. I place my hand back on her abdomen, picture the scans again, suffocate a quick, familiar twist of envy, followed by an inevitable thump of shame, and before anyone notices anything strange, I pull my hand away and walk back towards the break room.

"So how are you doing, Jack? Did you manage to get any sleep last night?" I lean towards Jack who sits opposite me in Sharma's office, catch myself biting my lip and force myself to stop. I don't want him to know I'm nervous.

He shrugs; he doesn't care about his sleep. He's in jeans and a navy sweater today. The color suits him. I wonder if Cassie bought it for him. He looks as though he's already lost weight with stress, his skin dulled by exhaustion and worry. He's broad but lean, dark and handsome in an obvious kind of way, like nature's blueprint for "a hand-some man."

"Thanks for agreeing to meet us a bit later. Mr. Sharma will join us in a moment; his meeting is running over a few minutes, but I thought it would be good for us to have a chat. How are you doing?"

He shrugs again and rubs the side of his temples. In hospitals people let their guard down quicker than in normal life; I doubt Jack would ever normally be so crumpled in front of someone he doesn't know.

"I think I'm still in shock," he admits.

"That's totally normal. Let me know if at anytime you feel you need more support. We can put you in touch with a therapist if you'd like to talk about how you're feeling . . ."

"No, look, my wife's in a bloody coma. I can't think straight, why would I want to talk to a stranger, a therapist about it?" He looks directly at me. "Sorry." His voice crackles. "It's just that, no, I haven't slept, and frankly I . . ." He clears his throat.

In the pause I say, "I don't blame you. If I was in your position I wouldn't want to talk to a stranger either. I just want you to know the offer's there in case you change your mind." He reads between the lines beautifully, possibly too tired to realize what he's saying.

"It's been over forty-eight hours now and I still don't believe it. Maisie's run off before, I kept thinking Cas would come home any minute, laugh at me for freaking out over nothing." He leans forward, his elbows on his knees and rubs his hands over his face like a washcloth before clasping them together in his lap.

He closes his eyes.

"Every time I shut my eyes I picture her in that stream, how cold she must have been." He shakes his head, his voice cracking like ice. "She must have been so scared to be hit and just left, left like that." He impatiently wipes away a tear with the back of his hand before it reaches his cheek. I thought he would be the kind of person to be ashamed to cry; I'm pleased I was wrong. We should have met in the family room where it would be all right to squeeze his arm. Here, there's a desk between us.

I lean forward towards him. "It would have happened so quickly, Jack, a split second."

With a sharp breath, he pulls himself together and raises his head again; he wants to talk.

"You know, I keep finding myself thinking all these stupid clichés like, 'this is a living nightmare,' and wondering why this is happening. It's the sort of stuff you hear about through the grapevine, and think, 'Thank God that's not me, not happening to us' and then wham!" He claps his hands together, "Here we are. Here we fucking are." His hands rub either side of his face as if trying to hold his head together. His eyes stare down at Sharma's desk. He doesn't look up as he says, "You know the police have arrested our neighbor, Jonny?"

I shake my head, and keep my eyes on Jack as he keeps talking.

"He's been saying his ex turned up at his place when he got back from the party, that she was with him when Cassie was hit, but she's not corroborating his story."

I realize now is not the time to tell him about the pregnancy; he's too exhausted. I want to think of an excuse to leave for a minute, to tell Sharma we have to wait until Jack's slept before we tell him, but it's too late. There's a gentle knock at the door and Jack stops rubbing his temples and looks up as Sharma strides behind the desk to stand next to me, a large envelope under his arm. Jack stands to shake Sharma's hand.

"Mr. Jensen," Sharma says, his face blank.

Jack nods his head, and I bite my lip as Sharma sits next to me. I move my chair a few inches away; I don't want Jack to think we're a double act.

"Mr. Jensen," Sharma repeats. Jack looks at him but his gaze is lazy, as though he doesn't have the energy to focus.

"Our test results show little change in Cassie's condition at present. The swelling to her brain is, I'm afraid, still substantial and doesn't appear to have decreased. That's not to say it won't, of course. Time will tell on that front." He sounds like he's reading the news on TV; enunciating every word, he talks with practiced empathy. Jack just stares at him, still frowning, Sharma seems to interpret the silence as an invitation to continue talking, so he does.

"There is another matter of some delicacy that has come to light during the course of our tests on your wife."

Jack's eyes flick from Sharma to me and back again to Sharma.

Sharma coughs gently before speaking. "Now, this may come as a shock but she is, it transpires, pregnant."

It's as though the words fly across the desk and sting him. Jack stands up immediately, to his full height. He's a tall man; I hadn't noticed before.

"What did you say?"

"She's pregnant, Mr. Jensen." Sharma opens the envelope

and starts to slowly lay the scans of the baby on his desk. Jack has his hand over his mouth. He starts moving recklessly around the room, turning in circles, as if we've trapped him in here and he's desperate for a way out.

He stops suddenly and fixes his eyes on me. "Cassie's pregnant?"

"Yes," I say.

"How . . . how many weeks?"

"She's twelve weeks."

"Jesus! Twelve weeks!" He spits the words out like wasps. "Twelve?!" he shouts.

"Yes, Jack."

He rests both of his large palms on the desk and hangs his head; he exhales long and heavy. I think he might be crying but he's shaking his head as he looks at the images.

"These are from a scan we did this morning, Jack. The baby is healthy and seems to be causing Cassie no extra stress."

Jack squints at one of the images. The little bolts of the baby's spine are visible and one of its hands floats in front of it; it could almost be giving a thumbs up.

"No extra stress?"

"Ms. Longe, a senior consultant obstetrician, who you'll meet, gave Cassie a thorough examination this morning," Sharma interjects. "From what we can see everything seems to be fine with the fetus and Cassie is naturally producing all the hormones needed to keep her pregnancy progressing. It does, of course, mean that we need to be more sensitive about the drugs we use for Cassie's comfort to protect the fetus. We're increasing her vitamin intake but, other than that, we don't really need to do anything apart from let nature run its course."

No one speaks for a moment or two. I stare at Jack's dark head as he bends forward over the desk. When he looks up, his face is flushed under his two-day-old stubble, the capillaries on his cheeks full of blood. He looks directly at me. He's picked up one of the scans. He's holding it so hard the edges crumple and fold towards each other. I want to tell him to be careful.

"But . . . but why didn't she say?" He looks to me again for an answer.

"Jack, many women don't know they're pregnant, even at twelve weeks." I want him to feel better.

Jack frowns, his eyes desperate. "She didn't know she was pregnant, did she?"

"That seems likely." I nod back at him, thinking the opposite.

He opens up his hand and the scan image floats like an autumnal leaf to the floor. He clutches clumps of hair between both his hands and looks at the image by his feet. "Fuck, fuck, fuck," he says, and I feel Sharma bristle with every "fuck."

Sharma stands up, opposite Jack. "We know this is a lot to take in, Mr. Jensen, but you need to . . ." Sharma is doing his two-handed "calm down" gesture, stroking the air with his palms turned to the ground, but it doesn't work on Jack.

"Don't tell me to calm down, Doctor, please. My wife is practically fucking dead and now you tell me there's a living baby?"

He sits heavily in his chair and looks at both of us for a moment, his eyes still wild, as if we just punched him, and then he rakes his fingers through his hair, bows his head and howls into his hands.

An hour later, Jack and I are sitting in the family room with two styrofoam cups of hospital coffee in front of us. He takes a sip and winces.

"I know," I say. "You think that's bad, you should try the food."

He nods his head with a tired smile. The rawness around his eyes accentuates the maple syrup brown of his irises; they're flecked with gold flakes like frozen petals. It strikes me as improbable that such a practical part of anatomy could be so beautiful.

"Sorry, I shouldn't have got so upset earlier," he says.

"Please don't worry about that at all, it would be strange if you weren't upset, all things considered."

"I told my mum, you know, about the baby. She burst into tears. She's on her way in now."

I nod. "It sounds like it's a shock for you both." I want to hear Jack say neither of them knew about the baby, but he just nods in an absent way. He looks as if he's trying to figure out how much to tell me. I smile and let him take his time to decide.

"We've been trying for a baby since we got married just over a year ago. We used to talk the whole time about the kind of parents we'd be. Cassie had irregular periods and stuff so we knew it might take a little while. She was pregnant over the summer, you know; we had a miscarriage just two days before the scan. It was just one of those things the doctors said. I still can't believe she didn't know she was pregnant." Jack shakes his head and smiles in the same tired way again.

I feel a sisterly tug towards Cassie, as I always do when I hear a woman has had a miscarriage. I like how Jack uses "we" when he talks about their miscarriage.

"That's so Cassie, though. She can be spontaneous, forgetful. She'd never keep a track of her periods and things. I think she got that from her mum. It drove me crazy sometimes but I still loved her for it." Jack takes a sip of his coffee and opens his eyes wide, as if trying to wake himself up, before he starts talking again.

"To be honest, she'd been going through a bit of a rough patch just before the accident. She was frustrated with her painting, and not sleeping well. Sounds so stupid to say that now, doesn't it?"

I shake my head. "How do you mean 'a rough patch'?"

"Oh, she could just get a bit down sometimes; nothing like depression, just a bit of a low mood. She'd always lived in London before we moved to the country. She found the change tougher than she thought she would, and she doesn't drive so she felt a bit isolated. I tried to cheer her up, but she sort of went a bit insular, distanced herself from her friends, that sort of thing. Cassie told me April could be the same; she could get pretty low even before the cancer diagnosis. I always think that must have been tough on Cassie, growing up with just her depressive mum, never knowing her dad."

"Cassie never met her dad?"

Jack shakes his head. "Cassie never knew who her dad was. April barely knew herself. He was some Norwegian guy April met in Mexico. I've seen photos of April back then when she was traveling and, if they're anything to go by, I'll bet Cas's dad was a proper hippie. Anyway, it was way before the internet and without a full name April couldn't track him down. Come to think of it, I remember Cassie saying April didn't know she was pregnant until she was pretty far along. The Norwegian doesn't even know Cassie exists. I always think that must be tough for Cassie, but she always said she didn't know things any differently so it didn't affect her too much. I think it's why she's so family-focused, why she's so close to my mum. She used to talk about how we'd have loads of kids, how things were going to get even better. She wanted what she never knew when she was growing up. Anyway, it's typical Cas not to think about doing a test or anything."

Jack's thoughts are jumbled but when he talks about his wife, his voice softens. He talks about her with a simplicity, a clarity, that only comes with real knowing, true intimacy. I remember my best friend Jess saying David's voice gets softer when he talks about me.

"So you think she didn't know, about the baby?"

Jack looks up at me. "Of course she didn't know. She'd have told me if she knew, I'd never have let her go after the dog and none of this shit would be happening." He seems to realize the truth in his words as he's saying them; all this could have been avoided.

"Well, pregnancy surprises a lot of women. It's important though, Jack . . . I mean it will be important to the ethics committee when they meet that Cassie wanted to be a mum. That'll mean her interests are aligned with those of the baby. A doctor will be talking to you more about this, but if Cassie wanted the baby, it should mean the pregnancy can continue without further discussion, assuming that's what you want as well?" I'd read up on protocols and NHS ethics committees, and where the mother is unable to make an informed decision about her pregnancy, decisions are deferred to the father.

Jack looks blank again.

This time, I nudge him forward. "Is that what you want, Jack? For the pregnancy to proceed?"

Jack nods. "Yes, yes, of course it is, yes. Cas wanted to be a mum, more than anything."

I'm surprised by how relieved I feel to hear him say it. Cassie's baby is a bit safer.

"That's good to hear, Jack."

"So what happens now?"

"Just like Mr. Sharma said, we look after Cassie as we would any other patient here, being more mindful of the drugs she has, of course, and we monitor the baby. There may be some meetings about it higher up the hospital food chain, but I wouldn't worry about that. As the father, if you want the pregnancy to proceed then that is what will happen."

Jack nods at me, and tears pool in his eyes. On the table in front of us Jack squeezes his hands together. "God, of course. Of course I do."

I smile at him.

"I just keep wishing she'd wake up, so I can tell her I love her, tell her I'm so sorry, sorry I didn't know, I should have guessed about our baby."

I hand him a tissue. "Jack, none of this is your fault. You mustn't blame yourself."

He nods as he wipes his eyes.

I wish I could ask him more about Cassie, about their lives.

But then he raises his head to me, calmer suddenly. "Where do you think Cassie's 'gone,' Alice . . . in her coma, I mean."

"You mean her consciousness?"

Jack nods his head. His eyes don't leave my face; they want answers. I think they want good, positive answers.

"Well, we don't know for sure. Every patient has a different experience, of course. Sometimes people don't remember anything, their coma like a long, deep sleep. Others report lucid dreaming and others say they go back to their lives, relive key experiences. It totally varies."

"I really hope she's not scared," Jack says.

My heart thumps; he's like Jonny, terrified of Cassie's fear. I wish I could hold his hand, think of something to reassure him, but Jack suddenly raises his hand to his heart.

"Sorry," he says, before he pulls his phone out of his pocket, clears his throat and looks at the screen.

"It's Mum, she's just arriving. I'd better go and meet her. She was pretty shaken up when I told her." He picks up the scans from the table and stands.

"Thanks for the chat."

I get up as well. "Anytime, Jack. Really, anytime."

We smile at each other before he leaves.

I have a sandwich on my own in the canteen, and afterwards I try to settle down at my desk. I've got a pile of admin, patients' notes to check and close, order forms to process, but I can't concentrate.

My eyes blur whenever I look at the computer screen, my mind a mess of all the things that could happen to Cassie and the baby: organ failure, miscarriage, an infection. The thoughts force me out of my chair and I look through the square window in the door that looks directly onto the ward. Cassie's curtain is drawn around her bed; Jack left about twenty minutes ago. Sharma told him about Jonny, said it wouldn't happen again. I watched as Jack gave the healthcare assistant at reception a weak little wave as he walked past. He didn't see me in the nurses break room as he walked away. The phone rings. I let reception answer it and walk onto the ward.

Charlotte's silvery head is facing the wall behind Cassie's bed. She's holding a slab of Sticky-Tac in one hand and a bundle of photos and cards in the other. Her clothes are as before, slightly too large for her, her navy blue jeans bag a little and she's wearing another unfitted striped blue shirt; she's still in emergency mode. She's decorated around Cassie's bed, a colorful shrine of photos and cards. Jack said Charlotte cried when she heard about the baby. I remember my mum cried the first few times I was pregnant. She hasn't for the last few, as if she's saving her tears for a few weeks later.

Charlotte turns towards me and smiles. "Oh, hello, Alice. I hope you don't mind," she says, gesturing towards the wall. "I did ask one of the other nurses." I close the curtain carefully behind me.

"No, no of course not. It looks lovely." Charlotte puts the Sticky-Tac and photos she's holding onto Cassie's bedside unit, before I add, "Can I have a look?"

She rests a hand on the metal frame of Cassie's bed. It makes her look frail suddenly; hospitals age even the most robust visitor. "Of course, please," she says with a nod, and gestures to the wall.

They're all of Cassie and Jack posed with arms around each other in different settings: at Christmas, in wellies on a walk, on a beach next to a palm tree somewhere exotic.

"Beautiful," I say.

Charlotte stands next to me, smiling at the photos. "Yes, yes, I know. She really is. One of those people who could light up any room. I can't believe their wedding was only a year ago." Charlotte looks towards a framed photo from their wedding day. Cassie laughing and beautiful in a tight white lace wedding gown, Jack, his head slightly tilted back, proud and smart, grinning at his new wife. She doesn't look like the kind of woman who'd scare easily. It's a solid silver frame, expensive and at odds with the clinical surroundings. I imagine their home is full of stylish frames from happy times. I'll have to move it later though; if someone nudges the bedside unit, it could fall onto Cassie.

"It looks like it was an amazing day," I say. I should suggest we go to the family room for more privacy, but I don't want to stem her flow; she looks comfortable here.

Charlotte nods. "In some ways, it's even more devastating for Jack." I think she's talking about the fact Jack and Cassie were married so recently, but she turns to me then and says, "You see, we lost Jack's dad, Mike." She breathes in deeply; she wants to talk, needs to share with someone. "He had congenital heart disease. Typical man, he was terrible at taking his medication, always forgetting. Jack found Mike collapsed on the floor. I was out doing the weekly shopping." She pulls a tissue out from her sleeve.

"I'm so sorry to hear that, Charlotte."

She shakes her head a couple of times, and pinches her nose with the tissue. She doesn't want me to be sorry for her. Charlotte takes her time as she continues, taking me arm in arm, strolling through her thoughts. "I fell apart, of course, couldn't imagine life without Mike, being a single parent and all that. But it was much harder for Jack. That's why we moved to Buscombe, for a fresh start. I was told the countryside would be good for him. It's pretty much the most damaging thing, you know, for a fourteen-year-old boy to find the dad they worship stone dead."

I nod. "I can't imagine how hard that must have been."

"We muddled through fairly well though, just Jack and me for twenty-one years, a tiny family of two, up until last year, of course." She looks briefly at the wedding photo before turning back to me. "It'd break him all over again to lose her," she says with a whisper.

I want to turn the conversation, to make her feel better, more positive, so I say, "It sounds like they have a happy marriage."

Charlotte breathes out. "Oh god, yes. They were always full of laughter. I've always adored Cas, knew she was the one for Jack the moment I met her."

We both turn towards some footsteps outside the curtain, Sharma perhaps, on his way to Ellen. Charlotte waits for them to pass before she glances at me, suddenly shy. She shakes her head at herself and pats my arm.

"Sorry, Alice. God, you don't want to hear all this when you must be so busy."

I place my hand gently on top of hers where it rests on my arm.

"No, please, it's really good to talk. I like finding out a bit more about Cassie."

Charlotte glances down at Cassie before she turns back to me, as if she doesn't want Cassie to hear. "She wanted to be a mum so much," she says quietly.

My heart shakes a little; I've overheard my mum say the same about me.

"I was holding my breath for a baby, especially after the miscarriage." She looks up at me. "Jack said he told you." I nod, and let her keep talking. "We were close, you know, Cas and I. We'd talk about everything. She told me about her irregular periods, that she was worried it wouldn't happen for them again. I just said they had to keep trying, be patient, let nature take its course. All the stuff people always say." Charlotte pauses for a beat before she adds, "To think she's twelve weeks and didn't know!"

Charlotte lifts her hand from my arm to wipe a tear with the balled up tissue in her hand. It's easy to imagine Cassie talking to Charlotte over tea or a glass of wine. A rare sense of calm surrounds Charlotte, a gentleness I imagine makes people feel safe, confessional with her. She's clearly ruffled by everything that's happened, but she hasn't lost her balance; she's too well grounded for that.

More footsteps and voices outside Cassie's curtain crack our delicate moment, and Charlotte heaves the smile back onto her face as she turns back to me.

"I'll let you get on, Alice. Jack said you're going to tell the other nurses about the baby today—" she glances at her watch "—and there's a bus that practically drops me outside my door in twenty minutes so please don't worry about me."

I must look surprised; I can't imagine Charlotte on a bus.

"You don't drive?" I ask, reflexively.

Charlotte shakes her silvery head, her hair catching the light.

"No, but I get along fine with buses, trains and the occasional taxi." She picks up her bag from the visitor's chair and says, "Poor Maisie will be desperate for a walk by now anyhow."

"Oh, have you been left in charge?"

Charlotte nods. "Poor thing, I think she was quite shaken up. She's a rescue; Cas had only had her for a few weeks. She told me once that she'd wanted a dog ever since she was a little girl, but she grew up in a little flat in Brixton so she never had one . . ." Her words run out as she looks down at her hands.

I had thought I might tell her about Jonny Parker coming onto the ward, but as I watch her put the now-shredded tissue in her pocket, I know now is not the time.

She's had all she can take today. She raises her hand to her mouth again as she says, "God, I am going batty. I almost forgot; I've got a few other bits and bobs here for Cassie from home. It was Jack's idea." Charlotte hands me a small, leather, overnight bag.

"He didn't want her waking up and not having some of her things with her." It always moves me when relatives bring things in from home. How hopeful they must be when they pack the bags that their loved one will brush their own teeth again, send a text, bend to put on their old slippers. I've seen relatives bring in condoms, old newspapers and arm weights before, but here, in this dehumanizing space, they're nothing but mementos from a lost life.

I take the bag. "That's thoughtful. We'll keep it in the break room so it's there if you or Cassie need it."

Charlotte nods, and I'm about to leave when she says quickly, in a flurry, as if she shouldn't ask, "What do you think about the baby, Alice?"

"To be honest, I think it's the closest thing to a miracle I've ever seen."

A smile breaks over Charlotte's face.

I worry I've been too honest so temper my next comment. "But we need to keep our fingers crossed. It's still all very uncertain."

Her smile fades only slightly; she breathes out. "You're right. You're right. Still, all being well, Jack said the baby could be with us in June?"

I nod. "That would be great but we will be preparing for the baby to arrive earlier, just in case it becomes risky for either of them. Only time will tell at this stage."

She nods and gives me a little wave goodbye before she turns back to Cassie and I leave them, the old Cassie in the frame, angelic, smiling down at her new broken self.

I'm home just after 7 p.m. David's running shoes are not in their usual place by the back door. He didn't take Bob with him this time. Bob wags his tail, delighted he avoided the run, curled up and warm in his basket.

It's cold, so I start running a bath; maybe David will hop in with me when he's back. My body feels slow and doughy; I must be about to get my period. I take my clothes off and put on my bathrobe, look at my phone to try and figure out the dates, whether I'm due this week or next. I count the dates twice. I definitely had my last period when we went to the carol concert in Brighton, which means that, yes, it's already a week late. Since we agreed to stop trying, I stopped logging the days until my period in my phone. I was surprised it didn't feel like a wrench; it felt like a relief, no longer monitoring day by day every hormone fluctuation, changes in temperature. But now, now I am late, eight days late.

I know there's still a test stored under the bathroom sink. I don't let myself think too much. The water filling our old Victorian bathtub thunders. I rip open the packaging and leave it on the floor for now; I'll hide it deep in the bin later. I've done enough of these things to ignore the instructions. I know this moment, know the sting of fear and sharp contours of anticipation. I have to focus on slowing my breath and stare at the ceiling for a few seconds before a small trickle starts to daintily fill the toilet, I move the wand into the stream and when I'm finished, I pull up my jeans and sit on the edge of the bath, feeling surprisingly calm as I wait for the letters to spell out the future.

Slowly, magically, the letters take shape and I read "Pregnant" over and over again and I start laughing and I must call out because a worried little black face noses the door open and even though he knows he's not allowed upstairs, he senses immediately my whooping was for something good, not for something bad, so his tail starts wagging and he trots towards me, his head low, knowing he's crossed the boundary line, but sensing I won't care. I hold his solid body and put my face in his muscly shoulder and it's as if I feel my heart take a huge breath in, and for one brief moment I let my hope soar.

After a few seconds, Bob pulls away from me and I look back at the dates on my phone. I'm only about three weeks. This is the most dangerous time for me; I've never got beyond nine weeks. I think of Cassie at twelve weeks, and try and imagine my own stomach, swelling, stretching around new life. Bob lies down in the corner, his head turned away as I do another test. I'm pregnant. I have an urge to call my mum; we haven't spoken for a while. I know she's busy helping look after Harry and Elsa but I long to hear her sound happy for me, long to make her proud. But I've done that before too early; there's nothing worse than hearing your own mum cracking inside in agony. No. It's too early.

I turn the bath off, hide the tests in their own plastic bag and drop them into the bin. Bob follows me lazily into the office. I don't know what to do. I feel fluid, new, shocked by joy. I wish I had someone to hug, wish I could tell someone who wouldn't be frightened for me. I wish it could be like the first time again, David spinning me around the room, Mum laughing with happiness down the phone. For one mad moment I think about driving back to the hospital, telling Frank and Cassie.

Instead, I sit in the office chair, and Bob collapses on the floor again by my feet. I turn the computer on. I suddenly want to see photos of Cassie, feel like I know her, as if knowing her—this woman whose baby survived against all odds—will help the tiny life in me.

I usually avoid Facebook, too many photos of babies and toddlers, I was going to close my account, but now I'm pleased I haven't. I find the search box and type "Cassie Jensen" before clicking on the magnifying glass search icon. I feel a bit foolish but remind myself that my sister says everyone looks at everyone on Facebook; it's legitimate stalking.

I scroll past a few other Cassie Jensens until I stop at a photo I recognize from Charlotte's display behind Cassie's bed. Jack is tanned and smiling; Cassie, less familiar to me out of a hospital bed, is wearing a bright blue sarong. She's less brown than Jack but she looks just as happy with Jack's arm around her shoulders, her hand touching his stomach. Her face is ablaze with sun freckles and her fair hair wavy with sea salt. I click on the "photos" icon and lean in towards the screen. The most recent photos were posted by Jack, just a few days after Christmas. Judging from Cassie's stark page, and lack of any security, Jack is a bigger Facebook user than his wife. Jack's Christmas album has thirty-four "likes"; Sara Baker has commented, "The perfect couple!", and Steve Langley asks, "Can I come next year?" My heart fractures as I read Jack's reply; he must have been so certain there would be more Christmases to come: "Cheers, Sara! Steve, mate, you can come see us anytime!"

There's a photo of Cassie holding a border terrier like a baby in her arms, and a selfie of Jack and Cassie outside in a white-dusted field, with the grumpy-looking dog between them. The caption reads, "Let it snow!"

I stop at a black-and-white close-up photo of Cassie placing a silver bauble on a plump, richly decorated

Christmas tree, her engagement and wedding ring glinting at the camera. Underneath, Jack's written, "My beautiful wife, tree decorating on our first anniversary" under the photo. The camera seems to have caught her mid-laugh, her smile so wide her large eyes crest. I think about what Jack said about Cassie having a tough time recently, but I can't see it, it all looks nauseatingly perfect. Despite my own happy Christmas and the fact I'm pregnant, I bite my bottom lip and feel another shock of jealousy and I remember why I never look at Facebook. I move forward in my chair, the photo pixilates but I keep staring at her fixed, unseeing eyes and I think she knew; she knew she was pregnant but she kept it secret. I think she waited, wanted to know the baby had a good chance. After she miscarried, I bet she wanted to protect Jack, her family, from more possible heartache.

I scroll through a few more photos before one catches my eye. Cassie's a few years younger, grinning at the camera as if she's on holiday, not in a hospice. She's got one leg raised up on the bed where an older woman, jaundiced and emaciated, lies, a bright blue headscarf wrapped around her bald head. They're holding hands. They don't look similar, but that's the disease. I know immediately the woman is April, Cassie's mum. On the other side of April is a man with longish white hair, the camera's caught him smiling but his eyes are closed. He's holding April's left hand as delicately as if a butterfly just landed on him and he wants it to stay. They're both wearing shiny gold rings.

"Facebook? You're never on Facebook." David's right

behind me; I'd been so engrossed I didn't hear him come in.

"David, you scared the shit out of me." I swivel round to face him, slap him playfully away, his T-shirt is sweaty, slightly damp.

"Oooh," he says, fending off my attack by grabbing my wrists. "So who are we looking at?" He leans towards the computer.

"Oh, no one really." I turn back to the computer, wiggle my right wrist free and close the page before he can see. While David starts half-heartedly stretching his calf I try and keep my voice normal. "God, I forgot what a weird thing Facebook is, everyone posting about their life."

"Yeah, but it's all window dressing, all carefully edited bullshit. People post photos of themselves wrapped around the partner they despise in an attempt to convince the world all is well, because if everyone else thinks they're happy, then surely they are?"

Can he not see it in me? Do I not look a little more alive? Like a light has been turned on inside me?

"Ahh, there he is . . . my very own little Grinch," I say.

"It's true!" He shrugs and releases his calf as he turns towards the bathroom, saying in a silly voice, "Ah, good little wifey running a bath for me."

I get up quickly from the computer. "Bugger off, it's mine!"

We race each other to the bathroom like children and he pulls the tie on my bathrobe until I shake it off, he puts his hand on my stomach but he still doesn't guess. I wrap my arms around his shoulders, kiss him full on the mouth. He's surprised—I usually avoid sweaty kisses—but I kiss him again and say, "I love you, David." He holds the back of my head, and he says, "I love you, A-Lice." I think of Cassie and think I might cry suddenly because, for whatever reason, the world has given us both another chance.

8

Frank

Sleep is hard to come by on 9B. The ward sounds like the Serengeti at night. I remember hearing it on a wildlife documentary, full of whoops and moans, and nighttime chatter. Here the commotion is led by Ellen, the old lady who goes back to the Blitz most nights. Because I can't move and my eyes are shut, I imagine it must seem that I sleep like the dead, but I'm just like everyone else; I have to be comfortable, which, most of the time, I'm not. I can't shift blankets if I'm too hot, or yell at the other patients to shut the hell up.

I must doze off eventually because when I open my eyes Alice is with me, chatting away about David, how he's started running. My head's slipped and lolls to the right, like a marionette with slack strings; I can see my Christmas cards and the photo Luce sent. I don't know what Alice is doing but she must be busy, buzzing around me; usually

she'd prop my head up straight away. There's a new lightness to her; she must still be all fizzy about Cassie and the
baby.

"Actually, that reminds me, Frank, I must get David
some reflective gear; I don't like him running on dark
roads . . ."

Someone clears their throat and, from behind the curtain,
Lizzie says, "Alice?"

Alice pulls the curtain back and out of the far corner
of my eye, I see Lizzie and Charlotte standing opposite
Alice.

"Morning, Charlotte," Alice says to the neat-looking
older woman. She turns to Lizzie. "Thank you." Lizzie
nods and goes back towards reception.

"The family room's free, I could make us some coffee?"
Alice asks Charlotte.

"Oh no, no I've only got a couple of minutes actually,
Alice. I just wanted to ask—" she glances at me quickly,
too polite to stare and her voice softens; she doesn't want
to offend "—about the private room for Cassie. Mr. Sharma
mentioned she would be moving a few days ago?"

Cassie's leaving? My heart falls.

"Oh, Mr. Sharma didn't update you?" Alice asks.

"Not since it was mentioned."

"The doctors have actually decided to keep her here,
on 9B."

Charlotte tuts, but lets Alice keep talking. My heart
balances again.

"The thing is, we have all the emergency equipment here
for her, in case we need it. We can't have those machines
on standby for only one patient; it may put others at risk.

And, besides, they were struggling to find a room with enough space for the machines we'd like to have available to her."

She's staying.

"What do you think, Alice, honestly?"

At least she won't be alone.

"I think it's probably the wisest decision. We have a minimum of two nurses here round the clock, the fastest access to equipment and meds; besides, it's such a small ward, it's pretty quiet here anyway, and we'll do all we can to make sure you and your visitors have privacy."

She nods again, looks up at me, as if for reassurance that I'm not going to be a nuisance.

I don't take it personally. She shouldn't worry; I'm a quiet neighbor.

"Actually, I wanted to talk to you about that as well," Charlotte says, turning back to Alice. "We've decided to keep visitors to a minimum for now."

Alice nods. "Yes, of course, if that's what you want."

"It was Jack's idea. He wants it to be just him and me for now."

I hear surprise in Alice's pause; Charlotte keeps talking.

"The phone is ringing constantly with friends asking how she's getting on, but we don't want lots of people knowing about the baby just yet, when we're still getting used to it ourselves. As you said, the most important thing is that we're calm and positive around Cassie, and to be honest, I don't want Jack dealing with streams of visitors. He doesn't need that just now. He told me about Jonny making his way onto the ward. We don't want anything like that happening again. We thought if she was moved and we limited visitors, he won't be able to . . . anyway, keeping it to just us two seems like the simplest option at present. Does that sound OK?"

"Yes, of course, Charlotte. Whatever you think is best. You can always reassess later if you want."

I feel a quick stab of disappointment, I was looking forward to seeing Cassie's friends, but if it means she'll be calmer, safer without people like her wild-eyed neighbor about, then so be it.

I spend most of my day staring at the foot of Cassie's bed, wondering where she is in her coma, if she's traveling in her subconscious, wondering if she, like me, is ever visited by the dead. Most of my visits happened on a plane. It was supposed to be my first flight, and I'm in my twenties again, on the flight I should have taken to America to start my new job, to start my new life. In the dream, the seat next to mine is always empty and I'm restless with fear unable to sit still, tapping the laminated emergency instructions I hold in my lap against a feverish leg that won't stop shaking. The smiling, pretty, flight attendants—packaged in their uniforms like plastic dolls, shiny hair and red lips—aren't even enough to distract me. The noise of 30,000 feet is not what I expected. It's a sort of white noise, a great long moan wrapped around the world; it stretches on at the same note, and my ears are full of it.

"C'mon, lad, shove over." I hadn't heard that gruff voice out of our tiny, paisley-printed sitting room—that smelled of airless hours in front of television mixed with something a little sweet, white bread maybe—since I was a teenager, but I'm hardwired to obey that voice so, without turning,

I move into the unoccupied middle seat next to me as my dad, who died when I was nineteen, eases himself with a wheeze and a wince into the aisle seat. I can't remember ever sitting so close to him when he was alive, his brown polyester slacks almost touch my stonewashed jeans.

"Your mother and me—" always his preferred opening line "—want you to get off this flight." I look at him then. He's looking forward, down the aisle towards a slim, blond stewardess who's bending down in front of her trolley to get someone a lemonade. His jowls spill over the top of his shirt collar, like extra pastry on a pie. There's a shock of white hair in his ears and I'm close enough to see hundreds of tiny blackheads on his nose that open out into larger pockmarks over the rest of his wide face. His deep-set eyes fix onto the blond woman's bottom and his gray eyebrows move as much as his mouth as he says again, "Yes, your mother and me . . . we want you to get off this flight."

"Dad." My voice far older, deeper than it was at twenty-seven. "What are you talking about? There's no way we can get off."

He pulls himself away from the blond then, and nodding, turns his wide face towards mine. His breath smells, as it always did, of well-stewed tea. "It's not safe, son, it's not safe. This is no way to go. You could be stuck on this thing for ever. It's not right, so it's best you come with me."

"Dad, this is crazy. We're somewhere over the Atlantic, it's not safe."

His eyes narrow at me.

"Don't argue with me, son. I know a way, you just follow me." He starts to heave himself up, but either he's too fat or the seat in front of him is too close because it takes him a few tries, and the whole bank of seats shudder with the effort. I look around at the other passengers—businessmen on laptops, cuddling couples, kids giggling at a film—but none of them seem to have noticed my dead dad.

He's waiting for me in the aisle now.

"Come on, good lad," he says.

I stand and start to follow him, bending my knees to move out of the row of seats and then I notice the blond stewardess has turned around. She's pulling her steel cart straight towards me, hips swinging in her high heels and she's looking straight at me. Underneath the makeup I can see it's June Withers from school. She dated my older brother Paul for a few months, which made me the coolest boy in my class for a brief moment, before June dumped Paul for a heroin addict. She was found a few months later face down in her own vomit at her mum's house. Now I think that story about the heroin and the puke must have been bullshit; she must have been training to be a stewardess all along.

Her red lips curl like a seashell into a smile, her teeth like pearls as she narrows her eyes in disbelief. "Frankie?"

"June?"

"Oh my god, it *is* you! How funny!" Her smile crests over me.

"Frank!" My dad barks like a pissed off terrier further down the aisle. I don't turn away from June, but she must see him over my shoulder because she says, "Is that your dad?"

"Oh, yeah. I think the altitude's got to him. He keeps saying we're not safe."

Her smile disappears immediately, and her face knots. "No, Frank, listen to him. We're safe, but you're not. You have to go with him or you'll be stuck on this plane for god knows how long."

She starts shooing me along with her manicured hands, saying, "Go on, follow him, Frankie, go on," and forcing me forward, pulling the trolley after her.

Dad's moved on down the aisle; he's waiting for me. When I reach him, he starts walking again; his brown cardigan and the way his stout neck has receded between his broad shoulders makes him look like a retreating mole. I'm pressed now, between my dad and June who still flicks me on, as if I'm an annoying fly.

We pass the toilets and rows and rows of people. I'm escorted by Dad and June to the tail of the plane, where there are more toilets and a little beige cupboard area. Two more trolleys like the one June is pulling are parked up and there's another stewardess sitting on a case eating some noodles. She glances up at us with bored, black-rimmed eyes and then looks away again. Out of the corner of my eye I see movement and, to my horror, my dad is braced, tense and puffing out through his cheeks. He's pulling the red handle of the emergency exit door.

I lunge towards him, but June's sharp hand on my arm pulls me back and she says with a little laugh, "Don't worry, Frankie; he's doing the right thing."

Then we hear a loud sucking sound and the light for the toilet flashes from red to green and the door concertinas as it opens and, after a second, my Luce walks out.

She claps her hands together when she sees me; she's

about twelve years old, her face round and flawless with youth. She reaches out to me and takes my hand.

"Come on, Dad," she says. "We'll be landing soon. Come and sit next to me." My dad stops wrestling with the door and June scowls softly by my side. They seem to know they couldn't stop me going with Luce, even if they tried. Hand-in-hand, Lucy steers me back to my seat. That's the last I remember from the dream. There are different characters, dead people from my life. Sometimes it's my nan, my Auntie Christina and, once that I recall, our little Scottie dog, Boots, tried to bark me off that plane, but Lucy always arrives and pulls me back in the nick of time.

It's Carol's high-pitched laugh that brings me back from remembering the plane, landing me again on the ward. Carol's usually in her office, but there's a shortage of health assistants today so it sounds like Mary's roped Carol into helping her change George's bed sheets. My eyes are only open a fraction. Mary moved my head so all I can see now is the end of my bed, and a small bit of the ward floor. My chin is almost pressed to my chest, but my ears are perfectly tuned.

"Just like old times, eh, Caz?" Mary says, and I hear George's curtain dance along its rail as she pulls it around George's bed. "Us two rolling up our sleeves."

Unlike other nurses, they don't count down before they lift George, and they don't remind each other to tuck in the sheet corners. These two have been around for long enough, they know all the steps to this dance.

"So did you speak to the police then, Caz?"

I get it. Mary is, of course, a bit of a gossip.

"They called this morning to say they've arrested that guy who found her, the neighbor." Carol's voice is lower than usual, a voice for saying things she knows she probably shouldn't. "They've charged him with drunk driving and attempted manslaughter. Paula says she's surprised it took them so long; she says she could tell it was him when he tried to barge his way in to see Cassie last week."

I feel movement behind the curtain, the tug as they pull away old sheets. The women pause.

"Well, you know what I think?" Mary doesn't wait for a response. Carol will hear what Mary thinks whether she wants to or not. "They were having an affair, weren't they? This neighbor and Cassie. It's obvious. She told him about the baby, their baby, and he panicked like a bloody idiot."

"Oh god, do you really think so, Mary?"

"I really do. It's just a pity we can't do a paternity test now, get it over and done with for the sake of Jack and his poor mum, but with Cassie in her condition it's out of the question."

There's a familiar swoosh as one of them floats a new sheet across the bed.

"It's heartbreaking. That poor man, he adores her. You know what Lizzie said the other day? She saw him reading one of those baby development books aloud to her? He'd be a lovely dad."

"I know, I keep thinking about his mum as well. They won't find out for months if it's Jack's or not, not until the baby's born. But you know, I'd rather know the truth, wouldn't you? I mean imagine raising a kiddie, thinking it's yours and then finding out years later it's someone else's. That's got to be worse."

Carol doesn't say anything for a moment, practiced hands slap over the starched, taut sheet.

"I just hope this neighbor does the decent thing and tells the truth before the baby comes along. Little mite shouldn't be born into all of this, should it?"

Moments later, carrying plastic bags with George's old sheets bundled inside, I see the two nurses' little white shoes pad across my narrow view. They stop whispering as soon as they're on the ward and I try and feel glad like them, relieved that justice is a little more in reach for Cassie and her little one, but I keep thinking of his face, his eyes wide, fiery with terror, desperate for a new image of Cassie to wipe the one in the stream, crumpled and bleeding, from his mind. I think about how he froze, tense as a deer who knows he's being hunted.

The afternoon rolls quietly into early evening. Jack visits Cassie. He plays her music. I can't hear what he's saying to her, if anything, over the music. The notes sing through my bones; I drink up every one like drops of nectar. At some point, my eyes shut and I drift away, to a place where a light breeze glances my skin, and Lucy is by my side.

My eyes don't open again until after dark. My head is resting slightly to the left, so I can just see the bottom right corner of Cassie's bed and a section of floor, made shiny by the light next to Cassie's bed. It must be late; Paula often opens the curtains between Cassie and me around midnight as it's easier for her to keep an eye on us that way. I'm counting along with my breath, in, out, in, out trying to trick my mind to sleep, to slip away to my dream again, to the outside sun and Lucy's little hand in my own, when I hear the ward door swoosh open. Thinking it's a nurse I go back to my breath. But then I realize something's missing. Whoever just came in isn't bustling around like the nurses always do. In fact, they're moving so quietly I can only just make out the lightest tap and squeal as they walk down the hard rubber floor. They pause at the end of the ward, before they start moving again and a shadow comes to hover in my view, a head, stretched long and weird by the light behind it.

Maybe it's a doc from another ward.

The figure moves to the foot of Cassie's bed. I can only see him from the hips down. He's wearing jeans; they bag around his legs like extra skin. He keeps his weight to his left, slightly wonky, nurturing his right. He moves gingerly towards her and out of my view.

I've never seen a doc in jeans, not here.

All I can see now is his shadow flickering in and out of my view, like a trapped flame. He's moving, he's doing something to Cassie and I can't do anything. I can't do anything but I imagine him pulling the tube out of her head, Cassie's blood spraying the ceiling bright poppy-crimson, my screams echoing, useless around my body. I long to turn away, to disappear in a puff of smoke, but this is it, this is what I must endure for being so fucking pointless, forced to watch but not quite see, whatever cruel thing he's doing to her, to them, prone and vulnerable on the sacrificial slab.

A phlegmy splutter from either Ellen or George and suddenly the shadow stops flickering. From behind her curtain Ellen shrieks, "No!" like an angry gull. "Not that!"

Ellen!

My heart seems to find itself again, slotting back into a rhythm as the shadow takes on form and the jeans flash back in my view.

Again, shout again, Ellen!

An alarm, from George, starts tunelessly screeching in a minor key. I will one of my machines to join the panic, to help get him far, far away from her. He moves too quickly; there's a tuneless clatter as he clumsily kicks a stainless steel trolley. My heart monitor starts beeping. We sound like an angry flock of birds, screeching at the intruder. It's too noisy and my heart is still flapping like a dying fish in my chest, so I can't hear him leave, but I imagine him, trying to move quickly, dragging his leg as though he's been shot, away from the ward.

"I'm coming, I'm coming." Paula bustles onto the ward. I imagine her shaking her head at the disturbed tray, and hear the wheels whine as she rolls it back to its place near Cassie.

She tends to the other patient before coming to me last. She dabs my eyes with saline and finally lifts my head up. My eyes leap on Cassie. She's still there; she's still alive. But she doesn't look serene anymore. Her facial muscles aren't relaxed; they're twisted, her mouth round, petrified in a noiseless scream and the truth hits me, clean as though I'd cut myself on the sharpness of the realization, that even here, Cassie and her baby aren't safe.

9

Cassie

"Must be left here," Cassie says, squinting down at the mess of lines on the map and looking up quickly, and down again, trying to spot some correlation between the bushy little lane they're bouncing down in Jonny's van and the capillary-like lines on the map that is spread out across her legs, her bare feet resting on the glove compartment in front of her. She feels Jonny turn to look at her, before he turns back to the road, still smiling.

"What are you smiling about?" she asks.

Jonny's smile broadens behind his sunglasses as he says, "You've got absolutely no idea where we are, do you? There is no left here."

Cassie drops her head again, frowning down at the map as if it lied to her.

"Jesus!" she exclaims. "Why call it Brighton when it's clearly the arse end of nowhere?"

"Good point, although I'm not sure the 'Arse End Food and Drink Festival' would draw huge crowds."

Cassie laughs. The boxes of jam slide in the back as Jonny swings the van, a sharp right down another small lane, hedgerows swaying with May flowers.

"All of these lanes look identical," Cassie complains.

"Let's just go with our gut, can't be far away," Jonny says as Cassie leans back on the headrest and turns to look at Jonny. He's in his denim cut-offs again. He threw his flip-flops in the back of the van before he started driving barefoot; even those flimsy things were too restrictive for him. His arms are already a burnt-caramel color, the hair on them as light as spiders" webs, a slightly darker patch of hair pokes up from the front of his faded T-shirt.

The world goes lightly with Jonny. He says it's because he spent too long in a suit, rushing through his life like it was something he had to endure. Now, it's as though he's come to an agreement with the world; I accept you if you accept me. Jonny says people always over-complicated everything. Cassie thinks of Jack. He hadn't slept well again last night; he was out of bed and hunched over his spreadsheets just like the last few nights, the glow from his computer screen highlighting his face sickly and anemic. He says issues at work are too complicated to explain, so he just turns back to his computer, and doesn't even try. She hasn't seen him like this before; his stress has a grandeur, an importance that Cassie doesn't know how to penetrate.

She talked to Jonny about it, on a "research trip" to a chili farm. Jonny had pulled his sunglasses off his face, nestled the arms behind his ears and looked straight at

Cassie as he'd said, "Well, it seems to me you have a choice, Cas. You can either confront him and say you need to work together to change things."

"Or?"

"Or you accept that this is a part of him for now and bring him a whiskey when he can't sleep."

Jonny makes everything sound so simple. Problem is, though, that somewhere in the journey between leaving Jonny and going home to Jack, Jonny's quiet logic seemed to twist and tangle, like a thin chain necklace, so even when she had used Jonny's words to explain to Jack how she felt, she'd sounded facile, childish. Jack had just frowned at her, rubbed his temples and turned back to his spreadsheets, and she'd apologized for bringing it up and had left him to his work. It wasn't like that with Jonny, though; he seemed to understand without her having to explain.

"Ah ha!" Jonny sits up in the driver's seat. "Do you see what I see?"

Ahead of them, there's the small Lego-like block of the racecourse building, and a plastic sign telling them they had, finally, arrived at BRIGHTON FOOD AND DRINK FESTIVAL.

Cassie picks up the map from her legs, exposing her thighs, and without bothering to concertina the map back into its folds, she throws it into the back, knowing Jonny won't care, and he grins as she throws her arms into the air, victorious, and says, "We made it! Arse End Festival!"

They pull into a small field to find a space to park. There aren't any close to the entrance so they have to drive further into the parking area. Cassie spots a familiar pink scarf and silvery bob. She tells Jack to slow down as she sees Charlotte walking towards the festival entrance.

"Charlotte!" Cassie calls out of the window. "You're here early!"

Charlotte looks around her, uncertain whether she did just hear her name or not, before she sees Cassie waving from the van. Charlotte holds the tablecloth she's sewn for Cassie a little tighter as she walks towards them.

"Oh, hi, Cas," she says, her eyes glancing over her daughter-in-law's bare legs, her feet still resting on the dashboard. "I got a lift with Maggie—you know, the hairdresser? She's helping at a cake stall. Here, I've got your tablecloth." She raises the red and blue striped cloth she finished seaming last night. Cassie slowly lowers her legs.

"Charlotte, you're amazing," Cassie says, lifting her bottom to tug her denim skirt back over her legs. She feels a shock, warmth, as Jonny's eyes flick down to her thighs again and bounce straight back up to meet Charlotte's gaze.

Jonny leans forward in his seat, hands on the steering wheel, past Cassie and calls out brightly, "Hi, Charlotte, we'll just park and be right with you."

Charlotte nods and takes a step back. As she watches the van pull forward, her thumbnail flicks against the fabric in her arms, and she feels the skin on her eyelid start to pulse, an old tic. It hasn't done that in years, and she feels a familiar queasiness in her lower stomach as she watches the van bounce across the field. She knows what it means immediately; she's worried for her son.

Jonny hauls most of the boxes inside to the two trestle

tables in the far corner of the main vestibule, while Cassie registers with the organizers and starts setting out her display. They know their roles now; this is the fourth event for Farm Jams, and Jonny's been by Cassie's side helping for each one. Cassie's careful to balance some of her newer, bolder inventions like chili chocolate spread and elder flower preserve with old favorites like raspberry jam and apricot. She positions the hand-labeled pots on the table in their kiln jars like tiny, sweet soldiers.

Over the last couple of weeks, Cassie has gone from eating mouthfuls of jam with a spoon straight from the jar to feeling like she'd puke at the thought of even smelling any jam. She must have overdone it, like listening to one song too many times. She'll get Jonny to open the taster pots today.

Cassie thought Charlotte was going to offer to help set up, but she hasn't seen her since Charlotte handed her the tablecloth and said she was going to see if Maggie needed help.

Cassie looks around the space. People are slowly starting to trickle in, but there's no sign of Charlotte. She heard a rumor that representatives from Flavor Awards were going to be coming today, incognito. Charlotte wouldn't leave without saying goodbye, would she? Cassie had hoped Charlotte would report back to Jack, tell him how good the stall looks, how hard Cassie's worked to make it look professional but still keeping the cottage, homemade feel.

"Right, that's the last one." Jonny, back in his flip-flops, shuffles towards Cassie with another cardboard box. He lowers it carefully on the floor behind the trestle table and wipes his forehead with the back of his wrist.

She briefly touches his back, feels his muscles move under her hands. She doesn't say thank-you; he knows she's grateful, just like he's grateful to Cassie.

He swigs from his bottle of water. Cassie took a sip from the same bottle earlier and almost spat it out, the water had a salty, chalky taste like clay. Jonny must have dropped an Alka-Seltzer in it before leaving home.

He'd been on the phone last night to Lorna, his wife in London. He always drinks too much when he talks to Lorna. Cassie knows things have been worse for Jonny since Cassie answered Jonny's home phone while he was out walking Dennis two days ago. Lorna went mental on the phone, called Cassie a bitch and a marriage wrecker before Cassie hung up and left the phone off the hook so Lorna couldn't call back. Cassie had been left shaken, but Jonny held her, reminded her that Lorna's unwell. He said it wasn't Cassie's fault as he poured her a glass of wine.

"You didn't see Charlotte anywhere, did you?" she asks Jonny.

"Not since we arrived," Jonny says, looking to either side of them, as though he expects Charlotte to be hiding nearby.

"OK." Cassie walks around their stall. "I just realized I left the flyers in the van. Can I have the keys?"

"I'll get them," Jonny says.

"No, no, I'll go, I want some air, I'm feeling sick again."

Jonny throws Cassie the keys and grins at her. "Great catch," he says with a wink, as her hands close around the keys in midair.

Outside, Cassie checks Maggie's stall and the ladies' toilet, before she looks in the pop-up coffee shop. Her mother-in-law is seated at one of the rickety-looking tables, her hand clasped around a polystyrene cup. Her eyes are cloudy, like she's lost somewhere in her memory. She only looks up, slightly startled, when Cassie puts her hand on her shoulder.

"Charlotte, I've been looking for you! You OK?"

"Oh, Cas, sorry. I just wanted to have a quick sit down."

"OK, well, I've just got to nip to the van quickly," Cassie says. "You won't leave without coming to see our stall, will you?"

Charlotte picks up her cup, drains the last of her coffee and says, "I'm finished anyway, I'll come with you now."

Charlotte stands and the two women walk side by side back to the van. The grass is flattened, tattooed with tread from tires. A mood Cassie hasn't met before hangs around Charlotte today like a fog; she doesn't know how to lift it, so it's a relief when Charlotte speaks first.

"What's the latest on Jonny and his wife? Jack said she's still in London?"

Cassie turns to look at Charlotte, but her mother-in-law keeps her eyes fixed forward. Cassie can't read her expression under her sunglasses.

"She's not very well. It became impossible for them to live together anymore, so that was a big part of Jonny's decision to move down here."

"What do you mean? Surely if she's not well she needs her husband more than ever?"

Cassie looks at her mother-in-law. Sometimes she can be quite unsubtle.

"This is confidential, but she's mentally unwell, Charlotte.

She became violent towards Jonny, started stalking one of his female colleagues at work before she was committed."

"Why? Was he having an affair with his colleague?" Charlotte asks, a clipped coolness in her voice.

Cassie frowns; Charlotte's usually so astute.

"Charlotte, I really don't think now . . ." Cassie was about to defend Jonny, but Charlotte has suddenly stopped walking.

Cassie walks back a couple of paces to stand opposite her.

"Don't be so naive, Cassie." The older woman pulls her sunglasses off her face like they're burning her suddenly. "Either he lied to his wife or he didn't."

Cassie realizes she's never heard her gentle mother-in-law angry before.

"Where is all this coming from, Charlotte?" Cassie shakes her head, she's only ever seen Charlotte's eye swell with happy tears. "You seem really upset."

Charlotte raises her eyes to something in the distance, over Cassie's shoulder; she squints as her eyelid starts pounding again.

"Cassie, look, I'm going to tell you something, because I trust you and because I think you should know so you can maybe understand my concerns about Jonny."

Cassie feels the fog lift slightly between them. Charlotte trusts her. She's OK. She nods and waits for her mother-in-law to keep talking. Charlotte's shoulders drop slightly, as if finally giving in to an invisible weight.

"After Mike died, a woman came to our house. She told me she'd been Mike's lover. That they were together on and off for years. She came because, after he died, she found out she wasn't the only one, that Mike had been having affairs with other women."

Charlotte pauses, her lips purse, pulling together as if they've been sewn by invisible thread. She breathes out before she starts talking again. It sounds sore.

"She told me because she knew now how it felt to be the other woman, how it felt to be lied to for so long. She thought she was doing the right thing." Charlotte shakes her head, a laugh, dry and mirthless, sticks in her throat like a shard of glass.

"The truth is, I think I knew already. Some deep, fundamental part of me knew he wasn't fully mine." Silence swells around them.

"Does Jack . . ."

Charlotte's eyes finally lock on to Cassie's face.

"Jack doesn't know a thing about it. I hated that woman for making me lie to Jack even more than I hated her for what she did with my husband. Jack had already lost his dad . . . had found him dead, for God's sake. He wanted to believe his dad was a hero. I wanted to keep his memory perfect; I saw no reason to take that away from him. I stand by that, Cas. I don't think it would have helped anyone for him to know then and it certainly won't help him to know now."

A couple of tears finally breach down Charlotte's face. Cassie puts her hand on her shoulder and, feeling no resistance there, pulls her mother-in-law towards her. She's glad Charlotte lets her wrap her arms around her. She hopes she can feel the love, the admiration Cassie feels for her. Charlotte releases her arms first and searches up her sleeve for a tissue, which she dabs underneath her eyes.

Cassie wants to know why Charlotte's telling her all this, why now. She wants to know, but she doesn't want to ask. So instead she takes hold of Charlotte's hand, the tissue bunching between their palms and she says what she had planned to say to Jack.

"Charlotte, you know, because Jack's been working so hard, Jonny's been helping me with the jam. We've become friends, that's a . . . I . . ." but she can't finish what she was going to say, because suddenly the world has started spinning and she reaches out for her mother-in-law to steady her. She hears Charlotte say, "Cassie, Cas? What's happening?" before the wave of nausea subsides and she's left with a crippling exhaustion so complete that it makes her knees buckle and she thinks she could collapse and fall asleep right here if Charlotte wasn't holding her up.

She wishes she could tell her mother-in-law to get Jonny, but she knows that would just make everything worse. So instead Charlotte helps Cassie into the passenger seat of Jonny's van.

Charlotte's about to sit behind the wheel next to her when Cassie says, "Charlotte, sorry to ask, but would you mind going to help Jonny? I'll be fine in a few minutes, but I just don't want him to be left on his own." A strong wave of nausea undulates from her stomach again; she feels her forehead prick with sweat.

"Really, Cas, I don't think you should . . ."

"Please, Charlotte, it's just my low blood pressure; I know it is. I'll rest for a while, have some water and I'll feel better. Come and check on me in fifteen minutes and I'll be fine again, I promise."

Charlotte looks stricken for a moment, unsure what to do, so Cassie repeats, "Please, Charlotte," before she at last leaves Cassie on her own.

Cassie sits motionless in the passenger seat for a few seconds as she lets the facts form a patient queue in her brain. She's sick, and her period's late. She feels one of her breasts; it's swollen and feels bruised as she squeezes it gently. Shit. She thinks about texting Jonny, telling him to come and find her, but that'd only make Charlotte more suspicious and she can't deal with anymore of that now. No, no she should do a test first. She needs to know for sure before telling anyone. She looks down at her gold wedding ring, turns it round on her finger and she fills her lungs with a big, shuddery breath. She'd imagined this moment before, used to fantasize about finding out she was pregnant, but she's shocked she can't feel any joy. Instead she feels another wave of nausea and she covers her face with her palms, as if trying to hide from the world, and sobs into her hands.

10

Alice

The female police officer, Officer Brooks, is standing at reception waiting for me. She'd already met with Elizabeth Longe for an update on Cassie's medical condition. It was Jack's suggestion I meet with Brooks afterwards. He said he wanted everyone to be clear on what happened. He wants to turn down the volume on the rumors and gossip that hums around the hospital ward like theme music to a movie, but I suspect there's something else. A muscle in Jack's jaw flexed and bounced when he told me Jonny has been granted bail.

Brooks has dyed her short hair a rusty ocher since we last met. I never know how to address police officers: "Officer," or maybe just "Brooks." "Jane" feels too informal for someone in police uniform.

"Hello," I say, adding, "How are you?" avoiding a name altogether.

Her thin lips smile briefly, and, for a moment, I see more "Jane" than "Officer Brooks."

"I thought we could go in here," I add, showing her into the nurses break room.

I was hoping we'd have a cup of tea, that we might talk freely to each other, if not quite woman to woman then at least as two female professionals working on the front line. But Officer Brooks sits rigid and impassive opposite me, her uniform like an armor between us. I get the impression she wants me to get straight to it, so I clear my throat.

"We were told the neighbor, Jonny Parker, has been charged."

"That's correct."

I'm worried I'm going to have to wring words out of her like a wet towel, drop by drop, so I'm relieved when she clasps her hands in her lap and leans forward in her chair towards me.

"Neighbors who attended the same New Year's party have provided witness statements," she says in a low, but clear, voice. "They saw Mrs. Jensen and Mr. Parker arguing outside the party. Mr. Parker says Mrs. Jensen walked home in the dark soon after they were seen. He stayed at the party for a couple more hours before driving home, five times over the legal limit."

"So he lives close to Cassie and Jack?"

Brooks blinks and nods at me, surprised perhaps I'm using their first names, like we're friends. She knows what I'm really asking.

"He drove down the same lane where Mrs. Jensen was hit, yes. The theory is he returned home, still catatonic,

147

but he let his dogs out so they could legitimately 'find' her."

"And what's he saying?"

"I'm afraid I can't disclose anything more."

"I thought Jack wanted . . ."

"Mr. Jensen wanted us to have this conversation because Mr. Parker is out on bail now and while his movements are of course restricted and he's not allowed to make contact with the Jensens, we can't place a limit on him coming to the hospital in case he's involved in a medical emergency. Mr. Jensen knows Mr. Parker tried to force his way onto the ward soon after the accident and he's understandably concerned he could make another attempt to see Mrs. Jensen, which would be very distressing for him and his mother. I've spoken to security here; they know to be extra vigilant but we thought it was a good idea to make staff on the ward aware as well."

"Do you think he'll try and come back?"

Brooks' eyes fix on mine for a moment. She seems to soften slightly, and I get the impression she's speaking more from personal rather than professional experience when she says, "Well, he said he wouldn't, of course, but I've seen his type before. They seem sane enough until they find themselves at home, alone and emotional, and the next thing they know, they're opening bottles and God knows what they'll do then. So just make sure your team is aware and monitoring all visitors, OK?"

Brooks bends down towards her feet and rips open the Velcro flap on her police bag.

"Mr. Jensen asked me to give you this as well. He forgot to take it when we met. He said he'd pick it up from you later." Brooks hands me a small brown envelope, the insides padded with stuffing. On the front someone has addressed the envelope to "Mr. Jack Jensen."

Brooks stands abruptly once I've taken the envelope. She doesn't ask me if I have any questions. She smooths her dark navy polyester trousers. "I think that's all for now," she says and she flicks another small smile towards me before she leaves.

I stay sitting in the windowless break room for a few minutes after Brooks leaves, the envelope in my lap, my forefinger twitching against it. It isn't sealed well; half of the envelope flap is unstuck, puckered and raised. I wonder if Brooks noticed it wasn't stuck down properly. I run my fingers along the opening, tease it open a little more. I know I should get some tape, seal it back down, but it's already almost open. Wouldn't it be better to put it in another envelope, one I can seal properly? It looks like it's been tampered with already. I don't want Jack to think someone he doesn't know has been fiddling with it.

Before I have time to talk myself out of it, I move my chair so my back is towards the door in case anyone comes in. I move my finger under the lip of the envelope, which tears easily. Inside, there's a small, clear, plastic evidence bag holding a turquoise ring. I've seen it before; it was on April's thin finger in the photo I saw on Cassie's Facebook—the one of Cassie, April and the white-haired guy in the hospice. The turquoise is marbled, the silver band worn and bumpy, as though it's full of stories. There's a white label stuck onto the front of the plastic bag. It says the ring was found on the third finger of Cassie's left hand. Her wedding ring finger.

My heart leaps as there's a knock at the door. I shove the bag back in the envelope and stand, holding the envelope behind my back. I turn towards the door as Sue, the ward technician, pokes her head into the room and asks if I've seen Mary or know anything about an order Mary made earlier today. I shake my head and Sue frowns quickly, muttering something about systems being in place for a reason before she closes the door.

I find a new envelope from the small stationery area and quickly write Jack's name on the front, just like the police did. As I hold the gummy edges of the envelope together I search for a coherent way into my thoughts, like trying to find the end of a ball of wool. I know there was something, something I saw about Cassie's wedding rings. Holding the fresh envelope, I walk back onto the ward and stop by Cassie's bed.

I pick up her left hand, feel where her wedding ring should be and finally my memory unfurls itself. I remember Jack the day after Cassie was hit; I see him again dropping Cassie's engagement and wedding rings into his shirt pocket. I remember how he patted the pocket, how the rings rested safe just above his heart. I thought the trauma team would have given them to him, but now I know I was wrong, Cassie wasn't wearing his rings when she was hit; she was wearing her mum's. Jack must have brought them specially from home.

I place Cassie's curled hand back on the top of her bed, and look at her withering face. Each day that passes is like a year on her, her skin graying and the lines carving deeper into her skin. I wonder what Jack was planning on doing with those rings; did he have them with him to feel close to Cassie? Or was he planning on sliding them back on her finger, reclaiming her as his own when no one was watching?

I think about Jonny running onto the ward; he would've thrown himself on Cassie if I hadn't stopped him.

As I pull the curtain around Cassie I remind myself that it's Jonny, not devoted Jack, I should be questioning, and I try to distract myself from the memory of his eyes, Jonny's eyes that were full of something like love.

It was Carol's birthday just before New Year so Mary and I take her for a drink after work. The Ox and Cart is a chain pub with spongy carpets and a slot machine that explodes every two minutes with tinny music and brash lights. The only thing in the pub's favor is that it backs onto the hospital parking lot. Mary and Carol are already at a round table for four; Carol's tight, black dress strained over her chest next to Mary's zip-up gray fleece make them look like unlikely companions. They're sitting on stools, a half-empty bottle of white wine in front of them. I forgot to bring a change of clothes so I'm still in my dark blue scrubs. I do a little pirouette as Mary whistles and says, "Sexy outfit, Alice!"

I buy a bottle of wine for Carol's birthday and remind Carol and Mary that I'm on "dry January" to avoid comments when I get myself a lemonade. Carol fills us in on Shane, her new man. They met on a dating site, a fact that seems to have turned Carol off even though she was on there herself.

"I know, I know it's irrational," she says. "I just feel a bit ashamed when people ask how we met, you know, that we don't have a sweet romantic story."

"So make one up." Mary shrugs. "Everyone lies about their life from time to time." Mary takes a gulp of wine.

"I don't," Carol says primly back to her.

"Well, that's my point. Maybe you should give it a go."

We always promise not to talk about work when we meet as friends but this evening we break quicker than usual as Mary says, "Bet even Cassie Jensen, with her gorgeous life, stretched the truth every now and then."

"Well, she obviously did about this baby. I still don't buy it that she didn't know she was pregnant." Carol shakes her head as she talks.

I clutch my glass and think about going to the restroom for a few minutes, in the hope the conversation has moved on by the time I get back. I know some of the nurses have been whispering about it; I'd probably join in if I didn't understand why Cassie didn't tell people about her pregnancy. She was protecting Jack, so he didn't have to go through the pain of another miscarriage. I know that takes guts . . . guts and a lot of love.

"Earth to Alice, whoohoo." Mary snaps her fingers in front of me. I blink twice and say, "Sorry."

Mary holds the stem of her wine glass between her index and middle finger like a pool cue. I'm craving a glass myself; lemonade just doesn't cut it when I'm with these two.

Carol leans forward towards me, conspiratorially. "We were just saying we've got some great gossip for you. It turns out she was in a commercial."

"Who was?"

"Cassie Jensen." Carol sounds vaguely irritated that I'm being slow, ruining her big news.

"A commercial?" I frown. My mind's blank; I can't think of any.

Mary rolls her eyes at me and leans forward, next to Carol. "Lizzie was going on about how she recognized Cassie and wouldn't leave it alone. Then suddenly it clicked and she said, 'There's the sun,' and that's when it clicked for me too."

Mary pauses. Carol smiles at me. Both of them want to catch the moment I figure it out.

I shrug at them both. "I don't get it." I have no idea what they're talking about.

"She's that girl, the girl from the orange juice ad, Juice-C?" Carol says it like it's obvious. "You know, the blond one who looks all miserable? Come on, Alice. You must remember. I mean, it was a few years ago, but everyone, *everyone*, was doing the catchphrase, even you . . ."

My mind is totally blank. I still can't think of any commercials, especially none I'd impersonate.

Carol holds her wine glass close to the side of her face. She takes a long sip, finishing off her wine in one draw. She exhales, as if sated, and says in a wispy Marilyn Monroe-style voice, "There's the sun."

I stare at Carol and then Mary.

Carol starts laughing again, delighted. "It's her, Alice! Lizzie looked it up. Cassie's the Juice-C girl."

Mary and I sip, Carol gulps. The fruit machine sounds like it's having a fit.

"You don't remember it, do you?" Mary sounds deflated.

"No no, I do remember something like that. I'll have to have a look when I get home. Was she in anything else?" I don't really remember but I want them to stop looking at me, expectant, like I'm about to perform some amazing trick.

"Not really, not that I know of. She's a bit like the Milkybar kid, isn't she? I don't think he was in anything else either." Mary's voice is already sticky with wine.

"What a weird old world, huh?" Carol turns to me. "The Juice-C girl on our ward, pregnant and in a coma. You couldn't make it up."

"Does anyone else know?" I ask. "About Cassie and this ad, I mean?"

Mary blinks at me and Carol shakes her head.

"OK, good," I say, "Sharma was going on about confidentiality to me again yesterday, *silentius maximus*."

Carol snorts on her wine and Mary scoffs, "*Arrogantius prickus*."

Mary moves on to tell us about her little grandson, Thomas, who has had the measles recently. He's been wailing so much Mary's daughter hasn't left the house in three days. Carol commiserates. Her daughter had it when she was little and it was a bugger to get rid of apparently.

I want to leave, to google the Juice-C ad, but now they're talking about kids I'll have to stay at least another fifteen minutes. I don't want them to feel bad or think that's why I'm leaving. I wait, trying to be patient, while Carol asks us for the tenth time if we think she should have laser surgery on her eyes. Mary tells her again that she's too young to have "reading glasses."

I probably haven't been listening long enough for them not to worry, but in what I hope is a happy voice, I say,

154

"Sorry, ladies, I'm going to leave you to the wine." I kiss them both. "Happy belated birthday," I say to Carol.

They tut and oh their disappointment that I'm leaving so early, but I reassure myself they'll be back to their stories as soon as I've picked my bag up off the floor.

I watch the ad on YouTube on my phone twice in my car. As soon as the mocked-up gray, 1950s, black-and-white street comes onto the screen, I remember it. An attractive young woman—more of a girl really—walks down the dull street, although they've made her skin light gray, similar to what it is now. She is undeniably lovely but a low-key, natural lovely. Her face isn't showy, demanding adoration, and her dimples and long neck are quietly gorgeous; there should anyone notice. Commercial Cassie walks close to the camera and appeals right into the lens, "Where's the sun?"

Immediately, a carton of Juice-C drops down from the heavens into her hands. She takes a good, long gulp through a convenient straw and, all of a sudden, the sky opens, the picture turns into brilliant color and out of nowhere, laughing, beautiful people bounce onto the street. Cassie is transformed. She's sparkling, her hair in a ponytail, her smile wide and her teeth California-white. A brass band marches behind her, cheerleaders twirl about, fireworks explode in the background and Cassie looks at the carton in her hand, her smile never shaking, and turns back to the camera. "There's the sun!" she says, with laughter in her voice.

The clip feels made to be annoying, aggressively catchy. I remember promoters outside a supermarket handing out free samples of the drink to anyone who did the catchphrase "There's the sun!" I just scuttled past.

I don't know this Cassie. She's too produced, too shiny, to fit with my idea of the strong, beautiful artist, who rose to all the challenges the world threw at her with dignity and grace. Trying to know Cassie is like wrestling with smoke; whenever I think I'm getting to know her, the image blurs and she comes back into focus as someone else.

My phone starts buzzing in my hand, it's David. Shit, it's already 7 p.m. Jess and Tim will be arriving at our place any minute. I turn the car on so David can hear the engine in the background and tell him I'm on my way. As I wait for the machine to read my staff card and open the barrier so I can leave the lot, an old SUV pulls up opposite on the other side of the road, in front of the entrance barrier. The man, who looks like he's in early old age, has parked too far away from the side of the barrier and can't reach the parking ticket. He kicks his door open and uses it to pull himself up to stand. He stumbles slightly as he leans forward to pull the ticket out of the machine. The wind blows his white hair as the barrier rises with a jerk and he holds onto the car door again as he lowers himself, with a wince of pain, back behind the wheel. Maybe he's at Kate's to have his hip seen to.

The car behind me honks for me to move on. I shake myself to wake up, and wave an apology at the car behind as I drive away.

Heat singes my face as I heave the lasagna David made out of the oven. It bubbles and pops so I leave it on the side to cool a little and turn to Jess, who sits at our kitchen table, cluttered with David's architecture magazines, candles and paperwork. She's cleared a little space to chop tomatoes for our salad. She's wearing a threadbare apron printed with little wild flowers that I've had since I was a child over her light gray fitted work dress. She's left her heels by the back door in favor of my slippers and her red lipstick is starting to fade to a diluted beetroot but her dark-chocolate bob is still sleek. There's still a hint of the Sony executive she's worked so hard to become.

"Should I slice the olives in halves or not bother?" she asks, taking a sip of red wine.

I sit opposite her. "Don't bother," I say, before handing her a cucumber.

She'd been telling me a story about a new boy band I hadn't heard of who have just been caught in the press with fifty-pound notes rolled up their nostrils, hoovering up cocaine.

"Anyway, looks like we're going to have to drop them. I feel a bit sorry for them really. It's all over before it even began. Too much too young. I mean, imagine if we'd had a million quid when we were twenty?"

I picture us when we met at Bristol University, me in my fake Doc Martens, dark eyeliner round my eyes, rarely smiling to hide the gap in my teeth, trying to pretend I wasn't giddy with freedom, and Jess next to me in the tie-dye outfits she'd picked up in Thailand, a joint permanently at her lips. She hated her hall so she moved into my room. We slept top to tail in my single bed for months. Back then, we'd try and picture what we would be like when we were married women with careers, families and now, almost twenty years on, we try and remember what we were like then.

Neither of us says anything for a moment. Jess carries on chopping and I take oil and vinegar out of the cupboard to make a salad dressing. Jess finishes chopping the cucumber and sits back with her wine cupped in her hands, her long legs crossed.

"So how're things at Kate's? How's Frank?"

"He's just the same. I get so nervous the doctor I was telling you about will get the PVS diagnosis he's after and that'll be it for Frank. Then it'll never be about rehabilitation for him, just management. He's only just turned fifty for God's sake, so young to have had such a massive stroke, and although it's unrealistic to expect a full recovery, I don't think it's crazy to think he could get some quality of life back. Otherwise he could have another thirty years just staring at the ceiling."

"Jesus." Jess picks up the bottle of red and waves it at me; I shake my head and pour myself another fizzy water.

"We've got a minor celebrity on the ward at the moment actually." It feels good to have a story Jess will appreciate for once.

"Oh yeah?" Jess doesn't look up as she pours herself another glass of wine.

I feel hot with guilt suddenly. Cassie isn't a "good story"; she's a patient. I'd be livid if I heard someone else talking about Cassie like that. I remind myself that Mary tells Pat everything, and besides, Jess is, most of the time, an expert keeper of secrets. She has to be in her job.

"It's that woman from the Juice-C commercial."

Jess looks blank for just a second before she says, "Oh god, not 'There's the sun' girl?"

I nod. "Strange, isn't it?" I tell her about the hit and

158

run, about Cassie, Charlotte and Jack. I don't mention the baby; that would be a breach too far.

"What are her mates like?" Jess asks, but her phone buzzes on the table. She expertly starts pecking away at the screen with her forefinger, immediately disinterested. But it's good timing; for once I'm glad her phone's distracted her and I don't have to answer her question.

I wish I knew some of Cassie's friends. I imagine them as bohemian creative types: people who probably lived abroad, maybe Italy for a while; people who practice mindfulness and have visited every theater in London. I'd like to meet some of them; they'd reassure me that Cassie is more like them, not like the Disney-style character from the ad.

Jess keeps tapping away at her phone before she turns the screen towards me. She's already found out Cassie's full name from the ad credits and found Cassie's account on Facebook. The photo is the one from Christmas, the close-up of Cassie in black and white decorating the tree. I feel another shameful twist of jealousy. Without doing anything, and despite everything, Cassie seems to have a knack of making me envious. To neutralize the feeling I say, "Beautiful, isn't she?"

Jess turns the camera back towards herself. She wrinkles her nose as she looks at the picture. "Yeah, but she doesn't look particularly happy if you ask me. I practically work in the business of fake smiles and that—" she jabs her finger at her phone, and I wish she wouldn't; it seems unkind, disrespectful somehow "—that is a fake smile."

I don't look at Jess. Instead I turn away and start shaking the salad bottle hard. I hear Jonny's voice, close, as if he was here in my kitchen, whispering in my ear. "She was scared."

Jess, thank God, drops her phone back on the table. She's finished for now.

"So what else is going on?" she asks.

I stop shaking the dressing. I want to tell someone. I want to tell Jess and, after all, I've been good not telling Jess about Cassie's baby, but I can tell her about my own; that's my choice. I put the dressing down on the table and bend my knees so I'm level with Jess. She looks slightly startled as I take her hand.

"I've got some news actually."

She knows immediately, but even Jess isn't quick enough to hide the frown, the concern that flashes across her face. We stand as she pulls me into a hug that lasts a bit too long.

"Oh, Ali!" she says, over my shoulder. "That's great!"

But I feel like I'm being consoled, not congratulated. I regret telling her immediately; the news curdles in my throat like a bad joke. Jess knows everything, of course, about all of my miscarriages. I feel I need to prove to her that I'm calm about it, that I know I'm still a long way from being a mother.

"I'm only about three weeks though. You're the first to know."

"Are you going to tell David?" she asks. Her phone buzzes again but she ignores it this time, keeps holding my hands, trying to gauge if I am genuinely OK.

I feel my face flush and think of Cassie not telling Jack. I think how brave, how loving she was to protect him. I want to do the same for David; he doesn't need to go through it all again. I shake my head at Jess. "No, not yet. In a few weeks probably." I shrug, and meet her gaze. "I'm

OK though, and I promise I'll let you know if anything changes."

We both turn towards the door; we can hear David and Tim laughing, about to come into the kitchen. Jess kisses me quickly on the cheek and I turn away from the kitchen door, busying myself finding the right tools to serve the lasagna, while I compose my face.

David and Tim burst into the kitchen. They're too full of their own conversation to notice my delicate news hanging in the air. David opens another bottle of wine and the men talk over each other as they explain a breakthrough they've just had with the building design. I serve up the lasagna with David, and, as we all sit down, I'm breathing steadier again because I know, despite all the fear, there's still a chance we might have a child, and I feel in my chest that old, familiar bud of hope beginning to bloom.

11

Frank

I remember the glass of water. In an emergency, there's always some poor sap who fetches a glass of water, isn't there? In my case, no one knew his name. He was just out for a quiet Tuesday pint, one of those lonely drinkers; most pubs have one. I was one of them for a while. He probably felt like he needed to do something, wanted to help. So he went behind the bar and poured a pint of water from the tap—no ice, no lemon—and plonked it down in front of my nose where I rested, surrounded by broken glass on the cool, slightly sticky stone floor. Some of the water slip-sloshed over the edge.

Could've got me a pint, mate.

I looked through the glass. The pub was softer this way. It had a magical, dream-like quality. Even Ange who was cradling my head in her lap and screaming louder than ever on the phone.

"How the hell do I know if it's a stroke?!" her fingers pressed hard into my neck—had a celestial quality to her. I wanted to ask if I gave up booze, seriously this time, would she take me back? That I need her help. Things are worse, way worse, without her . . . without Luce. But my voice came out in strange little barks like an annoying yapping dog. I didn't want to piss her off anymore so I gave up trying.

It started about an hour before Ange and I met in the Green Man. At first, I thought the pain was heartache because we were meeting to sign the divorce papers. I hadn't gone to detox like I promised I would and I'd failed Ange's ultimatum "booze or us" for a third and final time. Every time I told her I chose "us" I'd feel the creature limber up, protract its claws to test their sharpness, and lick its incisors. Honestly, I didn't stand a chance. Before I even got to the Green Man the pain was electric, gripping and releasing, gripping and releasing just behind my eyeballs, deep in my head, like I was clenching a block of ice between my teeth.

My second thought was that this pain was just a new flavor of hangover. So I decided to go to the Green Man early. I had plenty of time to down a few pints before she told me I failed, our marriage coffin arrived and we lowered the last twenty-three years into the ground.

A small group of teenagers, younger than Lucy, clutching sparklers, on their way to a bonfire party, smirked and giggled as they walked past me on the street. I knew how I must look to them—a scruffy, droopy-eyed man walking in rigid zombie steps towards the pub—but I was too close to care. Small mercies.

I tried to move my right arm to open the pub door, but it had grown distant, as if amputated from the rest of me. So I just threw my body against the door and almost fell into the comfort of the dark, damp-smelling pub.

This is one bastard of a hangover.

As I raised the pint glass to my mouth, I realized my hands had frozen rigid, like dinosaur claws. I had to use both of them to pick up the glass. The liquid streamed over my cheeks as I tipped my head back too far. It made my sweater wet.

Wherever I'd been, there must have been whiskey, and lots of it. I'm only like this when there's whiskey in me.

I finished the first pint, then had another. I felt every one of the billions of cells in my body, as it chimed against its neighbor like fine crystal glass, and I thought that was probably a good sign, the booze doing its job. So I ordered a third pint, skillfully avoiding eye contact with the barman, when Ange arrived. It had been four months since I last saw her. Four months since she'd got the phone call from the police. I'd been gone a week, and had ended up under Waterloo Bridge, apparently trying to find a building site I thought I was managing. I'd been out of work for a year. Without a word she drove me to a cheap hotel in Worthing, a few miles from home. She'd already dumped my clothes inside.

In the Green Man, Ange's blonde hair was longer than I remembered. I wanted to tell her she looked pretty but she curled her lip when she saw me, as if I smelt bad, and she didn't look pretty anymore. My hands, like claws, clung to the lip of the bar like a bat's thumb as I stood to hug her, but I misjudged it. Ange outstretched her arms to try and catch me, but I was too heavy. My pint smashed first, the liquid rebounding off the floor in a gorgeous amber wave. I remember thinking how much it's going to hurt when I land on that glass but then immediately I stopped worrying because I was on the floor already, and the glass must have slid quietly through my skin and into my body but I didn't feel it. Instead, every cell in my body melted with the cells from the stone floor, the boundary between my body and the floor no longer existed and I just wanted to stay, enjoy the feeling of my body evaporating, the creature curled and purring on the floor by my side. Even as Ange shouted down at me, that all-too-familiar look of shame and anger on her face giving away to horror as she started screaming for an ambulance, and despite all the heartache I've caused, all the embarrassment, and anguish, I let it all go, easy as exhaling cigarette smoke.

Pooff!

And it was the most tremendous relief.

That was the last time I remember seeing her. Alice tells me she came in quite regularly in the beginning, but patience never was one of Ange's virtues. For a while I liked to think she found it too hard seeing me like this, but Ange was always a pragmatic, practical type. She's right to move on with her life; she's spent too much time waiting for me to sort mine out.

Happily, Jack disturbs my wallowing. He's playing music from his phone connected to a little speaker for Cassie this morning. "Barber's 'Adagio for Strings,'" he tells her (us). It's only just started when his phone starts ringing through the speaker; he rejects the call. It rings immediately again. He frowns, irritated, and presses some buttons on his phone, presumably to stop it ringing a third time before he starts the music again from the beginning, holding the small speaker onto Cassie's stomach, like they tell you to do in the baby books. It muffles the sound quality but I can still hear. The strings soar. I imagine the tiny baby turning somersaults, wriggling inside Cassie. I'm glad Jack's here with her. It must be a comfort for Cassie that the night visitor won't come if Jack's around.

I've decided it was him, Jonny. He was desperate enough to run onto the ward before, after all. As I watch the baby grow, I keep thinking of his eyes and how panicked they were when he tried to get on the ward that first day, the life behind them like a fighting dog, who will either bite or lick if you put your hand too close.

There's only one reason he'd come to the ward, only one I can think of, and it makes all the hairs on my body rise and my organs clutch just thinking about it: the horror of him raising a pillow, or inserting something into Cassie's drip. He wants to finish the job and I'll be here, forced to watch.

Come on, Frank, get a grip!

It must be the music getting to me. I watch as Jack gazes at his wife. Every now and then, he smiles. I think he's reminiscing. I wish he'd do it aloud; from here, they look like happy memories, and I could use some of them today.

All too soon, Jack sits up straighter, clears his throat, and looking around himself quickly, he picks the speaker off Cassie's belly and kisses her forehead and strokes her cheek before he leaves us alone again.

I'm trying to replay the music, capture those soaring

strings in my head, when Alice draws the curtain back. She's humming; she must have heard the music as well. She turns my face towards her, the gap in her teeth visible. Small smiles keep escaping; they ripple across her face, and for once I wish they wouldn't. I need her to be serious, on guard in case she's here when he comes back.

She looks down at me and out of the corner of my eye I see her smile drop. She moistens my eyes, and the solution runs wet tears down the side of my head towards my temples. It feels wonderful, lately my eyes have been even itchier than usual. I hope I'm not getting an infection.

"Jonny Parker, Cassie and Jack's neighbor, has been charged, Frank."

I know, Alice.

She tells me about a ring that Cassie was wearing, her mum's ring. She tells me about Jack holding Cassie's engagement and wedding rings in his hands. I'm not too sure what she's getting at. Alice has to wear her engagement ring around a chain on her neck to work; there'll be a similarly perfectly innocent explanation why Cassie wasn't wearing hers; maybe the turquoise ring suited her New Year's outfit better. Jack probably brought her wedding rings in because he knew Cassie would want them in hospital with her, a talisman of hope for the future. If Alice knew, if she had any idea that Jonny's been in here at night, she'd change her tune. I think of my vocal cords lying useless as a tiny shipwreck in the back of my throat, how they and they alone could save Cassie, could save her baby.

I've amended my "getting better" fantasy recently. I still walk out of the ward, holding Luce's hand. We still stop at Alice, who hugs me as I thank her with all my being.

The difference is, before Luce and I walk home and leave 9B forever, I tell that policewoman about Jonny, about him creeping in here and take him away there and then. No bail, no getting out this time. Cassie, behind her big pregnant belly, smiles thanks at me. Cassie wakes up soon after me and gives birth to a beautiful baby girl and her, Alice, Jack and the little one come and visit me and Luce in our little house in the countryside.

Alice wipes the saline tears away from my face with some cotton and her cautious smile is back as she turns to look at me, her brown eyes sparkling with joy, and I know what she's going to say before she opens her mouth.

"I've got some more news, Frank. Guess what?"

Tell me, Alice.

"I'm pregnant!"

That's wonderful.

"I'm just a few weeks but I feel good, Frank, I really do. It feels different this time. I really think it's different." Her smile fades only slightly. "I'm keeping it quiet though, for now. Just you and my friend Jess know."

Promise I won't go blabbing.

She smiles at me again, before she presses her bottom lip against her teeth a couple of times.

What about a doctor, Alice. Shouldn't you tell a doctor?

But she's up out of my visitor's chair. She notes the readings from my machines before I hear another nurse calling her name.

She comes back to me just a few minutes later, the bounce back in her voice as she says, "You have a visitor, Frank."

I don't let myself think it could be her until I hear the

168

sweetest word, sweeter than any music ever composed: "Dad?"

Luce?

"If you sit in this chair here," Alice tells her, "and lean in, he'll be able to see you better."

Luce!

I hear some scuffle and shuffle as Lucy follows Alice's direction and then I see her. I see her. Her hair is darker, chestnut-colored, thick, and bobbed. She blows her hair off her forehead, just like she did when she was little and feeling nervous. Her skin is still milk-white and flawless. She's had her nose pierced, a silver ring in her left nostril. She fiddles with it; there's a red mark where it plunges into her, which looks painful, and I wince, despite myself.

"Well, Dad," Lucy says, smiling nervously. "I promised no tattoos but you never said anything about getting my nose pierced." She splutters a little laugh as a tear rolls down her face and drops on to the back of my hand. It feels glorious, a cherished, sad little kiss. She wipes another away with a quick hand.

Don't be sad, my love, don't be sad. I'm not! I'm so happy you're here.

"I'll be just at the end of the ward if you need me," Alice says to Lucy.

Lucy moves her eyes from me to Alice, and nods. She puts her hand over mine, where her tear just fell. Her hand's warm, healing, and she starts crying in earnest.

"Sorry, Dad. Sorry. I promised myself I wouldn't do this," she says, pointing at her tear-stained face.

You never need to be sorry with me, my love. You know that.

I can see from her face she's trying to remember Alice's advice, trying to remember how to talk naturally to me. She looks down briefly, playing with the tissue in her lap. She frowns. I see the little scar in the middle of her forehead where she fell and hit her head when she was a toddler. She looks up, visibly brightening a little. She's thought of something.

"I got a kitten, Dad! She's a rescue. The landlord doesn't know, of course, but he's never around and I've wanted one since I was what, like six? All my flatmates love her. I'll show you a photo." She carries on talking as she rummages in a bag I can't see.

"She's the sweetest little thing. I'm mad about her. It reminds me of that time we looked after our old neighbor's cats? You remember that one that crapped in the bath? Mum went crazy. Anyway, here she is. Her name's Betty." Lucy holds a phone screen in front of my eyes. She's wearing chipped, pink nail varnish. She's still biting her nails. The screen's too shiny, I can't see the photo. All I see is a skeletal face, reflected perfectly back at me, bones barely covered by translucent skin, like a saggy-skinned chicken before it's cooked. My eyes are sunken in their sockets, as if someone's taken the soft tissue out with an ice cream baller. I can't see any hair at all, and a blue tube, like a sick joke tie, pokes out from the lower edge of the image. My eyes are the eyes of a dead fish, filmy and vacant.

Take it away, Lucy, please move it.

But she doesn't. I'm forced to look at myself, an appalled narcissus as she chatters away about Betty.

"She's pretty good but she does shred *everything*." At last she takes the phone away.

Don't do that again, please, sweetheart.

"Anyway," she says, chewing her mouth, again trying to find something to say. "Uni's pretty good. I've met loads of brilliant people, Dad, and I love living in London. I'm going to have to get a job, maybe bar work or something. It's just so expensive . . ." She trails off and lightly places her hand back on top of mine, the best medicine.

"That's why I haven't been to see you for a couple of weeks. I'm sorry. It sounds so selfish, but I've just been so caught up in my own stuff. I decided to stay in London over Christmas. Mum wanted me home in Brighton, of course, but I just wanted to do my own thing . . ."

Lucy looks at me, frowning slightly. She chews one of her fingernails. My heart seizes. Something's on her mind; I can tell.

What is it, my love?

"Mum was going to come with me to see you today, Dad, but she bottled it at the last minute, said something came up with Gran and she had to go and help her." Lucy rolls her eyes at her mum's transparent excuse. We both know Ange's mum prides herself on never asking for help, and even if she did, we know she wouldn't ask her daughter.

"I thought she should tell you herself, but—" Lucy rubs her face with her hands, and shakes her head a couple of times "—Mum's got a new boyfriend, Dad. Craig. He works in insurance, and he's pretty much the most boring man I've ever met."

Ange has a boyfriend, a boyfriend called Craig. Strange, the simple sentence doesn't appal me, doesn't even surprise me that much. I imagine insurance man Craig, a lumpy face, the color of porridge, pulling his double chin away from the collar of a cheap polyester suit and I hope he'll succeed where I failed again and again. I wonder if he'll be able to make Ange happy, lift a life full of disappointment. I wonder if he can make Ange's mouth so often pursed as a tight knot finally loosen into a long-lost smile. I hope so. I'd like to think she could be happy; it would be good for Lucy to see her mum happy.

Lucy leans over me to look at the photo of us, me dressed as Santa, her on my knee, she laughs a small, wet laugh.

"We had fun, didn't we, Dad? You and me?"

Remember our fishing trip to Wales?

"Remember when we went to Wales? I caught, like, ten fish and you caught one tiny little thing." She laughs again before she looks down at me and her smile disappears. When I was with Lucy, the creature seemed to nap. I didn't want to drink when I was with her; didn't want to miss a thing.

She puts the photo back on my bedside unit and comes to sit back in the visitor's chair. Silence settles around us and I feel her struggle for something to say. Luce and I used to laugh at things no one else saw or understood: a jogger's funny run; a dog kicking clumps of grass in the air with their back legs after going to the toilet. Ange used to tell us to shut up. We used to be good in silence as well, Luce and I, but before the silence was chosen, not forced upon us like now. She fiddles with the ring in her nose, looks at her hands. I wish she wouldn't search for something to say; it makes me feel like we're not us anymore.

"I've started talking to someone, Dad," she says, not

172

lifting her eyes from her hands. "A uni counsellor. It's free so I thought I may as well." She shrugs and looks up at me, new tears falling fast as rain down her face. Her voice is a tiny, frightened little thing when she starts, but it gets stronger, practiced, as she keeps talking.

"I want you to know I forgive you. I forgive you for drinking, I forgive you for disappearing and I forgive you for lying to us. I know now that it's a disease, just like cancer or whatever. You couldn't help it. It's not your fault. That's why I forgive you."

She leans forward, and squeezes my hand. Her tears dampen my bed and I would die a happy man if the world would just let me stroke her hair once, or tell her I love her. But, of course, I'm asking too much. Her forgiveness chimes through my veins like a sugar rush neutralizing, for a while at least, the bitterness of my shame.

I love you, I'm so proud of you.

I say it again and again, my whole body pulsing with the charge, and I hope she senses the flavor of my feeling at least, which I think she does because she splutters a little laugh and smiles down at me.

We sit in silence together for a few minutes, Lucy cries some more before she kisses my cheek, sending the loveliest wave rippling through my blood.

"I'll come again soon, Dad. Love you."

No more piercings! That's an order!

She gives me a final little smile and then she disappears.

The space around my bed seems to ache with her absence and I am alone again.

12

Cassie

Cassie sips her coffee and stands back in the shed to look at the canvas, which glistens, wet with paint, before her. The coffee tastes processed, too meddled with. She's not used to decaf. She winces and puts it on the windowsill, careful to avoid the bumblebee that has been bashing itself uselessly against the window pane all afternoon. Every time she tries to rescue it, the stupid thing flies away.

She turns back to the canvas.

Inspiration struck for the painting while she was swimming in the sea with Jonny at Birling Gap. It was one of those freakishly hot June days and they'd been at a sweaty indoor market all day. Jonny had been nervous, and shouted at Cassie when she'd swam underwater. He'd said there were invisible rip currents, but she'd been hypnotized by how the sunlight, as seen from underwater, silvered the undulating surface of the water, weird and mercurial. She'd wanted to harness that mottled, refracted light on her canvas, and hoped it would fill the viewers' ears with the endless silence of the ocean. She'd wanted them to feel peaceful, held, safe.

Before she started painting, she imagined taking a photo of her work so Jonny would finally understand her vision, but now that feels needy, too desperate for praise, and besides she hasn't got it at all. The canvas is flat, one-dimensional; it looks like an A-level attempt. Complete shit.

Suddenly the shed feels stuffy, claustrophobic. She pulls off the old shirt she uses for painting. It slides to the floor but she can't be arsed to pick it up. She leaves the disgusting coffee on the windowsill. The shed door bangs shut behind her, and after a brief armistice, the bee recommences its assault, bashing itself against the pane again and again and again.

Outside, Cassie drops down onto the lawn between the shed and the cottage. Her bare toes rake against the grass, decorated with daisies and other wild summer flowers Cassie can't name. White clouds scud across the blue sky like cartoon drawings, and a beetle like a rusty, tiny bomber, rattles unseen nearby. Cassie always thought it was especially cruel that April died in the summer, a perfect sunny afternoon, two years ago to the day. April loved the summer. Cassie leans back, and opens herself to the sky. She closes her eyes and tries not to think too much. She feels weightless, as though she could lie there for ever.

She dozes but after a few minutes her phone rattles, fracturing the silence. She pulls it out of her pocket, hoping it's not Marcus calling again. She's already ignored one call from him today, lying to herself that she'd call him back later; ignoring a second call would feel too cruel. But it's not Marcus; it's Nicky. Her friend's name, as familiar to Cassie as her own, flashes on the screen, desperate for attention. She hovers her thumb over the "Accept" button, but she pauses and suddenly it's too late, it's gone to voicemail.

Cassie tells herself she'll call Nicky back later.

She lies back and closes her eyes again, trying to find her peace, but she can't. Her phone buzzes again, with Nicky's voicemail this time. Cassie peaks a hand over her brow against the sun as she presses to listen to the recording on her phone speaker. Traffic and the painful hammering of roadwork explode out of her phone, the noise dystopian and alien in the soporific summer slumber of the little garden. A longing twists like a knife in Cassie. London, the smell of molten asphalt, the distracted buzz of people, people everywhere.

"God, sorry, Cas. Hope you can hear me." Nicky's voice breaks just over the scream from traffic and roadwork. Cassie can hear her rushing, trying to get past the noise. "I'm at Victoria. Jesus, it's always a nightmare around here. I'm just calling to say I'm thinking of you and April so much today. I can't believe it's been two years already. It's nuts. Anyway, I really hope you're OK. It must be beautiful down there. You're so lucky; London's filthy. Maybe call me later if you can, OK? Let's sort out a date for me to come down again, yeah? Lots of love."

Cassie's arm drops heavy on top of her grassy bed. What's wrong with her? She thought she'd be OK today; after all, it's just another day, isn't it? Cassie remembers

Jack's line that "grief is a kind of art form." She rests her head back and thinks maybe there's some truth in it. Maybe now is a good day to try and give in to it. She's got April's diary from Mexico, when she became pregnant with Cassie. It's upstairs in a drawer. She considers reading it stretched out on the grass. That'd probably do the trick—release some of the tears she can feel building in her throat like a storm.

She's about to get up when her phone buzzes again. This time it's a text message from Charlotte.

Thinking of you and April today, Cas. Let me know if you need anything. All my love, C x

Charlotte and Cassie haven't talked about Mike's affairs again since their chat at the food festival, the spring grass under their feet, the oily tang from the cars and trucks parked all around them. Cassie wants to know more. How did Charlotte hide it from Jack all these years? How has she let him go on believing his dad was some kind of hero and not the slippery cheat he really was? Doesn't she want revenge? She has a new admiration for Charlotte, a new, dizzying perspective on the love she has for Jack, always putting his feelings before her own, even though at times her heart must have crackled and spat with anger in her chest. Cassie strokes her stomach. She hopes she's capable of the same love for her child, and promises the little life that, whatever happens, she'll try her best to be a mother like Charlotte.

Without warning, she hears the crispy crunch of wheels on the little gravel drive at the front of the cottage. She lifts herself up onto her elbows; her heart lifts. Jack. He's come home early as a surprise so she won't be alone! Her knees click as they bend for her to stand and, feeling better already, she runs on her tiptoes on the lawn and around the corner of the house, where she thinks she'll bound headlong into Jack's arms. She runs sharply around the corner and then has to skip herself to a stop. She knows the old Volvo parked in front of the cottage, but like a face she hasn't seen in years, it takes a moment for her to place it. The driver's door opens and a pair of long legs in corduroy trousers and round-toed brown leather shoes that look at least two decades old land on the gravel. Marcus uses the door to pull himself to his full height. She sees him wince as his bad hip takes on his weight. He opens his arms to her and she walks gingerly over the gravel towards him, trying to smile at Marcus through her surprise.

"Marcus, what are you doing here?"

She plants a carefully placed kiss on each of his cheeks, his face as wrinkled as his plaid shirt, far too hot for this weather. He smells stale, mothballs and wood smoke. The smell makes Cassie feel twelve again, disappointed he doesn't smell like the dad she always dreamed of, aftershave and expensive leather.

"What are you doing here, Marcus?" she asks again, feeling the gravel dig into her feet.

Marcus's eyes widen as he says, "Cassie!" as though she's the one surprising him.

"Marcus, I did not expect to see you!" she asks again, smiling so he doesn't feel foolish.

He frowns again, glances up at the cottage and says, "I

thought it would be nice to see you for a cup of tea. It's not that far really."

"You mean you were in the area?" Cassie asks.

Marcus shrugs. Cassie knows he wasn't. He drove two hours all the way from the Isle of Wight, "on the off-chance" she'd be in.

Marcus squints again at the friendly face of their redbrick cottage.

"Lovely place, Cas," he says. He's gained more wrinkles, his face a map of wiggly lines, the ones around his eyes most deeply riven. April always loved his white hair long but even she would bundle him off to the hairdresser's if she saw him now. It's crimped and wild, but flat at the back from where his head rested for the long drive. He's grown more fragile in the seven months since the wedding, as though the scales of his life have been weighted by his years and have at last tipped him into old age.

Cassie takes his arm. "Come on, I'll make us some tea," and she leads him, both of them hobbling slightly over the gravel, towards the cottage.

They sit on the old wooden table and chairs, greened with outside living. The table wobbles as Cassie balances a teapot, cups and saucers on top—the cups and saucers a wedding gift from one of Charlotte's friends, until now unused.

"So, you're painting again, Cas?" Marcus looks at Cassie's hands. She rubs her thumb over a streak of blue paint.

"Yeah, just for fun," she says, shy suddenly. "I've got a little shed over there where I work. I've got some of Mum's canvases in there actually, I'll show you in a bit."

"I'd like that. So you're still acting, are you?"

"Marcus, that was four years ago." He used to know exactly what was happening in her life. She's about to gently tease him for forgetting, but his brow knits, he's confused, he can't make sense of his thoughts. It must be the anniversary getting to him. She tries to lighten his mood. "You're just like Mum, Marcus; one stupid ad does not an actor make." She ennunciates her words, mimicking a Shakespearean actor, before she adds in her normal voice, "I think Mum genuinely expected the Academy Awards to call up with a nomination."

Marcus chuckles, and gently shakes his head as if at the memory, but he's a little too slow, his small laugh stiff. Cassie knows she's lost him.

"She was very proud of you, always believed in you," he says.

"I know, but seriously, ask Jack, I'm no actress. Painting's my thing. Just like Mum, remember?"

Marcus swats a wasp away from the table and leans back in his chair as he says, "Oh, I know what I wanted to tell you. I found the 'Fruit and Face' series recently. God, it made me laugh to see them again."

Cassie smiles, relieved to hear some of the old, sharper Marcus back in his voice. The paintings from the "Fruit and Face" series all came in pairs, one an image of a piece of fruit and the other the face of a person who resembled the fruit. One was of a fat man with a round, gouty face and dimpled chin next to a single, plump, red cherry; another of a woman with an oblong face and a high pony-tail like fronds over her head next to a pineapple. April said she could get away with painting rude portraits, said it was one of the very few advantages of having cancer.

Cassie remembers April giggling behind her canvas as she painted.

Cassie stands to pour the tea.

"So you canceled this weekend then?" she asks, trying to keep a lightness in her voice.

Marcus scrunches his eyes, as though he's rifling through a Rolodex of options about what Cassie could be talking about, so she adds, "Mum's anniversary, Marcus?"

Cassie keeps her eyes fixed on the cup as she pours milk, trying to hide a small flash of embarrassment for Marcus.

"Oh, yes, that. No, well, we can always do it next year, can't we?" he says, but it's as though the fractious pieces of his understanding still haven't quite meshed together.

Some of Marcus's tea sloshes over the edge of the cup as she puts it in front of him. She sits back in her chair, cupping both hands around her own tea, lifting her bare feet to the lip of her chair, so her knees press near her chin.

Marcus leans forward, puckers his lips for a sip and winces; it's too hot for him.

"So why did you cancel?" Cassie persists, sure eventually he'll click.

Marcus shrugs. "Too much going on, I suppose, Cas. Just too busy."

Cassie frowns, but he doesn't see. What is he talking about? He's too busy with what? Reading the papers? Doing his weekly food shopping? If anything, his life isn't busy enough. Maybe that's what's up, maybe he's just bored?

"Marcus, is everything—" but he interrupts her before she can ask him if he's all right. His face lights up and he turns to her, sparky suddenly, as though he just had a wonderful realization.

"I spoke to Lindsay recently, Cas," he says, jumping in. "We talked about that murder-mystery weekend your mum organized, remember?" Marcus tells Cassie the familiar story of the muddled weekend where April got all the characters and costumes confused so Marcus ended up playing a murderous vicar dressed as a racing jockey. He tells the story as though Cassie wasn't even there. His clumsy reminiscing, especially about April, makes her feel itchy. The table jolts to the right as she leans her elbow on the surface and rakes her fingers through her shoulder-length hair.

There used to be a time when she'd talk, really talk, to Marcus. She remembers once she told Marcus how abandoned she felt, essentially an orphan with no dad and now no mum, no living genetic relative that she knows about anyway. He didn't say anything, just hugged her, which was, she realized later—with a lick of guilt that she hadn't mentioned the fact she has him in her life—the perfect response. She felt her loneliness was complete, a bespoke pain, designed especially for Cassie. But that will change; she won't be on her own forever. She thinks of the small life, the size of an acorn, inside her. Jack picked her up when she told him, twirled her around the kitchen. He'd already started talking about names.

Marcus has finished with the costume story; he's looking at Cassie, frowning again and says apropos of nothing, "You know I'm always here for you, don't you, Cas?" The table lurches again as he cups his hand around the back of Cassie's. "I want you to know you never have to feel alone."

Even though she doesn't fully believe the words, she can hear the love in his voice, the care, and she smiles at him because suddenly she does feel a little safer. Maybe she could tell him about the baby? Maybe that would help with his strange grief?

But she doesn't have time because suddenly they both turn towards an unexpected voice across the garden.

"I thought I heard voices."

Jack walks around the side of the house holding a bunch of sunflowers, April's, and therefore Cassie's, favorite flower. He's undone his tie and taken off his jacket, but his suit trousers and light blue shirt are still incongruous, out of place in the garden. Beneath his light tan, he looks tired; one of the two project managers at work has been off sick for two weeks now, and it's doubled Jack's workload. An impenetrable aura of stress surrounds him. As Jack kisses Cassie she smells his busy day, a grabbed sandwich at lunch, too many coffees, Jack rushing from warm conference room to warm conference room.

"I thought I'd come home early to see how you're doing, love, but clearly I've been beaten to it."

Marcus stands, and the table wobbles as he uses it for balance to shake Jack's hand. They smile at each other but the lack of warmth from Jack towards Marcus is like a presence itself.

"Do you want tea, Jack?" Cassie asks, keeping her voice light.

"You know what, I think I'll grab a beer from the fridge," Jack says, giving her a kiss.

She takes the flowers from him. "I'll get you one."

"Thanks, Cas," Jack says as she walks towards the kitchen

and just before she reaches the door she hears Jack asking Marcus, "So what brought on this surprise visit?"

She rolls her lips between her teeth as she walks back across the dappled lawn towards them with the sunflowers in a vase a couple of minutes later, condensation from the cold beer wetting her other hand. Marcus is nodding, a polite, worried smile on his face, as though he's trying not to be rude to an overfamiliar stranger who thinks they're acquainted. Something's not right. Could it be he's just nervous? Marcus and Jack haven't seen each other since the wedding, after all. Jack said they hadn't spoken then, so it's the first time they've spoken since their argument over the magazine.

"I wanted the weekend to celebrate my wife, April, but you know Cassie—" he looks up and smiles as Cassie approaches the table "—this lovely young woman, my stepdaughter, was too busy so I dropped the idea."

"Are we still talking about this weekend?" Cassie says, putting the sunflowers on the table and handing Jack his beer. She rattles around her head for something else to talk about, maybe the "Fruit and Face" portraits or the murder-mystery costumes again?

Her stomach drops as she recognizes Jack's mood. He's not his usual measured self. He's querulous and stressed; always a bad combination.

Jack shakes his head at Marcus. "Oh, come on, Marcus. Don't put the whole weekend on Cas. If she didn't want to go, she didn't want to go. You could have gone ahead with it without her. End of story."

Marcus shrugs and frowns. "She said she was just too busy," he repeats.

"But that's fair enough. You can't put the fact you canceled on Cassie. You wanted to have the weekend and you chose to cancel, not Cas. Is that why you've turned up here like this? To try and prove she isn't busy?"

Marcus's frown deepens. He shakes his head. "What are you talking about?"

"Jack . . ." Cassie still standing, puts a quietening hand on his shoulder. He doesn't know how strange Marcus has been acting and she can't tell him now, in front of Marcus. But Jack can't feel her trying to calm him. Her hand falls away as Jack leans forward in his chair towards Marcus.

"No, I'm sorry. It's not fair, Marcus."

Marcus lifts his hand to his forehead and massages his temple with thumb and middle finger. Cassie had forgotten he does that when he's tired or confused by something.

"I just came to see Cassie, my stepdaughter, not you." Marcus's voice is quieter than Jack's but Cassie can hear how much effort he's putting into not shouting.

"She told you she was busy today, Marcus. Jesus, can't you take a hint?"

"Jack, calm down," Cassie says, but she can see the muscle in Jack's jaw bouncing and she knows he won't calm down.

"Cassie," Marcus says, glancing at Jack, "this isn't right. I don't know exactly what, but I know something isn't right here."

"That's enough, Marcus. You don't get to turn up at my home and start saying shit like that to my wife when this is a tough day for her already."

"I think I should go," Marcus says, his thumb and forefinger back to his temples as he stands surprisingly quickly, upsetting the table. Making the teacups clatter against their saucers.

"That's the only sensible thing you've said so far," Jack says.

Marcus keeps his head bowed as he starts to shuffle away.

Cassie stands and calls to him, "Marcus, wait don't go!" but he doesn't turn back; instead he keeps shuffling forward across the grass. Cassie feels a bruise settle over her heart.

She turns to Jack. "What the fuck was all that about?"

"I'm just fed up of him walking all over you. Look at you, you're shaking."

"That's because of you getting involved, not because of Marcus." Her voice is shrill. She doesn't care if Marcus hears them. She hasn't felt this angry for months and it feels fucking wonderful. "Something isn't right with him, Jack."

"Yeah, I know, he's a fucking weirdo."

"No, Jack, for God's sake, I mean I think he's not well. He's never been like this before. I was just going to ask him, suggest he goes to see a doctor, when you come storming in stressed from work and immediately having a go at him."

Jack stands, kicking his chair away with the back of his leg. It topples back on the grass like it's just given up. The muscle in Jack's jaw pops as he says, "I was just trying to defend you, Cas, stand up for you like I always do when you won't stand up for yourself; you never used to be like that."

"Oh, fuck off, Jack." Cassie turns to go after Marcus.

"With pleasure," Jack responds, and swigs from his beer bottle as he stalks into the kitchen.

Cassie and Marcus's abandoned teacups sit on the table, the saucers are full of tea. She never saw the point of saucers before, but now they suddenly make sense to her; many an argument must have started over a cup of tea. She has a powerful urge to smash the cups and fucking saucers against the side of the cottage. The sunflowers lean against their vase, their faces turned away as if shamed by what they've just seen here. Never has she seen such a pretty flower look so sad.

She hears Marcus start his engine and she desperately wants him to stay suddenly, to show him April's paintings like she said she would, to try and find out what's wrong, help if she can.

She runs round to the front of the cottage, calling his name, stumbling again on the gravel but she's too late; he's already signaling out of the small driveway and, as he turns away, an invisible force winds Cassie, like a strong gravitational pull on her lower abdomen, dragging. She clutches her stomach; it twitches and she knows something's changed, and that whatever it is it can't be good, because where she once felt a beginning, now all she can feel is the empty certainty of an ending.

13

Alice

"Please, call me Elizabeth," the obstetrics consultant says, as I open the door for her into the family room. She has a comforting Scottish accent at odds with her well-tailored suit. She reminds me of Jess and I wonder if people often misread her as I know they do Jess. I boil the kettle for tea as we wait for Jack and Charlotte.

"Actually, can I have coffee instead?" Elizabeth asks. "We're in the middle of the terrible twos at home and you know what it's like when you just can't get the little imp to sleep. I'm running on caffeine."

I smile and nod like I understand but I turn away from her so she can't see my face as I try and think of a way to change the conversation that doesn't seem rude, or force me to confess that, in fact, I don't know what it's like, not really. I've learnt most of the time it's easier to go along with peoples' assumptions.

"We're completely wrapped around her finger, of course. I've been told it won't last for long . . ." It sounds as though she's looking for reassurance from me.

I don't make eye contact as I hand Elizabeth her coffee, and thankfully, there's a knock at the door before I can answer her.

Jack's wearing a dark blue navy suit and tie. He's recently shaved; a different man from the one I first met. Charlotte is behind him in jeans and a fitted striped shirt. She holds a black coat over her forearm and has a dusty pink scarf around her neck. They've met Elizabeth before so we keep the introductions and pleasantries brief and Jack tells us he has to go to a client meeting in half an hour. His team has been covering him at work, but this meeting is too important for him to miss. I tell him to leave whenever he needs to; either Charlotte or I can fill him in on anything later.

Jack and Charlotte listen intently to Elizabeth, their heads cocked to the right at the same angle. Charlotte occasionally writes what Elizabeth is saying in a notebook. The gist hasn't changed. Cassie's just the same; the swelling around her brain has only decreased a little. The tube's been removed and Elizabeth has put Cassie on a vigorous physiotherapy schedule. The baby's growing well and we're going to prepare for both a natural birth and a C-section.

"We obviously want the baby to remain in utero for as long as possible," Elizabeth says, "but full term is unlikely. As the baby grows, it will place more stress on Cassie, but we really want to avoid the baby being born before twenty-seven weeks."

Charlotte traces her finger down her notebook, reading

aloud from her notes. Her questions are detailed, hinting at sleepless nights researching. She asks about the effect of anti-coagulants on the fetus, and if Cassie needs pain-killers, how will they affect the baby? If Elizabeth is impressed with the line of questioning, she doesn't show it; she'd never presume to be so patronizing. Jack sits silently next to his mum, like her overdressed assistant, strangely listless. Something's wrong. He scowls when his phone rings, interrupting Charlotte's list of questions. He cancels the call, but doesn't apologize. Probably his work. I've never seen his face so cloudy.

"Oh, yes, one more thing." Charlotte glances at her son for confirmation. "We've decided we've had enough surprises and so would like to know the sex of the baby."

Jack nods and drains his tea. He stands as Elizabeth replies.

"We can tell you for sure when she's sixteen weeks in a couple of weeks' time."

The meeting's over quite abruptly and hands are once again held and gently pumped before Jack kisses Charlotte on the cheek.

"See you later, Mum," he says, and I catch him as he whispers "love you" in her ear before leaving for his meeting. Elizabeth, with a quick smile and bow of her head follows him.

Charlotte sits back as if she's just got home to her sofa after a long day. She snaps her notebook shut, breathes out and closes her eyes briefly. There often comes a moment with relatives when they start talking without filter. Some do it to fill the silence, cover the beeps and ticks from the ward; others do it because they think we'll look after their loved one better if we know more about them. Charlotte is neither of these. I have the sense she talks because she has to, that she needs to unburden herself.

"You know the police have charged Jonny, don't you?" she says, her eyes still closed.

I nod and move my chair a little closer towards her. "The police said they knew each other well. Cassie and Jonny, I mean?"

Charlotte laughs, a tight laugh that suggests I don't know the half of it. She raises a palm to her temple.

"Oh, Cassie liked him, I think. He helped her with the jam business, drove her around, carried boxes, that sort of thing. He lived in a cottage on the farm. He was their closest neighbor. He moved from London just a few weeks after Cassie and Jack. It was good they all got on, but I always suspected it wasn't entirely platonic from Jonny's side. You know he was the one who got her the dog? Maisie?"

Suddenly Charlotte stops talking, she shakes her head, as if trying to shake out the thoughts that have settled there.

"Jack said she was a rescue?" My voice is gentle; I don't want to spook her.

"She is. Jonny helped Cassie get her from the same rescue center just outside Brighton where he got his own dog. It was good of Jack to let Cassie adopt Maisie. Jack's allergic, you see."

Charlotte picks up her tea; it must be cold now. She takes a small sip. I can tell she's finished talking about Jonny and Cassie. Her amber eyes flicker, like she's rifling through her thoughts, desperate to find one that has nothing to do with either of them. My arms are resting in my lap, my hands facing towards my lower belly; I don't realize until Charlotte's eyes cast down to where they rest. I pull them away and am about to offer to make her a new cup of tea when she asks, "Are you not feeling well, Alice?"

She asks with the quiet motherly confidence of someone comfortable showing people they don't know well that they care.

I look away from her, know if I look into her amber eyes, I won't be able to brush her off. I don't realize I'm smiling until it's too late.

"I hope you don't mind me asking, Alice, but have you got some news?"

I let my smile take over my face, as I turn to look at her.

"Oh, Alice, I thought you might be. You blinked every time Elizabeth mentioned Cassie's baby and your hands keep going here like a reflex." She lifts her hands to her tummy. She leans forward towards me in her chair and pats my knee. I hold her hand briefly in both of mine.

"What wonderful news," she says; her smile softens me and I feel the full weight of my joy again. "Is it your first?"

I nod, and as I do, a tear I didn't know was there falls from my eye and lands with a tiny splash on the knee of my polyester uniform.

Charlotte fishes a tissue out of her sleeve and hands it to me. "Congratulations, Alice." She stands, and my lower back immediately warms as she places her hand there.

"Oh, Charlotte, sorry, sorry." I wipe my eyes with the tissue. "It's just because I'm still only four weeks so I haven't told anyone yet, not even my mum or my husband.

It's just lovely to be able to tell someone." It's not true, of course; Jess knows and so does Frank, but Jess made me feel guilty, as though I'd willingly made myself ill, and Frank, well, Frank can't say anything at all. Telling someone new—someone who isn't worried for me, who isn't afraid to call my pregnancy "wonderful news" and mean it—feels amazing.

"I think Cassie must be a good omen," I say, holding Charlotte's tissue in my hand.

"Perhaps you're good omens for each other," Charlotte says with a smile and she pats my hand before she sits down opposite me again.

"Alice, I hope you don't mind me asking, but why haven't you told your husband?"

I start shredding the tissue between my fingers. The moment's past; the warmth cools. It's time for me to tell her the truth—this wise, kind woman, who seems to see the world in a way the rest of us miss.

"I haven't told David, my husband, yet, because I, we've, had a few miscarriages. Well, more than a few actually." I look up at her briefly; she's looking straight into me. "Eight in total." I'm surprised how easy it is to say those words, those three little words, too neatly summarizing the eight times hope ended in horror.

If Charlotte is shocked by the number, she doesn't show it. She just nods her head evenly.

"I'm sorry to hear that, Alice."

I nod. "We've had all the tests, of course; it's a chromosomal abnormality. There's nothing they can do. I'm thirty-eight. I had the last miscarriage last summer. I promised my husband we'd start thinking about alternative ways we could be parents. He thinks we've both had enough of trying to have our own. He was right, of course, and then just five days ago, I found out I was pregnant again."

Charlotte doesn't move her eyes off my face. "It reminds me of that saying, you know: you get what you want when you stop trying."

She looks away from me for a moment. I can tell she's thinking about Cassie, about her decision not to tell Jack about their baby.

She nods. "I can understand why you've decided not to tell your husband yet. How are you feeling?"

Suddenly my precious news seems to hang around us, too fragile in the stuffy air of this bland, windowless room. I can't protect it anymore; I feel the need to move, shift the space, lift the weight of what I just told her.

I stand suddenly. I feel Charlotte's eyes on my back as I start busily gathering up the mugs from the meeting, putting them in the sink too hard. They chime against each other cheerlessly.

The thrill of telling Charlotte has passed. I'll try and think of it as auspicious later but now I don't want to talk about my pregnancy anymore, not here where I'm more used to people dying than being born. Not yet, when David still doesn't know. I turn the tap on hard, the stream of water rattles against the stainless steel sink.

"I'm just keeping myself balanced and cautiously positive. We'll see. Anyway . . ." I remember one of my gynecologists littered his sentences with phrases like "cautiously optimistic" as I lay like a trussed turkey, my legs in stirrups on his table. My "anyway" hangs in the air. I turn the tap off and start washing up our mugs.

Charlotte senses the change in me. She stands as well and glances at her watch. "Oh goodness, it's almost eleven. I'll just go and see Cas and then I'm meeting a friend to take Maisie for a walk." Charlotte gathers up her coat and bag.

"You're still looking after her?" I ask, glad of the shift in conversation.

"Maisie, yes, she's with me at the moment. Jack's got enough to do and, to be honest, I think he finds it too hard to see her. She reminds him of Jonny, of everything that's happened . . ."

Charlotte shifts her bag up to her shoulder. She comes towards me, squeezes my forearm in brief recognition of the moment we just shared, and she says she'll see me tomorrow, before she leaves.

As the door clicks shut behind her I pull my dripping hands out of the sink, appalled with myself for not asking Charlotte to keep the news of my pregnancy to herself. I think about going after her, but then I remember her steady, calm eyes on me, the warmth of her hand on my back and I don't think I need to worry. She won't tell anyone.

There's a pile of paperwork waiting for me at reception. I should start leafing through it, but first I decide to go and see Cassie.

I'm careful to draw the curtain around us as I sit in her visitor's chair. Two weeks in this suspended place and her face is a colorless mask, her lips are slightly parted as if she fell asleep in the middle of an unfinished sentence. I've washed her hair three times now, but just a couple of days after the last wash, it already looks wilted. The cuts have healed on her arms, but her skin, now a light concrete color, is dry and scaly. I'll moisturize it later. Her hands are tight fists. I've curled her fingers around hand supports; even though I cut her fingernails the other day, there's still a risk she could hurt herself. She has extra inflatable supports under her arms and legs to ease pressure points and avoid thrombosis; her bed has become a mini bouncy castle. The baby, now fourteen weeks old, is just visible under the sheets, a sweet molehill.

I move close towards Cassie's head and look at the colorful display, like a dream of her former life, suspended just above her head. Either Charlotte or Jack have printed off the black-and-white photo of Cassie decorating the Christmas tree I saw on Facebook. It's stuck at the bottom of her display, resting just above Cassie's head like a halo. Cassie looks younger in the photo, her smile wide but slightly held.

I look at them both, Cassie in a hospital bed and Cassie in the photo. She looks like two different people. I think of Jonny's face when he came onto the ward. He had the nauseated, helpless look of someone who knows someone they love is in trouble. I look at the small hump of Cassie's tummy again and think about all the whispering on the ward. Perhaps Cassie wasn't protecting Jack from the possibility of another miscarriage; maybe she was hiding something else from him.

I hear him again; "She was scared."

The memory of Jack howling when he found out she was pregnant echoes round my head. I stand back, away from her suddenly, stung by the realization that I've been pulled into the lies myself. I feel vertiginous, unsure of the world suddenly, because the Cassie I thought I knew has disappeared, and the woman before me, this sleeping woman whose fate seems somehow inextricably aligned with my own, is a stranger to me and I know that to feel safe, for our babies to be safe, I have to know her. I have to find out who she really is.

14

Frank

It's official! Lizzie has a new boyfriend! She told me as she gave me a bed bath this morning, her voice sliding high and low like a xylophone with joy. My eyes have been getting itchier over the last couple of weeks. I lie here like a plate of spoiling meat, willing Lizzie to pause, to notice my sore eyes, and perhaps get something cool to soothe them, but she didn't look at me for long enough. She was too busy telling me about her new boyfriend, about Alex. It happened in the late January Ikea sales. Apparently, Lizzie likes to take prospective boyfriends to Ikea as a stress test. She told me about him as she soaped my starved skin. I'd listen to her all day, listen to whatever she wants to say, so long as she keeps wiping my skin with exquisite warm water.

Once I'm dry and tucked back up, I'm busy congratulating Lizzie (and Alex for passing the Ikea test) and thanking her for not cringing during my bath when, without warning, my vision goes black for a second. My burning eyes sing in relief, and then, as if nothing happened, Lizzie reappears, blurry but undeniably Lizzie, with the folder still open before her.

She looks up and smiles at me. "Hi, Mr. Ashcroft," she says before she turns her head back to her folder.

What the fuck just happened?

My eyes start to burn again; I imagine tiny flames inside my pupil and then, without any force—my ten-ton eyelids suddenly light as air—my vision goes black again as my lids slide down to meet each other.

Lizzie doesn't even look up.

Lizzie, I blinked! I think I fucking blinked!

I can feel the flames in my eyes starting to lick again, and I think it's my moment as Lizzie replaces my folder. I try and make myself ready, remember the rush of relief, the black, but, as Lizzie comes towards me with some damp cotton, my eyelids freeze.

Come on, Frank, do it now!

But it's no good. I've fucked it up. I've lost the sweet subtle point between trying and not trying and it's as if my eyelids are glued open again. She dabs my eyes with damp cotton as normal. For once I wish she'd shut up and just concentrate on me as she says in a voice gently taut with excitement, "Well, Mr. Ashcroft, there's some more wonderful news today. Alice said I could let you know that it's a girl, Mr. Ashcroft! Isn't that wonderful? Cassie and Jack's baby is a little girl!"

I try not to care. This was supposed to be my moment, but I can't help it; a vision of Lucy naked and newly born comes to me and then without warning my eyelids slide down, slow, amphibian. I have a moment of thick, blissful darkness before my eyes pop open to a view of the blank magnolia ceiling where Lizzie's head was less than two seconds earlier.

Goddamn it, Lizzie, look at me!

But she's off doing something else now, fiddling around with my bedside unit, her voice leaping octaves as she tells me about her auntie.

"She had loads of miscarriages, the baby just wouldn't stay until she had a little girl. My mum said all those babies she lost were probably little boys until she became pregnant with Sacha. Little girls are tougher," she says, finally turning towards me, with a smile, proud to be a member of the fairer, tougher sex.

Here we go!

But I see her head turn away just before I blink again, and she says, "Cheerio, Mr. Ashcroft." The sound of her walking away is like a pin bursting my bubble.

I blink a few more times throughout the day, but without anyone to see, to confirm this is happening, I stop myself from getting too excited. It could be my imagination playing tricks.

Congratulations from the nurses trickle after Jack like a waterfall as he arrives for a visit. I wonder if he's secretly a little disappointed; if he, like me, had been imagining kicking a football and playing with trucks and now the assumption of all that pink, the thought of bloody pretend tea parties, feels a bit lame, and not the story he'd pictured.

If I could I would tell him not to worry. Lucy had the

best left foot of her whole year and there's no love quite like that between father and daughter. I have a good view this evening. I watch him stroke Cassie's hair, a habit he's developed, before he places a hand on her stomach that is now undeniably a baby bump.

Looking towards her face, he says, "My little girl." He moves his hand round and round.

I'm not sure if he's talking to Cassie or the baby before he sits back in the chair, places his backpack on his knees and pulls out a small pile of colorful envelopes. He starts opening them one by one, glancing at the front briefly before showing them to Cassie and reading them out loud. I hear them all.

Some of them are formal, like they don't know Cassie well—"With best wishes for a swift recovery, Alan and Cathy Jones"—and others are more emotive: "I wish I could visit, Cas. You're in my thoughts every moment. Sending you all my love." Jack's not very good at reading out loud; he reads each card in the same monotone. He looks up at Cassie, every now and then, to say things about their friends: "That's sweet of Beth"; and "Typical Sam, eh?" A colorful paper pyre soon litters the area around his feet. He gathers the envelopes unceremoniously into a chaotic bundle before shoving them back in his bag.

He gives Cassie—and me—the daily update on his new life. He tells us it looks as though Jensen and Son are going to win the bid for the Brighton pub renovation Jack's been working on when he's not here at Kate's. He leans forward and strokes Cassie's hair back again, away from her forehead.

"Mum says Maisie's still sleeping with your scarf, love.

She misses you. She's eating better though. Mum said she had half a can of dog food last night, so that's a good sign that she's calming down, isn't it?"

I hear Alice walk towards him. She pauses just outside Cassie's area, behind Jack. She's looking at him while biting her bottom lip. She's nervous. It makes me nervous. My eyes burn and I blink again.

Over here Alice! Look!

Jack doesn't turn towards her footsteps; he can't hear her like I can.

"Hi, Jack. A little girl! Congratulations!"

He stands as Alice approaches him and he opens his arms to her, smiling. He looks delighted as he pulls Alice into an awkward bear hug. She releases him before he lets her go.

"It's wonderful news; the father/daughter relationship is really special."

Jack beams at her and she returns his smile, but it's not the smile of the Alice I know. Jack doesn't notice; he doesn't know her like I do. She's holding onto her smile. It looks effortful; she's lost her natural way with him.

"I was secretly hoping it was a little girl, to be honest. Cassie and I already picked a girl's name."

"Oh, yes?"

Jack bends down close to Alice and says quietly, "We both always loved Freya. So she's going to be Freya Charlotte April Jensen."

"Beautiful," Alice says.

She looks like she's about to say goodbye when Jack says, "Actually, Alice, I'm glad I saw you. Can I have a minute?"

Alice reapplies her smile. "Of course, shall we go to the family room?"

Jack ignores her question, but he lowers his voice and turns his back towards Cassie, so he's facing me, before he starts talking.

"I don't want to worry you unnecessarily, but I thought you should know that a guy called Marcus Garrett may try and visit Cassie."

Alice keeps her eyes fixed on Jack's face. She nods.

"He married April, Cassie's mum, just six months before April died."

"OK, so he's Cassie's stepdad?"

"She never called him her stepdad." Jack shrugs. "She's always found him difficult, but he completely broke down after April died and, to be honest, two and a half years later, he still acts like April died yesterday. He always made Cassie feel so guilty for moving on, for being happy."

"So he knows she's here?"

Jack nods. "One of Cassie's friends told him, apparently. The thing is, I've asked him not to visit, but Mum thought she saw him in the hospital café the other day. I just don't want him knowing about the baby. I think it could send him over the edge again."

Jack pauses, looks down the ward and bends his head lower, closer to Alice's ear.

"He turned up at ours completely out of the blue on the last anniversary of April's death. He really upset Cas, implied it was Cas's fault he canceled a memorial weekend for April, all sorts of shit." Jack pauses and looks at Alice as if to ensure he has her full attention. "There was an argument. I tried to defend Cas, get her to stand up to Marcus, but she got a bit pissed off with me, to be honest." Jack clears his throat and frowns. "Cas miscarried after he drove off."

Alice is nodding her head slowly, and, encouraged, Jack keeps talking.

"I know you said she might be able to hear us, and I don't want to risk her getting upset if she hears Marcus. I really, really can't let that happen."

Alice keeps nodding her head. She pats Jack's arm.

"It's all right, Jack. It's OK. We don't let anyone visit her without your permission anyway, as we agreed, but if you give this Marcus's full name to reception, we can be especially careful, OK?"

I blink again. The movement catches Alice's attention and she looks over towards my bed, looks me in the eye, but she just missed it.

So close that time.

"Thanks, Alice. I don't mean to sound cold. I just, you know, I just want to make sure Cas . . . Cas and Freya are safe. It kind of feels like the only thing I can do."

Alice nods again. "Of course, of course, Jack."

There's movement at the end of the ward. Jack and Alice both turn towards it. I can just see two doctors and a small herd of student doctors cluster like sheep for afternoon rounds.

Alice looks at the watch on her chest and says, "I guess that's our cue."

"Thanks, Alice. I appreciate it. And you like the name?"

"Very pretty." But Alice is back to biting her lip. As Jack starts to walk away, she says, "Oh, Jack?"

He turns back to Alice. "Yes?"

Alice looks lost, disoriented for a second, as though surprised to hear herself asking for Jack's attention again.

"You did pick up the envelope Brooks left for you?" she asks after a pause.

Jack looks slightly relieved, as though he anticipated bad news. He smiles at Alice. "Yes, I picked it up over a week ago. It wasn't anything too important." He gives her a little wave and walks away.

Alice watches him leave. She goes back to biting her bottom lip again, pulling at the skin with her teeth, her eyes slightly narrowed.

I recognize that look; I've seen it on Ange's face too many times. It's the focused, slightly pressurized look of someone who thinks they've just been lied to.

Paula's on shift again tonight. I know it's around 3 a.m., because Paula's a woman of habit. She carefully positions her second snack to give some relief to the final part of her night shift. It sounds and smells like popcorn this morning. I hear the door slowly open just as the first kernels start to pop; it makes for a strange soundtrack. My heart clutches and I know it's him; he's back.

Paula has left me with my chin to my chest, so I see more of him tonight as he limps towards Cassie like an injured shadow. Her curtain sways as he moves to the side of her bed, where Alice stood just a few hours before. I think about Jack warning Alice about Cassie's stepdad, Marcus, how worried Jack was that he'd get onto the ward. It's him. It must be him.

He stands grimly over her bed. He doesn't move for a few minutes until I start to see him shake, his shoulders pumping up and down.

He's laughing. He's fucking laughing, the sick bastard.

Jack made him sound a bit weird, but he never said he was a complete fucking mad man. I can do nothing but stare as he moves closer to her, and lowers himself slowly down into her visitor's chair.

My skin senses the air tighten around me, like the air itself is being slowly sucked away. I squirm within myself as he props his elbows onto the edge of her bed and he presses the heels of his hands into his eye sockets as his head starts shaking back and forth, back and forth. His shoulders rise up and down and I hear him suck in a damp-sounding chesty breath, and I realize he's not laughing, he's sobbing.

"I'm sorry, I'm so, so sorry."

At first I think I've finally lost it, that my brain has short-circuited but the longer I watch and the more I hear those words, "I'm sorry, I'm sorry" the more convinced I am that this is real, that the night visitor isn't Marcus at all, and it can't be Jonny, because whoever it is begging for Cassie's forgiveness is a woman.

15

Cassie

Cassie sits at Jonny's old pine kitchen table, the surface almost completely covered in scraps of paper, handwritten sums in pencil, receipts and invoices. She planned on bringing it all home with her, but it had started raining and it just felt easier to stay at Jonny's rather than hauling everything down the lane in the rain. Besides, they keep most of the equipment—the sterilizers, jam pans—at Jonny's now. There's more space and Jonny doesn't mind the mess like Jack.

OK, where to start?

She picks up a torn piece of paper, an "I owe you" written in Jonny's billowy hand, for some money he took from the jam jar full of coins they jokingly call "petty cash" to pay for breakfast one morning. He's doodled in pencil at the bottom of the page, more of a sketch really. Cassie stares at it and recognizes her own ear, slightly indented at the top. April always called it a "pixie ear." Strands of hair float around her ear, and she recognizes the small diamond studs Jack gave her on their wedding day. She lifts her hand to stroke the fleshy drop of her lobe between her thumb and forefinger. Jonny doesn't miss a thing.

Cassie, concentrate!

She puts the scrap piece of paper back down on the table and pulls her laptop out of her backpack. Jack's been on at her for ages about starting some sort of financial spreadsheet to keep track of all the Farm Jam money. She reckons they've made around two grand this summer, her and Jonny. Not bad for what was supposed to be just a hobby, a way of getting involved in the community, meeting people. She's not sure she can account for all that money now, not since they've gotten into the routine of going to the pub after most events, eating whatever they want and drinking expensive wine.

How different things could have been; she'd be around seventeen weeks by now, thinking about buying prams and baby names, not trying to decide between the Shiraz or the Pinot Noir.

She gets up and flicks the kettle on.

Right!

She opens Excel on her computer, and various boxes flash up at her, asking to be updated. She cancels them all. Maybe Jonny was right; she should have gone to meet the "Pick Your Own" farmer to talk about taking on their surplus raspberries instead of Jonny. He'd probably build them a financial template in half an hour. But she'd felt fractious and cold this morning, the change from summer to autumn in her bones, and she wanted to cave it up.

Staying in Jonny's warm cottage with Dennis snoring in his basket was much more appealing than going out in the rain to look at soggy raspberries.

She must be hormonal. She makes a cup of tea. Jonny always has chamomile, her favorite. She flicks the radio on.

The free-template table options on the screen in front of her blur. Maybe she's going about this wrong. She should first organize all the scraps of paper and then try and figure out how to record them on the computer. She closes her laptop and moves it to the end of the table. Jack would laugh if he saw her faffing like this.

Over the last month, his weekdays have become a complete mystery to her. He usually leaves before Cassie's awake. A damp towel from his shower and already-hot water in the kettle from his first coffee is the only proof he was home at all. He spends his days in site meetings, talking about things like steel reinforcements and sewage connections, and speeding up to London to meet potential new clients. Everyone wants to do building work in summer so it's always the busiest time for him. He usually doesn't come home until after 9 p.m. She's quiet in the evenings, especially after an event, pretending to be more sober than she feels. Charlotte thinks it's good they're both busy. She hugged Cassie for a long time when they told her; Charlotte said miscarriage is sometimes sadly part of having a baby.

They just need to keep trying she said.

Cassie's organized the papers into a pile and taps the bottom edge against the table, a pretence at order.

Her feet feel chilled on the stone floor. She lifts them to her chair, rubs them, but it doesn't make any difference.

Dennis raises his head from the basket as the stairs creak under Cassie as she makes her way up to Jonny's bedroom in search of socks. She's worn some alpaca ones of his before, a gift from Lorna a few years ago, when they were still in love. She opens a drawer and sits on the unmade bed to roll them on.

Dennis is waiting for her at the bottom of the stairs. She picks up the pile of papers again.

Right. Now she'll divide it into income and expenses.

But she remembers she hasn't replied to a text from Nicky that came through earlier that morning. Can't wait to see you, what time will you be home? xxx, her friend had written.

She was coming down from London tonight for the weekend, a long overdue catch-up. Cassie thought about calling her a few times since the miscarriage, but Nicky was in New York for a whole month over the summer, partly for her new job as Executive Assistant to a self-made web entrepreneur and partly for a holiday. It didn't seem right crying over the phone when Nicky was finally doing better and, besides, Jonny had been there for Cassie.

She types, Me too! It's been forever, home about 6ish. What time does your train get in? Text Jack, he said he'd pick you up after work. xxx The message makes a whoosh sound as it sends.

Laying the two piles of paperwork in front of her, she opens her computer again and chooses a template, one that separates the rows into dates, starting from today and counting back.

God, is it really the middle of October already? She scrolls down the document, counts eleven weeks since the miscarriage. She hasn't told Jack that she's spoken to Marcus on the phone a couple of times. Neither of them mentioned the argument. He sounded better on the phone, but she still should find a time to go and visit him. Even bringing up Marcus's name still makes Jack thunderous; she knows Jack blames Marcus for the miscarriage. She can't be bothered to have that argument again, trying to defend Marcus to Jack. He just needs time. Nothing bad has happened to him since he was fourteen, it's understandable the miscarriage shook him up. Staring at all those neatly rowed days and weeks since her miscarriage, Cassie realizes her last period was an unfeasibly long time ago. Cassie looks at the calendar on her phone. The hair on her body rises and her skin prickles as she realizes she's completely neglected to keep track.

Oh my god!

She has to get home, get home before Nicky arrives so she can do a pregnancy test, find out for certain one way or the other. She doesn't know whether she's thrilled or terrified, or both? She pulls on her walking boots she left on the back doorstep.

"Sorry, Dennis, you're staying here." His tail drops as she holds him back and closes the door in front of his nose. She puts the spare key back in its place under the mat; she'll message Jonny later to explain that she had to dash off.

She pulls her hood up, the rain patters loudly against the thin shell of her bright red raincoat. She decides to go along the lane; it's the quickest way, the stream bubbling like a caldron by her side. She keeps going over the dates again and again in her head. Each time she's at least three weeks late.

How had she not noticed?

Cassie knows there are a couple of tests left over from last time in their en-suite. It's only 4:30 p.m., far too early for Jack to be home. He hasn't been back before 7 p.m. for weeks so she'll run straight upstairs, do the test and know either way before he collects Nicky from the station. Perfect.

The rain is getting into its pace, flowing freely, hitting the earth rhythmic as a metronome. She steps over a couple of newly made puddles as she turns into their driveway, breaking into a little jog at the end of the drive. There's a light on in the sitting room. Strange; she's usually good at turning everything off. As she gets closer, she sees a figure move like a ghost downstairs. The windowpanes have tiny vertical rivers of rain running down them; the person's image is distorted and stretched by the water. As she gets closer, she recognizes Jack's broad outline.

He must be ill; there's no way he'd be home otherwise.

Through the steady fall of rain she watches as her husband sits back on the sofa. He slouches back as the sofa gently folds around him, crossing his right leg over his left and ruffling his hair. He raises a bottle of beer to his lips, his mouth curling around the rim, smiling at someone sitting next to him who Cassie can't see. He hasn't looked so relaxed in months.

He can't be that ill if he's having a beer, Cassie thinks primly. She's close to the window now. She pulls her hood down off her head and feels the rain wet her crown like a baptism. She's about to lift her fist to knock against the window, but she pauses because the person sitting next to Jack is stroking her husband's leg with beautiful long white fingers. Jack looks down at his leg and interlaces his fingers with the woman's. She pulls him towards her and he gives in easily. Cassie watches, paralyzed, as they come together in a way that looks inevitable, the pressure too great to not put their lips together, for his hands not to hold her face as he kisses it, her red hair cascading between his fingers like lava. He's kissed Cassie like that so many times. She touches her face, almost expecting to feel his hands there, where they should be, holding her face, not holding Nicky's. Cassie can't move. It's as though her mind has been cleaved clean away from her body. She watches them push and pull against each other, watches as her friend smiles behind her kissing mouth and her fingers fall to Jack's fly, like they've been there before.

Cassie's heart dilates and contracts painfully, like the organ itself has been thumped hard. The force shoves her backwards, and she grips the window frame to stop herself falling.

The movement catches Nicky's eye. Her head raises, away from Cassie's husband, and her hand whips away from his fly. Her red hair flows down her back as she sees Cassie, and she says one, short word before Jack turns.

His face is blanched, already pale, eyes made round, cartoonish with shock. He leaps up as though the sofa is suddenly burning him and comes close towards the window. He's shaking his head and he keeps saying her name over and over again, a cloud of evaporation frills around his palm as he places it against the cold glass.

But Cassie isn't looking at him. Through the rain-streaked window she's staring at her best friend who is now standing perfectly still in the middle of the sitting room, and Cassie can't stop staring at her because Nicky's body must be possessed by someone, something else. This can't be the same person who slept in the same bed as Cassie for a month after April died, because her mouth, which used to call Cassie her sister, was just kissing her husband.

Cassie watches as Nicky's lips make the shape of Cassie's name again and then she turns away from the window and she runs as fast as she can back into the weeping day.

16

Alice

I'm running, my feet rhythmic and steady on the road. My body feels taut, energetic, as if I could run forever. The lane narrows and becomes foggy and I see a figure in front of me, another runner, just a few yards ahead. I can't see her face; it's a woman with a bouncy, blonde pony tail. The small, wiry-haired dog—the same one in her Facebook photos—trips around her feet, and then I know who it is.

"Cassie!" I call out.

She stops in the middle of the lane, slowly turning around, which is when I see that her face is all wrong. Her features are frozen like a death mask, her mouth twisted in a noise-less scream, her skin a flawless gray. Her eyes are only half open, red veins like weird lace lattice the whites of her eyes; I can't see the iris.

Our room is pitch-black, the bed sheets clammy with

my sweat. I turn on my bedside light and David stirs but doesn't wake.

Jesus.

5:40 a.m. I try closing my eyes. They burn with exhaustion and my body aches for more sleep, but it's no use. My mind is cracking like a whip, so I grab my dressing gown and pad downstairs.

I've always loved the peace of early morning, the privacy of being the only one awake. As if the dial has been turned down on the world, the early morning feels like a suspended space, a pause, a chance to catch up with myself.

Without turning on any lights, I stare out of the kitchen window. The morning sky is still a deep indigo. It's freezing outside, the lawn covered in petrified, icy blades of grass. Something—a rabbit, perhaps—has left a sweet little trail of paw prints heading into the cypress bush; Bob will enjoy trying to flush it out later.

I know some nurses struggle not to bring work home with them, but it's never been an issue for me. As soon as I step out of my uniform, I strip my day, and other people's pain, off with it. I never thought it was unusual; most people live in at least two worlds. But it's different now, with Cassie. I want to stay close to her, like the survival of her baby is a good omen, as if some of her magic, just a tiny bit, might rub off on me. I pour myself a glass of water and go back upstairs to the study; I turn the computer on, the light from the screen stark, cold in the dark room.

I open Facebook and search through Cassie's friends. There's no Jonathan Parker or Jonny Parker; either he's not on Facebook or he's deleted his account. All of Cassie's photos have been posted by other people, mainly Jack in the last two years and, before then, by someone called Nicky Breton.

I look at the older ones, the ones posted by Nicky. This is the Cassie I don't know so well. Her face is fuller, more girlish in the photos, her skin's even, taut with youth, and her hair is buttery and long, falling either side of her face. Her clothes are different in the older photos; they're colorful, made from natural fabrics, tie-dye and floaty, the kind of clothes people buy at festivals.

One of the photos of Cassie and April is a close-up of their faces. They're both staring at the camera like they've been told to be serious, but they look too giggly, like trying to be serious makes them laugh. They have the same eyes, blue with nuggets of hazel. April is wearing a bright blue headscarf—maybe she'd just started chemo—and strands of Cassie's hair dance like sprites around her face. In the background there are slick rocks, jagged as incisors, a foam of white water around them. The two of them look like they belong there, by the sea.

I scramble, a Facebook amateur, to the more recent photos, stopping at the now familiar photo Jack posted of Cassie decorating the tree, her hair bobbed and smooth. People have left comments like "Wow!" and "Beautiful!" underneath, but there's nothing from Cassie, no thanks or acknowledgement. I zoom in on Cassie's frozen face, just a foot away from my own; she's almost to scale on the screen. A lump forms in my throat as I stare at her. She looks different to me now. I remember what Jess said about her smile looking fake. I can see it now. In the photo, Cassie's wearing the sort of smile that must make her jaw ache. She's flexed, rigid, as if she's grinding her teeth. She looks like she's holding onto her smile. I imagine it falling away as soon as the camera was lowered. There's something mildly intrusive about the photo, the glint in her eye like a secret.

The lump drops down into my thorax. I remember what Jonny said when he came onto the ward. What was she scared of? Of Jack finding out the baby wasn't his? Or of Jonny finding out the baby was his? Has Cassie been lying? Playing the doting wife but messing around with Jonny? I think about her baby. I pray again that I'm wrong, that Jonny isn't the father. A mum in a coma and a dad in prison? I don't want that for Freya and I don't want that for Jack.

Without warning, my phone vibrates in my dressing-gown pocket.

"Hello?" My voice small in the dark morning.

"Alice?" Sharma's accent sounds thicker over the phone.

I retie my bathrobe around me. He sounds disconcertingly close.

Without waiting for me to respond he asks, "Have you seen the *Sussex Times* this morning?"

"No, what is it?" I move the little arrow wildly across the screen, guilty suddenly, as if Sharma can see me snooping around Cassie's life. I shut the pages down.

"Just have a look and come in as soon as you can, will you? I'm on my way now." He doesn't say goodbye before he hangs up and he didn't say anything in Latin. Something must be up.

The headline, *Local Celebrity in Coma: Pregnant*, seems to leap off the page and slap me. I have to read it twice.

I scan the article. I'm not interested in most of it; I go straight to the bit that means something.

"A source close to Cassandra Jensen who wishes to remain anonymous . . ."

I sit heavily in the chair. They've used her real name, they know about Juice-C, and the article mentions Buscombe, and a "Jonathan Parker," described as a "close friend" (I imagine the journalists winking at each other when they chose that phrase) and a known local drinker who has been charged with driving under the influence and attempted manslaughter. It feels like catching myself talking in a mirror. A familiar story but framed all wrong. The lump seems to twist and turn; it makes my whole chest ache.

I don't realize I'm muttering "shit, shit, shit" until Bob's strong black nose pokes up in the crook of my arm.

"Uh oh, that doesn't sound good. What's up?" David walks into the study just in his boxer shorts. He puts his hand on my shoulder and frowns at the computer screen. I stare with him.

"God. How horrific." He turns towards me. "Is she one of yours?" and I feel a twist of guilt for not telling him about Cassie, guiltier still for not telling him I'm pregnant.

I blink my eyes, forcing them to focus.

"So this is why you haven't been sleeping. God, I didn't even know this was possible. Why didn't you say anything?"

"I can't tell you everything about my patients, David," I snap, irritated to be interrupted when I want to read the article again.

"Yeah, but this? You tell me about the guy with the

religious nut wife, the patient who has no visitors, but you don't tell me about a pregnant woman in a coma?"

He moves back, as I get up from the chair, creating space between us. It feels awkward, icy.

"Why didn't you tell me?" he asks, a little wounded.

"Oh, come on, David, she's not some juicy bit of gossip. She's a patient. You know why I didn't tell you."

"Because you think I'd worry too much?"

"No! Because of patient confidentiality! Look, I don't have time for this, I've got to go to work." Before I get to our bedroom I hear David mutter, "Bollocks."

I don't bother with a shower and brush my teeth while I try and get ready, which doesn't save anytime. I dribble toothpaste on my clean uniform by accident; it looks like bird poo. My mind whirrs over who could have told the press. It could have been any number of people; the ward is always busy with visitors, student doctors and porters.

I feel eyes on me. David is staring at me from the door frame, his head perched quizzically to one side, like Bob when a rabbit he's been chasing disappears down a hole.

"Sorry, Ali, sorry for being a prat."

I stand and move towards him. He bends forwards, closer to me so I can wrap my arms around his neck and kiss him quickly on the mouth. He smells slightly musty, someone who was recently fast asleep.

"It's OK," I say, over his shoulder. "You were partly right. I didn't want you to worry."

"Are you OK with all this? It's pretty crazy, pretty close to home."

Now would be the time to do it . . . to tell him. Now, Alice!

But instead I pull away and start shoving pins in my hair. I'm not going to bother with mascara. I shrug at myself in the mirror.

"She's a remarkable patient, but to be honest, it's still just work, that's all," I lie. I kiss David again, tell him not to worry and by 6:15 a.m. I'm in the car and driving too fast down the quiet, still dark roads towards Cassie.

Lizzie was on night shift last night with a bank nurse. She hands me a cup of coffee. She's so young the night doesn't show on her face at all. I look and feel like the living dead after a night shift.

"Mr. Sharma said you'd be in soon, so I thought you'd want one."

I thank her. "Have you heard, Lizzie?"

"Mr. Sharma told me," she says, nodding. "I've just been reading the websites. Other newspapers are starting to pick up on it, the *Daily Mail* and the *Sun* . . ." The exhaustion might not show on her face, but her voice is clipped; she sounds startled.

I nod, take a sip of burning coffee.

"You know, there'll probably be reporters around the hospital for a few days so we'll need to be extra careful, especially with visitors, OK? If anyone asks you anything you just say—"

"No comment?" she interrupts me. "Just like on telly."

I nod. "Just like on telly."

As I start making my way towards the break room, Lizzie asks, "Has anything like this happened before?"

I think for a moment. "There was a guy, a couple of years ago, an old seventies drummer who gave himself brain damage after a massive drink-and-drug binge. The local press got hold of that one. The poor receptionist actually drew a reporter a map to the ward." Lizzie's eyes widen, as I add, "The receptionist was fired."

I knock on Sharma's door and it takes him a moment to answer.

"*Intrare!*"

His ear is glued to his desk phone. "Incredible." He shakes his head at the receiver, holding it towards me.

I hear a distant, tiny voice from a recorded message.

He points at the receiver. "The Trust's Head of Communications still clearly has no idea what's going on." Sharma replaces the phone with a sigh and another shake of his head. "And I still haven't got ahold of the head of security." He looks up at me with a quick smile; a spark, excitement, animates his face.

"How do you think it got out?"

We're interrupted by an uncertain, quiet knock at the door.

Sharma isn't interested in what I was saying. He calls, "*Intrare!*" again, and Lizzie's full, young face appears.

"Sorry to disturb you," she says to Sharma. She looks at me. "But Charlotte Jensen's just arrived."

Charlotte's back in the ill-fitting jeans and oversized shirt with pockets I recognize from the first few days after Cassie was hit.

"Oh, Alice," she says, frowning as if she doesn't under-stand what she's saying. "I'm afraid Jack's rather upset about the whole thing. He's on the phone to his office.

Apparently reporters have already started calling. He's trying to figure out how best to deal with it." Her small hand flutters up to her temple.

"I'm afraid it's all a bit of a mess, isn't it? As if we haven't been through enough." I steer Charlotte by the arm into the family room and Jack comes in a moment later like a typhoon. Charlotte motions for him to sit, but he ignores her and stays standing.

"I know who it was," he rages. "Cassie's stepdad, Marcus Garrett, I'm absolutely sure of it. He told the papers, his way of saying 'fuck you.' It's obvious, because we wouldn't let him see her."

Charlotte sits down, her tone balanced. "Cassie always said he could be tricky, but she never made him sound vindictive. Do you really think he'd go that far?"

"Oh, come on. Don't you remember how weird he was with Cas? He is vindictive and he's delusional and—" Charlotte raises her palm to Jack for him to stop.

"That's enough, Jack." She doesn't have to raise her voice as well.

"We can't just pin this on Marcus without thinking of other plausible solutions. I mean, it's always so busy here." She turns to me. "I hope you don't mind me saying, Alice, but could it have been, I don't know, not a nurse or a doctor, but a porter or cleaner or someone?"

I nod. "Yes, I had the same thought, to be honest."

Jack doesn't say anything. He's got his man; this discussion is just to keep his mum happy. A muscle in his jaw jumps with tension. A hospital PR person joins us; they talk about what is likely to happen, advise Charlotte and Jack on how to handle the reporters. Charlotte and Jack spend the rest of the morning with Cassie, and I help coordinate a staff meeting. We're getting our own security person for the next few days and everyone is reminded that visitors who are not related to a patient have to ring ahead and have family permission before they can visit.

After the meeting, I join Carol and Mary in the break room. Carol fills the kettle from the tap as Mary reads aloud from her phone screen. She pauses to look up briefly as I come in.

"This is the one I was talking about," she says. "Here in the comments section this guy who calls himself Peckham Tim says that Jonny Parker was a big drinker."

Carol nods judiciously, and, forgetting I was there that night, she wrinkles her nose as she says, "Paula said she could still smell it on him."

"Yeah, but here, this is the bit." Mary starts to read aloud from her phone. "My ex-girlfriend didn't like him; he always made her uneasy. He groped her one night in the pub and when I confronted him he denied it, which led to a fight, and that was the last time we saw him. He's a nasty piece of work. Lock him up!" Mary and Carol look at each other, their faces animated, delighted by their villain.

"Bastard," Carol says, shaking her head. The kettle rumbles to a boil. "You having tea, love?" she asks me. I nod, and Mary keeps talking.

"On the *Mail* website people are saying he was obsessed with her, wouldn't leave her alone. There are witnesses from the party who saw them hugging, just as the clock struck twelve, before they had a row and Cassie got upset."

"Who were?" I ask, feeling myself frown. "Arguing, I mean."

"Ali, catch up! Jonny and Cassie; loads of people at the party saw them. They rowed just before she walked home . . . was in tears and everything. He stayed drinking for another hour before driving towards home absolutely steaming drunk and, more to the point, pissed off with Cassie . . ."

"You don't think it was an accident?"

Mary raises her eyebrows in a look that says, in her story, it definitely wasn't an accident.

I don't realize I'm shaking my head until Mary asks, "What is it? Why are you looking like that, Ali?"

"I just . . . I don't know." I think of Jonny. I've seen enough to know what real tragedy looks like; I know it can't be faked. "He just seemed so devastated."

"Of course he was!" Mary snorts at my ignorance. "Devastated because he knew he'd be caught." She picks up her tea and takes a sip as she sits down at the table with Carol. I leave them with their eyes glued to their screens, hungry for more details to smear all over Jonny.

An hour later, both Mary and Carol have left for the day. I go to the break room to collect my coat and bag when the locker we keep for patient items catches my eye.

The leather bag Charlotte brought in for Cassie has the earthy smell of animal; it's wrinkled and old, as though it's been on many adventures. I move it to the desk and open the zipper. Charlotte folded everything beautifully inside. I take out a carefully pressed pair of blue striped pajamas, a packet of white cotton briefs, a plain bra, a cashmere sweater, bed socks and a pair of cotton sweatpants. Everything is so well laundered it all looks brand new. There's a Kate Atkinson novel and a toiletry bag with an electric toothbrush and some half-used Clarins products. Charlotte packed thoughtfully for her daughter-in-law. I feel disappointed; pajamas can't tell you the truth about a person.

As I'm repacking the bag my fingers find an internal pocket hidden in the seam, there's something in there. I slide the zipper back and slip my hand inside and pull out a small envelope. There's nothing written on the front but the back is well sealed. I look up at the door as I slide my thumb under the flap. No one will know. The paper tears easily. Inside, there's a piece of white paper, torn out of a book. The note's short, written in black pen. Jack, I'm going away for a while. I don't know how long. I need space. Please don't call or look for me. I'll be in touch when I'm ready. C

I read it three times, turning it over, looking for any other clues. My heart's beating fast, as though it's trapped inside my ribcage. There are voices outside on the ward; they sound like they're getting closer. I shove the clothes, toiletry bag and book back in the bag, not bothering to fold them again. I put the bag back into the locker just as Lizzie opens the door. She doesn't see me fold the envelope into my pocket.

"Alice, there you are. I've been looking for you. I was hoping to have a quick word?"

"I was just about to go . . ." but then I look at her. She looks wired, as much as her round, open face will allow her to look wired, and I know this is important.

"Sorry, Lizzie, of course. What's up?"

Her brow furrows. She's about to break into tears. I stand, put my arm around her shoulders, guide her into a chair and hand her a tissue.

"Lizzie, what's happened?"

"Oh, god, sorry, Alice. I'm just . . ." She fans her hand in front of her face and dabs her eye with the tissue. "Sorry, I know you're busy so I'll be quick." She breathes out. "I'm going to hand in my notice."

I frown. "I'm sorry to hear that. I thought everything was going well. You seemed happy here."

She nods emphatically and blows into the tissue. "I am, I'm really happy here."

"Then why, Lizzie?"

She looks at me, her eyelashes slick with tears. "It was me, Alice. It's my fault the press found out about Cassie."

I frown harder. "What?"

The tears start again. Lizzie is shaking her head, saying, "Sorry, I'm so sorry. I didn't mean to, I honestly didn't."

"What happened, Lizzie?"

"I was out with Alex, you know, my new boyfriend? We went bowling with his brother and his brother's girlfriend and, to be honest, Alice, I was really nervous because his brother's girlfriend is gorgeous. I mean she really looks like a model, and she's funny and everything. Anyway, I was an idiot. I always thought she looked down on me for only being a nurse, so I told her about Cassie; I wanted to prove I had big things going on. I didn't know her dad's a reporter for the *Sussex Times*." Lizzie's breath comes out in ragged little puffs; it sounds painful.

"Oh, Lizzie," I say, and she's back to shaking her head, whimpering into the tissue. I stand up, put an arm around her, and rub her shoulders. "Come on, just breathe."

After a couple of minutes she's calmed down enough to hand me a letter.

"What's this?"

"My resignation letter. I thought it best to make it official."

"Well, I don't accept it, Lizzie."

She looks at me, her face puffing up in confusion. "What do you mean?"

"I won't accept your resignation because there's no need for you to resign. Look. You're happy here and you're a great nurse. You've made a mistake. Definitely. A big mistake. You've broken patient confidentiality and it's had terrible consequences, but you're owning up to it, and I know it won't happen again, will it?"

Lizzie doesn't take her eyes off me. She's still shaking her head, but this time she's saying, "No. No. It won't. I promise."

"So. No one's been disciplined for talking to the press. If someone is accused, then we'll need to step in but that's unlikely to happen. When these kinds of things have happened before, it's blown over quite quickly."

Lizzie stands and hugs me, her face damp against my own and says a few more thank-yous and sorrys, before she at last walks quietly out of the little room.

I stand in the middle of the room for just a moment, before an auxiliary nurse hurries in to get her belongings before heading home.

I walk back onto the ward. I think about going straight to Cassie but I decide to let the discovery of the note and my conversation with Lizzie settle in my mind before I do.

I pull Frank's curtain carefully behind myself and sit down in his visitor's chair. Lizzie's combed Frank's hair and cut his fingernails. I appreciate these little touches and I bet Frank does too. His eyes are closed but I still gently turn his face towards me. I feel the envelope crinkle in my pocket and I know I can't ignore it. I promised I'd look after Cassie and her baby. I lean in closer towards Frank so I'm sure he can hear.

"I found something, Frank. A note from Cassie to Jack. It says she needed time away from him, a break from their marriage. It was hidden in her bag, like she was going to give it to him or put it in the mail. Everyone is so convinced it was Jonny, but I just don't believe it."

I look at Frank's pale face. I know him well enough to know he's not asleep; his face looks focused, concentrated.

"But that's not all, Frank, I just found out Jack was wrong. It wasn't Marcus who told the police. I keep wondering what else he could be wrong about. She'd taken off her wedding rings; she was wearing her mum's ring instead. Remember when Jonny came onto the ward, Frank? Jonny said something to me, Frank. He told me she was scared, that Cassie had been scared."

I wonder what Frank's thinking, what he makes of all this, and then the truth slices, clean and sharp like a knife. I think of the black-and-white photo, how tense her jaw looked, her smile forced and hard and yet the comments below called her "beautiful" when she looked like she was on the brink.

"She was scared." I lean in, closer to Frank and whisper because I can't quite believe I'm going to say the words aloud. "Cassie wasn't looking for her dog, Frank. She was scared. She was running away."

17

Frank

Sharma, the pompous ass, is calling the episode "the media breach."

The nurses have started using the phrase and I don't need to see them to know they punctuate it with quick glances and carefully concealed smiles. Sharma seems oblivious, though; I suppose sarcasm can't be taught.

He was right about the national newspapers, though. They picked up on the story pronto. By then, print versions of the articles were banned on the ward, but the nurses told me plenty. The papers knew about Juice-C. They were calling Cassie a modern day Sleeping Beauty. Cassie has become the new face of a local road awareness campaign, and sales of Juice-C have almost doubled.

Hospital staff talk about reporters now as casually as they talk about the weather. I picture them, these reporters, skulking around the corridors, fiddling with their phones in the waiting areas, hoping to catch a nurse's eye, someone who might know about Cassie; ideally, someone who even works on the ward. They aggravate the nurses like wasps at a picnic.

At any other time, the "media breach" would be welcome entertainment, a new soundtrack to accompany the endless hours I stare at the magnolia ceiling, but I can't enjoy the whispers and the gossip because even though I know she's gone, that woman seems to hang in the air around the ward, the woman who hit Cassie. It's as though that woman's left a charge here, as though her visit has changed the cellular make up of the ward: the air feels squeezed, the oxygen forced into my lungs thinner, less nourishing somehow. Like fearing a virus hanging in the air, I don't trust 9B anymore; it's not safe enough for Cassie, not safe enough for her baby.

I think about her constantly, that woman. I don't know anything about her, didn't see her face so couldn't pick her out of a crowd, but I know her voice. How softly she spoke those words she probably hoped would soothe her burning guilt, at least for a moment: "I'm sorry, I'm sorry."

I know those kinds of apologies. I've tried to give them myself to Lucy and Ange for the times I abandoned them, all the times I fucked up as a dad, as a husband. I know when someone is sorry from their soul, and I heard it that night. I hear it still now: "I'm sorry, I'm sorry."

How do you forgive someone for almost killing a pregnant woman? For letting someone else take the blame? If Alice's theory is right, and Cassie was running away, then this woman hunted them down and I don't care what she says or where her apology comes from, there can be no forgiveness, not yet, not until everyone knows the truth, and for now, at least, the truth is locked, trapped inside me, pitiful and useless as a butterfly trying to fly through a window pane.

Today is a quiet day, a sluggish Sunday, a little heavy. Everyone prays for Sundays to be like this as most senior staff are at home, eating roasts, glugging back the red wine.

Ellen was wheeled away for the last time a few days ago, off to an old peoples' home, Alice said. It's a strange, lonely thought to think she could die and even though we'd spent weeks side by side, I'd never know.

George Peters has been moved to another ward. His wife Celia kissed all the nurses before they left. It's the first time I've been on 9B with two beds free—it's just me and Cassie—and I wonder if patients who would've been here have been moved to other wards . . . if the hospital is trying to protect Cassie from the reporters. Small mercies. The Jensens haven't been in today yet so there's less coming and going and Alice is in a quiet mood, moving slowly, which is good because she'll be more likely to catch me.

She checks Cassie's curtain is closed before she sits in my chair. She doesn't say anything; she doesn't need to. She looks at me, the skin under her eyes the color of heavy rain clouds. She's thinking about Cassie, I can tell. She's always thinking about Cassie. I wish she'd think more about herself, about her own health for once. But maybe, maybe soon I'll be able to help her. I'll tell her about the woman, get her to call the police, sort this Cassie mess out and I know this is my moment! This is the moment I tell her she was right to trust her instincts, that I am here, that I've been here all along; I blink!

Come on, Alice.

But she doesn't see because she's looking down at her hands and telling me about Officer Brooks, about how she took the letter she found to her. Alice kneads her hands as she tells me that Brooks implied the letter doesn't change anything, she says they knew Cassie and Jack had their troubles. They all think Jonny's the cause. His alibi still mustn't have come good for him. Alice's bottom lip is livid, sore, the color of raw meat as she pulls it through her teeth. She hasn't told anyone else about the letter; she thinks no one will listen. I know how that feels, to know and be silent.

See me.

She's looking up at me now and I know I don't have long so I call on every cell in my body to rally and join in the effort and I blink!

She stands up like she's been electrocuted.

"Frank?" Her face is above mine and I can see that sweet little gap and her dimple, and I think I've got enough in my energy reserves to give it another shot so I do, I blink again. Fireworks explode and a tiny brass band starts marching in my head because she's grinning down at me. She's laughing now!

"You blinked, Frank! You blinked!" and she's stroking my face and calling to Mary and it's like something celestial has awoken in me because for the first time in months I've sent a message, a tiny telegram to the world, that I still exist! I'm here!

Mary's little face appears next to Alice and she asks me

to blink again and I do, and Mary says, "Oh, Frank, you absolute winner, Frank," and she puts her arm around Alice who's still stroking my cheek and smiling at me in a way that looks like tears are close behind.

"Can you try one more time, Frank?"

And like the star in the football team I go for a hat-trick. My vision goes black but something's wrong; my eyelids are too heavy. I've lost the controls; I can't open them. They're frozen shut and I scream around my body, like some crazed insect trapped in a jar because the moment's gone and I can't see Alice smile or hear Mary call me a "winner" again. I'm in black, and I can feel their disappointment on my face, like sunburn. It doesn't last too long, though, because Alice is talking about getting me a scan today, while Sharma's on leave. They hurry away to call radiology and to find out which registrar is on duty.

I realize I've been so focused on someone seeing me blink, I hadn't thought too much about what would happen immediately after: scans, tests, more prodding and poking. How long will it be before I can tell them about the woman? How long will it be before I can thank Alice for everything? How long before I can hug my Luce again? I know enough now to know it won't be like the films. If the blinking is anything to go by, my rehabilitation will be slow, painful and appallingly frustrating, and the first step is a scan. I'm not sure I'm ready, but all of a sudden I hear her voice again—"I'm sorry, I'm sorry"—and it dawns on me that this woman, whoever she is, is in some way my redemption. I'll work even harder to get better, and won't rest until I can tell the world about her . . . about what she did to Cassie and her baby. Perhaps that'll even the scale, the bad I've done finally balanced with this new good. Perhaps I would finally forgive my own fuck-ups?

Clipped footsteps interrupt my thoughts and suddenly, without warning, my eyelids are peeled back like skin on a lychee and a piercing light is shone straight into my pupil.

I can't see him but a gentle male voice with a French accent tells me, "Mr. Ashcroft, I am Matthieu Baret, the specialist on duty today."

Matthieu releases the eyelid and goes straight on to the left, colors flash within my head like the inside of a kaleidoscope. Then Matthieu asks me to blink, which seems a bit rich after he'd been pulling back my eyelids like he was trying to peel them off my face, but to my astonishment and with relatively little effort, I blink. For a moment I see that Matthieu is a slightly overweight but kindly looking black man, that Alice and Mary are grinning at me from behind him. Matthieu knocks me about a bit to check my reflexes and he's telling Alice and Mary to book me in for a PET with CAT scan, which sounds reassuringly thorough. Before he leaves he leans in close enough for me to feel his warm breath on my skin.

"Mr. Ashcroft," he says in an overly loud voice, as if speaking to a five-year-old, "if you can hear me, you should know you are in the hospital. You've been in a coma. You are safe and we will look after you."

My fillings rattle as his voice booms around my head, and then I feel him move away towards Alice and Mary.

"Well, let's hope some of the 9B magic rubs off on the

rest of the hospital." He chuckles and Alice laughs with him just so he's not laughing alone.

The call from radiology comes in sooner than they thought as there's been a cancellation. I don't dwell on why someone's appointment was canceled; no time to think, no chance of clinging to my bed covers.

They use a hoist to get me out of bed, and like a grotesque sculpture, I'm craned onto a portable bed. Alice guides my tracheotomy trunk and Mary is on the IV and heart monitor, a complicated tangle of tubes.

I haven't left the ward in months; a perky-looking elderly woman twists in her wheelchair to look at me as we pass each other in the corridor. Her mouth hangs open when she sees me, a mixture of curiosity and horror filling her face, clear as if the very words were tattooed on her wrinkly skin. I decide I don't want to see anymore and shut my eyes.

An hour or so later, and I'm back in bed, my eyelids slide open a little, I haven't blinked since before my scan, Alice told me Lucy was on her way so I've been saving my energy for her.

I hear my girl approach and I think, this is it! This is when Luce will believe in me again.

My curtain rattles back and Lucy comes into view, her hair is pulled back from her face, and her cheeks are flushed. She says, "Dad!" and I blink and immediately she starts crying.

Oh, Luce, don't cry! This is good! Look, watch!

I blink again and I start doing a little jig inside because she's laughing more than crying now. She clutches my hand and kisses it and I wish I could laugh and cry with her but I can only blink, which makes her hang her head over me. She leans forward, her face towards mine, and a couple of her tears fall onto my cheek, as though she knew what I was thinking and she's crying for me.

Alice appears behind Lucy and puts her hand on Lucy's shoulder.

"Remember what I told you, Lucy. Only time will tell and we still need to get the scans back."

Lucy sits up and wipes her eyes with the back of her hand. All the crying has made her irises an even richer brown.

"Blink if you can hear me, Dad," she whispers close to my ear.

I blink. It's a good one—purposeful and complete—and Lucy splutters a wet, teary laugh, and Lucy turns to check Alice is still there, that she's seeing it as well.

"You've been here all along, haven't you, Dad?" and I blink again, for yes.

Lucy's bubbling over with questions now. We strike a deal: one blink for "yes," and two for "no." I can't tell her I haven't tried a two-blink blink yet.

"Are you in pain, Dad?" Lucy asks, and I'm about to blink once for yes, even though I'm not, because it might encourage Alice to get the morphine out, but my eyelids have turned to stone. I strain, quivering inside with the effort, but it's no good. Show's over for the day; my eyes clamp shut. I'm glad I don't have to see the disappointment on Lucy's face.

"He's probably exhausted," Alice says gently. "It's been a huge day. He'll just need to rest until tomorrow."

After a pause, Lucy asks, "Can I sit with him for a bit?"

"Of course, take as long as you like."

Alice walks away and Lucy's soft hand spoons the back of my rigid claw.

Lucy moves close to my ear, her voice warm little puffs on my cheek. When she was small, she used to wake me up like this. She'd come over to my side of the bed and whisper so as not to disturb Ange. Her breath would tickle my ear as she told me she had a surprise for me in the kitchen, and I absolutely had to get up straight away so as not to miss it.

"I'm here, Dad," she says now. "I'm not going to leave you for so long again. I promise. You're going to get better, Dad, I know you are. One day, you're going to walk out of this place and I'm going to be right by your side cheering you along and we're going to go home, Dad. We're going to go home."

I'll try, Luce, I'll try to make you proud of me.

For the first time I see it; I can see us, hand-in-hand, walking out of here. I can feel the rush of fresh air on my face as the hospital doors finally slide open to spit me out. Still closed, I feel my eyes start to burn as something crests, breaches from my right eye, spilling fatly onto my cheek. It traces a wet line down my face. I haven't cried in years, but, hey, from today, I'm a whole new me.

18

Cassie

She opens her eyes; she must have fallen asleep with the bedside light still on. Her mum's diary from Mexico—full of adventures involving peyote and hitchhiking in a goat truck to the Yucatan—lies splayed open on the top of the bed. Through the half-closed curtains Cassie can tell it's very early; the day's still inky with newness, and Cassie's eyelids feel too big, swollen in their sockets. The pain wasn't what Cassie expected. She thought she'd be livid with it, but the betrayal turned out to be more subtle, a gummy tumor of disappointment she still carries around everywhere.

She pulls herself up to sit, and Maisie stirs in her basket and lifts her little gray head towards Cassie, her coarse beard stroking the basket the rescue center said she'd slept in all her life.

Her eyebrows seesaw at Cassie. "Do what you like, but

don't think I'm getting up yet," she seems to say, and with a little sigh she falls back on her side.

Cassie had thought about telling Jonny about Nicky and Jack last week when he'd driven her to the dog rescue center to collect Maisie. Jonny had asked about Jack's change of heart in getting a dog, Cassie had thought about telling Jonny the truth, that Maisie is a symbol of Jack's guilt, his olive branch, but instead she'd shrugged his question away. It hadn't felt like the right time to tell him about Jack and Nicky when Jonny had been away for the last month in London trying to appease Lorna for a final time. Lorna had been back to her delusional tricks, turning up at Jonny's old office again, demanding to know what happened between Jonny and his poor colleague. Apparently the colleague had tendered her resignation as a result, which Lorna had taken to be proof of her guilt. Jonny had started divorce proceedings the next day in the hope it might shock Lorna into getting some proper help.

Awful as it is to admit, it was a relief for Cassie to hear someone else's problems, to pause momentarily the video in her mind of the two of them on the sofa.

Without warning, the spare room door opens and Cassie listens as the hallway floorboards creak under Jack's weight as he goes to the bathroom. He always wakes at 6 a.m., even on Sundays. He's been home, sleeping in the spare room for two weeks now. He said he couldn't justify work paying for a hotel room for any longer than three days. There's a brief silence as he pees before the toilet flushes and the floorboards creak again as he goes back to bed.

Even though he wouldn't be able to hear her, Cassie holds her breath. She promised they'd finally talk today— that she'd listen to what Jack has to say without shouting at him, or slamming the door—but she wants the morning to steady herself first.

Maisie paddles her legs in her basket, lost already in a dream. Cassie lifts herself out of bed and pulls on her jeans and a gray cashmere sweater Charlotte gave her, saying it was too small for her. She uses an elastic to pull her hair into a messy bun. She's decided to grow it long again, like she had it before she met Jack, and she glances down at the little dog and wonders whether Maisie's dreaming about running towards something or whether the little dog dreams of running away.

The shed smells different now that November has arrived; the summer stuffiness has been replaced by the sorrowful, earthy smell of damp leaves. Cassie puts Maisie on the floor and offers her a cushion so she can carry on sleeping, but Maisie stands rigid in the middle of the shed, back slightly raised, her tail stiff and unwagging, her eyebrows plump with confusion.

Cassie flicks the two floor lights in the shed and turns the space heater on, just for a few minutes.

"Go on, Maisie," Cassie says, looking at the cushion, before finally the little dog, nails clicking against the wood chip floor—the dog equivalent of walking on tiptoes—moves slowly over to her temporary bed.

Cassie blows into her hands as she sits on the swivel chair—Mike's old office chair—and looks at the thirty-odd canvases that fill the room like a colorful crowd. Two

242

days ago she pulled them out of the attic where Jack stored them and arranged them in the shed. They're all her mum's work, an assortment of different sized canvases, and they all feature Cassie in some way. Cassie standing tiny next to a London bus; Cassie about five years old in a ballet tutu; a still life of Cassie's crumpled Doc Martens, titled, "Cas's boots." About half of them feature a figure in a khaki-colored coat, looking at Cassie. She used to think he looked sinister, but now she can see her mum painted him with love, a single black line for his gently smiling mouth. Maybe at some point April tried to tell Cassie who he was, but Cassie probably just skipped away, consumed by her own life. There were so many things she'd never know.

Her phone buzzes in her pocket. She looks at it. It's another message from Nicky. A familiar hollow feeling, like grief, settles over her, before she shakes it away and deletes Nicky's message without looking at it and turns her phone off. She knows it'll be just like the emails and the voicemails, begging Cassie to speak to her, to let her explain. Cassie only replied once requesting Nicky delete her number, not contact her again, but she doesn't even respect Cassie enough to do that.

She'll go into town next week to change her number, and she should set herself up a new email too; the first few steps towards the new Cassie, even though she doesn't know herself yet who that person might be.

She stands and lifts her own easel into the middle of the space; she sketched in pencil some of the outlines yesterday on the large white canvas. She'll paint what she sees before her, a little homage to her mum's work, to their

life together, and a preparation for the new life she'll share
with her tiny secret.

Maisie starts to gently snore. Cassie moves quickly as
she prepares her paints; she doesn't want to think too
much. After smearing the tip in a violent red, she picks up
her paintbrush and starts to paint great slicing cuts across
the canvas.

She doesn't know how long she's been painting for when
Maisie lifts her head towards the door and a soft, brief
knock follows.

"Cas?"

Cassie rests her paintbrush. The door starts to open
slowly and she says, "Give me a sec." She stands quickly,
and the feet of the easel wobble as she slides it against the
floor so it faces away from the door. It feels too intimate
now for Jack to see what she's painting.

He's nudged the door open a few inches and a French
press of Guinness-black coffee floats around the door.

"I thought you might like one of these."

She pulls the door open. Jack, in his dark blue bathrobe,
lowers his arm holding the coffee. She blinks at him, aware
suddenly that her eyes still feel pillowy, her face swollen
from another sleepless night. She pulls her hair out of its
little bun, and nods. He's slightly more grizzled than
normal—he reminds her of someone but she can't quite
think who—but apart from the stubble, he looks just the
same, as though the last three weeks haven't happened at
all. He hands her a mug, half full with warmed (not hot!)
milk, just the way she likes it. They don't say anything as
she holds the mug and he pours her coffee.

"Thanks," she says then.

"How's it going in here?" he asks. He glances over her shoulder; she used to love showing him her work.

"Yeah, fine, fine."

He nods, and his eyes dart back to her, his head dropping a little, like a wilting flower.

"Cas, I was hoping we could talk this morning if that's OK with you?"

She winces. She wishes she could turn off Jack and his pleas for forgiveness, cut him out of her life, just like she has with Nicky. She knows the chat she's promised him will fix the mood for the whole day, that it'll be almost impossible for her to get her head back into this sweet numb space.

"Give me a couple of hours?"

He nods and takes a step back, and says, "OK, shall we say ten then?"

She nods, vaguely, "OK, ten." She pulls her foot away, so the door shuts in his face before he can turn away from her.

At 10:15 a.m. she opens the shed door. Fallen autumnal leaves stick to her boots as she walks across the wet lawn towards the kitchen. Maisie, more awake now, jogs behind her.

Jack's already sitting at the kitchen table when she enters, the Sunday papers before him. His eyes flicker up to the clock on the kitchen wall, and she notices with a small flash of satisfaction that he's sucking his cheeks and his neck looks tense. He's nervous. Good.

She hasn't had any breakfast, and it's starting to make her feel queasy, so she opens the fridge and finds a Tupperware from Charlotte. She puts a chocolate muffin on a small plate. Jack folds away the papers and she sits down opposite him.

"OK," she says, picking at the muffin with her thumb and forefinger. "Ready." She looks up at him, and he tries to smile at her, to soften her, but she looks back down at her muffin. She'll cry if she smiles back and she doesn't want to be the one to cry again.

He breathes out.

"Cas, we have to talk about this. This can't go on."

She nods, tries to blink the saltiness from her eyes, and looks up at him.

"OK, how do you propose we do that?"

"I want to tell you everything from my side again, and then I want you to figure out if you can forgive me."

"You said you'd already told me everything, about how lonely you felt, how it's my fault for spending time with Jonny, the miscarriage, you working so hard, that you'd given in when Nicky, the person I used to call my sister, forced herself on you in some sort of weird jealousy trip against me."

Cassie can feel the anger heating her already, rising quickly through her body to her head like mercury in a thermometer.

"Cassie, please. We're never going to get anywhere unless you actually listen to me."

She breathes out. He's right, of course. She knows she's being obstructive, but the truth is, she's still too angry, and there's a part of her that, it turns out, really relishes being angry; it's so much clearer than sadness.

She balls crumbs from her muffin together on her plate and nods.

"OK," she says, looking up at him. He's leaning forward towards her, hands clasped together on the table. "OK, you're right."

He breathes out, fully emptying his lungs before taking a deep breath and starting to talk.

"Nicky called me at lunch, said she was coming earlier to surprise you. I thought it was a bit weird, but she said she wanted to make supper for you, have it ready when you got home like she used to. There weren't any taxis so she called me when she got to the station. I'd had another shitty day and felt like I was going to implode if I didn't have a break. So I thought I'd pick her up, take her home and do some work while she did whatever she wanted to do in the kitchen for you."

"But then she gave you a beer and you just couldn't control yourself."

"No, Cas. Come on, you said you'd listen. Look, it felt good just to talk to someone, like releasing pressure. I never thought running the company would be like this; I knew I'd be busy but the stress isn't about the workload. I'm responsible for other people's families now. If we don't succeed I have to let people go. My dad never did that once in his whole career, did you know that? Then of course we lost the baby and I felt I shouldn't feel so sad about it, had no right when it must have been so much harder for you, but you didn't talk to me about it, you talked to Jonny." He pauses, rubs his face with his hands. "She didn't say anything. She just listened to me and then she kissed me.

"I promise you, Cassie, we only kissed that one time. It never went further."

"That's not how it looked."

"Cassie, please, it was all so quick. One minute I was saying how much I missed us, you and me, missed feeling like a team, then the next minute she was kissing me and then I saw you and my heart died."

"Sorry for interrupting you."

Jack knows better than to challenge her sarcasm.

"Nicky's jealous of you, Cas. I'll bet she always has been."

"How the fuck can she be jealous of me? No dad, no mum, only a fucking weirdo stepdad and now, thanks to her, a fucking cheat for a husband."

Jack props his elbows on the table, rakes his fingers through his hair, and says, "Oh god, Cas, please don't say that, I know you're angry, you have every right to be, but I'm terrified you're going to throw everything we have away because of this stupid mistake."

Cassie slaps both her palms down on the table as if she needs to wake Jack up.

"She was my best friend, Jack. My best fucking friend."

His hands still hold onto his hair and he starts shaking his head.

"I know, Cas, I know, but you have to forgive me." He wipes his eyes.

"No, I don't."

He looks up at her, his eyes stormy.

"Come on, Cas, don't destroy our life because of one stupid slip-up."

"I haven't destroyed anything," she replies, feeling the mercury inside her soar, but then he looks up at Cassie, his eyes contoured in red, and she realizes how alone they both are.

"Look, do you want me to stay in the office for a while?"

"Why don't you stay at your mum's?" she says, but she knows the answer already.

He's back to shaking his head again.

"You know I can't tell her about all this; it'd upset her too much. You promised she didn't have to know."

Cassie knows he's right of course; Charlotte would be devastated, more than even Jack knows, if she knew her beloved son had done exactly what Mike did to Charlotte. No, she couldn't bear hurting Charlotte like that.

"I won't say anything to Charlotte," she says, feeling Jack's eyes as they pull up to her face, "and you can stay here but I really want you to give me space for the next few days, OK?"

Jack nods and splutters a small thanks, a grateful smile playing across his lips.

Cassie pushes the half-eaten muffin away. It tastes bitter; the chocolate roils around her stomach like dirty washing.

"And I think we should focus on getting through Christmas and everything and assess in the New Year." She'll be about twelve weeks by then, and the baby will be safer. She'll have to tell Jack then, make a decision about her and her child's future.

Jack nods, a faint smile cracking his face.

"That's good to hear, Cas, really, so good to hear," before he adds, his voice slipping into poorly concealed jealousy, "I'm assuming you've told Jonny all about this?"

Cassie looks at her husband who now seems so ordinary, so much smaller somehow, than the man she remembers marrying.

"Jack, it's none of your business what I choose to tell my friend."

"I just thought maybe we could keep it between us."

Cassie laughs at him, but it doesn't feel good. It burns her throat.

"I hope you're fucking joking, Jack."

He goes back to rubbing his face again and suddenly, without knowing she would, she says, "I just realized."

He looks at her to keep talking.

"This morning, when you brought me coffee, you reminded me of someone and I couldn't place who it was but now I know exactly who I was thinking of."

Jack, anticipating another attack says, "Let me guess, I reminded you of a fucking idiot?"

Cassie smiles. "Well yes, obviously," she says, but then she shakes her head, almost flirtatious, before a coolness curls itself around her heart again, and she realizes she's completely serious. "You reminded me of your dad."

Jack's face drops, heavy as a stone, and suddenly she wishes she could pull Jack towards her, pull the words she just said out of his ear, and bury her face in his chest, tell him she didn't mean it, bring him back to safety.

"Why? Why do you say that?" he asks. The lines around his eyes narrow in pain and Cassie notices a flicker, a recognition, pass behind them and she thinks, not for the first time, that at some level he knows about Mike, who his dad really was: a liar who broke his promise to Charlotte every time he booked a hotel room, every time he unbuckled his belt.

"Just because you look like him more now, with the stubble, that's all," Cassie says.

She shrugs and stands up from the table. Jack stands as well, mirroring her, Maisie in her basket raises her head and Cassie knows Jack's sadness is morphing, curdling into something more familiar and dangerous.

"You can't say something like that and just walk away," he says, walking towards her in two quick steps. He tries to grab her arm but Cassie's moved away from him, and he can't reach her.

"Jack, calm down," she says, turning towards the sink. "I'm just getting a glass of water."

"What do you know about my dad?" He follows her around the kitchen island, vying for attention.

"Jack, all I said is that you remind me of Mike, or photos I've seen of him, that's all."

"Yeah, but why are you bringing him up now, when we're talking about all this? It just seems weird."

Cassie runs the tap for a moment, puts her finger in the water to check the temperature. What if she told Jack what Charlotte said, about Mike's affairs, she wonders. He seems halfway there himself already; maybe it's time for him to know the truth, maybe that would either save them or finally drop the guillotine that hangs over their marriage. But then she thinks of Charlotte; she's spent the last twenty years lovingly preserving Mike's memory for Jack's sake. Cassie may know the truth about Mike, but she also knows it isn't her story to tell. She puts the glass under the tap.

"Stop fucking ignoring me!"

Jack pulls Cassie's forearm towards him and the glass she's holding hits the side of their enamel sink and a large shard snaps away from the edge and bites into her hand.

She drops the glass in the sink, the water still running. A tiny bloom of blood flowers by Cassie's thumb.

Jack takes a step back.

"Shit, Cas, are you OK?" He hands her some kitchen roll, but she shakes her head and sucks the little cut instead. It fills her mouth, the metallic zing of blood.

"Cas, sorry, it was an accident."

Still keeping her lips to the small cut she nods at him before pulling away. He's never grabbed her in anger before. The cut's tiny, the bleeding already stopped. She holds her hand away from Jack so he can't see and says, "I'm fine, Jack, I'm fine . . ."

"Are you sure? Let me see." He tries to take her hand but she's backing away from him.

"Please don't fuss about it, Jack. Just let me go back to my painting like you promised, OK?"

She doesn't look at him again, leaving him to clean up the shattered glass, and she walks back out towards the garden.

The shed door bangs behind her and she catches a movement in the little mirror by the door, her own reflection startles her, weird as a stranger walking too close behind her. She stops to stare at herself, the light gray sweater, her blond hair already below her shoulders, unbrushed but still so straight. Like a light on its dimmest setting, the woman in the mirror looks ready to fade away completely. She looks like Charlotte. She flicks her head forward, rakes her fingers through her hair again and again. She pulls off Charlotte's sweater, and slaps her face between her hands to bring some color to her cheeks. She flicks herself back up. The woman who looks back at her now is scruffier, less composed, her eyes smeared with old mascara, her hair sticking up at angles like a distressed clown. She smiles at herself because she sees April again, her brave mum, and she realizes how long she's been away, and how much she's missed her.

19

Alice

I pretend to still be asleep when I feel David get out of bed. I'm working a night shift tonight, so there's no urgency to leave our warm bed. David starts running a bath; I can smell my posh bath oil, which I know he hates, so the bath must be for me. I winch open one eye and he smiles and kisses me.

"Hop in," he says. "I'm going to make some breakfast."

The bath is a little too hot. I'm still cautious enough to heed some old midwife stories, so I add some cold before sliding in, feeling the water encase me, holding me in amniotic warmth. My belly rises a little above the water; I'm almost nine weeks now. Being busy has had its advantages. I wonder if Cassie had to pretend she was off booze, and how she explained her early pregnancy tiredness away.

I make a little wave of water and watch it glide over my belly. My pregnancy (it feels too dangerous to think of it as "a baby") is always on my mind but in a subtler way than ever before, like a secret when the keeping of it is more satisfying than sharing. I listen to David whistling and clinking mugs and plates in the kitchen and I think, maybe now, this morning, is the time to let him know. I could reassure him that this is the best it's ever felt, that this time it's different, and try and make him believe it will be different.

But when I put my bathrobe on and join him in the kitchen and watch him make coffee, he seems so unencumbered— smiles and laughter come easily to him—and I know how that will change if I tell him. He'll grow shadowy, a fear will settle around us like fine, thick dust, a fear neither of us can express because to talk about it out loud might jinx us.

The last time it happened, we hardly spoke to each other for a month. I imagined us like cartoon characters, sad stick people with a black cloud hanging over each of our heads, the words "what is the point?" written inside.

So instead of saying anything, I kiss him on the lips. A news program on Radio 4 runs through the headlines. At the end of a bulletin about the latest political scandal they play the clip I've heard countless times already. Jack's rounded, deep voice asking for privacy during this "most difficult time."

I played it to David for the first time last night; he said Jack sounded like a character from an afternoon radio play. I didn't tell David I knew what he meant; instead I said it was the stress making Jack's voice vibrato, stretching the pauses in his speech. I don't know why I defended him. Maybe because I still want to be wrong, I want Cassie's baby to have one healthy, free parent.

David changes the radio station, and Jack's voice is replaced by the clear notes from a piece of piano music. David wants me here, fully here, with him this morning. I have to be fair; I have to try. He's laid out croissants, prosciutto, melon cut into little pieces, along with freshly squeezed orange juice.

"If we weren't already married, I'd think you were about to propose," I say, pulling out a chair, and picking up a piece of melon with my fingers.

"Shit." David smacks his hand to his forehead. "We're already married, aren't we?"

I make a "you're an idiot" face and pick up a croissant.

"Sorry," I say, pouring us both some orange juice, "I know work has taken over recently."

David sits opposite me, takes a sip of juice and says, "It's fine, Ali. I get it, it's important." Around a mouthful of ham he asks, "So what's the latest then? Press still sniffing about?"

The buttery croissant melts in my mouth. "It's easing off a bit now." I look at the radio. "They're playing repeats." If they were playing the full interview, Jack would be talking now about how Cassie and he enjoyed living in such a close-knit community, how grateful he is for all the support.

"And how's Cassie?"

"She's . . . she's just the same really."

Now Jack would be saying how much they wanted to be parents, how Cassie wanted to be a mum.

David frowns at me. "Alice, what is it? What's on your

mind?" He knows—of course he knows—that there's something I'm not telling him.

I force myself to turn the radio station off in my head.

"There's just some stuff I keep thinking about."

"Like what?"

I might not be able quite yet to tell him about our baby, I think, but I can tell him about Cassie at least.

"When Cassie first came in, Charlotte, her mother-in-law, brought in a bag of pajamas and stuff for her."

David nods for me to keep talking.

"I found a letter, from Cassie to Jack, saying she wanted a break, some time away."

"OK."

"She'd taken her engagement and wedding rings off. I think she was running away, David."

"Seriously, Alice?"

It all sounded so paranoid out loud, not the quiet sense it made in my head.

"I thought she was looking for her dog?" He pauses. "Don't forget how crazy Bob goes when he hears fireworks. A rescue dog in a new home would be really jumpy, and remember when you thought you'd lost your engagement ring?" He gets up, pours himself another coffee.

I'd forgotten about that. I'd left my engagement ring in my jeans pocket when I went swimming one day, and spent the next week pulling the house apart trying to find it. I grab a second croissant.

"And you know, every couple has their tough times, don't they? The fact that she never gave Jack the letter is telling. Maybe she wrote it for catharsis and never meant to give it to him."

My conviction evaporates like a magic trick. I decide not to tell David about Jonny's eyes, how he looked like a man losing someone he loved, or about the gossiping on the ward about paternity.

"Sorry." I shake my head. "I don't know why I'm . . ."

"You're just protective, Ali. Of course you are. It makes total sense; the stakes are even higher with this patient than they are normally. I get it." He hands me a coffee, and I take a sip; it's caffeinated so I put it back on the table.

He sits opposite me again, and crosses his legs. He's moving faster than normal; he's nervous.

I narrow my eyes at him. "Why are you so jumpy?"

He uncrosses his legs and rubs his hands over his cheeks; he's smiling. Something's up, and he's excited about something. Maybe he's got a dream client? Maybe we've finally got enough in our holiday fund for the long trip we're always promising ourselves?

"I've been thinking, Ali . . . I'd really like it if we could fill out the forms for the adoption agency."

Our eyes meet and I look away again immediately; every cell in my body seems to perform a little jump. David keeps talking.

"I know you couldn't think about it before, but that was over a year ago now. Remember, they said the process will take quite awhile, so I just thought I'd fill out the initial form at least, get it off and see what happens."

I picture a row of children before us, David and I pointing to one of them and taking him or her by the hand, to be scanned like at one of those self-checkout machines. We'd bring the child back here to try and make them our child.

What if we didn't bond? What if the child didn't like me? I try and feel the life inside me, to remind myself that none of that will happen; none of it will need to happen.

"Ali, it's just the initial paperwork. I promise, we will not adopt a child unless we are both absolutely certain it's what we want." He curls his palm around my hand. "But we always agreed it could be an option for us."

I nod, smile at him, try to look happy, excited even.

"No, it's a good idea. We should get the paperwork off, get the ball rolling . . ."

David grins at me, and I fold the last of the croissant into my mouth. He kisses me and says, "Love you," as he grabs his keys and leaves for his morning meeting.

I do some admin during the day, eat a sandwich, and in the afternoon try and nap before my night shift, but I can't settle; my mind keeps flicking like a faulty switch to Jack's radio interview. He talked about the close-knit community in Buscombe. I've never been, but Buscombe is only sixteen miles from here. I heard they've got good walks, and I owe Bob a long walk. I look at my watch; I know I should try to nap again if I'm to have any hope of getting through the night. But I'm far too wired to rest. I work out I've got enough time to drive there, back home and on to Kate's in time for my night shift. I tell myself I'll just drive through quickly, see the place Cassie called home, and then find a wood or a field for Bob to have a good run. He clatters to his feet as I lift his lead off its hook by the back door.

Most of the journey is on anonymous four-lane roads, past fast-food shops and cinemas, but eventually they trickle away. Following signs, I turn off the main road and the world seems to open up, like a large powerful lung taking a deep breath; the earth seems to have more oxygen out here. Early tufts of emerald seedlings in the fields catch the light like fish scales, and daffodils and snowdrops quiver in the grass banks. I slide my window down; the breeze itself smells green out here, cold and new.

The center of the village is positioned around an open patch of grass called Buscombe Green; large Georgian houses sit around the green like elders around a meeting table, wisteria buds creep around their doorways like waxy whiskers. I can imagine Charlotte walking out of one of these front doors. I drive all the way around the little rectangle, passing five or six shadowy little lanes that could lead to the cottage. My phone has no reception so I can't load my maps; I have no idea where to go from here.

Not wanting to admit to myself I'm lost, I take one of the turnings off the green and am immediately faced by an old 4x4; I'm looking around over my shoulder, wondering how we can pass each other, when its lights flash and I can see that the larger car has already reversed, expertly tucking away into a spot where the lane is a little wider. I drive up slowly and wind my window down. It's a woman, about my age, on her own in the car; there are empty booster seats in the back. She already has her window down so it's easy for me to lean across and ask directions to Steeple Lane. I have to go back to the green, she says, and take the turn just by the pub. She asks where exactly I'm going, but I don't want her to know, so tell her not to worry, I'll know my way from there, and I thank her for her help. As I make a clumsy three-point turn, I wonder if this woman knew Cassie, if they were friends.

Except for the little stream that runs busily along, Steeple Lane looks much like all the other roads around here. The lane itself is narrow and dark, the hedges thick with branches. It's like traveling down an artery. The road opens up after a mile or so, wide enough for two cars to pass, slowly, side by side.

A little wooden sign in the hedge reads "Warning, deep ditch." On my left there's an ancient-looking farmhouse, black beams crisscrossing the house, contrasting with white walls, a couple of scraggly trees in the garden. A sign outside says "Steeple Farm." I remember that Charlotte said Jonny rents one of the farm cottages. I keep going. I don't want to look too closely; he could be there now. I keep going for another mile or so, eventually crossing over the little stream, until the road starts to narrow again and I see a sign on my right: Steeple Cottage. I'm here. This was Cassie and Jack's home.

I can't see the cottage at the end of the drive from here; I have to park my car somewhere on the lane. I pull in close to the side of the lane and tell myself I'll just have a quick look. I just want to see it for a moment, that's all. I wind the window down for Bob and ignore his outraged bark as I lock the door behind me.

The drive to the cottage is surrounded by trees; it's graveled and bends sharply to the left, before opening up in a small circle in front of a light-colored stone cottage. I called the hospital on the drive. Jack, I know, is with Cassie, but I still don't want to be out in the open, so I lean my back against one of the trees that seems to huddle around the cottage as if trying to keep it away from the world.

The cottage is older than I'd imagined and perfectly symmetrical. Two large rectangular windows dominate the ground floor, either side of the stone porch. Two more windows are directly above, where I imagine the bedrooms must be. At the top of the cottage, a round window peers out of the attic, like a Cyclops. Delicate daffodils prettily punctuate the front flower beds, I picture Cassie on her knees planting the bulbs, her hands in the earth. I don't know why, but the image makes me feel lonely for her.

Angry clouds gather overhead, sucking away the light. Sparrows dip and soar and a lone bat dive-bombs for invisible insects. I move towards the house; moss under my feet muffles my steps until I get to the path. Immediately, a security light flashes on and I'm bathed in brightness. Blinded, I forget I'm not doing anything wrong. Suddenly I'm an intruder. The house doesn't want me here. It's spotted me, and its warmth has cooled. I turn away from it, back down the path, my feet too loud on the gravel. The security light is strong on my back, like the presence of the cottage behind me, pushing me away. The trees have changed too, almost black in the approaching night. Their branches look painful, like arthritic hands. Their leaves, disturbed by wind, shake the gossip of my visit to each other. A rabbit leaps across the path a few feet in front of me, flushed out of its hiding place. It looks startled, and I think I do too. I want to run but I'm worried running would expose my fear, and that'd make it worse. I round the end of the cottage path towards my car.

It's not until the car door has clicked shut that I breathe out. Bob's crept onto the passenger seat, and his tail wags.

I feel my heart beating inside my chest; I'm safe now. I pull Bob closer towards me, kiss his head and laugh a little at myself. I've always been good at freaking myself out. As a girl, I'd imagine sharks in a swimming pool or zombies in the wardrobe. Thank God David and I didn't move out here; I'd hear the wind calling my name in no time. I wonder if Cassie ever thought she heard hers whispered through the silver birch trees, if she ever felt loneliness cover her like a cold blanket. I look in my rearview mirror. The cottage is still lit up, like searchlights in a prison. How long do the security lights stay on? Surely they must click off soon.

Bob whines next to me and presses his paws up and down on the front seat, reminding me I promised him a walk. I put the keys in the ignition and drive slowly up the lane, away from the cottage. I pull in after a few hundred yards. It's started to rain a little. I remember the weather forecast said it'd only get worse towards dusk. I'll let Bob out now, just for a quick run, and then dash home to get to Kate's for my shift. Bob bounds straight over me, and leaps down onto the lane as I open my door. I think of Maisie running away and call his name to keep him close but he ignores me. I follow him and call his name again, picking up my pace as I turn a corner.

Bob's spotted someone. He's trotting towards a man in a dark waxy-looking jacket, standing on his own by the side of the lane, next to a small mound of what looks like trash. The man turns towards Bob as Bob parks himself, sitting on his hind legs right in front of the man, chest puffed like a centurion, his tail wiping back and forth against the asphalt. He's straining towards the man, sniffing, led by his nose.

"Oh god! Sorry," I exclaim, breaking into a slow jog to pull Bob away. "Bob!"

But the man's smiling down at him. He's got longish white hair poking out from under his hat, and the nurse in me spots a failing hip in the way he favors his left side. I've seen him before. He was the man who caught my eye outside the hospital. Then he turns his face towards me and I stop, my stomach lurching, because the man is Marcus Garrett and he's smiling at me. He has no idea who I am, and why should he? He strokes Bob's silky head.

"I think he can smell the pastry I got in the village." He chuckles, pointing towards a brown paper bag that pokes out of one of his large pockets.

I stare at him, and Marcus looks up at me again, brow raised, waiting for my answer. I walk closer and grab Bob's collar with one hand, and clear my throat to try and shake the surprise from my voice.

"Oh, pastries are his favorite. My husband and I have a joke that Bob's more pig than dog, don't we, Bobby?" Bob doesn't take his eyes off Marcus's hand as it goes towards the bag in his pocket, breaking off and taking out what looks like half the pastry.

"Mind if I give him a bit?" Marcus asks.

I shake my head and let go of Bob's collar and he lunges greedily, as though he's never been fed, towards the sizeable chunk of beige, glistening pastry.

Marcus keeps smiling as he bends to pat Bob's shoulder, saying, "There's a good lad."

I see that what I thought was trash is actually a small shrine by the side of the road, this unremarkable little patch, with the stream gurgling and hissing like something injured. This is where she fell. The flowers aren't flowers anymore; most have turned to soggy brown mulch. I imagine no one has the heart to throw them away. Marcus follows my gaze and I realize that I'm not in my uniform. To Marcus I'm just a woman walking her dog. I'm free to ask things I normally couldn't.

"That's why you found me here, I'm afraid," he says heavily as though the words themselves have weight as he nods towards the pile of dying flowers.

I steel myself; I can do this. I remind myself I'm lying for Cassie's sake, not for my own benefit.

"Oh god, was there an accident? Someone you knew?"

Marcus shakes his head, as though he wants to shift the thoughts that have settled there. When he talks I recognize the same relief I've seen in hundreds of shocked, wide-eyed relatives I've met at Kate's, longing for comfort, even from a nurse they've never met. Marcus is so desperate; he'll talk to a stranger walking her dog.

"A young woman, a beautiful young woman, my step-daughter, so yes, I knew her," he says. "I knew her," he repeats, as though he needs to confirm the fact to himself.

"Is she going to be OK?"

Marcus shrugs. "I don't know, I really don't know." His voice cracks like a shell.

I let the silence ask my question for me.

"Her husband doesn't let me see her." He turns slightly towards me and looks at me. "I never liked him. He's got a temper, a real temper, on him. They never should have married. He pretended he loves her but he never really knew her, not like me."

The rain makes a pat-pat sound against my coat. I think of Jack, how certain he was that it was Marcus who told the press about Cassie. Hearing Marcus talk so freely, as though he's saying his jumbled thoughts out loud unedited to me, a stranger, I understand now why Jack was suspicious of him.

Marcus breathes out, slowly, by my side.

"So I come here instead to think about her, to feel close to her. You see, I promised my April I'd look after her."

He's staring down into the stream, like he's lost something in the water. I follow his gaze to where Cassie fell. Raindrops fall fatly into the stream, making perfect circles dance on the glass surface of the dark water.

"I used to do this before, you know . . . before the accident. Just kept an eye on her every now and then, just to make sure she was doing OK." Marcus looks up at me quickly.

I ask, "And do you think she was? Doing OK, I mean, before the accident?"

Marcus drops his eyes back towards the lane, and his head droops as if in sympathy with the flowers and I realize he's turning away from me because he's crying.

"She wasn't happy. I remember now. I knew she wasn't happy. I wanted her to know I was there for her, that I'd help her when she realized her mistake."

"What mistake?"

Marcus lifts his head to me, but doesn't wipe the tears from his cheeks as he says, "Marrying that man."

I tense. I don't know why Marcus can't say Jack's name.

"Marcus, who do you think hit her?"

I realize my mistake as soon as I've said his name but Marcus is too emotional, too confused to realize. Instead he turns to me, his eyes darkening.

The raindrops are even heavier now, striking down from the sky like tiny fists as rain turns to ice.

"He always seemed angry with her. I don't think he wanted a wife, I think he wanted freedom. That's why he . . ." Marcus turns to me, his mouth open, as though appalled to see me, listening to him there. "You said my name, just now." His face clouds. "Who are you?"

"No, no, sorry, I . . . you misheard . . ." Shit, shit, shit. But I've lost him.

Marcus shakes his head and starts backing away and he glances up at the sky, as if for guidance to a higher power, as though he thinks his April is there in the clouds. He raises his shoulders to his ears, trying to protect himself from the hail, protect himself from me.

"No, I promise, I'm . . ." but Marcus turns sharply away from me, and I watch as he limps as fast as he can down the lane before I turn back to the pile of flowers, my breath leaving me in thin clouds. Alice, you idiot. Despite the balls of ice that fall from the sky, I feel clammy, too hot in my coat suddenly, as if burnt from meeting Marcus. Something isn't right with Marcus, something more than grief and age.

Bob whines by my feet. We should go back to the car but I need a moment. I look down at the flowers and bend to pick up a photo propped next to a bunch of browning sunflowers.

It's of Cassie, around the time of the Juice-C ad, her face full with youth, and the red-haired woman I saw on

Cassie's Facebook, Nicky Breton. Nicky's turned to look at Cassie; she's smiling at her friend, awed, as though she's close to something celestial. Cassie seems oblivious to the light she casts; she's turned fully towards the camera, smiling as though there could never be anything wrong with the world.

Bob's whine becomes a bark; he starts turning circles in alarm by my feet, appalled by the hailstorm, urgently wanting to feel safe again. I put the photo back against the flowers, trying to shield it from the weather, but it's no good; the photo is hit and flicked by tiny balls of ice. I've never been religious, but standing there, at the place where Cassie was hit, my hope turns fluidly into a prayer and above the hammering of the hailstorm and the swell of my own fear I whisper quickly, "Please, please." I don't know if I'm begging for Cassie or for myself.

I feel my fear creeping up on me again; like eyes on me, it builds up behind me like smoke, and I wonder whether Marcus has left or if he's still watching me like he used to watch Cassie. I shiver. I glance one more time at Cassie's flowers, before I call for Bob and start walking back towards my car. The approaching night feels like dark hands, pushing me away. I want to run, the tarmac iridescent and slick, a pathway to safety before me. A car growls, restless behind me. They haven't turned their lights on. Can they see us? I grab Bob's collar and press us both hard against the bank on the other side of the lane to the stream. Marcus only flicks his lights on as he drives past us. I stare at him, but he keeps his eyes fixed forward, as though he's searching for someone else.

*   *   *

The oil cracks and pops in the pan as I add the chicken thighs, skin side down. Bob sits on his hind legs, chest puffed out, eyes fixed on me. Every now and then he works his chops noisily as if to remind me how very, very starving he is. We both know I'll give in eventually. I move the chicken around in the pan and try and iron out my thoughts.

Marcus isn't well and he keeps turning up without warning. He was there before Cassie had her miscarriage. I know he's been at the hospital, and now, today, again at the place Cassie was hit. My stomach curdles, as I remember what he said, that Jack didn't want to be married, that he wanted freedom. But Marcus was confused, acting strangely. Can I trust him? The noise of the frying meat gets louder, more urgent. Bob, not a fan of strange noises, even if they smell delicious, retreats to his basket in the utility room.

I remember Marcus behind the steering wheel, how he forced us against the side of the lane like a bully, his eyes fixed and unseeing.

My phone starts vibrating on the table, shifting around like an upturned beetle. It's Jess. I hold it in my hand. I'm not sure if I'm in the mood to speak to her; she always knows when something's up and I don't feel like justifying myself. Just as I decide not to answer, a pain like being simultaneously bitten and kicked in the abdomen jolts through me, and I call out, "Oh, Jesus!" as I fall to my knees. The shock sucks the air out of my lungs, my arms fold around my belly, as if all this pain needs is a good, reassuring hug. My right hand, still clutching the phone, smudges against the screen. I must press the answer button because I can hear Jess's voice in miniature, shrunken on the line, asking, "Ali? Ali? Are you there?"

I call out again as another clash of pain rips through me. It feels like I'm being eaten alive. I can hear Jess calling for me—"What's happening Ali? Are you there?"—and I let out a groan that becomes Jess's name and I look down at the phone, and with a shaky finger press the speaker button. My kitchen is filled suddenly with all the life in Jess's kitchen. There's music in the background, something with Spanish guitars. Tim must be on the phone or have someone over because his laugh, deep, resonant and usually so reassuring, echoes through the receiver and into my ear.

Ha! Ha! Ha!

Now it sounds mocking.

Ha! Ha! Ha!

"Ali? Alice?" and then Jess pauses and says, away from the receiver, "For God's sake, Tim, will you shut up? Something's wrong with Ali," and I let out another moan as the pain starts to feast deeper inside.

Tim always listens to Jess; the laughing stops immediately and the Spanish guitars are snuffed out as well. Bob comes to see what's the problem. His black seal-head hangs low. He sniffs me uncertainly. I'm frightening him; all this noise is frightening him.

"Ali, is it happening again?" I was at Jess's house when I had the sixth one; she recognizes the groans. All I can do is grunt confirmation and try and whisper, "It's OK, Bob. It's OK."

Refusing to hang up, Jess calls David from Tim's phone to tell him he needs to go home. He'll be a little over an hour she tells me in a breathy voice she must think is controlled, reassuring. Jess wants to call an ambulance but I yell out, "No, no ambulance," and she knows I mean it, she wants to drive over, but it'll take her almost as long as David at this time and, besides, I know this battle and I need it to be a private one. Between gasps of air, I persuade her she's more help on the phone.

The only clear thought I have is that David mustn't find me squashed and wailing on the kitchen floor. It'd upset him too much. So slowly, like a maimed animal, I pull myself up on the cutlery drawer. Bob's tail starts cautiously wagging. Still bent over double and now holding the phone towards my stomach so Jess's voice is muffled, I stagger, stooped over like an old woman, and shuffle to the spitting stove. The meat is ruined, cooked through from one side, the skin carbonized. Tiny sprays of fat leap from the pan and sting my face. I could weep at the waste, but there's no time. I know I don't have long to get to our bathroom before another spasm. I turn the stove off and using the wall for guidance I pull myself upstairs. It starts again just as I get into our bedroom, forcing me to bend over as my abdomen is ripped to shreds, but it doesn't quite wind me and I make it to the bed, tossing the phone down on the duvet, Jess reminding me in an authoritative voice to stay calm. I sit on the edge of the bed and look at my feet as I puff air in and out. Labor breath comes instinctively even though I never made it that far . . . never had the lessons.

After a few minutes, I think I'm strong enough and stand again, my body shaking like a taut string, my skin slick with sweat, and, grabbing the phone, I stagger faster this time, more urgent, to the drugs cabinet in the bathroom.

I kept some strong painkillers from last time, as if I knew in my marrow this would happen again. I swallow a couple of pills and then feel the first falling away deep inside me, a detachment in that deep middle-belly space, the horrifyingly familiar sensation of being turned inside out. I manage to sit on the toilet as the blood comes quickly and focus on the pain that in a few months would have been happy, welcome pain, but now is just an agonizing reminder of a truth I've refused so many times and I hold my head and I let myself cry.

This is how David finds me, hunched on the toilet, my face puffy with sorrow. He doesn't ask any questions, not now. He sees the pills, which are now kindly distorting, softening everything for me.

He picks up my phone. Jess is still on the line; he tells her he's home, that I will be OK. She reminds him, like I asked her to, to call Kate's to tell them I won't make my night shift before he hangs up. He cleans me, puts me in pajamas, all the while he's telling me it's going to be OK, that he's here now, that he loves me.

He carries me to bed and lies behind me, spooning me, and it's only then I feel his body tense and release, tense and release, as he sobs, and I want to turn to hold him but the pills are too strong, and I let go and fall deeply into a violent, chemical sleep.

When I wake, there's just a twisted strudel of bed sheets next to me. I sit up.

"Hi, Ali," David says gently. He's pulled the armchair over towards the bed. His face is swollen from lack of sleep. I feel as if I drank two bottles of heavy red wine the night before, a headache like a gathering storm pounds just behind my eyes. The cramps have quietened to dull thumps in my lower abdomen. My tongue is sticky, so I reach for the water but David intercepts.

"How are you feeling?" he asks as he hands me a freshly poured glass.

I find I can't answer, and just gently raise my shoulders, shaking my head, I don't know how I'm feeling; I haven't been able to place myself just yet.

"Why didn't you tell me, Ali?" His face messy with lines and confusion.

"That's what I've been trying to figure out all night—why you didn't tell me. I . . ." He hangs his head.

I feel my heart crack as he starts shaking his head. I move forward, across the bed, and put my hand in his curls, trying to soothe him as best I can, when the pain, like a memory from last night, ripples through me, and all I can say is, "I'm sorry, David, I'm so sorry."

He moves to sit on the bed. I fold around his torso, and he wipes his eyes with his thumb and forefinger.

"I've been thinking, I'll have a vasectomy to stop this from happening. I can't go through it again, watch you suffering, me totally incapable of doing anything to really help . . ."

Neither of us says anything as we grip onto each other and I find that, instead of the familiar sense of loneliness where my hope used to rest, I can feel something else there, a feeling of possibility for change, a spark of something different.

Moving away from this terrible routine scares me less

than being locked in it, and although it feels blasphemous to even think, I realize I'm ready to wave a white flag, ready to surrender to the truth that my body can't carry our child.

We stay in bed for the whole day, taking it in turns to cry and soothe, until David falls asleep again by my side, and I listen to the rise and fall of his breath and hope for sleep to come.

20

Frank

Lucy's kept her promise; she's visited every afternoon since my first scan four days ago. Today she's curled up in my visitor's chair chewing her fingernails, her feet tucked underneath her. She's flicking through a glossy manual for a rehabilitation center in Birmingham.

"It says here, Dad, that they've got a special swimming pool to help residents regain muscle strength." She looks at me. "Ooo eerr," she says, like I'm headed to a decadent spa. I imagine people like me floating around like jellyfish.

I'm trying to blink twice for "no" because I can't blink "never, ever put me in a bloody swimming pool" just yet, when Lizzie approaches the bed.

"Hi, Lucy. Hi, Frank," she says. "This is Dr. Sarah Marsh, our senior speech therapist. She's going to introduce you both to the blinking board I was telling you about."

An older woman with wiry gray hair and glasses that look like they're about to slide off her nose and fall on me smiles down.

"Hello, Mr. Ashcroft. May I call you Frank?" she asks.

I blink once and she shakes Lucy's hand.

I zone in and out of Dr. Marsh's instructions. The blinking board is a large piece of plastic with the alphabet divided lengthways into different color bands. Red for letters from A–D, yellow for letters from E–H and so on. Dr. Marsh gets really excited when she tells us that soon Lucy can personalize the board for me, adding words I commonly use so I can just look at them without having to blink through the whole bloody board.

"I hope you don't mind swear words!" Lucy says brightly.

Dr. Marsh frowns and says, "Let's just try, shall we?"

She positions the board right in front of my face and in an overly loud voice that makes my skull vibrate she calls out, "Red."

I blink.

"Right, so that means his letter is in the first row of letters," Dr. Marsh says in a normal voice to Lucy before booming back at me, "A."

I blink.

"A. So we know he wants his word to start with 'A.'"

I get over excited and screw up the next letter, blinking too soon on "K" instead of "L" so the next letter "I" makes no sense.

"A, K, I?" Dr. Marsh sounds uncertain.

"Aki, Dad? I can't think of any word that begins with Aki . . ."

They both turn to me, confused, worried perhaps that I have lost it after all.

I try a double blink for "no" but I'm too exhausted so I just let my eyelids glide shut.

"I think it's knackered him out," Lucy says.

"It's a big step." Dr. Marsh sounds disappointed although she's pretending not to be. "Best to take it slowly. Today was just a little taste."

Dr. Marsh leaves and I hear Luce mutter, "Aki, A.K.I," quietly to herself a couple of times.

In the blackness, I worry that Lucy will question whether I am getting well or not, that she'll start to think my blinking was just muscle reflex after all.

But then a doctor I don't know comes to the bed and tells us a recent brain scan was encouraging, that there seem to be some small shards of light in the pulpy mess in my head.

There's something very intimate about having a brain examination. I hope they're not too accurate; I'd hate to think what they'd see. I imagine the white coats wincing over the results: "Oh dear, look, purple there for regret and those big flashes of red? Rage. Frank Ashcroft is not a peaceful man."

Lucy gives me a peck and says, "I'll be back tomorrow, Dad. We can try again with the board then. It's so exciting to think you might say a word soon!" I hear her smiling, a big smile to egg me along, to keep our spirits up.

I listen to her walk away and wonder where Alice is. She's been gone for three days now. I overheard Carol telling Lizzie it was "one of her migraines," which is news to me; Alice never said she got migraines. My plan is to sort this "AKI" mess out, to blink what I obviously meant to blink, that'll cheer her up, make her forget her migraine, if that is what's wrong.

The last four days have been busy. I try to keep my eyes open now as I'm wheeled to my daily scan. I need to get used to people staring at me. Even after all of this, I'm surprised to find I still care what strangers think. When I'm not being scanned or with Lucy, I'm being prodded and pushed by an energetic physical therapist, or my pupils are investigated by some visiting doctor. The main difference is that now they tell me where they're going to prod or poke instead of just cracking on like before. Small mercies. They ask me before every session "How are you, Frank?" which is bloody annoying because I'm still strictly a "yes" or "no" man.

Just as things have heated up for me, they have cooled for my neighbor. The reporters, it seems, have mostly lost interest, for now anyway. They're pointing their cameras and microphones towards a local radio host who it turns out is overly fond of young girls.

Jack comes everyday. He sits by his wife's side, plays her music, calming classical stuff mainly, or reads her the newspaper. He only reads political and sports updates out loud for her. All the war and misery he keeps quietly to himself. I'm grateful for that.

Charlotte comes everyday, too. She likes to keep herself busy. She files Cassie's nails, washes her hair, but sometimes she just waits—hands poised over Cassie's stomach and her eyes fixed on Cassie's face—for any sign from the baby. She cried the first time she felt the baby kick. They're so consumed with their Cassie, I don't think they even know I'm here; I could turn bright purple with pink spots overnight and they wouldn't notice. Fair enough.

The lazy February sun has long gone and I've had a sleep since afternoon rounds, so I reckon it's early evening when Alice arrives. She pauses by Cassie's curtain before coming to me. My head is tilted forward so all I can see is the thin outline of my useless legs, but holding both sides of my head, she pulls my gaze up so we look directly into each other and I know as soon as I see her; it wasn't a migraine.

She's gaunt, as though she's been emptied drip by drip of spark, her Alice-ness. She looks me straight in the eye and I see her eyes swell behind her eyelids. She bites the skin that peels painfully away from her bottom lip, looks deep into me and shakes her head a couple of times and that's all it takes. I know. I know it's happened again. She wipes an escaping tear from her cheek and lowers her eyes for a second before we both hear the rattle of Cassie's curtain opening.

"Alice, you're back?" Charlotte asks. She's visiting later than normal this evening.

I watch Alice's face change in an instant; Alice the professional is back. She turns toward Charlotte, and all I can see now is the back of Alice's head as she walks towards the older woman.

"Charlotte, hi, yes, sorry. I've been off with a really terrible migraine, I'm afraid."

Charlotte's hair falls to the side as she tilts her head slightly, listening to Alice.

"Doing much better now though," Alice continues, "so

I thought I'd just pop in quickly, see how everyone is, then I'll be back for my shift tomorrow morning."

Alice's voice is clipped, efficient. I hear a small warning to Charlotte not to ask questions.

Charlotte's eyes narrow slightly. I don't think she believes Alice, but she seems to have picked up on the warning in Alice's voice; she knows not to pry.

"Well, make sure you don't overstretch yourself, Alice. I was supposed to leave a little while ago, actually, but the little one's been so busy tonight. I've just been standing there feeling her kick. Honestly, it's amazing how much energy she has. Come and have a feel."

Alice follows behind Charlotte to Cassie's bedside but she keeps her hands laced behind her back, away from Cassie's baby. I know she means well, but I wish Charlotte would leave Alice alone.

"Actually, Charlotte, I'm really not planning on staying long. I . . . I'm still not really myself, so I think . . ."

Charlotte stares at Alice. Her eyes narrow again, like Alice is a puzzle she's trying to work out. Then she looks down at her hands, resting on the top of Cassie's bed, and I think Charlotte knows there's something else wrong. Maybe like me she's seen the new absence in Alice, the loss in her.

Charlotte nods and looks up at Alice, tries a small reassuring smile, and says, "Of course, Alice, I understand. You should go home and get some rest. Get that husband of yours to make you supper."

Alice nods, and raises a small but empty smile to Charlotte.

"You're going to stay for a bit longer?" she asks Charlotte. "I'll let Paula know you're here."

Charlotte nods. "I bought that cream I was telling you about, the one that helps skin stretch? I think I'll just pop some on her now and then I'll head home as well."

"Well, I'll see you at some point tomorrow," Alice says. She casts a final expert glance over Cassie, her eyes resting on her bump for just a second. Her smile fades as soon as she turns away from them. She closes the curtains most of the way around them but she wants to get away quickly now and she doesn't pause to fully close the gap. She only looks up at me quickly to smile goodnight.

My heart breaks for her; her footsteps sound so lonely as she walks away.

I try and become interested in what Charlotte's doing, to distract myself from the terrifying free fall of Alice's loss. I watch as she takes off her coat and lays it carefully on the visitor's chair. From her handbag she takes out a white tub, and starts picking at the seal until the lid finally releases with a little sigh. She pulls the sheets carefully off Cassie, bunching them around her ankles. Cassie's legs look thin, the sort of thinness old people have when their muscles wither like overripe fruit. Charlotte lifts her nightdress, exposing Cassie's swollen stomach. I haven't seen the bump like this for a while; Cassie's tummy button has popped out like a small, juicy grape. Her stomach is impressive, dwarfing Cassie's form. It looks bigger next to her shrinking muscles, as though it has its own presence, as if the baby's here already, which in a way, I suppose it is.

Charlotte doesn't sit in the visitor's chair. She stands above Cassie as she dips her hand into the jar and pulls out a large handful of white cream. She warms it in her hands before she starts smearing it on Cassie's stomach in fluid, round motions, as if icing a cake. She keeps her eyes fixed on her work as she looks down at her hands and Cassie's stomach, both of which are now covered in cream. She starts muttering, her voice taut, lower than I've heard it before.

"Oh, my little Freya," she says, smiling down at Cassie's bump. But then her hands stop moving and for a brief moment they become tense. "I want you to know your daddy never wanted any of this to happen." She looks up briefly at Cassie's face, and the warmth in her voice cools to a hiss. "I tried to warn her." And then she starts moving her hands again in small circles, Cassie's stomach as innocent as a shelled boiled egg, white and glistening with the cream.

21

Cassie

Jack, handsome in his tuxedo, a dark red silk scarf splashed over his shoulders, opens the taxi door for Cassie and then, with a flourish of his hand, offers Charlotte the passenger seat. As Jack lowers himself next to Cassie, Cassie sees Charlotte smiling at her son in the side mirror, proud of the fun, chivalrous man she's raised.

This year, the theme of the Clarks' annual New Year's Party is "The Roaring Twenties." Cassie had forgotten to do anything about an outfit, so now she's wearing a strange assortment of clothes that never should be worn together: a black velvet dress she bought at a second-hand shop ten years ago; red, satin gloves from Charlotte; and her raincoat in case it's still raining when they walk home later. The synthetic material of her dress lies scratchily against her skin, and she can feel her tights already slipping down her hips, making an uncomfortable web of fabric between her thighs. She wishes for the hundredth time that she hadn't agreed to go to the party, that she could stay at home under a blanket, warm and safe with Maisie. But she'd promised Jack in a weak moment that she'd go, so here she was. Christmas had been a slog. Guilt had turned Jack into a cheesy sitcom version of himself. He'd been cloying for weeks, acting like he couldn't do enough for her. He'd bought her an expensive red coat for Christmas they couldn't afford and she hadn't really liked. He'd cleaned the house and tried to give her massages. He'd gotten her to pose for photos that he posted to Facebook, and typed "beautiful" next to them. Judging from the comments, no one seemed to have noticed how much effort Cassie had put into holding up her smile. People only see what they want.

Cassie doesn't know this version of Jack. Is this his way of covering his back, so, if their marriage dissolves, the world will believe he did everything he could to make it work? Cassie doesn't know anymore. She has no idea what's going on behind those amber eyes, what he's capable of.

In the back of the taxi, Cassie's phone buzzes in the pocket of her raincoat. She still hasn't got round to changing her number. She looks at the message and sees the first line reads "Happy New."

"For fuck's sake," Cassie whispers under her breath as she deletes Nicky's unread message. Her mother-in-law hasn't seemed to notice how forced and unnatural things are between her and Jack. She turns in her seat to look at Cassie, frowning slightly at Cassie's swearing.

"What a treat to be out with my two favorite women," Jack says, leaning over to pat Cassie's knee, in a strange matey way, but Charlotte doesn't notice. In the side mirror, Cassie sees her smile at her son again.

Cassie imagines what she'd say if her mother-in-law wasn't in the car with them. Maybe: "Oh, we're your favorites tonight, are we?" or, "Where does Nicky rank?", or similar. Instead, she moves her knee away from Jack's hand and, the taxi driver says, "Off we go" and as they start to pull away, a premature firework bangs and Cassie's heart tenses as she hears Maisie bark in alarm from inside the cottage.

The Clarks' farm is arranged around a flagstone yard, the huge tiles uneven as bad teeth. The family gave up rearing livestock over a decade ago and have since turned the old barn into a bed and breakfast. Many layers of pastel paint haven't been able to cover the rust-and-silo smell that seems to flow through the arteries of the old farmhouse. By the back door there's a huge collection of muddy welly boots, and also a stack of old newspapers, Cassie has no idea what for. She doesn't recognize the dozen or so guests who have congregated in the kitchen glinting in cheap art deco headdresses and hastily bought stick-on moustaches. They look like they've arrived at the wrong party next to the decades-worn pine table and farmhouse dresser.

Jack and Cassie are each handed a glass of sparkling wine by the flustered hostess who has forgotten they came last year, just back from their honeymoon. She points them towards the door through to the barn before she turns to show a young man dressed as a sailor the way to the toilet. The atmosphere is charged, as if everyone has been shaken up like soda in a can over Christmas, and, tonight, the final festive night, the metal ring is being pulled slowly back.

Couples and families, bloated and wired by togetherness, look at Jack and Cassie as they walk into the main barn with a blend of recognition and solidarity.

God, is that us? Cassie wonders. Do we look like that to them?

She takes a sip of sparkling wine and thinks they probably look worse.

A couple's loneliness together is vivid. It screams, especially loud to those who know it themselves. Cassie knows that now. Fast jazz vibrates out of huge black speakers. Cassie feels the hairs on her arm rise as the music sends jarring vibrations through her skin. She's always hated jazz; it makes her feel edgy.

Jack finishes his sparkling wine in just a few gulps. Cassie watches his brow soften as she hands him her glass, pretending it's too sweet for her. She knows he'll take it as a good sign, that things may finally be thawing between them.

He turns to her, holds her wrist.

"Cassie," he whispers, "I just want to say that I really appreciate you coming tonight. I want more than ever to make a fresh start. I promise I'll make everything up to you."

"The lovely Jensens!"

They both turn to face Martha, an old friend of Jack's who grew up just outside Buscombe, and her husband Paul. Cassie wiggles her wrist out of Jack's grip. Martha's broad shoulders are draped in a black silk shawl with a long fringe, and Paul is wearing a monocle that falls off as he politely kisses Cassie's cheek.

Cassie has bumped into Martha a couple of times over the last year and realizes now, with a small slap of shame, that she never replied to Martha's text asking Cassie for a drink. Should she apologize now? Or just act like she never got the text? She feels out of her depth, as though the last few weeks have wiped the rules of social interaction from her memory.

Martha, as if sensing Cassie's discomfort, doesn't try and talk to her, and instead jokes with Paul and Jack, and Cassie is left marooned on the edge of their little conference, her raincoat hot over her arm. None of them seem to notice as she walks away, towards the drinks table; her throat immediately feels freer. She picks up an orange juice.

At the drinks tables she bumps into Maggie, the local hairdresser, breasts jostling for space in a tight purple dress at least five decades later than the party theme. Maggie natters away about how bad the roadwork in the village has been for business. Cassie grinds her feet into the floor to keep from running away as Maggie lifts a corner of Cassie's hair between her fingers as though she's picking up someone else's rubbish, and tells Cassie with a little sigh of forced patience that she still needs to trim even if she's growing her hair long again. An older woman takes Maggie's hand and Cassie stands back as the two of them start talking simultaneously at the same high pitch over each other.

A saxophone screams through the speakers.

Cassie looks over to Jack. Paul's disappeared, but Martha's nodding and smiling as Jack whispers in her ear. It looks like a secret. What's he saying?

The orange juice burns her stomach like acid.

This isn't her place; she shouldn't be here. She feels like she's woken up in someone else's life.

Behind her she hears two men laugh like honking geese at each other. It sounds forced, mirthless.

Jack's right; she does need to start again, but she's starting to think she needs to do it alone, ball up this life like a scrap piece of paper, chuck it away and start again.

She scans the room. Where's Jonny? she wonders. He was with his mum in Edinburgh for two weeks over Christmas. She won't survive unless she sees one friendly face tonight, but all she can see are raised eyebrows, lips curling into unkind smiles. She feels exposed, naked, as though everyone knows her husband cheated on her with her best friend. Ha! And she's pregnant and doesn't know what the fuck to do. Ha, ha ha!

Underneath her jacket she clenches her fists so her nails bite into her palms; the pain steadies her and she keeps her eyes fixed on the door as she walks towards it, turning sideways to squeeze past bloated bodies. She wades through the noise of the party, so loud it's almost physical, like a jelly, the hot wine breath, the laughter, the clashing music.

She opens the door and the last few minutes of the year seem to open up to her like a cave. She takes in big greedy mouthfuls of freezing air. The lawn is a modest little rect-angle, raised slightly from the house, and, at the far end, Cassie sees Jonny smoking in jeans and a white T-shirt, talking to an older, whiskery-looking man who holds a cigar like a pen. They look like the only two who have completely ignored the dress code.

Cassie breathes out a long white cloud of relief. She's about to call Jonny's name when a hand on her shoulder stops her. She turns and sees Charlotte, whose eyes have the same questioning, unsettled look they had in the car on the way over.

"Cassie, are you feeling OK?" she asks, her head falling slightly to one side.

She'd be fine if she was just allowed to go and speak to her friend, she thinks. Instead she pulls her lips into a smile.

"Just a bit of a headache, Charlotte. I'll get some air for a few minutes and then I'll come back in."

Charlotte's eyes dart up to where Jonny's standing. They both watch as Jonny flicks ash from his cigarette onto the lawn and rocks on his heels, nodding and laughing at something the older man says, embodying the foppish twenties gent even without an outfit. Charlotte pauses like she wants to say something, her eyes darting around Cassie's face like she doesn't recognize her daughter-in-law suddenly.

Inside, someone has turned the howling music down and a male voice calls out, "OK, everyone; get a drink and get in position for the countdown!"

"You should go back in, Charlotte. I'll be right behind you."

She feels her mother-in-law's eyes crawl all over her back as she turns away and walks across the lawn towards her friend.

The older man, thank God, has already left; he's probably gone inside for the countdown. Jonny's seen Cassie at last, waves and starts walking towards her. They meet halfway across the lawn.

"I've been looking for you!" he says. His grip as they

hug softens before hers. She doesn't want to let go; it feels so good to be held by someone she trusts, someone who knows her. She kisses his cheek.

The noise drops from the party; a charged quiet, the fidgety kind that can't stay still for long exudes from inside.

"Oh god, I can't tell you how pleased I am to see you," she says, holding onto his hand.

He looks down at her, his smile slightly lopsided. He swigs from a bottle of wine and takes a step back. Cassie recognizes the absent look behind his eyes, as though Jonny's stepped away from himself, his gestures weird and exaggerated.

"Me too, Cas," he says, squeezing her hand. "You won't believe the shitstorm I've come back to, though. Christmas has made Lorna even loopier than normal. Somehow she's made the connection that you're the Juice-C girl and she went mental on the phone to me earlier, saying we've been sleeping together . . ."

Inside, the crowd starts counting down 10, 9, 8 . . .

Jonny, drunk enough to forget what he was just saying, grabs her other hand and joins in for "5, 4, 3, 2, 1. . . Happy New Year!"

He picks Cassie up and spins her around, his feet unsteady beneath them, and he's laughing so he doesn't hear as she slaps his back and shouts for him to put her down. Everyone inside starts singing a slurry version of "Auld Lang Syne." As Jonny spins her, she sees a few people huddled round the back door, drinking champagne, still hugging and kissing as if congratulating each other for surviving another year. Jonny finally rests Cassie back on the grass.

"Jesus, Jonny, urgh. That made me feel really sick," she

says, holding her head. He offers her his wine bottle. She shakes her head.

He narrows his eyes at her and asks, "What's up?"

"Your wife thinks we're having an affair, that's what's up."

Jonny wags a wonky finger at her. "Ex-wife."

"Jonny, don't be so fucking flippant, I'm serious."

"So am I. The only way to handle such stupid accusations is to seriously laugh at them."

She thinks she might cry suddenly. She'd been looking forward to seeing Jonny for two weeks and now he's so drunk, so preoccupied with his own troubles again, she feels like there's no room for her, but she needs his help. She has to try and talk to him at least.

She takes Jonny by the wrist and pulls him to the corner of the garden. There are more people outside now. A woman dressed as a flapper is handing out sparklers. Cassie doesn't want to risk someone overhearing her telling Jonny she's pregnant, that she's considering leaving Jack, that she needs Jonny's help.

But Jonny misinterprets her hand on his wrist. He raises his hand high in the air and pulls her into an awkward jolting dance, his wine bottle pressed against the small of her back. He spins her around and catches her in his arms before he tries to drop her over his arm, but they're out of sync, their weight unbalanced, and he has to lean forward, pull her up to a hug to stop her from falling. He holds on to her, laughing, his breath stale with wine against her skin, his heartbeat quick against her chest. She pushes him away.

"Jesus, Jonny! Fucking stop it!" she says. A stinging heat is starting to gather and burn behind her eyes; she feels the bovine gaze of other guests on them. Her heart drops because she knows she can't tell him now, not when he's like this, too sloppy and careless with booze for the delicate secret she's protected for twelve weeks now.

Jonny finally quiets as she wipes big, rolling tears from her face. They travel quickly, trapped for too long. She's not crying for herself, though; she's crying for her unborn child. "The secret." She won't let her child be born into all this suspicion. Jonny, suddenly serious, puts his arm around her.

"Shit, sorry, Cas. Why are you upset?" he asks, but Cassie shakes his arm away.

"I'm upset because I'm fucking scared, Jonny. I'm scared, OK?" Over Jonny's shoulder she sees a couple of people staring at them in the vacant way people stare at trashy TV, worried perhaps they might miss something terrible happening to someone else. Fuckers. She instantly regrets telling Jonny she's scared. Now is not the time to tell him about her fears for her child's future. She doesn't want a scene. She turns her back towards the crowd, but she can't stop crying. The tears feel too good, exorcising the broken little person she's terrified she's become since she saw them together.

"Oh god, Cas," Jonny says, his eyes widening but his voice fudged with wine. "Sorry, I didn't mean to . . ."

"Don't worry, it's not that, it's . . . I'm fine, really. Look, I'm totally overreacting. I'm just going to head home." She nods her head at Jonny. "I just want to go home," she says more firmly.

"OK, I'll drive you."

Her face is wet now, her hands stained black from mascara. She smiles at his worried face, but she shakes her head.

"No, no," she says. "Jonny, seriously, I promise you, I'm fine, OK? We can speak tomorrow when I've had sleep and you've got a stinking hangover. I'll need your help more then, but I'll walk back now. It'll take fifteen minutes max. I'll be fine, OK?"

"Please let me drive you home."

If it was only her decision she might have said yes, but it's not just her safety she has to think about anymore; she has to get her baby safely away from here.

She strokes the side of Jonny's worried face.

"No, I want to walk. It'll do me good. I promise I'll be fine."

"You're not going to tell Jack you're leaving?"

A firework in the field next to the farm bangs, followed by a small shimmer of light. The crowd makes a shy "ooh" sound.

Cassie shakes her head.

"Don't tell him I was upset, will you? I don't want him to worry. If you see Charlotte or Jack, just say I went home to check on Maisie, that I was worried about her with the fireworks and everything."

Jonny searches Cassie's face for reassurance, but his gaze is blunted by alcohol, his eyes unseeing.

"Have fun," she says, squeezing his arm, "and I'll come over tomorrow, OK?"

"Happy New Year, Cas," he says, kissing her cheek before she starts walking down the path, towards the gate that

leads directly onto Steeple Lane. Eventually the noise from
the party fades and she can hear the stream, swollen from
all the rain, alive ahead of her. Her phone buzzes with a
message. She thinks it'll be Jack, already wondering where
she is. She looks at the screen. But it's not Jack, and it's
not Nicky. It's Marcus.

> Happy New Year, Cas. I'm just having a quiet one at
> home but just wanted you to know I'm thinking of you,
> Marcus. x.

She feels her eyes swell again, and her tears fall, landing
like water bombs on her screen, distorting Marcus's
message. She pictures Marcus in his silent sitting room,
balancing a whiskey on the arm of his favorite old chair,
with only his failing memory for company. She realizes,
with a jolt of surprise, that she wishes she was there with
him. She wants to be in the house her mum called home
and she wants to be with the man who was her mum's
husband, the man who loved her and knew April almost
as well as Cassie knew her. Marcus needs her and she
needs him.

Of course. She almost laughs as she drops her phone
back in her pocket; it's so obvious. She can't decide her
future, her child's future here. She needs a break, some
time and space away from her suffocating life and she'll
be able to finally get Marcus to a doctor. She starts walking,
invigorated with the energy of her decision. At last she's
going to honor her mum's wishes; she'll look after Marcus
and she'll let Marcus look after her. She'll call Marcus first

thing in the morning, and tell him she's going to come and stay for a while; he'll be delighted. Then she'll go over to Jonny's, before Jack's even awake, and get him to take her to the train station. If she's lucky and his hangover isn't too bad, he might even drive her all the way to Portsmouth. The Isle of Wight will be peaceful. She'll have space and time to think and paint if she wants. It's where her mum found solace after all.

She lets her hand drop to her lower belly; she pictures her mum, traveling back from Mexico all on her own, her belly already swollen with Cassie. Maybe she'll pick up on some of her mum's courage if she's by the sea, walking those high cliffs they both loved so much.

She's at the gate now that leads to the lane. She's about to open it when she hears a branch crack. She stops. She feels a slightly itchy sensation prickle her back, as though she's being watched.

"Hello?" Her voice is small, lonely in the night, but there's no reply, just the creak of the trees and the distant hum of drunk party laughter. Another firework explodes, gaudy in the sky. It lights up the space around her in an unnatural pool of brief light.

She's on her own after all, Steeple Lane directly ahead of her, the stream hissing by its side. The fireworks die in the sky and the darkness settles around her again. She turns left onto the lane, towards the cottage. It feels right to be walking on her own, away from the crowd, into the first night of the New Year, towards a future she realizes with a surge is entirely her own. The wind picks up and Cassie shivers. She pulls her jacket tighter, freezing against her skin. Her breath coils around her in dense white clouds, each icy inhale electrocutes her lungs. Her mouth fills with an unusual taste. It reminds her of something, something metallic, and as she walks deeper into the night, she knows what her mouth tastes like. It tastes like blood.

22

Alice

"Alice, what are you doing here?" Paula is looking up from where she sits at the reception desk, yesterday's papers spread before her. If she's pleased to see me, she doesn't show it; her pale face folds in on itself like cake mix in confusion. "I thought you were off today?"

I try and ignore the flicker of amusement I see shadowing her wide-set features; I'm probably getting a reputation for always being on the ward, not having a life outside my shifts.

I shrug and lie. "I left something in my locker so thought I'd just pop in for it."

"For God's sake, it's seven in the morning, Alice!"

"Paula, I got an early night, woke up early, OK?"

Now it's her turn to shrug, before I ask, "How's Cassie's night been?"

Paula folds up her newspaper.

"Oh, she's quiet as a lamb," she says with a sigh. "It's Frank who's taken a turn, I'm afraid. The specialist was with him for a while earlier." Paula wrinkles her nose. "I've never heard his lungs like this, I would have sworn it was pneumonia but the doc said it was most likely an infection brought on by overexertion over the last few days, not enough sleep and all that. I've just cleaned his trach, given him his antibiotics and made him comfortable." She pauses, before adding as an afterthought, defensive perhaps that I caught her slacking, "I just finished his notes, before you arrived. They're all up to date." Then she licks her thumb and forefinger and opens her newspaper again.

Paula's left Frank slightly turned towards the left. His eyes are open, as though he was expecting me, or someone else. He blinks as soon as he sees me. Paula was right, his lungs are congested; they rattle with every breath. I drop my bag on his visitor's chair and move him to a more central position. Veins wriggle across the whites of his eyes like tiny red rivers. He's exhausted.

"Frank, what's going on?" He stares at me and I kick myself—idiot—for not asking yes or no questions.

"Is something wrong?"

Frank blinks yes.

"You want the board, Frank?"

Blink.

"All right, we can try for a little while, but after you must promise me you'll try and rest, deal?"

Blink. I have the feeling he's only saying yes to get me to shut up and get the board. I pick it up from its place behind the frame of his bed.

He starts blinking as soon as I've raised the board in

front of him. He moves too quickly. I don't know the board well enough and have to keep looking at it and back at Frank so I miss his blinks. I don't know what he's trying to say. I feel a rip in my chest, and I'm worried I might cry suddenly: he needs me and I don't understand.

"I'm sorry, Frank, I . . ." I look at him; there's a ferocity behind his eyes I haven't seen before.

"Shall we start again, Frank?"

He blinks, weaker this time. Each blink draining a little more energy.

"OK, try going slower," I tell him before we start to work again. I think he blinks "L" but then he blinks a shaky series as his eyelids spasm with exhaustion and I think I've got it wrong again. His eyeballs shudder in their sunken sockets. I can hear the effort within him—the congestion echoes through his chest—and I know we can't carry on.

"Frank, I'm sorry. But that's enough for now. You need to rest. I'll come back later, we can finish then, OK? I promise."

Frank blinks twice for "no" but, as he does, I hear Mary calling good morning, warning Paula to watch out for roadworks on the A27 and I know it's time for me to go. I can handle Paula's disdain, but I know Mary will see through my weak excuses. She'll know something is up and I don't have the energy to try and convince her I'm OK. I grab my bag from Frank's chair, ignore his furious blinks, put my hand against his cheek and tell him again, more firmly this time, that he has to rest. I promise him that I'll be back later and it's only when I hear Mary go into the nurses break room that I pull Frank's curtain back and walk quickly off the ward.

Mary was right; the traffic even so early in the morning is bad and it takes me twice as long to get home as normal. I'm still worried about Frank, but I tell myself that once the antibiotics take hold he'll calm down as his infection starts to clear. In stationary traffic I watch early daffodils shake their heads on the grassy edge of the road, and my thoughts turn again, magnetized, back to Cassie, and I know what I'm going to do with my day off.

As soon as I get home, I bundle Bob into the back of the car. David won't be home until the afternoon. The trains have been bad into the city recently, so he stayed at a hotel in London last night to make an early morning meeting. I told him on the phone last night that I was going to take Bob for a windy beach walk today, perhaps to Birling Gap, but as soon as we pull back into the traffic, I know I won't follow signs for the coast. Instead, I stop at a gas station and buy a big bunch of red and yellow tulips and follow the signs to Buscombe.

The morning sky is a storybook blue against the peacefully sleeping mounds of the South Sussex Downs. Bob pokes his nose out of the car as I open the window; the air feels cool and new, a fresh batch. Visiting a local village isn't a crime, is it? It's a Wednesday so Jack will be working and even if I bump into Charlotte, I'll pretend I'm visiting a friend who lives nearby and if she doesn't believe me, then I don't really care. Now I know I'm not going to be a mum, I feel strangely invincible, bolder in my new, toughened skin. I may not be able to protect my own child, I know that now, but I remind myself I can still try and protect Cassie's as I turn down into the dappled shade of Steeple Lane.

I press my foot to the brake as I pass the sign for Steeple Farm and Cottage, Jonny's place. Bob pokes his nose out of the window towards an elderly-looking Alsatian lying on the short rubbly drive that leads up to the farm. The Alsatian creaks arthritically onto his paws and, tossing his head in the air like he thinks he's still a puppy, he trots down the drive, barking all the while at Bob, to either stop and say hello or to get off his patch. I'm just about to accelerate away when a man I can't see shouts, "Dennis!" The man whistles and then says, "Come here, boy!"

Bob almost clatters off the front seat as I slam on the brakes. My mind flips through my nurse's training. Did I miss the class on "not visiting the main suspect in your patient's manslaughter case?" Have I gone completely fucking crazy? The Alsatian is still barking, shaking his mane at us and ignoring the voice that keeps calling for him, getting closer. I can't move. I have to see him. This is why I'm here; this must be why I'm here. Bob whimpers in the front seat to be let out. I just keep staring past him, towards the Alsatian as a tall, blond-haired man in cut-off denim shorts, with old, tan, leather boots that gape around his lower calves, walks in long strides out onto the drive. Jonny.

"Dennis," he calls, a warning growl in his voice. At last, Jonny looks up. I'm not sure if he sees me peering out at him through the window over Bob's shoulder. He stands up straight, lifts a hand to his forehead to shield his eyes from the sun and neither of us moves for a few seconds. I wonder whether this is the moment I'll look back on and regret. Will my future self scream at the memory of this moment to "turn the fuck around, Alice." But I don't. I can't. Dennis looks thrown, turning from Jonny to Bob and back to Jonny, before he breaks the armistice and starts running towards us, which makes Bob dance on the spot in the front seat and bark.

Jonny starts cautiously following him. His long legs and arms sway by his side, as though they're only held in place by thin string. From a distance, there's a boyishness to his movements, but when he gets closer, I see how his cheekbones protrude from his face like stumps and how worry has carved its telltale lines all over his face like battle scars. I roll down the window a little further, and hold Bob's collar, pulling him back as he shoves his neck through the opening. Jonny curls himself down towards the window and we peer at each other over Bob's shoulder.

"Can I help you?" he asks, politely.

His face darkens as soon as he sees me. He recognizes me but I'm not sure he knows where from.

"Jonny?" My voice is small.

He frowns, immediately on guard; I know his name. Dennis picks up on his hesitation and growls by his side. Jonny rests a quieting hand on his head.

"Who are you?" he asks.

Bob bounds out of the car with me; I have to pull him by the collar to get him back onto the passenger seat, closing the door, before I walk around the car to Jonny. He looks at my face, his brow furrowed and his eyes full of warning. He has the shady uncertain look of someone who has recently learned not to trust people. I stand in front of him and say simply, "I'm Alice." He looks at me like I'm stupid for a second before I add, "I'm one of the nurses looking after Cassie."

His face breaks in knowing at last and he waggles a finger towards me and nods as he says, "That's right, that's right . . . you were there when I tried to see her."

"That was me," I say, nodding.

"You didn't let me see her."

"I couldn't, Jonny. You see, we have to be . . ."

He interrupts me gently, raising his hands, "No, that's OK, I understand. It was a stupid thing to do, in retrospect. Didn't do anyone any favors, least of all me." His face gathers itself and comes to rest in newly furrowed lines. "Is she OK? God, has something happened?"

I bite my lip and realize I have one chance, one chance before he spooks and turns his back on me.

"Would it be OK if I pulled my car into your drive, Jonny? Perhaps we could go inside and have a chat?"

There's a twitchiness to him, a jerkiness to his movements, as though he's drunk too much strong coffee to stay awake. I get that sometimes. Although he looks about a decade older, I recognize the look on his face from before, when he came crashing onto the ward. It brings a certain light to his eyes that can't be feigned, and I know—as I did that first time I saw him—that he loves her, not necessarily in a romantic way; he just simply loves her.

He nods but says, "Please just tell me, she's . . ."

"She's still alive, Jonny."

He breathes out and closes his eyes, briefly, a quick thank-you to the universe before he turns towards the cottage and asks, "You'll tell me how she's doing? I can ask about the baby?"

"Yes, I'll tell you whatever you want to know."

He stares beyond me for a moment, as though searching for an answer on the lane behind me.

"Come on, then. I'll put the kettle on."

Jonny tells me his place is where the herdsman used to live when the farm was still a working dairy. It looks as though Dennis has had the run of the place for a while. I step over a large, well-chomped stick; splinters litter the floor. Half the table is covered in open leaves from newspapers like broken wings from huge dead insects and the other half is dominated by a small army of empty wine bottles and cans. The sink is full of cups and pans, their surfaces iridescent with grime. A small circus of flies buzz around the overflowing bin in the corner. One has crash landed; it fizzes on its back across the sideboard. Jonny knocks the washing machine door closed with his leg; it bounces open again, knocking against some clothing that spews out of its opening.

"Sorry it's such a dump at the moment," he says, turning the kettle on and peering optimistically into a cupboard for clean mugs. "I haven't been here for a while. I hate being here now, for obvious reasons." He turns back to me. "Do you mind tea in a glass?"

I shake my head, still standing.

"Bollocks, I don't have any milk. Is chamomile all right?"

"Perfect," I say and he clears a sweater, dog food and a couple of maps off a chair.

"I always got chamomile for Cassie," he says as he motions for me to take a seat in the space he just cleared. "It was her favorite."

I smile at him, grateful for this small detail, grateful to him for making her a little clearer to me. As I sit down, I imagine her here, sitting on this chair, drinking her chamomile tea, looking out of the little window across to the farmhouse. This space was their friendship HQ, where she made her jams, somewhere she felt safe. I want to keep him talking about her so I ask, "Did she come over a lot?"

"Yes, over the summer especially. We kept all the stuff for the jam in the spare room here. She'd use my spare key so she could come and go, even when I wasn't around." He puts a glass in front of me. The inside of the glass sweats with condensation, a tea bag floating in the middle, flaccid as a jellyfish. Jonny makes a clicking sound with his tongue as he gently wakes a pissed-off-looking tabby cat I hadn't even noticed, dropping her to the floor so he can sit in the chair opposite me. His collarbones stick out painfully under his T-shirt and I notice the skin around his fingernails is scabbed and bitten. He doesn't have tea.

"OK, so can you tell me how she is?"

I breathe out. I've come this far; I can't lose my nerve now.

"I will, Jonny, I promise, but first I want to hear what happened that night. I want to hear from you."

He looks up at me, alarmed, and rakes a hand through his hair. I've changed the deal and feel cruel, but I know I can't help Cassie if I don't have the truth. I lean forward across the table towards him.

"She'd taken off her wedding ring, Jonny. I don't think she was looking for Maisie, I think she was leaving Jack and someone surprised her on the road. You said she was scared."

Jonny nods and leans back in his chair, closing his eyes for a moment before rubbing them hard with both hands.

"She cried at the party. Everyone thought I made her cry because there was something going on between us, but that's bullshit. I think she cried because—as we now know—she was pregnant, and I don't think she knew what to do."

"About the baby?"

"No, not about the baby. I know she wanted the baby, especially after her miscarriage. She didn't know what to do about Jack."

"You think she wasn't happy with Jack?"

Jonny interlaces his fingers between his hands, and looks at his nails as he picks them. I imagine he did the same when he was interrogated at the police station hour after hour.

"Looking back, I think something changed. I don't know what, but she went from seeming happy to being distant. I was away a lot and had so much shit going on with my ex; I'd talk and talk to Cassie about Lorna, about how crazy she could be, but now, of course, I wish I'd asked her more, listened more." He pauses and looks up from his hands. "The only person who can tell us now what was going on between them is Jack and there's no way he'll say what was really happening, so . . ." Jonny shrugs. "You know, when you think about it, Jack, moving down here . . . all of it was a bit of a curveball. She'd spent her whole life in London; she got together with Jack just a couple of months after her mum died. I think he offered her a ready-made life, a way out of feeling on her own. A home, a husband . . . a chance to make a family of her own. So different to the way she grew up. I think he made it seem like he understood her, that he knew her grief, but he didn't, not really."

He stops talking, and in the pause I ask, "So what changed?"

"I don't know, exactly, but I think the baby made her wake up, realize the life she had with Jack, although seemingly perfect, wasn't really who she is."

"So you think she tried to leave that night. You said she was upset?"

"I meant she was upset because she was scared, scared of the future, scared of making a decision about whether to stay or leave Jack."

"But she chose to leave."

"That's what I think. She told me she was fine, that she wanted to go home and check on Maisie and she just left. Asked me to tell him she'd gone."

"But why did Cassie have to leave that night. Why not wait until the morning?"

Jonny shrugs. "That's what I can't figure out. She told me before she left the party that she would come over the next morning, that she'd need some help, but she didn't say what with."

"What happened after she left the party?"

"I stayed for a couple more hours, then I drove home, around three in the morning. I've admitted that—I should never have been driving—but I remember the whole journey and nothing happened. I must have driven straight past her." He pauses and digs into his thumbnail with his other hand so hard that he draws blood. He winces and wipes his hand against his shorts.

"When I got home my ex-wife was here. She's not well, has a habit of making a scene. I was too drunk to cope with her, to keep calm, and I said some stuff, some awful stuff to her. She left saying she never wanted to see me again. She didn't corroborate my story with the police until now to make me suffer. After Lorna left, Maisie turned up at the back door. Maisie went nuts when she saw me. As soon as I opened the door, Dennis ran outside with Maisie and they wouldn't come back when I called for them. I thought it was the fireworks freaking them out, but they went racing off down the lane, barking their heads off."

"They found her?"

"They knew she was there. Maisie must have seen the whole thing. I shouted down at Cassie. I thought it was some fucked-up stunt at first; she looked weirdly peaceful, like she was meant to be just floating there. But then I saw the blood . . ." Jonny closes his eyes briefly, as if he wishes he could close his mind, wipe the memory away.

"You didn't see anyone else?" I ask, desperate for him to keep talking.

"No, like I told the police, I passed an old SUV, parked on the side of the lane just near where she was hit. I remember it because whoever was driving had their beams on high; they almost blinded me in my rearview mirror." My insides feel eely.

"Could it have been a Volvo, Jonny?" I think about Marcus heaving himself out of his Volvo when he arrived in the hospital parking lot. I think about him driving past Bob and me on the lane . . . how vacant he looked.

"Yeah, it could have been. I've been over and over this. I can't say for certain what make it was, but yeah, something like a Volvo. Why? Do you know—"

But I cut him off; I want him to keep answering my questions before I answer any of his.

"Did Cassie ever talk about her stepdad, Jonny, about Marcus?"

"Not much. I mean she told me he'd just completely crumbled when her mum died, that he couldn't handle his grief at all. She said she was a bit worried about him, that he was getting confused. My grandma had dementia and from what Cassie said it reminded me of when she first got ill." I nod at him; I've thought the same. Jonny keeps talking. "I think Cas felt guilty for not seeing Marcus more, but whenever she did see him, it kind of screwed with her head. It was obvious as well that Jack and Marcus never got on." Jonny pauses. I have the feeling he's weighing whether to tell me something or not.

"What is it?"

He shakes his head, like his memory isn't worth saying.

"What?" I repeat.

"I was just remembering this one time when Cas was talking about Marcus, and she kept going on about how differently people cope with the shitty things that happen in life. Cassie said Marcus had let his grief destroy him, but Charlotte, whose husband died when Jack was a teenager, had risen above her own grief for Jack's sake." Jonny pauses. "She really admired Charlotte."

I think of how calmly Charlotte handles her world, as though she isn't spinning around on it like the rest of us. She's easy to admire.

"So let's say she made the decision to leave Jack. When she said she was scared could she have been talking about him or could she have been talking about someone else?"

Jonny looks at me. He shakes his head, like he knows the terrain of these questions well.

"She was talking about Jack. She told me Jack has a temper. He's not used to not getting what he wants."

"You've told the police all this?"

"Of course, but they don't believe me. I'm a drunk driver. I'm scum to them. Me hitting Cassie was such a neat conclusion for them. It's taken them weeks to finally get the truth out of Lorna, that she was here with me that night, that I couldn't have hit Cassie."

He moves closer towards me across the table, his eyes pressurized and desperate like when he came onto the ward.

"How is she, honestly? How's the baby? I'm not allowed to know anything apart from whatever bullshit is in the papers."

I tell him how well the baby's growing, how active she is. I tell him that we play music to Cas and the baby, how all the nurses are getting extra training for the arrival, that we're planning for every possibility. He nods occasionally, even smiles when I tell him it's a girl and says, "good, good," a few times.

I want to ask him more questions, about Jack and his temper and about Marcus, but we're interrupted by a phone in another room, the volume turned up loud, and Jonny excuses himself to answer it, his tone changing, becoming professional, with whoever it is on the other end of the line. He lets them talk for a minute and says, "Good." He breathes out, the relief in his voice palpable as he says, "that's good news," before telling them that he's actually in the middle of something and asks to call them back in a few minutes.

When he comes back to the table, I can see the phone call has changed him. He grasps his upper arm, releases it and moves the same hand to his hip.

"That was my lawyer. He says they're taking Lorna's statement. He thinks the charges will be dropped any day." He starts to rub his thumbs into his temple as he speaks, and his eyes glisten.

I don't know what to say.

He raises his head as he says, "She says the police are looking at early statements again. I bet they'll be talking to Jack. I have to call my lawyer back so . . ."

"You must be so relieved, Jonny," I say, and stand so he knows I'll leave.

He shakes his head, like he doesn't understand what's happening, and I think he needs to be alone to let his mind work around the news, to believe it.

I want to hug him, but instead we shake hands. I hold his upper arm briefly; he's thin and his muscles leap in surprise, as though no one's touched him for a while.

"Look after yourself, won't you, Jonny?"

"What are you going to do now?"

It's a good question; I wasn't expecting it. "I'm going to take my dog for a walk," I say dumbly, as though this is just a normal, pleasant day off for me, as though we haven't just been talking about manslaughter, before I add, "but then I'm going to call Officer Brooks, tell her she needs to speak to Jack again."

Jonny's eyes widen and he nods quietly and as soon as

the door closes behind me I hear Jonny gasp, a big chesty sob of relief that he's going to have his life back.

Gravel crunches under my feet as I walk slowly back to my car. Bob is fast asleep in the back seat, only waking when I pull the door shut. I drive us slowly back to the place where Cassie was hit. It's so different today, the light shining through the new leaves like stained glass, the water in the stream gently flowing. The small shrine is still there. I bend to place my plump tulips at the front, obscenely healthy and alive next to the brittle, brown remnants of the older flowers. They totter in their place and, as I try and make them sturdier, I notice a photo at the back. I didn't see it before; someone must have left it in the last week. I recognize it from Cassie's Facebook page; it's the one from the hospice, the day Marcus and April married, April withered but smiling in her bed, Cassie on one side of her and Marcus on the other, proudly holding April's left hand in his own to show off their new wedding rings.

I pick up the photo; it isn't at all weathered. I turn it over, and on the back in black ink, someone's written just two words, filling the whole of the space with their regret: "I'm sorry."

I fold the photo in half, put it in my pocket and stand still for a moment to let my breath settle. She was scared of Jack. He thought she was having an affair with Jonny and he went after her that night. I bow my head and close my eyes, listen to the wind ripple through the trees, like a slow steady breath. I believed him. I thought his trauma couldn't be faked. I was wrong. The wind picks up. I feel it like a guiding palm at my back; it gently pushes me towards my car and for the first time in a long while I feel clear, because I don't have to choose what to do anymore. My promise to Cassie has made my decision for me and the wheels of my car bounce on the uneven surface of the lane as I drive away as fast as I can.

23

Frank

The color alphabet board floats before me; the colors blur with Lucy looking worried behind it. She watches my face for every flicker, almost as desperate as me for every painful letter. I only manage to get to "J-A" before my head starts to fizz and whirr again with the effort and my eyelids clamp shut. Still, it's progress and much better than before with Alice. I feel Lucy lower the board. I wish they'd turn my breathing machine up again, the oxygen doesn't feel strong enough to get through the mess in my lungs. That doctor last night told me I have an infection from over-exertion. He didn't see me blink twice for "no" when he said the nurses would give me strong antibiotics directly into my IV to fight the infection off.

I don't want the fucking antibiotics!

But, of course, that's not my choice to make. My body doesn't belong to me anymore; it belongs to the people in white coats. Mary injected a second round of drugs directly into my IV soon after Alice left this morning. I can feel the drugs tickling my veins and no matter how I fight against it, everything starts to soften and slow, as though the world is made of cotton. My lungs feel heavy and useless; they've turned into two hanging pieces of well-chewed gum. I feel them, slimy and dripping. But that doesn't matter, I can't rest—mustn't rest—until I tell someone about Charlotte, what she said to Cassie. I may not know what Cassie's laugh sounds like, whether her eyes are green or blue, how she takes her tea, I may not know anything about her, but I do know she's not safe. She's not safe and I'm the only one who can help.

I force my eyes open and feel my lungs bubble with the effort. Lucy's lovely face looks worried in front of me; she tucks some strands of dark hair behind her ear before she dabs my eyes with saline pads like Mary showed her.

She smiles once she's finished and says, "Hi, Dad, how're you feeling?"

I blink once to try and fool her, reassure her I'm fine. She fiddles with her nose ring for a moment, her forehead crinkling in thought.

"Alice told me you don't want me to tell Mum or Grandma Ashcroft or anyone that you're getting better, that you're blinking, Dad. Are you sure? Don't you think it would be . . ."

But I interrupt her with two hard blinks—No!

"But, Dad, I think Mum might . . ."

Blink, blink—No!

Lucy looks down at her lap for a moment, disappointment

rippling across her face, and I feel my heart crumple like balled-up paper.

"Alice said it's because you want to wait until you can communicate a bit more, say more words before we tell anyone else. Is that right, Dad?"

Blink!

Yes, my sweet one, I need to be better to tell the world about the night visitor, about Charlotte trying to warn Cassie, to tell the world it was Jack who tried to kill his wife. If we start telling people, they could find out I know the truth about Jack. So far, neither Charlotte nor Jack have asked about the extra attention I'm getting on the ward. Maybe they're so focused on Cassie and the baby that they haven't even noticed.

My eyelids feel weighted again and I hear Lucy say, "That's it, try and rest please, Dad."

But as soon as my eyes are closed, the night visitor sweeps into my thoughts like bad weather, begging forgiveness from Cassie again and again, for what? The question sparks my adrenal system; adrenaline pushes through the drugs, forcing my eyes open again. Is it something to do with Jack? Were they together that night? And I know I can't rest, not now.

I blink for the board. Lucy shakes her head at first.

"No, Dad. You have to rest."

I blink again, good steady, determined blinks.

Lucy looks down at me, her brow troubled.

I'm sorry, my love, but I need you to do this for me.

I blink a third time for the board.

Lucy turns to look down the ward, seeking advice, but we're all alone; Mary's busy talking to a white coat just by the new patient's bed. I don't know their name—they were wheeled in this morning just after Alice left—but it sounds like, whoever they are, Mary isn't happy about them being here. I hear parts of their conversation—"multiple organ failure"; "nurse shortages"—and it's clear to me that Mary's worried about having another patient with very high care needs with only two nurses here on 9B.

Lucy turns back to me and picks up the blinking board.

"OK, Dad, but only for five minutes. Then I'm going to leave you to have a good rest. Deal?"

Lucy asks, knowing I won't waste a blink to confirm that it's a deal.

"So from last time we have J, A so we'll keep them and get going." She fixes her eyes on me so she doesn't miss a precious blink, and traces a finger down the board, as she recites, "Red . . ."

Blink.

"OK, Red . . . A, B, C . . ."

Blink.

"C, OK, so we've got J, A, C . . . I could go on, Dad, but are you trying to spell Jack, like Cassie's husband?"

Blink!

You did it, Luce!

Lucy beams at me and calls out down the ward, "Mary, Mary! Dad just did another one!"

Mary hurries over; she's out of breath when she arrives at my bedside.

"I don't call this resting!" Mary tuts at Lucy, and then winks at her, before she turns to me. "Come on, Frank, I could use some good news. Tell me you finally spelled out my name?"

317

The excitement has given me another rush of energy. I manage to blink twice. "No."

"Cheeky bugger," she says to me, in her mock West Country accent. I love that she teases me.

Lucy laughs, impatient to share our news.

"No, he spelled Jack! I think he's trying to tell us that he knows even more than we think, that he's aware of what happens here on the ward to other patients, to Cassie. Am I right, Dad?"

I manage one blink before my eyelids fall and darkness billows around me again.

Yes, my clever girl, you are. You're right. But there's more I need to tell you.

I've nudged a little closer to saying what I know. It's my most important word yet. Now I need to think how to link it to another word, and what should that word be? Bad? How can I tell them "bad" refers to "Jack"? Maybe if I try "Police" . . .?

But Lucy kisses me and says, "I'm going to leave you to rest now, Dad." She ignores me blinking for her to stay. Mary's already disappeared, so I'm on my own and feel my mind soften again into the drugs; like melting ice cream, my thoughts drip from my brain. At least my lungs feel less sticky now. In, out, in, out. I count along with my breathing machine and I find myself imagining where Alice is now, on her sunny day off. Perhaps she's gone to the coast, throwing sticks for Bob, the wind making her hair dance around her face. Soon someone will tell her that I blinked Jack's name and then she'll know what I was trying to tell her earlier; she'll understand that Jack has fooled us all and she'll go to the police and this whole sorry mess will be wiped clean. Is that an expression? I'm not sure. My mind slops and sloshes back to safety again; it finds Alice's face. I imagine Alice smiling, the gap in her teeth, how proud she'll be of me for helping. How much better she'll feel about everything. In, out, in, out and, at last, I give in, and slide into the endless black.

I wake to a wet sucking sound, like boots walking through wet mud. It takes me a moment to realize it's coming from my lungs. I feel like I've been asleep for a long time; someone's cleaned me while I was out, but my lungs must be filling quickly. I feel the darkness tugging me towards it again before I remember her hands, brittle above Cassie, and a bolt passes through me, making my heart patter and, over the noise of my organs, I hear some unfamiliar footsteps approach. I'm sure Mary said they'd canceled my physical therapy because of my infection, so I tell myself to calm down, ignore them, assume they must be for Cassie, when I hear my curtain pull back and Lizzie saying, "Frank, good news: your niece is here to see you."

Niece?

"So bear in mind, he's a little woozy because of the infection . . ."

I know Paul's got boys, I know I've got nephews, but I don't remember a niece.

More than one alarm starts ringing over the new patient's bed, and feet immediately start pounding down the ward, drawn to the noise.

"Oh, god," Lizzie says. "Sorry, we're a little shorthanded today. I'll be back soon as I can . . ." and Lizzie scurries off, joining the stampede to save whoever it is.

Perhaps the little brain coil with my niece in my memory died in the stroke, or melted with the drugs.

I'm still turned towards the window, on my right, so depending on where she's standing, I can't see this niece of mine, but I feel her come closer. Her footsteps are heavy; it sounds like she could be wearing leather boots. She smells smokey but sweet like incense. She smells like a hippy.

God, don't let my niece be a hippy.

She moves around my area, coming to where I'm turned at the right side of the foot of my bed. She's wearing jeans. Her legs are long and slim but she stands solidly through them. She's wrapped in a green coat, which she peels off and leaves to rest on my visitor's chair. Her long red braid bounces down her back like a snake, but it's hard to make out anymore details from my position; my eyes are gummy and ache with exhaustion. I hear her pick up the well-thumbed folder the nurses use for my notes before slotting it back into place at the foot of my bed. Then she comes close, studies me like bacteria through a microscope. She breathes through her nose, long and deliberate, and, placing a cool hand on my forehead, she bends low and just an inch from my ear, says, "Hi, Uncle Frank."

My organs squeeze. Recognition slices through me clean and quick as a razor.

She's back.

I remember her bending over Cassie, how she shook with remorse.

What did you do?

I swear up a storm inside, but to her, of course, I must seem as still as a millpond. I'm forced to look at her; she stares down at me, as thorough as if looking at an X-ray.

She has large, solid-looking features and alabaster white skin, patterned with freckles.

Why are you here?

At the end of the ward, there's a white board with all our names written on it. I remember she paused there, the first time she appeared. She must have seen my name there. She inspects me, her eyes narrow slightly in curiosity, but she doesn't wince; she must have a strong constitution. The alarms from my noisy new neighbor at the far end of the ward keep screaming.

She picks up a framed photo on my bedside stand; it's of Lucy and me from our fishing trip to Wales. Lucy brought it in yesterday; she left the frame on my nightstand, too high for me to look at, and all I can see now is the black velvet back of the frame. I know what photo it is, though; I remember it was one of the happiest days of my life. Lucy's about ten in the photo. I'm kneeling down by her side and we're both wearing one of my dad's old flat caps. We're smiling at the camera; Lucy's smile is so wide her eyes are almost closed. We're each holding up a sea trout we caught in the River Towy behind us. Lucy caught tons, and the one she holds up to the camera is twice the size of my one and only catch, which always made Lucy laugh. The woman only looks at it briefly before she lets out a sad little sigh as she places it back where it was before, out of my sight.

Then she looks sharply away from me, and I know why she's here.

No!

Our curtains twitch with her movement, but she walks almost silently, even in her heavy boots, across the ward to Cassie.

She casts her eyes over Cassie. I watch as she strokes Cassie's cheek just once with her forefinger and then she says, "It should have been me, Cassie, not you. It should have been me."

"It should have been you who what, Nicky?"

I'd been listening so intently to this woman, this Nicky, trying to catch her words over the noise of the new patient's alarms that I'd missed Charlotte's clean footsteps on the ward floor.

Nicky spins around to Charlotte and at that moment, one or two of the alarms stop; only one keeps up its mechanical wail.

Charlotte moves forward towards Nicky. She tries to pull Nicky's arm, to move her from Cassie's side, but Nicky corkscrews her arm away. It's Nicky who leads, followed by Charlotte, back to my bedside. As Charlotte walks behind Nicky I see Charlotte's face fall, from her held smile, livid and hard as a fist. Charlotte carefully closes my curtains before she comes to stand on the other side of my bed, opposite Nicky.

Thank God, Cassie's safer.

"What are you doing here?" Charlotte asks, her voice thick, her question as uncompromising as a stabbing knife.

"I had to lie to see her," Nicky says. "Jack wouldn't let me visit, so I had no choice." Nicky pauses; her face crumples into a frown but her voice softens as she continues. "I've tried to be there for him, for the baby. I thought he'd need me now, now that he doesn't have Cassie. But he won't let me help him. He ignores me, just like Cassie did."

Charlotte leans across the bed, towards Nicky. I can hear the effort it takes for her to keep her voice steady as she says, "Is that what you meant when you said it should have been you? You wanted to be with Jack?"

Nicky looks up at Charlotte. She shakes her head, and her eyes fall away from Charlotte's face.

"I never wanted any of this," Nicky says. "All I wanted was to make things right between us. She wouldn't answer my calls, my texts. I saw no choice. I came down that night to make her talk to me."

She was there that night.

Nicky keeps her arms locked by her side, occasionally flexing her hand open before making a fist. She's nervous and it's obvious Charlotte can sense that.

"You drove that night . . ." Charlotte says, her voice strained.

In that moment, Nicky's face is wiped clean, strangely naked of all expression as she realizes what she's said. She takes a step back, the corner of my bedside stand jars hard against her hip. It must have been painful, but she doesn't wince.

"You drove down that night, Nicky, but not to apologize to Cassie. You came to try and take my son away from his wife. When you saw Cassie with her bag on the lane, you saw an opportunity, you thought you could have what you've always wanted: Cassie's life for yourself."

It was her.

At last, Nicky's face ruptures. She gasps, her breath too fast. She starts hyperventilating as she says, "No, no, no, no . . ."

I was right from the start.

But Charlotte talks over her. "It was you . . . it was you, Nicky. You tried to kill her!"

Nicky holds the side of her temples with both hands, her eyes wild and her voice becomes a long attenuated cry before she shouts, "I came to say sorry for what she saw!"

Charlotte stops talking suddenly, like she wasn't expecting Nicky to say that. She keeps her eyes fixed on Nicky. Nicky's breathing is becoming more frenzied; her chest beats like something inside her is trying to escape.

"What did she see?" Charlotte's voice is clear.

"She saw me and Jack." Nicky's hands drop from her head, her voice fragile. "She saw us."

I feel my sheets shift as Charlotte grips the top of my bed.

"How do I know you're not lying?" Charlotte spits the word at Nicky.

"She saw us together, Charlotte, back in the autumn. I was coming to stay for the weekend and arrived a couple of hours earlier than planned to surprise Cassie. Jack was home. I was glad to have some time with him. He'd had a bad day, left the office early. We were talking on the sofa. He was telling me how stressed he'd been at work, with the miscarriage, how he knew Cassie wasn't happy and he didn't know what to do. I don't think either of us knew what was happening, but suddenly we were kissing and Cassie saw us. She was at the window. She saw us kissing."

I watch as fine cracks spread across Charlotte's face like fault lines. Her smile drops and her gaze flicks, sharp as a whip, across Nicky's face, searching for a lie.

Charlotte suddenly moves, walks around the foot of my bed and comes to stand on the same side as Nicky. I think for a crazy moment that Charlotte might hit Nicky, there and then. The violence I saw in her the other night is back, like something has been released and won't be caged again.

"He isn't . . . he isn't like that." She talks quietly, but it sounds like she wants to scream. Her jaw snaps around her words.

Nicky just stares at Charlotte. Her hands make fists.

"He is, Charlotte."

"You made him. You made him do it." Charlotte's face twists ugly around her words,

"I'm not blameless—I'm not saying I'm blameless—but I didn't make him, Charlotte," she responds, before she adds weakly, "It was just a kiss."

"You say it was just a kiss? It's never just a kiss."

Nicky flinches as Charlotte comes closer to her.

Charlotte strains like a dog on a leash against herself. She looks like she could bite into Nicky's neck. She points her hand violently towards the curtain, towards Cassie.

"She wouldn't have left him that night." Charlotte hisses the words through her teeth. "We wouldn't be here now if it was just a kiss."

Charlotte's anger doesn't have the rawness of a fresh rage. She doesn't seem shocked by it; it is familiar to her, almost rehearsed, as though she's practiced similar scenes in her head late at night many times before, and finally, now, Nicky has given her a stage.

Nicky's gaze drops to my bed, away from Charlotte. Her eyes pool; her sight must be blurred. The words come cleanly out of her, like they've been simmering under her skin for a long time.

"I left a party just after midnight. Picked up my car and started driving. I was still too late by the time I got to the cottage. There was no one there. It was cold. The security lights flashed on outside. Ice had started to settle everywhere—" she pauses, catches her breath and looks up at Charlotte "—but it hadn't formed on Jack's car. I put my hand on it. I knew he was there because he'd just been driving. His car was warm."

Jack.

"What are you saying?"

"I tried to tell myself there would be a reason why his car was warm, tried to tell myself after Jonny was arrested that it was him, Jonny who hit her. Deep down I think I always knew it was Jack. I don't think I was the first, I think there were other women before me. He didn't want Cassie anymore . . ."

"Stop it. Nicky . . ."

"He drove after her, didn't he? I know it was him."

Charlotte speaks slower than Nicky, her voice authoritative as she says, "I can call the police right now. They'll watch the tapes. They'll see you driving down. You'd been drinking . . . you had a motive."

Nicky lifts her hands to her head again, as though Charlotte's words are needles pricking her ears.

"You thought you could take him, but it hasn't worked has it, Nicky? Look at you, still on your own . . ."

But suddenly, Charlotte's voice fades and her head whips around towards my curtain. Footsteps approach and as Lizzie pulls my curtain back, Nicky drops her hands from her head again.

Charlotte smiles at Lizzie as the nurse moves forward

next to my bed, as though Charlotte had just been passing on supportive words to Nicky and smiles to me all along.

"Oh, hello, Charlotte." I can hear a small frown, surprise, in Lizzie's voice, but she doesn't notice the atmosphere that hangs in the air like pollution.

"Um, so sorry to leave you, Ms. Breton," she says, adding in a more discreet voice, "little emergency, I'm afraid."

Nicky at last lifts her head, her eyes red. She shakes her head, knocking my bedside stand again as she moves. "No, no, that's OK, I have to go now anyway."

Her voice shakes, but Lizzie doesn't notice as Nicky grabs her bag from the floor, clutching the strap like a lifeline as Charlotte says, "Well, it's been good to talk, really. Such a relief to be understood, isn't it?" Charlotte's voice doesn't waver; she doesn't flicker or blush, her lies indistinguishable from the truth.

Nicky doesn't say anything and she doesn't look at Charlotte. She just nods quickly, her head bowed as she pushes her way past Charlotte and Lizzie. Nicky's boots sound heavy again against the floor as she rushes away and I know Nicky wasn't here to defend herself. Nicky was here to finally tell the truth.

Jack's car was warm.

Lizzie blinks, surprised by Nicky's abrupt departure. "Oh, bye then," she says to Nicky's back before she turns to Charlotte. "Was it something I said?"

Jack wanted Nicky; he wanted other women.

Charlotte's eyes stay fixed on the space where Nicky just stood and she shakes herself briefly, as if she's just woken up and, turning to Lizzie, she smiles and says, "She's a bit emotional, that's all. I think she found it hard seeing her uncle like this."

Cassie was in the way.

The phone starts ringing at reception. Lizzie looks towards the noise, hoping someone else might take the call, before she says to Charlotte, "God, it's one of those days, I'm afraid," and she hurries away from us again, towards the reception desk.

As soon as she's gone, Charlotte seems to deflate as she exhales long and deep. She grips onto the end of my bed frame by my feet with both hands, and closes her eyes, and says a quiet mantra, "She'll pay, she'll pay." Still with her eyes closed, she shakes her head gently, back and forth as she says, "No one saw, no one knows. It wasn't his fault."

Her words sting like a swarm of bees inside my head.

She's not accusing Nicky because Nicky did it. She's accusing Nicky to protect Jack.

I think she feels my stare, because she opens her eyes and I know she's seen a shadow, this small ghost of Frank Ashcroft pass behind my dull stare and without meaning to, I blink.

Shit.

She stares at me.

"You blinked," she says, her voice dumb with shock. She keeps her eyes fixed on me and I focus on the muscles around my eyes, forcing them to keep still, to not even flicker.

But she doesn't smile like everyone else when they see me blink. No, her expression hardens like it did with Nicky.

She turns around, behind her, and calls, "Lizzie!"

She pulls my curtain back

"Lizzie!" she shouts again, agitated now, and Lizzie appears, slightly flushed from exertion.

"Sorry again, Charlotte. Honestly I don't know what's going on today—"

"He just blinked," Charlotte says, interrupting Lizzie, pointing a finger towards me.

Lizzie's young face turns towards Charlotte and breaks into a wide smile, as though she's just about to reveal the most delicious secret. She nods her head.

No, Lizzie, don't!

"Frank's wanted to keep it quiet, haven't you, Frank? Until he's well enough to say proper words." She turns to me briefly before turning back to Charlotte. "But I suppose you basically guessed, Charlotte, so I can tell you that, yes, Frank is getting better!"

Stop, Lizzie!

"But Mr. Sharma said he was in a permanent vegetative state." Charlotte's voice is bald with shock.

"Well, that's what he thought but, no, I'm happy to say he was wrong this time." To prove her point, Lizzie looks down at me and says, "Isn't that right, Frank?"

I keep perfectly still.

"Oh, he's probably just a bit tired. He's got an infection at present, so he's probably feeling the effects of the antibiotics," Lizzie says as she picks up my file and opens it to start taking my readings.

"To be honest, I'm surprised you and Jack didn't know something was up, Charlotte. He's an absolute superstar. He's starting to blink out words. Even though he's got this infection, I heard he was absolutely determined today. Mary said it was like he was on a mission. He would not rest until he blinked Jack's name!" She turns to Charlotte and frowns briefly because Charlotte's not smiling, not like she thought she would, but it doesn't stop her talking.

"Frank's been here all along. He knows everything we're saying, understands everything perfectly. Isn't that right, Frank?"

Jesus, Lizzie . . .

Both women turn to look at me: Lizzie's face smiles down at me briefly before turning back to my machines; Charlotte looks blanched, queasy, her mouth small and twisted, like she's straining to keep it under control.

"In fact, the doctors think he's got supersonic hearing; they figure he could hear a pin drop on the ward. But don't worry, Frank's promised me he won't give away any of our secrets. Isn't that right, Frank?"

They both turn towards me, but again I don't move. Lizzie glances down at me before looking at Charlotte. She's disappointed; usually Charlotte's full of smiles.

"Charlotte, are you OK? You've gone really pale suddenly."

Charlotte's eyes stay fixed on mine, and her focus burns my retina worse than any of the doctor's flashlights.

"I'm fine, Lizzie, really. Just happy for Frank and surprised we didn't know." Charlotte's voice has a new, mechanical quality like an automaton.

"I keep thinking, maybe by the time the baby's born, Frank will be able to talk to us all! Won't that be something!" Lizzie says, her smile fading because Charlotte hasn't lifted her head away from me. Lizzie frowns, before she remembers what she's supposed to be doing and starts scribbling down the numbers from my machines while Charlotte keeps her eyes on mine, hard as bullets.

I can tell she knows what I'm thinking.

I heard you warning Cassie.

I feel her thoughts running alongside my own.

I heard everything you said to Nicky.

"You heard," she says to me, so softly I can hear the saliva move around her mouth.

"Sorry, what was that, Charlotte?" Lizzie looks up from her folder.

His car was still warm.

"I was just saying what wonderful news this is." Charlotte smiles at Lizzie and Lizzie smiles back, delighted that Charlotte seems to finally understand.

He wanted her gone.

From the other end of the ward, an emergency alarm starts to screech again, the sound panics the air around us.

It was Jack.

Lizzie drops my folder in its slot at the foot of my bed.

"Oh god, not again," she says glancing down at me briefly.

No, no, Lizzie you can't . . .

I blink twice, and I blink again, but Lizzie doesn't see me because she's turning to leave already, to join the other urgent feet that pound the ward as the doctors and other nurses run back again to the end of 9B.

But Charlotte sees me.

The alarms seem to ring through my organs. My heart monitor starts to beep as I watch Charlotte look left and right before she closes my curtains quietly and, coming back to me, she brings her face so close to mine I can feel her words as little puffs of warm air against my cheek, as she says, "You heard. You heard me talking about Jack."

I think of Luce, of Alice; I have to keep still for them, I have to keep still for Cassie, for her baby. Charlotte keeps her eyes on mine. She's fixed, deep inside me, as though she's seeing something in me even I don't know.

"I know you're there, Frank, I know you heard things you shouldn't have."

Her eyes widen around the truth and, as if in sympathy, her own eyelid starts to tic. She shakes her head and stands away from me, turning so I can't see her. She's not talking to me anymore as she says, her voice desperate, "My god, he knows, he knows."

Then the air around my bed becomes still and the silence is worse than anything she's already said, and I feel my heart turn to ice in my chest because I hear her thoughts before I hear her words.

"Frank, I'm sorry. Really, I'm sorry."

You're sorry your son almost killed his wife?

"You shouldn't have heard any of it, Frank."

Or are you sorry for lying to protect him?

Then she moves again, so she's above me, staring down at me. She's strangely absent behind her eyes, like she's temporarily walked away from herself. Her eyelid keeps pulsing; she's concentrated. Even though I can't move, I still freeze.

At the end of the ward, a man, a heavy-sounding man, shouts out numbers; he's giving the new patient CPR. Through the high-pitch squeal of the alarms and the voices shouting orders, I hear a lower, crunchy sound, like he's snapping twigs as the patient's ribs break beneath him. I will one of them, someone, to turn away, to know what's happening here.

Charlotte hangs her head forward.

"I'm sorry you heard me, Frank," she says again. She speaks in a hissed whisper that finds its mark quicker than normal speech. "But you have a daughter. You know how hard you'll fight to protect your child. You'd do the same if you had to, Frank. You'd do the same."

Time seems to yawn, stretching out before me. I don't hear the noise from the new patient's drama anymore, or the shouts from the people told to save her. I keep my eyes steady, unflinching. Her hand shakes as she starts twisting the valve on my tracheotomy; my stomach crawls and writhes like it's full of maggots.

No, no Jesus, no.

My throat starts making an unnatural gurgling sound, like water being sucked down a drain.

Please, please, Charlotte.

Then, suddenly, there's no breath, no noisy rattle from my chest, and it's a novelty until my lungs seize in panic. My breath has disappeared. I've been still for months but this is different; it's an unnatural kind of still, like a wave that's suddenly frozen.

I don't want to go like this.

Boiling molten metal is poured into my lungs, and then they harden.

I was going to tell Alice everything.

Charlotte is cowering in the corner by my chair, her hands raised to her mouth like she's trying to muffle a scream.

I was going to make Lucy proud.

Tears flow freely from her eyes, but she keeps them fixed on my face. My vision starts to blur, colors run like wet paint, which is a relief; I don't want her face to be the one I take with me.

I was going to walk out of here one day, next to Lucy.

Everything melts to silence; even the weird orchestra of outraged alarms falls away to peace.

Sorry, Luce, I let you down again. I'm so sorry.

Lucy must have known I need her because she comes running up to my bed.

Ah, Luce, there you are!

She's a little girl again, her hair poking out underneath one of my dad's old flat caps. She's missing her front two teeth and her cheeks are flushed with fresh air and she laughs as she takes my hand and pulls me up. We're not in the hospital anymore; we're on the plane again but this time she doesn't want me to sit back down in my seat. She wants me to jump; she wants me to jump out of the plane with her. I tell her she's crazy, but as I look at the clouds below I think what a relief it would be to let go, and I know it's the right thing, the only thing I can do. Lucy wriggles her little hand in mine. She turns to me, her eyes dance with joy, and she laughs. "Ready, Dad?"

And we fall.

24

Cassie

Maisie's whole body trembles with adrenaline. She leaps with every distant bang and fizz from the fireworks, as if she's terrified of the New Year itself, fearful of the changes it may bring.

Cassie wants to pack for the Isle of Wight before Jack gets home. She doesn't know how long she has so she only pauses to soothe the little dog briefly. She looks at her phone; it's after 1 a.m. already. She took her time walking home, breathing in the rich night. The darkness felt nourishing; she felt like she could walk forever, at last in tune with the earth beneath her. She pulls her mum's old leather bag out of the spare room cupboard; its familiar animal smell wafts up to meet her. She'll only take what she needs for a week or so. She opens drawers and lays out a couple of pairs of jeans, underwear, sweaters and T-shirts. She puts her mum's photo album and diaries into the bottom of the bag; maybe she and Marcus can look through them together. Her toiletry bag can wait until early tomorrow morning, just in case Jack comes into the bathroom and notices her things are missing. She doesn't want to risk raising the alarm tonight. That would only complicate things, muddy her decision with shouting and tears, when practical action is so much clearer, so much easier. In spite of everything, she wants to minimize the hurt she causes Jack. She doesn't think he's a bad man, not really. He's just misguided, and so was she.

Cassie concentrates.

What about the shed? She thinks of her paints, smeary and twisted in their tubes, her paintbrushes stiff from lack of care. She'll treat herself to some new ones in a day or two. She'll leave with Maisie early in the morning, as soon as it's light. If all goes according to plan, she won't even have to see Jack. She could be at Marcus's house by lunchtime.

The bag is only half full. She could take so much more but she likes the idea of traveling light, leaving with just the essentials. She shoves the bag under her bed. Good. What next?

She picks through her jewelry box until she finds her mum's old turquoise ring. Her engagement and wedding rings seem to suck onto her finger, like they don't want to leave her. She twists her finger to get them off and doesn't pause as she drops them into her jewelry box. Let Jack find them and realize how serious this is. Her mum's turquoise ring is heavier on her finger, the metal cooler, more substantial and sure of itself than Jack's thin rings. It feels right.

How is she going to let Jack know she's going away for a while? Depending on how hungover he is, he probably won't get up until about 10 a.m. and, after checking the shed, and finding it empty, he'd call Cassie and then probably Jonny. Jonny's already involved enough as it is. She can't expect him to be the one to tell Jack she's gone away; he'd have to bear the brunt of Jack's anger, and that wouldn't be fair. A text is far too dismissive, too casual. Jack deserves more than that. It'll have to be a letter.

She changes out of her scratchy, synthetic dress and into pajamas. She coaxes Maisie out from under the bed where she shakes, cowed and vulnerable, even though the bangs from the fireworks have at last quieted. Downstairs is murky; the furniture and their possessions seem to spy on her like guards. She turns on a lamp, turns on the kettle and tears a page out of the book they used for notes to their cleaner, scrawled reminders to buy dish soap and paper towels. She finds a black pen and starts writing. She doesn't plan it; she just lets the words come. They follow her satisfyingly practical mood: Jack, I'm going away for a while. I don't know how long. I need space. Please don't call or look for me. I'll be in touch when I'm ready. C.

She pours boiling water over a chamomile tea bag; she'll keep the letter with her tonight and leave it on the table early in the morning for Jack to find when she's already left. She's about to turn the light off and go upstairs when, from outside, a yellow light pools around the kitchen, as though it's searching for something. For a crazy moment, Cassie thinks it's someone outside with a flashlight, Jonny maybe, come to check on her, before she hears the low crunch of wheels grinding against tiny rocks and she knows the light is from car headlights. Shit. Is Jack home so early? If she crept upstairs now, she could get into bed, pretend to be asleep and avoid him altogether. She slaps her hand against her leg and calls "Maisie" but the little dog has disappeared again, her stubby tail poking out from under the sofa. Cassie will have to pull her out by the collar to get them both upstairs in time, but it's too late. There are a few muffled words, the slam of a car door, rocks rubbing against each other as the cab turns around, and then the metallic chatter of a key in the lock. Cassie feels exposed. She wishes she could hide like Maisie, crawl under the sofa. Instead she shoves the letter into her pajama pocket and picks up her tea as the door opens. Her heart eases as Charlotte walks through the front door.

"Charlotte, what are you doing here?" Cassie focuses on keeping her voice light. "I thought you were Jack." Charlotte moves slowly, glinting in her sequin dress as she hangs her black coat up on one of the pegs by the door, and, through the window, Cassie watches the cab as it pulls out of the driveway. Why is she here?

Charlotte takes off her kitten heels by the door. She's pulling off her gloves as she enters the kitchen; she looks small suddenly, like a child playing dress-up in her mum's sparkly dress. She looks up at Cassie briefly and, seeing her mug, says, "Oh, could you make me one of those, Cas?"

Cassie doesn't move. Instead she says, "Sorry, Charlotte, I was just about to go up to bed actually."

But Charlotte ignores her, and sits at the table with a small exhale, before she says, "I just need to talk with you for a few minutes. You left early tonight. Jack was looking for you for ages."

"I just wasn't in the mood, that's all, and I was worried about Maisie with all the noise."

Charlotte looks up at Cassie and then she looks at the chair opposite her.

"Come on, Cas," she says, "I wouldn't be here at this hour unless it was important."

Cassie moves into the kitchen. They don't talk as Cassie makes Charlotte a cup of herbal tea.

Even though she strains to be alone again, Cassie decides she doesn't want Charlotte to worry, so she puts the tea in front of her mother-in-law and lowers herself into the chair opposite Charlotte. She'll listen to her for a few minutes, gulp back her tea, and in ten minutes she'll be upstairs, checking over her bag one last time before she can get into bed and wait for the sun to rise.

But first, she has to deal with Charlotte, who rests her palms on the table and is staring at Cassie as though she's seeing her for the first time.

"Whatever is going on has to stop, Cassie."

Cassie feels a frown crest over her whole face.

"Please, Cassie, be respectful. Don't pretend you don't know what I'm talking about. I've seen you and Jonny together. I saw you all those months ago at the food festival, the way he looked at you. I didn't think anything had happened then, but I could see he wanted it to; that's why I told you about Mike. I thought you'd understand. I didn't tell you just for the sake of it. I was warning you to be careful."

Cassie stares at Charlotte's mouth, too stunned to say anything herself, so Charlotte keeps talking.

"I wanted you to see how hard I'd worked to protect Jack, the sacrifices I've made so Jack could keep believing his dead dad was this hero, this perfect man. I wanted you to hear it from me; I thought it'd make you think, stop you from destroying your marriage. Ever since you lost the baby, you've been different. That was understandable at first, but now I see you and Jonny, messing around like you did before." She looks up sharply at Cassie as she says, "I won't let you ruin my son."

Cassie almost laughs in outrage.

"I'm sorry, I can't listen to this." Cassie shakes her head, stands up from her chair, but Charlotte is too fast. She grabs Cassie's wrist.

"Don't you ignore me."

Cassie wriggles her wrist away from her mother-in-law and slaps her hand down hard on the surface of the table.

"Charlotte, you're so blind! You still think it's me having the affair? Talk to Jack, ask him what's really been going on. I've had enough. I'm going to bed."

She whistles for Maisie who creeps out from under the sofa and trots, head down, not making eye contact, towards Cassie. Maisie trembles by Cassie's feet. She looks like she's been scolded. Cassie bends to rest her hand on Maisie's head; it's like she's a completely different dog, shell-shocked and terrified of life. Cassie looks at the turquoise ring on her finger, heavy on Maisie's head and she realizes that if she leaves like this, no matter what she did, Charlotte would always blame her. She'd be blamed if their marriage broke up, if their child grew up in two homes. She thinks of the baby, twelve weeks old; even if Cassie's life here is over, she's going to be inextricably linked to Charlotte and Jack forever. Charlotte needs to know the truth. She can't be complicit anymore, protecting Charlotte from the truth about Jack and protecting Jack from the truth about Mike. She turns back to Charlotte who is sitting back at the table, her hands wrapped around her mug, her gaze still fixed firmly on Cassie.

"Charlotte, it was Jack who had an affair, not me. It was Jack and my friend Nicky. I saw them."

Charlotte's eyes flash at Cassie; something phantasmic passes behind them, like the truth has roused something dormant within Charlotte, and it doesn't like what it hears.

"You're lying. You're lying to protect yourself." Charlotte stands suddenly. She leans forward over the table, opposite Cassie. Maisie, smelling tension, creeps around the door and curls herself gingerly in a little "u" shape at the bottom of the stairs. Charlotte looks different to Cassie suddenly; where she once saw strength she now sees something tremulous and unpredictable resting behind her eyes. It feels familiar somehow; she's seen it before in someone else.

"Charlotte, I think you should tell Jack about Mike, about his affairs. I think it's only fair he knows. He's a grown man now, not a little boy." More gently she adds, "He'd be angry at first, but then he'd calm down and be honest with himself. I think he already has suspicions."

Charlotte's eyes snap up to Cassie.

"You told him?"

"No, no, I swear I didn't tell him anything." Cassie raises her hands to her mother-in-law, baring her palms, trying to calm her.

Charlotte comes up close to Cassie; her words make Cassie's hair sway.

"If you told him any of it, Cassie, what I told you in confidence, I . . . I . . ."

Charlotte's words are swallowed by her anger; she can't finish her sentence, just like Jack.

After a pause she shouts, "I just want to protect my son!"

"Well, I think it's time to stop." Cassie breaks the gaze first. Anger crackles between them, making it harder to breathe; she feels her heart bounce in her chest.

Charlotte is still staring, her gaze fixed on Cassie across the table.

"What do you think all this is going to achieve, Cassie, really?"

"I . . ." Cassie pauses, and in the pause she thinks she might tell Charlotte about the baby, tell her that she wants her child to grow up in the truth, like she did, even when the truth isn't pretty, but instead she says, "I'm going to go and stay with Jonny tonight."

Charlotte's face twists again, but Cassie raises her hands once more to her mother-in-law and says, "You can think what you like, Charlotte, I don't give a shit anymore." The honesty of her words rings true through her whole body. She doesn't care! Suddenly she can't wait to be a memory here. She turns towards the stairs. Maisie jumps up, startled by all the unexpected movement, and follows Cassie up the stairs. As Cassie runs away she hears a sharp crack as Charlotte's mug crashes against the kitchen wall.

The room spins around Cassie as she grabs, unseeing, at the things she was going to take in the morning.

Toothbrush, face moisturizer . . . she throws them into her bag. She remembers the letter she wrote to Jack, and shoves it into the inside pocket of the leather bag. She can't leave it here anymore; she doesn't want Charlotte reading it. She takes off her pajamas and grabs the jeans she wears for painting and pulls on a sweater, simultaneously wiggling her feet into her old sneakers. She tries to text Jonny that she's coming to his house now, but her reception has dropped again. She'll text him on the walk over. She knows she needs to move fast, before her heart slows and her resolve trickles away. Everything looks different again, the colors and banal everyday shapes of the room she used to share with Jack made new and bright by her decision to leave now, right now. Suddenly it feels like someone else's bedroom, a stranger's space. Her body feels indestructible, oiled with strength. She's shoving Maisie's leash and treats into the bag when she hears the back door slam. It makes her freeze immediately, her ears strain for any other noise. She thinks she can just about hear the clock in the kitchen, but there's nothing else. The cottage is completely silent. She's gone, Charlotte's left; she must have decided to walk home.

The zipper seems to laugh in relief as she pulls the bag closed in one long tug and throws it over her shoulder. Maisie hovers by her ankles as Cassie walks out onto the landing where they stop to listen again at the top of the stairs. There's nothing. The quiet has the complete quality of no other living, breathing thing filling the space.

Her feet seem to echo as she walks down the stairs. Charlotte went out the back door; she always takes the footpath across the fields and over the little bridge to meet up with the village path that leads to her house. She'll be home in ten minutes. Jonny's place, thank God, is in the other direction, along the lane. Charlotte's left the lights on in the kitchen; a large wet mark drips down the white wall opposite the kitchen table. Cassie steps over the broken porcelain and tries not to think about Jack coming home drunk and cutting himself on the shards. She opens the drawer where they keep all the miscellaneous home stuff; she searches through a mess of old chargers, lost pieces of string and instruction manuals. The flashlight is missing. Fuck it. She's got Maisie and the light on her phone. They know the route well; they'll be fine. She needs to leave now before her excitement turns into fear and fogs her clarity. Her eyes dart around the kitchen one last time before she sees a flash of blue and walks over to the simple silver frame.

Maisie barks, thinking the sound of the glass smashing against the kitchen island is another firework. Cassie shakes the shards to the floor like tears before she carefully plucks the photo away from the smashed frame. She looks at April's face, in her bright blue head scarf. She looks like she's smiling encouragement at Cassie, urging her on, and as she shoves the photo into her pocket, she knows that tonight her mum would be proud of her.

She opens the front door and feels the darkness again pull her forward as she walks quickly down the drive and onto the lane, deep into the thick night. The air electrocutes her lungs with each icy inhale, and her legs feel confident, sure of their new direction. The stream bubbles jollily along by her side, while the branches from the silver birch trees creak above her. She doesn't use her phone's flashlight after all. The clouds have passed while she was inside, and the moon itself is extra bright tonight, like it's been polished, ready for the New Year. Surprising herself, she starts to hum, something made up, childlike; it's a nonsense but she doesn't care and she doesn't feel ashamed.

Maisie's scampered off, and her humming turns into a call for the little dog.

"Maisie!" She listens before she calls again, listens again. She keeps walking; Maisie will be scampering around in a field somewhere, lost to everything except the smell of rabbits. The bag's digging into her shoulder. She lifts it, rolls her neck a couple of times.

The flash from the car lights behind her is a surprise at first, like they're intruding on her private moment. As she turns, they blind her. The shape of the car looks familiar; it's the car she sees everyday, parked outside their cottage. It's the car that drives Jack to work and home again. Shit, shit, shit. She has no choice; she waves at him, casting shadows on the lane, her arms preposterously long. He must be pissed, driving after her like this. Maybe Charlotte called him, told him about their fight, that Cassie told her about Jack and Nicky. She decides to run to the wider part of the lane, but Jack must be livid, he must want to scare her, because instead of slowing, he starts driving faster. The car lights bounce up and down on the uneven surface. She waves again, screams his name, her bag falling from her shoulder. The car bites into her side, the impact making her spin, an insane pirouette to the edge of the stream. Her feet can't keep up and she falls back, thorns shred her useless hands as she clutches the hedgerows for support. She hears herself scream, distant, as if it's coming from someone else far away, her head sounds like a piece of meat as it hits something hard. The water, like a million freezing needles pierces her, but the stream welcomes her. She opens her eyes, watches the white clouds of her breath disappear into the dark sky. She puts her hand between her thighs and raises it, but she can't see any blood there. It's still raining. Maisie barks and her leaden lips try and whisper her name to calm the little dog, but she doesn't make a sound. Instead she hears the car door open, and clipped footsteps above her. They pause for a moment. Relief crests over Cassie as she hears the click, click as the footsteps walk away again. The car roars into life above her once more and Cassie's heart at last eases because now, finally she is on her own. She can rest. She is free.

25

Alice

Bob wakes up as I pull into our drive at last. I open the back and, even though it's started raining, I let him run around the garden for a while. He never did get the walk I promised. David still isn't home, which is a relief; he'd know something was up as soon as he saw me. He'd be full of questions I wouldn't be able to answer.

It's just before 5 p.m. I go upstairs to find the business card Officer Brooks gave me in the office and walk back downstairs, pour myself a glass of water and keep my eyes fixed on Bob as he gallops around the garden, delighted to be out of the car, as I dial her direct line. She answers on the second ring.

"Brooks," she says her name like a reflex, as though she's distracted by something else.

"Hello?" I say, unsure again how to address her.

"Who is this?" She doesn't have time for civilities.

"It's Alice Marlowe, the nurse from Kate's, caring for Cassie Jensen."

"Ah, yes. How are you?" I have her full attention; it makes me feel more confident.

"I know Jonny Parker's charges are going to be dropped."

"Did Mr. Jensen tell you that?"

I don't answer her; where I heard it isn't important now.

"I have some information I need to share with you."

"OK," she says, "can you tell me over the phone?"

"No, no, I want to see you in person, if that's OK? Can I come to the station now?"

She pauses, weighing up perhaps if I'm worth postponing whatever else she had planned before she leaves for the day. I add, "I can be there in an hour."

"OK, Nurse Marlowe, that's fine. I'll meet you at the station at six o'clock."

"Thanks," I say into the receiver, but she's already hung up.

I bribe Bob inside with some leftovers from our curry last night, and ignore the pull on my heart as he whines from inside as he hears me locking the door. I'm just about to get back in my car when a strange buzzing from my bag makes me stop. It's like someone has slipped their phone into my bag; the beep is persistent, unfamiliar, demanding attention. I dig around inside my bag and pull out my emergency work pager, flashing red and wailing. It's never gone off before, reserved for critical use only, and I know immediately what it means; it means something has happened to Cassie.

"Oh, god," I say to no one, staring at the pager, dumb for a second before I open the passenger door and, dropping my bag on the seat, start fumbling again in my bag, this time for my phone.

I start calling 9B as I sit in the driver's seat and turn the key in the ignition. My heart floats up into my throat, and my mind starts to flip through images of what could have happened. Cassie in cardiac arrest, the baby's heart rate dropping or speeding up, a too-early emergency C-section.

No one answers the phone on 9B reception. I reverse to turn around, skidding the back wheels on the lawn, and as I pull out of our drive, I try 9B again. I don't look properly before I pull out and another car screeches to an emergency stop to my left. "Crazy lady," the driver calls out of his window before he drives away shaking his head at me on my phone, but I don't care; I hardly see him. Neither Mary or Carol answer their cells so I call the main hospital number, but they just put me through to 9B reception again.

"Shit!" I shout and throw my phone onto the passenger's seat. All I can think about is Cassie, that she needs me—she needs me right now and I'm not there—so I keep my foot on the accelerator and ignore the honks from other drivers as I barge my way through the rush-hour traffic.

I'm just a couple of minutes from Kate's when my phone starts ringing. I grab it, hoping it's Mary or Carol or at least someone from the hospital. But it's David. I pause, think about not answering but I know he'll be home now, wondering where I am. I know he'll just keep calling until I answer.

"David?"

"Ali? Where are you? I thought you said you'd be—"

"David, there's been an emergency," I interrupt.

"An emergency?" he asks, immediately tense.

"It's Cassie. I'm driving to the hospital now. I don't know when I'll be home. Look, I'm almost there, I've got to go. I love you."

I don't wait for his response; I hang up the phone and turn it off. I know he'll call back and I can't bear to hear the worry in his voice, not now. I pull into a space outside the hospital and, leaving my bag and coat in the car, grab my hospital ID before I start to run across the parking lot, through reception, down the corridor towards the ward. My heart pounds around my body; it seems to spiral in my chest. I'm out of breath, I have to force myself to walk the final distance towards 9B. The little waiting area outside the ward is empty apart from one small figure, slightly hunched and rocking back and forth in one of the plastic chairs, like something driven crazy from being caged for too long. She looks up at me, but I can tell even from a distance that Charlotte's gaze is unseeing; I must be a blur to her. Where's Jack? I think briefly about stopping to ask her what happened, but then I think of Cassie's baby, and I know I have to find out for myself, and I start running again.

The ward reception is abandoned and all the curtains are drawn around the beds. The lights are on their brightest, cruellest setting. The fluorescent lights are on in the nurses break room as well, but I can't see anyone inside. The ward has never been so empty; it has the stopped, frozen quality of a recently abandoned space. My nerves grip, forcing me to slow to a walk.

I reach Frank's bed; I want to see him first suddenly, as though a glimpse of him will give me courage. I pull his curtain back. His bed is still there but I see there's just a twist of sheets on his bed. His letter board has fallen to the floor. His machines, which were so critical, stand by, suddenly useless, just clumps of metal and blank screens. His heart monitor blinks like it's shocked by Frank's sudden absence. I hold onto the end of his bed for a moment to stop the room from spinning before I turn around towards Cassie's bed and tug her curtain back in one motion. I hear myself cry out as my hands cover my mouth and I feel all my veins constrict because where Cassie's bed should be there's just a little halo of photos and another gaping empty space.

"Alice?"

Lizzie is standing at the end of the ward, her face plump with sorrow, her hair made wild by the terrible demands of her shift. She's walking towards me fast. She looks like she's about to throw her arms around me, but instead I take hold of her wrists and force her to look at my face. I can't comfort her now, not until I know what's happened here.

"Where are they?" The words feel fragile in my mouth.

Lizzie's face is blank, her eyes wide, as though she can't believe what she's saying.

"Frank's dead, Alice. We don't know what happened: a complication with his tracheotomy; his infection must have gotten worse . . ." Her voice trails away, the words too new, too difficult to say.

"A new patient was admitted today, multiple organ failure. She kept crashing. Mary and I were so busy with her. It was Charlotte who raised the alarm, told us something was wrong with Frank. She was the last one to see him alive, him and his niece." Lizzie sniffs hard through her nose, before she says, "Sharma's talking to the technicians now, trying to figure out exactly what happened."

I stare at Lizzie; my legs feel like rubber, as though they could give way any moment. I grab on tighter to Lizzie's arm and force myself to ask. I have to know.

"Cassie?"

Lizzie nods. The movement shakes more tears from her eyes.

"She's OK, she's OK. Her blood pressure rose. Ms. Longe thought they were going to do a C-section, which was when we paged you, so she's down in prep, but as soon as she was taken away from here she leveled out again. They're keeping her down there just in case, but she's OK; they're OK."

At last, I loosen my grip on Lizzie's arm and I stare at Frank's empty bed. I want to feel someone alive, so I pull Lizzie in close and feel her shake in my arms as I hold her. There's so much wrong; my brain wheels. Frank's bed seems to pulse with his absence. He was here, just a short time ago. He was here, but he wasn't alone. I pull Lizzie away from me, sharper than I meant to.

"You said his niece was with him?"

Lizzie nods.

"I checked her ID, Alice; it matched the name she gave. Nicola something. I was glad Charlotte was here—" but I cut Lizzie off.

"Was it Breton, Lizzie. Was her last name Breton?"

Lizzie nods vaguely, surprised at how my words sting. She starts to cry again, her hand shakes as she wipes her eyes.

"She seemed nice, but then when I came back and saw her talking to Charlotte she left really abruptly. Charlotte just said she was upset at seeing her uncle so unwell."

"They were alone together, Charlotte and Frank?"

Lizzie nods, and the skin around her eyes wrinkles; she's terrified she's done something wrong.

"Yes, but not for long, Alice, I promise. The new patient, she was arresting, I had to—"

I cut her off again. "Tell me what happened when you got back to them, Lizzie. Tell me exactly what happened."

My urgency makes her widen her eyes in panic, but she takes a deep breath. Her eyes flicker as she tries to remember.

"Frank's niece, that Nicky woman, she left and, as I took Frank's readings, I talked to Charlotte for a bit. She called me over because she saw Frank blink. I know he didn't want people to know yet that he was getting better, but Charlotte guessed! So I told her that he hears everything."

Lizzie looks like she's about to crumple into sobs again as she corrects herself. "*Heard* everything."

I hold onto her upper arms and encourage her to carry on.

"What next, Lizzie? What happened next?"

"The new patient started crashing again, so I left Charlotte with Frank and then a couple of minutes later Charlotte came running down the ward shouting that something had happened to Frank." Lizzie at last breaks into sobs and lifts her hand to her mouth. She starts mumbling something about Jack into a tissue in her hand.

"I can't hear . . . what are you saying, Lizzie?"

"I was just saying, only this morning he blinked out Jack's name."

Lizzie's shoulders start heaving again. Out of my peripheral vision the ward seems to shrink. I remember the morning. The cold look that replaced the usual playfulness in Frank's eyes. Even though he must have been struggling to breathe from his infection, even though the drugs would have made him feel tired, he wouldn't stop. He wanted to tell me something. I promised him I'd come back, but I hadn't.

I can't speak. My hands drop from Lizzie's arms as she keeps sobbing into her tissue, the muscles raised in her neck. Behind her the ward seems to vibrate. I think of Frank's face, twisting with the effort of each slow, painful letter. I could have saved him; I should have been here.

"He heard everything." My voice sounds distant but it makes Lizzie look up from her tissue and nod at me.

"I think he heard much more than the rest of us put together."

Lizzie's right; Frank knew Jack, and he knew Cassie, probably better than any of us.

I stare at Frank's ruined bed, and picture him from the morning, how his eyes strained, how I got it wrong. He wasn't blinking "L"; he was trying to blink "J." Of course, he was trying to warn me. He was trying to spell Jack.

I have surprisingly few thoughts, as though the words I just heard are in a line, waiting to move from my ear into my brain to be processed and assimilated into something coherent.

Frank knew it was Jack and Charlotte found out Frank was getting better.

I ignore Lizzie as she calls out, tears still thick in her throat.

"Where are you going, Alice?"

But I'm running now, to the end of the ward, past Mr. Sharma's office, past reception and left through the doors. The small, hunched figure from before is still rocking back and forth on the chairs.

Charlotte's aged; the lines on her face like scars, and her hair hangs by her face in a limp curtain. Her eyes are red and the skin underneath puffed as though she's been punched hard.

I stand in front of her and for the first time, we don't smile when we see each other. Her fingers twist her wedding ring, round and round her finger. I walk slowly towards her, my body heavy. I stand before her for a moment and then I hear myself say, "Frank's dead, Charlotte."

The words feel cold in my mouth. Her hands still and she raises her eyebrows towards me and she nods, like she was expecting those three words, before her shaky hands keep on with their work, twisting her ring round and round. They don't pause as she whispers, "I'm sorry to hear that. I tried to get help."

My eyes stay fixed on her pinched face; keeping my gaze on her seems to strengthen my resolve and stops the world speeding around me.

"You were with Frank, weren't you, Charlotte."

Her lips quiver like she's about to speak, but she doesn't make a sound; she just keeps twisting her ring round and round.

"You know, Jack's name was Frank's last word."

She turns her eyes up slowly, but she still doesn't look at me. It's as though my words are too heavy; she doesn't have the strength to raise her eyes to me.

She knows.

Her hands, at last, still as I keep talking.

"But he didn't blink to prove he knew Jack's name. I know now; he was trying to warn us."

She lets her hands drop to her lap.

"All this is her fault. Nicky. She lied to see Cassie. She can't handle her guilt."

But I won't be distracted, not anymore.

"Jack hit Cassie," I say, feeling how strange it is that such short, simple words can change the way the world spins. "Frank knew it was Jack and you panicked."

She stands up suddenly, her face set, a ferocious mask of the kindly face I thought I knew. She points her finger down the hallway, where Nicky would have walked, not long before.

"All this is her fault. She tried to take what wasn't hers. I was protecting my son." Charlotte frowns, then, as she looks at me, her face cracks into a frown. I know that look well; I see it in my family, my friends. Charlotte pities me: in spite of it all, she pities me.

"This must be so hard for you to understand—" her jaw clicks around her words "—the maternal instinct to protect is stronger than anything you could possibly imagine. You have no idea what it's been like, coming here day after day, praying the baby is ours, my granddaughter, Jack's daughter, but still not knowing for sure who her father is."

Neither of us hears him approach; his voice is so small, our concentration so firmly fixed on each other, that it takes us both a moment to turn towards him when Jack says, "I'm Freya's father."

His voice shocks Charlotte like electricity. She turns,

stronger on her feet suddenly, and moves towards her son, opening her arms to him. They beg to hold him. But Jack shakes his head; he takes a cautious step away from her.

"Mum, what is this?" Jack looks at his mum, at me. He sees the muscle twitch in Charlotte's face and I know he senses the horror I feel in my chest. "Mum!" he says again louder this time.

"Jack. Nicky was here. She was telling lies, all sorts of lies about you. But it's OK. It's all going to be OK." She tries to make her words sound soothing but it doesn't work.

Jack's face darkens. "She told you what happened between us."

Charlotte nods and says, "But I know it was her, Jack. I know all of it was her."

"No, Mum." His eyes wrinkle in pain as he talks, but I can also hear a fullness to his voice; it sounds like a relief as he looks at Charlotte and says, "Nicky's right. I betrayed Cassie in the worst way possible. I have to live with that fact, that I failed her, for the rest of my life." He lifts his eyes to meet mine and I know, the way I know I have to keep breathing, that he loves her. He keeps staring at me as he continues talking. "But I'll do anything to make it right. I was too ashamed to tell anyone about Nicky. She kept calling me. She wouldn't leave me alone. I was worried the police would think we were really having an affair, and that would be a motive for me to hurt Cassie. I was terrified that Freya would be born with no parent to love her."

At last, he lifts his eyes away from mine, to stare past me, past Charlotte. His gaze seems to travel down the corridor, towards the ward, towards where Cassie used to lie.

"I'm not good enough for her. I thought about leaving her for her own sake. Then decided I'd try harder over Christmas. But that only made Cassie pull away from me even more. I knew I was coming on too strong. I didn't know what to do. I was frustrated, angry with myself, wasn't ready to accept what I secretly knew. She didn't love me anymore. I should have let her go."

"No, Jack, no. It was wrong of her to try and leave you that night. She deserved it!" Charlotte's voice is brittle as though it could snap on any word.

Jack frowns at his mum as though he's seeing with new eyes and he says, "I've just come from the police station. They've been questioning me about that night. They asked me where I usually keep my car keys at home. I told them I keep them in the little bowl on the side table in the hall. I thought it was a weird question." He stares at his mum. "But then I remembered. You told me Cassie had gone after Maisie. I wanted to go and look for her. But I couldn't find my car keys. They weren't in the bowl. You had them. Didn't you, Mum?"

Charlotte doesn't move. Her face is frozen, her eyes fixed on her son as he keeps talking.

"You said I was drunk. But I remember, your hand was shaking as you poured me a glass of water."

"Jack . . ." she says, raising her palm to her son, trying to calm the storm we can both feel building within Jack, but it's impossible; she can't stop it now.

"But Charlotte, you can't drive," I say quietly. Jack turns to me, his eyes golden, their color accentuated by the force of his realization.

"She always says she can't drive but that's not true, is

it, Mum?" His gaze shifts from me to Charlotte and it's like a flame that was burning, hovering over my skin, has at last been snuffed out.

"It's not that you can't drive, it's that you don't. Dad always drove you everywhere. Then you had that accident after he died. I was in the car, it scared you shitless and you never drove again. Until that night."

My veins grip under my skin, as if they've been pulled taut, like puppet strings. Charlotte starts shaking her head, as though Jack's words can't settle as long as she keeps moving. Jack doesn't take his eyes off Charlotte because at last her head slowly stills. Her eyes are glazed, as though a transparent film has developed over her irises and she's replaying the scenes from that night.

"She was going to see him. She was doing to you, Jack, what Mike did to me and I couldn't . . . I couldn't let her. Not after everything we've been though, Jack, not after all this time. I was going to walk home, but it was icy, dangerous in my heels. So I went back to the cottage. That's when I realized she'd gone. She'd left you. So I drove after her. I wanted to stop her, that's all, to make her change her mind; but she started running when she saw the car. She must have thought I was you, Jack. She was running away from you. She had a bag with her, just like Mike. It was like she was throwing everything back at us, all the love and care we'd shown her. Mike wanted to run away too. I told him not to try and leave, that I wouldn't let him. It was easy to swap the heart tablets in his medicine bottles for aspirin. They were almost identical, little white pills. I thought if he had a scare, he'd know how much he needed me. How much he needed us. I wanted to scare Cassie too, so she'd know how much she needed you, Jack . . . I thought they'd both come home."

I want to run away suddenly, but the air seems to have weight, stopping me from moving. I want to force the world back to a place where I admire the way Charlotte loves, a world where Frank is getting better.

Jack's body is rigid, trying to absorb the shock of the demolition as his whole life crumbles to ruin with each one of his mother's words.

But we're not finished, not yet. There's still more I have to know.

"Frank was getting better, Charlotte," I say, my own voice foreign in this new world.

Charlotte doesn't take her eyes off Jack. I feel the walls start to move in out, in out, as if the hospital itself is breathing as she says, "I only turned his machine down a little. I thought he'd pass out . . . forget what he heard. That's all. He thought it was Jack." She pauses before she says to Jack, "I had to protect you. You'll understand when you're a parent yourself." She looks at me, and her face twists. "They didn't tell us he was getting better. It's their fault. They should have told us he could hear."

The walls keep pulsing, faster now, in time with the beating in my chest. I'm too winded to say anything.

Jack shakes his head at the woman he has trusted, unquestioningly, all his life. "Don't say 'us,'" he says quietly. "I'm nothing like you."

Charlotte moves towards him again, but he takes another step back, away from her.

"Please, Jack, don't be like that."

In my peripheral vision, the breathing walls seem to tremble; like the whole hospital, everything I know is going to disintegrate and we're all going to turn to dust with it. Jack feels it, too. I watch as his composure dissolves. He sways on his feet. He falls to his knees. I see the life behind his eyes splintered like a dropped mirror. He frowns at his mother, as though his vision is distorted and he can't see her anymore. Charlotte drops to her knees opposite him; she's saying his name, shaking his shoulders, begging him, over and over: "Jack, oh Jack, please, Jack."

And as I turn away from them, the musical soprano of an ambulance siren shrills the air, on their way to another tragedy, away from here, and even though the violent noise hurts my ears, I'm grateful to it for drowning out Jack's screams.

26

Cassie

She doesn't remember walking out here, so far out on the rocks; the sea waters slosh, guttural and thick fifty feet below, as the waves wash in and out. Come to think of it, she can't even remember how she came here at all, but then she looks up, and how she got here doesn't matter anymore because the sunset is so gorgeous, the sky full of pink and orange as if it's flushed with embarrassment at its own beauty.

Her feet have gotten used to the pitted, sharp volcanic rock and she keeps clambering to the end of the crop, where she can see her mum, waiting for her. Her mum's wearing a bright blue swimsuit, facing out to sea, her hands on her hips, her hair thick and her cheeks full, flushed with life. She's well again. A crab scuttles scared across her path, making Cassie yelp. The noise makes her mum turn around, and Cassie sees her whole face is glowing, laughing in joy like she used to.

"Come on, Cas!" she calls to her daughter. "Look, it's the most amazing sunset!"

Cassie's close to her now. In just a couple of seconds she'll reach out and touch her, she thinks, but then, without a sound, her mum leaps off the edge of the cliff and a moment later there's a splash as the sea swallows her whole. Cassie's at the edge now, where her mum just stood, and she calls, "Mum?" but there's just a wedding dress of white foamy water where she jumped. Panic grips Cassie before her mum's head pops out right in the middle, a watery bride. She whoops and laughs and twists in the water, agile as a dolphin.

"The water's perfect," she calls up to her daughter. "Jump in! It's even more amazing from here!" Cassie knows her mum sees her hesitate, and she calls again, "Come on, Cas! It's totally safe."

Her toes shuffle shyly to the edge of the rock. She looks up again; the calm sea stretches weird as mercury all the way to the horizon where it meets the sky in a blaze of color. She can almost see the curvature of the world; she imagines it rolling on and on, an occasional cloud puffing across the view like forgotten pieces of blowsy cotton. The water is dark as an oil slick, but the waves seem calmer suddenly; she hears it gulping on the rocks below, like something thick and delicious mixing in a huge bowl. Her mum's on her back now, swimming like a happy otter. She's humming, her eyes shut. Cassie wants to hold her hand, swim next to her, but she's frightened of the fall and, looking around, she can see no way of getting out once she's in. Typical of her mum not to think about anything practical.

A man startles her so much she almost leaps off the edge in surprise.

"Hello, Cassie," he says. He's got a strong West Country accent.

She turns to look at him. He's older than her—nearer to her mum's age—but he's familiar somehow. She scrambles around her head for a name, but finds nothing. Water runs off his tanned skin like rain on glass and there are little droplets in his mahogany hair and eyelashes. Cassie looks down at her own skin, and realizes she's covered in dry sweat; compared to him, she feels stale, grubby. He's smiling out at the view.

"Quite something, isn't it?" he says softly. She feels safe standing next to him. He turns his smile to Cassie's mum who's now windmilling her arms behind her in a splashy backstroke. The man turns back to Cassie and asks, "You jumping in?"

Cassie turns to look at him, and tries to smile before she shrugs her shoulders.

"Come on, Cas, it's so much better from down here!" her mum calls, before she dives under the surface, her body shimmering in the fading light as she swims, a mermaid in the clear water.

"The water's perfect today, so refreshing. Come on, you'll love it," the man says, and, without asking, his wet hand reaches out for Cassie's dry one and it doesn't feel strange because he holds her hand so gently. She wishes she could remember how she knows him . . . understand why she trusts him. Cassie looks down again at her mum who's treading water now, smiling up at them.

"Come on, you two!" The sound of her voice makes

Cassie nudge her toes closer towards the edge. The man looks at her and starts counting.

"One, two, and three." They don't let go of each other. Their clasped hands punch the sky as they leap into the warm, pink air and in that brief flightless moment Cassie knows they were right to make her jump. She wants to be clean; she wants to feel new.

And they fall.

Epilogue

Bob licks my hand as I load the final suitcase into the car. He's been sitting in the back, his eyebrows raised in worry, surrounded by boxes, for the last hour, terrified that we're going to leave him behind, along with the house. He still hasn't forgiven us for our two-week vacation in Italy. It's a steaming August day, the leaves curl in the heat and the asphalt is like molten treacle. It's a day for lying in the shade with a book and a beer, not for moving to a new house, but the movers have already left and all we have to do is drive down to our new tiny seaside cottage. David promised we can go skinny dipping as soon as we arrive. I want to start our new lives feeling free, because we are free. With David's exit package and the sale of the house, we've figured out we'll be able to get by fine for the next year. The plan is for David to finally set up his architecture practice from the small, converted stables next to the cottage, and I'll do community nursing part-time while I start my psychotherapy course at Exeter. This time, we mapped out our future from our dusty rental car driving through the lazy hills and vineyards of Tuscany and Umbria. Experience has taught us that even if the whole plan doesn't fall neatly into place, we'll find our own way; we'll be OK.

We left for Italy just after Frank's small memorial. David held my hand as his coffin was carried past us, the photo of Frank and Lucy from their fishing trip perched on top. I didn't get to talk to Lucy; her relatives glued themselves to her all day, like they didn't want to miss a moment of her mourning. I only let go of David's hand to wave goodbye to her as we left. She waved back, a small, confused wave, like she'd forgotten who I was, didn't recognize me outside of Kate's. The day Frank died is always with me. I carry my broken promise around with me like a shard of glass stuck firmly into my side. I don't know if I'll ever get it out. I think about him everyday. It was him who led us to Charlotte. Without Frank, Charlotte may have been able to keep the truth hidden. In a way, he saved us all.

Freya was born, as if in homage to her maternal grandmother, on April 29, just shy of twenty-nine weeks. Ms. Longe performed the C-section; she'd held off for as long as they could. Cassie had been deteriorating for a while; both Cassie and Freya's pulses consistently erratic ever since Frank's death. Jack invited me to meet Freya when she was just two days old. She was in an incubator, preposterously big for her. Her tiny body covered in a fine blanket, her eyes wide, life a completely unexpected surprise. As we stood side by side, in front of her incubator, I noticed a new peaceful quality to Jack, as if he wouldn't need anything again if he could just stay there, by her side forever.

Officer Brooks didn't have to wait long for me at the police station. The call came through about Frank from the hospital; they told her it was related to Unit 9B and she knew it had something to do with Cassie, with me missing our meeting. It was Officer Brooks who took Charlotte away. She didn't try to resist, her arms were limp as Officer Brooks clicked the handcuffs around her wrists. Charlotte kept her gaze fixed on Jack, begging him to look at her, but he didn't look up at her once.

Charlotte has pleaded guilty to all charges. David told me her sentencing date keeps being pushed back due to her poor mental health, some form of repressed post-traumatic stress. The media couldn't believe their luck when they found out. "Charlotte Jensen" has become a byword for "evil" in the cheap magazines ever since.

I haven't worked out what I think about that yet, and I don't know what happened to Nicky; she only crosses my mind fleetingly, like a bad memory every now and then. When she does, I wonder if she's found any peace, a way of forgiving herself. Officer Brooks said that Jonny's moved back to London; she didn't say where exactly, and I didn't ask. I think it'll take some time for him to rebuild his life, but I think he'll get there. I hope he's happy.

And now here we are. I move my sunglasses onto my head and sit for a moment on the back of the car, playing with Bob's velveteen ear and look at the house we no longer own. I remember the day we unpacked our lives here almost eight years ago. I was so full of the future, planning a nursery and where our children would play, and now, here we are, just us, leaving again, our lives so different from how we planned.

David's still inside so I open my purse and take out the two envelopes from Jack addressed to me at Kate's. Mr. Sharma wanted to open them, apparently, but Mary managed to wrestle them off him before he got the chance.

Jack and Freya live in Brixton now, not far from where Cassie grew up. If they stay, Freya could go to the same preschool her mum went to. Sometimes, every now and then, life does seem to cough up another chance.

Jack told me in his letter that Freya's doing well, putting on weight but she seems too in awe of the world, too fascinated to sleep much. He didn't mention Charlotte. He enclosed two photos, one of Freya, in just a onesie and a white sun hat, her face somewhere between a laugh and a squeal at the person taking the photo, her sweet rolls of baby fat like a built-in crash mat. The other was of a group of about thirty people in bright clothes standing barefoot in a semicircle on a cliff top, the huge sky a swirly watercolor of setting sun behind them, the sea stretching all the way to the horizon to meet the sunset. Jack wrote that the photo was from Cassie's memorial ceremony on the Isle of Wight; April's ashes were scattered there as well. In the photo, some people are holding hands; some have their eyes closed as if in prayer. Marcus is amongst them, his eyes cast down, a faint smile on his face. He's holding Freya in a light blue onesie; she's grabbing chubby fistfuls of white hair. I wonder if he has a diagnosis. I hope someone is looking out for him. I put the letter and photos back into my purse, next to the adoption papers I completed late last night, as David comes out of our empty house with the final box. He closes the door behind him for the last time. He moves slower than normal, squinting in the bright sunlight towards me. He moves the box onto the back seat before he comes next to me, and leaning his back against the car, he places his hand on my bare knee.

"OK, that's the last of it. Ready to go?"

I nod and we kiss briefly on the lips and I know that even if our lives aren't as we planned, they are still just as rich as we hoped.

As we drive away I look over at David, already singing along to the radio next to me, and just like I did eight years ago when we arrived here, I feel full of the future, entirely blessed because this is it, my tiny family, and I know it's all I need.

Acknowledgments

I would like to start by thanking my brilliant agent, Nelle Andrew, who believed in this book before even I knew I could write it.

Great thanks to the hugely talented Lucy Malagoni at Little, Brown for always going above and beyond; and to the whole Little, Brown team for all their work and dedication.

Thank you to my godfather Tom Shields for his sage advice—"Don't not do something just because it's a hard thing to do."

Thank you to my dear friends who always make me laugh and for providing ever-absorbent shoulders; and to the Stonehouse for giving us all shelter over the years.

Great thanks to my wonderful sisters—Laura Pettifer and Catherine Williams—together we'll always be the Elgar girls.

In deepest gratitude to my incredible parents Edward and Sandy Elgar who have been absolutely unshakeable in their faith in this book and their love for me throughout my life.

Finally, to my dear husband James Legend Linard for being by my side every day. I love you.

About the author

Read on

Insights,
Interviews
& More . . .

About Emily Elgar

Originally from the Cotswolds, Emily
Elgar studied at Edinburgh University
and then worked for a non-profit
organization providing support services
to sex workers in the United Kingdom.
She went on to complete the novel
writing course at the Faber Academy.
She lives in East Sussex with her
husband. *If You Knew Her* is her first
novel. ∽

A Conversation with Emily Elgar

Have you always wanted to be a writer? How did you get started writing fiction?

I think there was always a secret, yearning part of me that wanted to be a writer, but it took a long while for me to feel courageous enough to say it out loud! It always felt too audacious, strangely pompous (which I now know is complete rubbish because for many, writing fiction is to put your ego through a mangle every day). I was working in London as a support worker for male, female, and transgender sex workers when I decided to make a real go at writing. My job was fascinating and challenging, but I felt like I needed something other than my work and home life. I signed myself up for two courses, one in Latin dance and the other in creative writing. I strained my groin in the first class and fell in love with writing in the second. This led to more creative writing courses. When my dear grandad passed away, he left me exactly enough inheritance money to enroll in the Faber Academy novel writing course. At the end of it, I met my brilliant agent and it all went from there.

How did you come up with the idea for If You Knew Her? ▶

A Conversation with Emily Elgar *(continued)*

About ten years ago, I was sitting in my ancient car outside a London supermarket on a—very rare—sweltering summer's day. I'd just started listening to an ethics program on the radio and, despite the heat, I couldn't stop listening. It was about a woman who was in a coma and pregnant. The discussion was about who should be the doctor's main focus of care—the woman or her unborn child? I was gripped, saddened, and quite overwhelmed by the idea that this could happen to any woman. Over the next few days and weeks, I read many amazing true stories about women who gave birth naturally while in a coma, and about women who recovered from a coma and discovered, to their amazement, they had a new son or daughter! I wasn't writing at the time so I pocketed the idea. A couple of years later, while attending the Faber Academy, I started writing a piece of historical fiction. I thought it was *brilliant*, but no one else shared my view and it was completely—and rightly—panned by my peers and course tutor. It was bruising at the time, but now I'm infinitely grateful as it made me pick myself up, dust myself off, and finally open the brain drawer where I'd been storing the idea that eventually became *If You Knew Her*.

Do you plot out the whole story before you write it? Did you know how the

novel would end before you set pen to paper?

I've learned so much about myself as a writer and a person while writing this book. One of the main lessons about myself, as a writer, is that I have to plot out what I write *before* I write it. I am far too liable, like Alice, to chase a white rabbit down an interesting looking hole and end up somewhere completely baffling. For the first draft, I didn't plan ahead at all and ended up in all sorts of weird places. When I rewrote the book under the guidance of my fantastic editor, I started to realize how important it is for me to plot. This doesn't mean that I don't allow myself to be surprised by subplots and interesting new ideas along the way. It just means that I know where I want to end up and have a map to help me find my way. For future books, I've promised myself to make sure I have a map in my back pocket before setting off.

I knew some of the ending, but not the entire thing, for a long while. In fact, the ending was, for me, the hardest part to write, and I wrote quite a few drafts before we finally felt it was ready.

What are you working on now?

I'm working on a new novel and completely love it so far (but ask me ▶

again in a few months and I may well have changed my tune!).

Do you have any advice for aspiring novelists?

As I say in the acknowledgments to *If You Knew Her*, don't give up just because writing a novel is widely considered a tough challenge. I think many things—like raising children or establishing a career—can feel completely overwhelming if you're focusing on the "whole." How will this baby ever become a functional adult? How will I ever be a director of this company? That's why I always try to focus on the writing day before me, how I'm just going to quietly concentrate on taking the words out of my head and juggle them around a bit before I like the way they sit on a page. The next day I'll do the same thing, and the day after that, and the day after that until slowly, slowly a book starts to emerge. That's the idea anyway.

The other thing is know when you're writing and when you're editing. They're different skills and require different tools. I think writing should be (bearing in mind the map!) an exploration, a crazy dance where you give yourself permission to move however feels good without worrying what you look like. Editing is the complete opposite—it is the careful tidying, the mopping up and rearranging because you've danced so hard you've knocked a vase of flowers onto the floor. Sometimes it's tempting to clean up immediately after you've made a mess, but it might be a waste of time if there's more dancing to come. ∿

Reading Group Guide:
Discussion Questions for *If You Knew Her*

1. Elgar has created three distinct points of view. How do these various viewpoints help to reveal these characters and unravel the mystery? How does the author withhold information about Cassie from the reader in her sections?

2. Which characters did you relate to the most? Why?

3. Which character did you trust the most at the beginning of the book? Which character did you trust the least?

4. Did you feel that Alice crossed the line of ethics in her quest to help solve the crime? Is it ever justifiable to do so if it means that a crime is resolved?

5. To what extent do you think the media is drawn to Cassie's plight because she's young and beautiful? Is the author saying something about why the news focuses on certain victims and ignores others?

6. How would you characterize Frank's relationship with his daughter, Lucy? Are his parental shortcomings compensated for by his deep love for his child?

7. In this book, more than one character lies to his or her spouse. Is it ever acceptable to lie to a loved one, even to protect him or her?

8. Were you surprised by the revelation of who was driving the car that hit Cassie? Why or why not?

9. Though the novel has an optimistic ending, these characters have suffered many losses. Do happy endings ever help to mitigate grief? Why or why not?